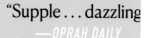

"Supple . . . dazzling
—*OPRAH DAILY*

"Original, intense, powerful, disturbing,
and **utterly mesmerizing**."
—*BOOKLIST* (STARRED REVIEW)

"Some of the most **original thriller writing** about Arctic
environments since Peter's Høeg's . . . *Smilla's Sense of Snow*."
—*LOS ANGELES TIMES*

"Uniquely imagined in a spectacularly unforgettable
setting that simultaneously filled me with **wondrous awe** and
absolute terror. I couldn't turn the pages fast enough."
—*LISA GENOVA*, *NEW YORK TIMES* BESTSELLING AUTHOR
OF *STILL ALICE* AND *REMEMBER*

"An excellent, **thrilling mystery** . . . With its fascinating science
and compelling characters (one or more of whom may
be a murderer), *Girl in Ice* demands to be read in one sitting."
—*BOOKPAGE* (STARRED REVIEW)

"**Exemplary** . . . Trenchant details about catastrophic
climate change bolster a creative plot featuring
authentic characters. . . . Ferencik outdoes Michael Crichton
in the convincing way she mixes emotion and science."
—*PUBLISHERS WEEKLY* (STARRED REVIEW)

"*Girl in Ice* is a novel of secrets. It is also an allegory for what human
beings are doing to the natural world and the terrifying possibility
that Mother Nature might one day strike back in unpredictable ways.
All in all, this is a memorable and **literally chilling** read."
—*BOOKREPORTER*

Praise for *Girl in Ice*

"*Girl in Ice* is a lot of things: a psychological suspense novel, a linguistic thriller, and a scientific puzzle. . . . Ferencik describes the Arctic topography with a poet's awe, and some of her set pieces—the procession of a huge herd of caribou, an Arctic dive gone badly awry—are breathtaking. . . . A singular sensation."

—*The Wall Street Journal*

"Hauntingly beautiful . . . *Girl in Ice* uses the subtleties of translation to draw us into different worlds and ways of thinking."

—Sarah Lyall, *The New York Times Book Review*

"Ferencik infuses every page with her research in the fjords of Greenland (where the Inuktun word for climate change translates to 'a friend acting strangely'). That plus a writer's eye for the telling detail have produced some of the most original thriller writing about Arctic environments since Peter Høeg's 1993 novel *Smilla's Sense of Snow*. As science-driven thriller and probing exploration of fear, language, and family bonds, *Girl in Ice* will not be easily forgotten."

—*Los Angeles Times*, "The 7 Best Crime Novels of the Winter, 2022"

"An excellent, thrilling mystery . . . With its fascinating science and compelling characters (one or more of whom may be a murderer), *Girl in Ice* demands to be read in one sitting."

—*BookPage* (starred review)

"*Girl in Ice* is a novel of secrets. It is also an allegory for what human beings are doing to the natural world and the terrifying possibility that Mother Nature might one day strike back in unpredictable ways. All in all, this is a memorable and literally chilling read."

—*Bookreporter*

"An inherently fascinating and deftly crafted novel by an author with a remarkable flair for imaginative, compelling, and narrative-driven storytelling."
—*Midwest Book Review*

"Whether I was desperate to solve a mystery, marveling at a beautifully described part of the northern scenery, or absorbing some fascinating tidbit of knowledge, this book held me rapt from start to end. Already one of my favorite books of next year, I'll be thinking about this one for a while."
—Fiona Cook, *Mystery and Suspense Magazine*

"This dark, suspenseful, visceral thriller combines the pressing issue of our time—human destruction of the environment—with a gripping and beautifully written mystery set in the frigid far reaches of the Arctic Circle. Unflinching, devastating, but ultimately hopeful, *Girl in Ice* grabbed me and didn't let me go until the very last page."
—A. J. Banner, *USA Today* and *Publishers Weekly* bestselling author

"With its jaw-dropping premise, unique locale, and great emotional depth, Ferencik's latest adventure thriller is riveting from the first page to the last."
—Robyn Harding, bestselling author of *The Perfect Family*

"This gorgeous, captivating thriller sets a dangerous, precious environment against an inner landscape of grief and longing. Moving, provocative, and breathlessly entertaining, this journey lingers long after the last page is turned."

—Kassandra Montag, author of *After the Flood*

"Ferencik's beautifully written suspense chiller held me in its icy grip and wouldn't let go. Meticulously researched, rich in scientific detail and Inuit folklore, this moving human story is one you won't soon forget."

—Catherine Burns, author of *The Visitors*

"This fiercely intelligent thriller delivers an ice-cold shot of adrenaline. Erica Ferencik takes the reader on an unforgettable ride through the Arctic, where the menace of the starkly beautiful landscape is matched by that of the human psyche."

—Lexie Elliott, author of *The French Girl*

"A propulsive, utterly unforgettable, jaw-dropping thriller."

—*The Patriot Ledger*

"This haunting tale of love and obsession is peppered with lines so beautiful and profound that sometimes I had to stop and catch my breath."

—Zoje Stage, *USA Today* and internationally bestselling author of *Baby Teeth* and *Getaway*

ALSO BY ERICA FERENCIK

Into the Jungle
The River at Night

GIRL
IN
ICE

ERICA FERENCIK

SCOUT PRESS

NEW YORK   LONDON   TORONTO   SYDNEY   NEW DELHI

Scout Press
An Imprint of Simon & Schuster, Inc.
1230 Avenue of the Americas
New York, NY 10020

First Scout Press trade paperback edition November 2022

SCOUT PRESS and colophon are registered trademarks
of Simon & Schuster, Inc.

For information about special discounts for bulk purchases,
please contact Simon & Schuster Special Sales at 1-866-506-1949
or business@simonandschuster.com.

The Simon & Schuster Speakers Bureau can bring authors to
your live event. For more information or to book an event, contact
the Simon & Schuster Speakers Bureau at 1-866-248-3049
or visit our website at www.simonspeakers.com.

Interior design by Michelle Marchese

Manufactured in the United States of America

1   3   5   7   9   10   8   6   4   2

The Library of Congress has cataloged the hardcover edition as follows:

Names: Ferencik, Erica, author.
Title: Girl in ice / Erica Ferencik.
Description: Scout Press hardcover edition. | New York : Scout Press, 2022.
Identifiers: LCCN 2021001122 (print) | LCCN 2021001123 (ebook) |
ISBN 9781982143022 (hardcover) | ISBN 9781982143039 (trade
paperback) | ISBN 9781982143046 (ebook)
Classification: LCC PS3606.E68 G57 2021 (print) | LCC PS3606.E68
(ebook) | DDC 813/.6—dc23
LC record available at https://lccn.loc.gov/2021001122
LC ebook record available at https://lccn.loc.gov/2021001123

ISBN 978-1-9821-4302-2
ISBN 978-1-9821-4303-9 (pbk)
ISBN 978-1-9821-4304-6 (ebook)

For George

How shall the heart be reconciled
to its feast of losses?

—STANLEY KUNITZ

In ice is the memory of the world.

—JAMES BALOG

GIRL
IN
ICE

one

Seeing the name "Wyatt Speeks" in my inbox hit me like a physical blow. Everything rushed back: the devastating phone call, the disbelief, the image of my brother's frozen body in the Arctic wasteland.

I shut my laptop, pasted a weak smile on my face. There would be no bursting into tears at school. Grief was for after hours, for the nightly bottle of merlot, for my dark apartment, for waking on the couch at dawn, the blue light of the TV caressing my aching flesh.

No, at the moment my job was to focus on the fresh, eager face of my graduate student as she petitioned for a semester in Tibet, a project in a tiny village deep in the Himalayas accessible only via treacherous mountain passes on foot and maybe yak, all to decipher a newly discovered language. As I listened to her impassioned plea—trying to harness my racing heart—an old shame suffused me.

The truth was, I'd never embarked into the field anyplace more frightening than a local graveyard to suss out a bit of Old English carved into a crumbling stone marker. And even then I made sure to go in broad daylight, because dead people—even underground—frightened me too. Never had my curiosity about a place or a language and its people overridden my *just say no* reflex. Citing schedule

conflicts, I'd declined a plum semester-long gig in the Andean mountains of Peru to study quipu, or "talking knots"—cotton strings of
differing lengths tied to a cord carried from village to village by run-
ners, each variation in the string signaling municipal facts: taxes paid
or owed; births and deaths; notices of famine, drought, crop failure,
plague, and so on. I'd even passed on the once-in-a-lifetime chance
to deconstruct a language carved into the two-thousand-year-old
Longyou caves in Quzhou, China.

Why?

Anxiety: the crippling kind. I'm tethered to the familiar, the safe,
or what I perceive as safe. I function normally in only a handful of
locations: my apartment, most places on campus—excluding the
football stadium, too much open space—the grocery store, my father's nursing home. During my inaugural trip to the new, huge,
and sparkly Whole Foods—chilled out on a double dose of meds—a
bird flew overhead in the rafters. All I could think was, *When is it
going to swoop down and peck my eyes out?* I never went back.

Ironically, I was the one with the power to give or withhold
the stamp of approval for my students' research trips, as if I were
any judge of risk and character. Watching the glistening eyes of the
young woman before me, one of my favorite students, I stalled a
few moments—tossing out a couple of insipid questions about her
goals—an attempt to soak up her magic normalcy. No such luck.
I signed off on her trip to Tibet wondering, *How does she see me,
really?* I knew she was fond of me, but—that casual wave of her
silver-braceleted hand as she turned to leave, that look in her eye!
I swear I caught a glint of pity, of disdain. It was like she knew my
secret. Her teacher was a fraud.

I'M A LINGUIST. I can get by in German and most Romance tongues,
and I've got a soft spot for dead languages: Latin, Sanskrit, ancient

Greek. But it's the extinct tongues—Old Norse and Old Danish—that enrapture me.

Languages reveal what it is to be human. This desire to make ourselves understood is primal. We make marks on paper, babble snippets of sound—then agree, by way of miracle—that these scribblings or syllables actually mean something, all so we can touch each other in some precise way. Sanskrit has ninety-six words for love, from the particular love of a new mother for her baby to one for unrequited romantic love, but it has twice as many for grief. My favorite is *sokaparayana*, which means "wholly given up to sorrow." A strange balm of a word, gentle coming off my tongue.

Though words came easily for me, I tended to miss the patterns that were staring me in the face. The fact that my ex genuinely wanted out didn't hit me until divorce papers were served. The fact of my father passing from just old to genuinely ill with lung cancer and not-here-for-much-longer didn't sink in until I was packing up the family home and found myself on my knees in tears, taken down by *dolor repentino*, a fit of sudden pain. The stark realization that my twin brother, Andy—the closest person in the world to me—had been pulling away for months came to me only after his death and at the very worst times: lecturing in an auditorium packed with students, conversing with the dean in the hallway. When it happened, these vicious, sudden, psychic stabs, I'd briefly close my eyes or turn away to cough, repeating to myself: *sokaparayana, sokaparayana*, until I could speak again.

I felt safest in my office, alone with my books, charts, runic symbols, and scraps of old text; and when I deciphered a chunk of language—even a word!—a thrill of understanding juddered up my spine. The distance between me and another human being, just for that moment, was erased. It was as if someone were speaking to me, and me alone.

For two decades, these glimmers of connection had been enough to sustain me, but over time, they began to lose their shine. These private revelations no longer fed me, warmed me like they had. I yearned to be drawn closer to the human heart. Not through words—however telling or ingenious—but in the living world.

AT PRECISELY EIGHT o'clock that night—the end of office hours—I got up and locked the door. Squared my shoulders, smoothed my skirt, and sat back down. Outside my window, remorseless late-August sun cast long shadows across the drought-singed grass of the quad.

I clicked open my email. The subject line was blank, but then, Wyatt had never bothered with niceties. My head pounded with end-of-summer-session exhaustion. I was in no mood to hear from Professor Speeks about my brother, his fond recollections of mentoring Andy through the rigors of grad school, or even some funny thing Andy had said or done during their year together on the ice.

I considered deleting the message without reading it, but a tingling buzzed my fingers. Something said: *Don't.* Still, I resisted until some darker knowledge swarmed up from the base of my spine, warning me it would be a terrible mistake not to open it.

From: Wyatt.Speeks@ArcticGreenlandScience.org
To: VChesterfield@Brookview.edu

Hey Val, hope you're doing well, all things considered. Something's happened out here. We found a body in the ice out on Glacier 35A. A young girl. We were able to cut through the ice and bring her back to the compound. Val, she thawed out alive. Don't ask me to explain it, I can't. She's eight, nine years old, I'm guessing. And she's talking pretty much nonstop, but in a language I've never heard before. Even Pitak, our supply runner from Qaanaaq, had no idea, and he speaks Inuktun. Jeanne's stumped, too, so we're both just keeping the girl fed and nodding our heads a lot and trying to figure out what to do next.

I've pasted here one of her vocalizations. Maybe you can figure out what she's saying? You're the expert. Give it a try, then call me as soon as you can. And please don't tell anyone about this.

Wyatt

The MP3 stuttered across my screen like a city skyline. The girl *thawed out alive?*

Sweat bloomed on my brow, even though the air conditioner was blasting. I got up, walked to my window, sat back down. Checked the time: too early for a pill. I knocked back the remaining swallow of stale coffee in my mug, rattled open my file drawer, extracted a bottle of Amaretto, and filled the cup halfway. The sweet, warm alcohol hit my empty stomach fast. Smoothed away the sharp edges.

I thought about all the times I'd let Andy's voice play in my head these past five months, how he was still so alive for me in this way. Memories of us as kids chasing each other through the lake house in upstate New York, T-shirts still damp from swimming. Or cozied up with our beloved mutt Frida, playing go fish and Monopoly while our parents got tight and happy on cocktails: a rare glimmer of joy during their disintegrating marriage. And so we were comforted, sharing the delusion that if we were just good enough, they would stay together.

Little by little I'd pored over the photos, letting myself "feel everything," as my shrink instructed. Mourning every shirt and shoe, I gave away or got rid of his clothes and belongings; though, there were a few I couldn't part with, his drawings especially. The only other place he lived on was in my phone: a dozen saved messages remained.

Now, on my screen, the forward arrow on the voice clip throbbed red. My finger trembled as it hovered over the play button. I steadied it, pushing down.

The first slam to my gut was the panic in this high, sweet girl voice that—even if you didn't understand a word she said—made you want to reach out and wrap her in a hug. The tremulous ache in her utterly foreign words only intensified in the twenty-eight-second clip, as if she was pleading for something. I tried to picture this child trapped in the ice, to imagine what horrors had brought her there.

I played it again.

What language is this?

Of course, West Greenlandic was my first guess, but I heard no correlation. It wasn't Danish, either—Greenland had been settled by Danes—but no, this was Danish put through a blender and mixed with what, *Finnish*? Not quite that, either. The vowels were too long, the accent on the last syllable. It wasn't Norwegian, clearly, and it was too clipped and choppy to be Swedish. I pulled up some Old Norse, the language of the Vikings, and listened alongside the girl's quavering voice. The cadences were similar in places, but I couldn't match up a single word. This language was completely new to me.

I was lost.

I listened again.

And again.

My face grew hot. Breath clouding the screen, I leaned in close, as if proximity might help.

Nothing—all I understood was raw emotion.

I sat back. Tried to recall all I knew linguistically about where Wyatt was—where Andy had died.

Three main dialects of Greenlandic were spoken in Greenland: West Greenlandic, East Greenlandic, and Inuktun, which had only about a thousand native speakers. In grad school, I'd been fascinated by this culture built from animal skin, sinew, bone, stone, snow, and ice, but in the end, I became more of a generalist. I deciphered languages quickly—given enough context and clues.

I got up and paced, holding my drink. The reality was, I didn't *have* to do anything. I could pretend I never opened the email. Ignore Wyatt's calls. All I wanted was to crawl back home and hide with my booze and my misery and never come out.

If only I hadn't heard her voice! I could have forgotten the whole thing. But even after the clip stopped playing I could still hear her, feel the sound, a high thrum in my jaw. Talking to Wyatt—even emailing him—brought back all the horror with Andy, but *who was this girl?* And why no picture or video—was there something he didn't want me to see? I turned, taking stock of the four walls of my tiny world. My achingly familiar posters, bookshelves, knickknacks— even my framed honors and awards—both comforted and repulsed me. *It's just a phone call, Val*, I thought. *For the love of God, you can do this.*

I knocked back the rest of my Amaretto and picked up the landline to dial Wyatt halfway around the world at his climate research station on Taararmiut Island, translated "land of shadows," off Greenland's northwest coast. Already my palm was slick with sweat as I listened to the odd *dud-dud-dud* of the international call. If it wasn't too cloudy, and the antennae hadn't been ripped away by the near constant fifty-mile-per-hour winds, the satellite call would go through, and there would be simply no going back.

two

I pushed through the doors of my father's nursing home, wondering how many more Saturday mornings I would spend with him—out of a sense of obligation, an old, warped love, or some fantasy that one day he might actually like me. Or, more practically, how many more Saturday mornings he would be here on earth.

Head down, I signed in on a clipboard at the nursing station counter.

"Hey, Val," said Carla, the head nurse, sliding the window open and peering out at me. "How's it going?"

She knew about Andy and was a good person, but I plastered on a fake smile as an answer because I just didn't feel like sharing for one second how it was actually going. "How's my dad today?" I asked.

"He's good," she said, moving on briskly to business—with relief, it seemed. "Hates the new activity schedule. Then again, he hated the old one, too. Skipped breakfast again." She glanced over a form she'd been filling out when I walked in, before looking back up at me. "He's in the lounge."

"Thanks," I said, now fully anticipating a dad storm cloud and suddenly glad to be sneaking in a box of caramels, which were his favorite, though forbidden on his diabetic diet.

A rehabbed hotel built in the twenties, the home retained the tang of disinfectant, air barely cooler than the heat-blasted day. Sad zebra fish mouthed dully against the glass of an aquarium as they swam in a fog of their own excrement, exquisite combs fluttering.

As if he'd become part of the furniture, my ninety-one-year-old dad, Dr. Joseph Chesterfield, climate scientist, once a strapping six-foot-four hard charger with a fierce intellect and fiercer temper, the terror of climate research stations around the world, sat motionless, sunk deep in the belly of his favorite wingback chair, knobby knees jutting up higher than its arms, several inches of hairless shin on display between pant cuff and fraying polyester sock. He'd dragged the chair to the window for a view of the outside world, a place I knew he missed desperately.

He was fast asleep. I considered my options. I could catch up on some grading back at the office, Marie Kondo my spice cabinet, ride the stationary bike in my bedroom for precisely three miles—

He opened one aquamarine eye. "You said ten o'clock."

"I lost track of—"

"It's ten past eleven," he stated firmly, with no watch, clock, or phone in sight. I glanced up at the wall clock behind him. Exactly ten past eleven. He hitched himself up to a slightly more organized position, swept back cottony wisps of hair, and gestured to a matching chair. "Sit," he said. "Contemplate the universe with me."

My escape plans flying away in sad little thought bubbles, I dutifully lugged the chair toward where he sat in full blazing summer sun.

"So, why aren't you eating, Dad?" As if I ate like a normal human being anymore, either.

"I don't eat when I'm not hungry."

I handed over the caramels. Side-eyeing the staff, he scratched at the cruel cellophane wrapping.

"Hang on, Dad, let me get some scissors or something."

"Never mind," he said, gnawing at one end of the box. "I got this." Inordinately pleased with himself, he tricked open the flap at one end with an eyetooth and tore off a clear strip of plastic. He popped a piece of candy in his mouth, almost reluctantly holding out the box in my direction.

"No, thanks."

"Watching your figure?" His eyebrows waved, as if he thought this might be a good idea.

"They're for you, Dad."

He chewed aggressively, jaw muscles flexing and dancing. "What's new, kiddo?"

A petite, nearly toothless elderly woman, as tall as he was sitting, and wearing an apron with little yellow ducks on it, walked over and gave him a tennis ball.

"Not now, Marie," he said, handing the ball back to her, but she thrust it back at him, her face fixed in a fragile smile.

"Maybe just take it, Dad, if it makes her happy," I said in low tones. Marie had Alzheimer's but was clearly in love with my dad. Back when her mind was clearer, they'd discussed playing tennis on their respective high school teams. Some part of her mind had hung on to this fact.

"Thanks for the ball, but I'm visiting with my daughter now," he said loudly, as if her problem were her hearing. He took the ball and wedged it next to his bony hip. Marie nodded eagerly and hurried away. He shook his head, muttered, "Christ, to think of the women who used to follow me around. World-class beauties. Now I've got Marie. It all comes to this. Complete and utter shit. Take note, okay? Take note." He blew his nose into a soggy handkerchief, took me in with watery eyes. "What have you got to say for yourself?"

"I talked to Wyatt last night."

His eyes widened, then dimmed with pain as he squinted into

the sunshine. "Some kind of what . . ." His voice quavered; he cleared his throat. "New information?"

"Not . . . about Andy." I sat straighter, considered not telling him a thing. "Dad, have you ever heard of someone thawing out alive after being frozen?"

He glared at me, blurted, "Is this a joke?" Several nurses and residents glanced over at us.

"No," I said softly, hoping he would mimic my tone. "Why would I joke about something like—"

"Is Wyatt losing his mind out there? God knows I would, after what happened with Andy and wintering over the year before. Asshole didn't even come home for the funeral."

"He couldn't leave . . . the research, remember?"

He glared at me as if I were too stupid to guess some obvious truth. "I never liked him." He tossed the box of caramels on a nearby table. "Who called who? He called you?"

"I called him, because he sent me an email about finding a girl frozen in the ice." I leaned a little closer to him. "She woke up alive, Dad. She's speaking, talking all the time, but Wyatt can't understand what she's saying, neither can Jeanne—"

"Jeanne? That tough old bird's still out there?"

"Dad, listen. He sent me an audio clip. I can't understand a word of it."

"Even *you* can't sort it out?"

"It's like nothing I've ever heard before."

"First of all, I don't buy this horseshit about thawing out alive, so let's put that aside for now. Where did he say he found this girl?"

"Glacier 35A—"

"He's hundreds of miles from anything. There is no indigenous population there. Never has been."

I stared through the picture window at a little girl half pulling her elderly grandmother along the sidewalk; the girl looked about seven years old. She looked so small. "Dad, Wyatt's not crazy. He's a lot of things, but he's not that."

My father leaned forward in his chair. I glimpsed the old fire in him. "We only had his story, Val, you know? Anything could have happened out there."

"He wants me to come up. Try to talk to the girl. He'll pay my expenses, any loss of income. He wants me to come right away."

"Greenland? The Arctic Circle? *You?*" he snorted. "You've never been out of Massachusetts."

My voice got small. "I went on that trip to DC. In high school."

"Oh, yes. DC. When you refused to get on the plane home? I had to leave work, drive down to pick you up, then drive you all the way back."

I felt helpless and sad. What good did it do to tell him I'd been on a plane a few times since then—miserable and zonked out—but showing up for exactly one wedding and one funeral before scuttling back home like a hermit crab to its shell? No one had to remind me of my shortcomings, especially my father. I knew which twin had been the favorite, the most charismatic, charming, funny, brave.

But I was the one left alive.

"Dad, I'm just telling you what he said. Of course I can't go. I've got school, and I've got . . ." I trailed off pitifully. What *did* I have? No husband, no children, just my father, and my rage-aholic ex, Matt. After our breakup and a few months of reveling in my conviction that I'd done the right thing, I'd begun to miss him and come frighteningly close to drunk dialing. But thanks to Facebook, a few taps of my wine-sodden fingers and there he was, hooked up with some hard-looking blonde with an endless forehead. Work was weird, too—a sabbatical freed me from upcoming fall and spring semesters to work on a project I had, over time, grown to care less and less about. Translating a series of books of Aramaic poetry had lit me up when I applied for the gig months before Andy's death;

now, the idea of spending six months dragging meaning from the texts—which tilted a bit heavy on love poems—felt tedious. I had a great sucking nothing keeping me here, except visits with my father, or coffees with Andy's bereaved fiancée, Sasha, but I felt her pulling away too. Each time she saw me, she saw Andy, which only cut her to ribbons.

Dad sank deeper in his chair, his long-fingered hands forming a steeple against his forehead. "Something's going on."

"Yeah, well, clearly—"

"No, Val, listen to me." His voice grew deep and gravelly. "Wyatt is up to something, and it has to do with your brother. I know it. I'm sure of it. He's a wily son of a bitch." He levered himself to his feet, his reedy length swaying back and forth until he grabbed his walker.

This resentment over Wyatt's closeness with Andy was not a new theme with my dad. Sure, he'd been grateful when Andy's prof had helped him navigate graduate school, keeping on him to finish assignments on time (Andy couldn't have cared less what day it was), relentlessly mentoring him until, one fine day, Andy earned a doctorate in climate science. Everyone in the restaurant at his graduation dinner could feel their affection for each other. Teacher and student acted like father and son.

Which was the problem.

"Come on." My father's face grew rigid with determination. "We're going for a walk."

Hunched over his walker, he clomped his boxy orthotic shoes down the brightly lit hallway, his sharp shoulder blades slicing at his thin summer shirt like the wings of an extinct bird. I grabbed my purse and followed. At the door, he turned to me and—even though I wanted to—I couldn't look away. For just a moment, all the rage, grief, and despair I couldn't bear to feel was etched into his once-handsome face. His son, his heart—the boy who melted him in ways I never could—had taken his own life, and only I was left.

I matched his halting pace out the double doors into the brutal heat, where we made our way along a manicured sidewalk under drooping elms, their slender leaves curled with thirst. Summer on the North Shore of Boston, unrelieved by any trace of rain or sea breeze.

"You know, Val, that I don't believe your brother killed himself."

"Yes, Dad. But what are you saying?"

The lines of his face drew tight with rage.

"Dad, it's too hot for this—"

He banged his walker on the concrete, devolving into a coughing fit. "Your brother," he said, pausing to catch his breath, "was not depressed. He was not the type—"

"How can you say that, Dad? Of course he was depressed. He'd been depressed for years. You didn't know him—"

"*I knew him!*" he shouted, blinking, spitting droplets in the sizzling air. His eyes grew wet. The little girl visiting her grandma looked up in alarm. "Andy was my son, and I knew him, and I loved him."

I rested my hand on his heartbreakingly thin forearm. "I know, Dad. I know."

He pulled his arm free and ran a shaking hand over his skull, patting down wayward tufts. "And he would never, ever, do something like that."

"Dad." My voice verged on a whisper. "Maybe we don't talk about this now." Sometimes I thought his grief would strike him down, take his last strength, kill him, and I wouldn't be able to survive it.

"Let me talk, for Christ's sake." He leaned heavily on his walker, which, even with its legs fully extended, wasn't tall enough for him. "Your brother loved this world too much. . . . Yes, he was sad about what we're doing to the planet, but he loved it. He—he would *never . . .*"

He wobbled, the walker's rubber tips catching here and there on the pavement as he tendered small steps forward. I caught his arm. "Dad, take a second. Sit."

I held him gently by his narrow torso, torqued him a bit, and he let gravity sink him onto a bench, which was, according to its inscription, dedicated to a Mr. and Mrs. Gerald K. Waterston.

"Listen, kiddo, if I wasn't such a decaying old heap of garbage, I'd be on that plane today to pay Dr. Speeks a little visit. *Right this second*, do you hear me? And god*dammit* if I wouldn't get the truth," he said, searching for his handkerchief in all the wrong pockets.

His paranoia about Wyatt's role in Andy's death made no sense to me, but he had always tended toward the suspicious. For years, he'd harangued Mom, convinced she was running around on him while he was on assignment in Antarctica. But she was crazy about him, always had been. So what good would it have done to remind him that, after what was described as a normal March evening at the Tarrarmiut Arctic Science Station, where the temperature hovered at twenty below with fifty-five-below-zero wind gusts, Andy was found outside at dawn, curled up on his side, barefoot, wearing only boxer shorts. Frozen to death. No signs of a struggle.

"It's hard to accept, Dad, but—"

"But you, Val. You're young. You're strong, even though you're wasting your life pretending you're not. And you've got that break coming up at school. Whatever you call it."

"Sabbatical—"

"You *go*, understand? He's even gonna pay your way. And you know why? Because he knows you'll be able to figure out what that girl—wherever he found her—is trying to say, because *that's what you do*." His voice caught, but he continued. "That's what you've spent twenty years of your life getting good at."

Sweating in my too-heavy cotton shirt and skirt, staring at the heat-stroked roses and clipped-too-short browning grass, I realized that the reason I'd even told him about the call was because I *wanted* him to change my mind, to push back at my obstinate, stuck self. Talk some smack to the person who ate the same damned dinner every night—Caesar salad with grilled chicken, no croutons—because new foods frightened her, who joylessly counted her steps on the StairMaster as she watched the women in Zumba swivel and shake their hips with incomprehensible abandon. The person who clung to her routine of rigid control: up at six, never in bed later than ten after a *Columbo* rerun, only to stare into the dark wondering, *Why am I always so afraid, and what, exactly, am I afraid of?*

I could feel my dad watching me, waiting for an answer, while I indulged in my age-old disappointment that his fondest wishes had nothing to do with me. On top of that, he wasn't concerned about my safety or happiness. I was an implement of justice, only.

"Go, Val," my father said, gripping, then releasing the handles of his walker, veins bulging. "Or don't bother coming to see me anymore."

THAT NIGHT I lost count of how many times I played the twenty-eight-second clip. Slowing the girl's voice down, speeding it up, trying to sync it with every known language in the world, or at least the ones in the northern hemisphere. No matches, no overlap, nothing. *What is she saying, what does she want, what has happened to her?*

As I got drunker and more exhausted, the lines blurred, and she became me as a little girl, hidden behind a brother I adored and resented in equal measure, giving inchoate voice to my own anguish. I got so drunk I finally played Andy's voice mails. I may as well have stabbed myself with a pair of scissors.

But the next morning I woke sober and clear. Over coffee, I played each voice mail again, erasing them as I went. I would never see or speak with Andy again. But this girl—no matter where Wyatt had found her—was alive. The pleading in her voice unmistakable, her suffering clear. And Wyatt had a temper—a couple of hair-raising stories Andy had shared jumped to mind. *How was he with little kids?* Jittery, I opened my bottle of pills and dumped them on the counter. Two weeks' worth. I'd need enough for a month, maybe more. Double doses for the plane. It could be done.

I pulled down the thick notebook of Aramaic poetry I'd committed to translating over the next six months. Opening to the first page, my eyes glazed over even as I translated the first line—something about a sunset, the ache of unrequited love. I pictured the ancient crypt where the original text had been found, the bones of the poet lying nearby ground to dust by time, his passions, musings, longings now my task to reveal. It would be impossible to devote myself to this. Almost irrational. How could I stay here, knowing I might hold the key to unlocking a living human child's desperate needs, tragedies, secrets?

I showered, dressed, and just before leaving for class, wrote to Wyatt to ask about arrangements to get to Greenland.

He booked me on the next plane.

It left in eight days.

three

After a ridiculous series of security checks, I stood swaying under the harsh lighting of the military waiting area of the airport, a bleary, semi-destroyed version of myself. It was just past four in the morning, a barbaric, unreal hour. All night I'd packed and repacked my bag, trying to cap it at forty-three pounds—my limit, I was told—and still bring all I needed. Smacked down by Ativan, I reminded myself over and over that I only had to do one thing: *Get on the plane.* I rubbed salve on my hands—my skin always a bellwether of my sanity—though no amount of lotion seemed to touch this eczema.

A monstrous cargo plane the near black of a wet gravestone brooded on the rain-slick runway, red and orange lights blinking along its wings. No windows except those for the pilot. Maybe that would be a good thing. Workers loaded crate after shrink-wrapped crate of machinery and supplies into its low-to-the-ground belly through a two-story-high cargo door. *How will this beast lift itself from the earth?*

The flight to Thule, Greenland, the US Air Force's northernmost base, was only the first leg of the trip to Wyatt's frozen island eight hundred miles north of the Arctic Circle. I'd scrolled up and down Wyatt's email that spelled out flight details; no return trip was scheduled. In our call, he mentioned wanting to be off island by the last week of October, when the sun set and didn't rise again until February of the following year. I shot off a panicky text. He assured me that the local flights—the ones from Thule to various villages or research stations—were arranged more casually and according to need, so there were no strict schedules per se. As to getting home, we were at the mercy of these military flights.

The day after I agreed to come, my government-issued polar gear arrived in the mail: quilted overalls, high-tech leggings and long-sleeved shirts, an orange parka, vest, and hat. Immense Gore-Tex gloves came most of the way to my elbows, and giant orange boots looked like ones Goofy might wear. I shivered to think I would need all of it just to survive.

"Hey," came a lilting female voice behind me.

I whipped around, nearly smacking my knapsack into a young woman.

"Are you by any chance Valerie Chesterfield?" she asked in a British accent so sparkling I thought of champagne freshly poured in fluted crystal.

"Yes," I said, reaching out to shake the hand she offered me.

"I'm Nora, and this is Raj." A slight, handsome man with a ropy sort of strength under his Polartec sweater held out his hand with a bright smile. He wore round gold-wire spectacles that emphasized the intelligence in his deep-set brown eyes.

Nora was slender and hazel-eyed, with a wide, somewhat crooked smile and beautiful teeth under a slightly hooked nose. Shining black hair fell past her shoulders in natural waves—a real beauty in a charmingly imperfect way.

In a last-minute email, Wyatt had informed me I'd be meeting married polar marine scientists Nora and Rajeev Chandra-Revard at the gate before our flight. This news helped normalize the situation slightly: it wouldn't just be me, Wyatt, the girl, and Jeanne—the mechanic—with whom I'd be living for seven weeks out in the middle of nowhere.

"So, this is all quite thrilling, isn't it?" Nora said, hiking her daypack higher over one shoulder. She fizzed with energy and excitement; I did my best to mirror back something like it.

"A little, yeah." A fresh influx of military men and women queued up for the flight, sniffer dogs weaving among them.

She laughed, eyebrows knitting slightly. "Just a little?"

"Won't this be an incredible opportunity for you?" Raj said in an equally charming British cadence. "To decipher some unknown language? Wyatt told us you were quite the expert."

Nora cast him a sidelong look. "Come on, darling, best not to discuss that here, remember?"

Maybe they'd signed the same government contract I had: it stipulated keeping mum about the girl anywhere except on-site.

"What about you? Are you excited?" I asked.

"Well, of course we are!" Nora said.

Her shiny, non-Ativan'd self nearly knocked me over.

"This is huge for us. Competition is brutal for any assignment in the Arctic. We're all killing ourselves to be chosen, you know? We've been in Antarctica once but never Greenland, and even better, it's such a remote island, never really explored before."

"Being in the lab all the time gets tiresome," Raj said. "I'm jumping out of my skin half the time."

"Same for you, right?" she asked brightly. "Don't you leap on the chance to study languages in the field?"

"Absolutely."

"Boarding for Group A," an exhausted-sounding voice droned over the loudspeaker. I looked at my ticket: Group A. My last chance to run. To escape back to life as I knew it: circumscribed, safe, terrifying. As Nora and Raj turned toward the gate, I told myself, *Take deep breaths so you don't vomit. Keep your eyes on the floor. Just follow Nora and Raj—along with dozens of others who are clearly not the least bit afraid to board this plane.*

Don't think.

Just walk.

Our footsteps echoed on the corrugated metal floor of a long, gray umbilical passageway into the plane. The small digital recorder where I had downloaded the girl's twenty-eight-second vocalization rested in my jacket pocket. I reached in to hold it, the heat from my hand warming the narrow plastic cylinder. With every step, I told myself, *This is why you're going to keep on walking: this girl needs your help.*

Steep, narrow stairs led to a vast, poorly lit space, like a hollow whale made of steel. A domed ceiling soared far above. Chained-down parts of polar stations, machinery, stacks of cut wood, even snowmobiles, jammed the center aisle. Berths fitted out with army cots bolted to the floor flanked the mountains of gear, a sleeping bag rolled tight at the base of each, but no seats. Passengers—either in military gear or suited up for polar conditions—mulled around, trying to get comfortable. Those used to this arrangement promptly claimed their spots and laid out their belongings. Nora and Raj grabbed a berth; I snagged the one next to them. A few people immediately got down to the business of sleeping, some women but mostly burly, suspendered men in skullcaps bundled in their sleeping bags, faces wind-bitten and red, arms folded against remembered cold. Others lay with their heads propped up on one elbow, reading, or: headphones on, iPads out. I wondered what they were reading, or dreaming about, or working on; what were their reasons for traveling halfway around the earth?

We blasted off into the night. Without windows, it felt surreal, as if we were in a rocket ship hurtling to Mars. I bit an Ativan in half and chewed it like candy. Marveled at everyone around me who appeared to be in a state of utter indifference to the fact that we were shooting off into the sky carrying enough equipment to birth a new world on another planet. Again I wondered why I hadn't told anyone except my father where I was going; again concluded that it seemed impossible to say I was headed to Greenland and not talk about the girl who had thawed from the ice.

Nora and Raj curled up together on their cot under a sleeping bag, every now and then whispering to each other as they read by headlamp. An hour later, Nora was asleep on Raj's chest, her paperback spread-eagled on the sleeping bag, his arm around her, the other cradling his head. He gave me a little smile as he glanced over, eyeglasses glinting in the dim light, then went back to his book. They seemed altogether smitten with each other, and I envied their intimacy.

Shivering, I curled up on my cot, searching for comfort in the drafty space that smelled of crankcase oil, bad breath, and warmed-over chicken noodle casserole—supper served in a TV dinner–style tray distributed to us by pimpled recruits who looked barely high school age. I freed my cartoon-orange government-issued parka from my pack, balled it up, and stuffed it under my head for a pillow. A symphony of snorers held sleep at bay, as did the grinding roar of the engine that kept hundreds of tons aloft.

Hot in my hand: a quarter-sized, heart-shaped piece of lead, formed in the gizzard of a loon in the lake where Andy and I spent our childhood summers. Loons ate fishing sinkers thinking they were fish, dying as a result. He'd found this one in the skeletal remains of a loon along the shore. He gave it to me for my birthday—our birthday, really—when we were ten. At the time I said it was a weird, sad present, but he told me that everyone loved loons and that the heart shape was a sign that it was time for us to love them back.

I've carried it with me ever since.

AS I BEGAN to pore over my language books, I was reminded of the complexity of West Greenlandic. Most words in this language are composed of multiple elements called "morphemes," word parts that often create "sentence-words"; the longest stretches to over 200 letters. Nouns are inflected for one of eight cases and for possession. Eight moods as well as the number and gender of both the sentence's subject and object inflect every verb. Subdialects spring like weeds. Translation? Sure, I had all my downloaded dictionaries and American movies with Greenlandic subtitles, but in all honesty, I felt screwed. The learning curve seemed impossibly steep.

Fresh cracks on my fingers throbbed. The thin red lines looked like nothing much in the dim light, but often woke me at night with pain. I rummaged for my salve, which gave me a few moments of relief.

To distract myself, I scrolled through images of tiny West Greenland coastal towns—many with fewer than three hundred souls—barren, rocky hillsides dotted with small, brightly painted wooden houses, the great Greenland ice sheet in the distance. In the past, delicacies included fermented meat or fish and fermented seal oil, which apparently tasted like blue cheese. Seal eyes were a treat, as were the half-digested stomach contents of walrus, and fully formed chicks in their shells. I reminded myself of the reason Greenland was called Greenland. One theory held that when the Vikings discovered Iceland, they fell so in love with it they wanted to keep it a secret, so they gave Greenland its attractive name, hoping to lure explorers away from Iceland and to this nearly seven-hundred-thousand-square-mile block of ice—two miles deep at its center—ringed by black, craggy mountains that shot straight up out of the sea.

People still hunted and fished to survive: caribou, musk ox, seal, polar bear, and narwhal. These hunters were so skilled they could read the attributes of polar bears, or "ice bears," by their footprints: not only their age—but whether they were starving. The culture teemed with myths, but as usual, the language told me more than any single fact. It even betrayed a wry sense of humor: the island with a name that meant "not enough moss to wipe your ass with"; the first known term for missionaries: "he who talks too much." *Taimagiakaman* referred to the "great necessity": that of having to take the lives of animals to feed people and their dogs. The word in Inuktun for climate change translates to "a friend acting strangely"—what a personal and beautiful way of describing a relationship to the natural world.

The legendary plethora of words for snow is no myth, but the number of words for ice—topping 170—taught me more. There were words for dense, old ice: ice that was safe for a hunter and his sled and dogs to cross; words for grease ice, water in its earliest stage of freezing, which won't support a person but will allow seals to break through and breathe. Dozens of other terms specified various ice floes by shape and size, even by movement: were they rolling, swept along by the current, or stuck among their brethren? There was even a word for a crack in the ice opening and closing due to ocean movement beneath. Perhaps inspired by the necessity of knowing what kind of ice you were dealing with, there were a dozen words for fear, because the reality was that even seasoned hunters could die in a flash if the ice gave way and were often found frozen clinging to the edge of a floe. Among these flavors of fear were words for being at sea in a puny sealskin kayak as a storm barrels down, the fear of calamitous violence as when facing death, a fear so powerful one cannot move to defend oneself, and a fear of someone who must be avoided at all costs. I could certainly have added a few varieties of my own.

The words that stopped me cold, though, were *nuna unganartoq*, which meant "an overwhelming affection and spiritual attachment to the land and nature." Something as simple as the warm feel of a rock face baking in the sun, to an emotion as ineffable as the sense of infinity when witnessing a heart-stoppingly beautiful vista. A sensation of being no less a part of the land than a stone, a sprig of moss, or driftwood plying the waves. *Nuna unganartoq* was something I had never experienced, but I knew where I'd seen those words before.

It was how Andy had signed all his letters.

When we were eight or so, we had a fight and I ran to our mother to tell her how much I hated my brother. She said, *Well, he doesn't hate you.* She pulled a box of photos down from a high closet shelf, dug around until she found what she was looking for: an in vitro scan of the two of us curled up against each other. I was busy saying, *Yeah, so what*, until she pointed out that, even in the womb, his arm was draped protectively around my shoulders.

But in life—in grown-up, real life—who protected whom?

THE LAST TIME I'd seen him, just over a year ago, I'd been working late correcting summer-session papers in my office, my green banker's lamp the lone light on campus at nine at night. In a swirl of whiskey-smelling air—no knock—Andy barreled in, plopping down across from me in the chair my students used to dispute their grades or garner advice, usually some thinly veiled version of *I want to change majors.*

Even drunk and distraught, Andy was so much more handsome than I would ever be beautiful. Burly and strong, but with an athlete's grace. A solid six-footer, he had hair that grew wavy and thick, a rich auburn; mine was thin and fine like wispy smoke. His features were well defined, expressive: full lips, aquiline nose, deep-set, haunted eyes; without makeup I was washed-out, thin-lipped, snub-nosed, and tiny-eyed. So why did I feel like I was looking at myself when I looked at him? Why, after spending the day to-gether, was some part of me taken aback to glance in the mirror and see myself? At the time, I didn't understand it. The sensation felt oddly out-of-body, disturbing and sad at the same time. Was it because he—at his best—possessed so many of the qualities I could only dream of?

That evening he wore baggy khaki shorts I recognized from high school days and a filthy cotton madras shirt, one sleeve partially torn off. His skin glistened, as if he'd been running. The tang of Andy sweat, Andy panic, filled the tight space. Eyes red-rimmed and wild, he perched on the edge of the seat, leaning so far toward me he had to rest his elbows on my desk for balance. No air re-mained in the room.

He said, "Am I interrupting anything?"

It was the manic Andy who'd come to see me that night; it put me on guard and exhausted me. "What's up?"

"You know it's over, right?"

I exhaled and began to pack up my papers for the night.

"We've passed the tipping point. It's already too late."

"Please, Andy—" It's not that I wasn't freaked out about what was happening to the planet—I was—but I'd heard this rant count-less times, and there was no stopping him once he started.

"It doesn't matter anymore, Val. How much I talk about it, how much I lecture to my students, how much research I do, how many papers I write, presentations I give, how much I yammer on social media. It doesn't matter how much *anyone* talks about

it. Game over. It's useless. This world, this beautiful world . . ."
He dropped his head as if its weight was too much to bear. Stared
at the rug, until he lifted his gaze, refocusing his unblinking eyes
on mine. "Millions upon millions of animals are going to die,
understand? Are dying. Each of them, big and small, in agony.
Slow deaths. Starvation, thirst, disease, heat stroke. It's happening now. Musk oxen breaking their legs crashing through melting
permafrost. Polar bears drowning as they swim for sea ice that's no
longer there. Already ptarmigan eggshells are so thin they burst
before the chick is ready to be born. Countless sea creatures—
whales, shark, dolphins, octopuses, turtles, fish by the billions,
Val—they'll wash up on beaches, dead. Thousand-year floods will
be yearly, catastrophic. Hurricanes like no one's ever seen before,
can even comprehend. And for us?" He shook his head. "Climate
refugees in the millions, maybe billions. Water wars. Worldwide
crop failure, starvation, more pandemics. Oceans will be acidic
cesspools. . . ." He looked up at me imploringly, as if there were
anything his one-minute-older sister could conjure to comfort
him. Finding nothing, he leaned back in the chair and gazed out
my window with an expression of vague disgust. Slipped a can of
Red Bull from his roomy shorts pocket and gunned it down with
a shaky hand, forehead awash in sweat. "You want to know the real
reason it's hopeless?"

"Sure."

"Because even if we got rid of fossil fuels tomorrow, which we
won't, fix everything that's broken, which we *can't*, the problem is,
no one can fix human nature. We're greedy, selfish, stupid, so, *so*
fucking stupid, and shortsighted by *nature*. And that's what's going
to kill us all. Hopefully."

I stood and zipped my briefcase shut, snapped off my lamp. The
lights from the soccer field filled the room with an eerie yellow glow.

"What do you want me to do about it?"

He chewed on a fingernail, assessed me. Scratched a bug bite on his leg; a constellation of red marks covered one thigh. *Has he been sleeping outside?* Eyes on the soccer field, he asked, "Can I stay with you tonight?"

I sagged a bit, leaning on the back of my chair, feet aching in my pumps. "Well—why? Can't you go home?"

Andy's eye twitched. "Sasha kicked me out." He swirled the dregs of Red Bull and sucked it down.

"For Christ's sake—"

He jumped to his feet. "You know what, Val? I will *not* bring children into this world." He jabbed his finger in my direction as if I'd been badgering him about this. "I will not do it. Sasha's been riding me on this for months, and it all came to a head, and so, fuck it." He plopped back down in his seat, crossed an ankle over a knee, waggling his big Teva'd foot crazily. "I've got a better plan anyway."

I sat back down; my overstuffed leather chair giving a little *poof* of defeat beneath me. This was bad. Andy plus "a better plan" *always* equaled sirens and flashing red lights. We both drank too much; the difference was he did it in public.

"You're tapping my last nerve, Andy."

"Come on, Val. Hear me out."

I propped my chin in my hands. "What's the plan?"

Frenzied hope took over, animating his face. "It's about Wyatt."

I raised an eyebrow: *Go on.*

"He's stationed in Tarrarmiut. It's an uninhabited island off the northwest coast of Greenland. He's still doing his climate change study, getting some of the oldest ice core samples of anybody up there, but he's discovered something amazing. Totally by accident. Something to do with his pet mouse, honest to God. I wish I could tell you more, but I can't. Val, this is going to change everything. You've heard about the ice winds, haven't you? It's been in the news. Those three hikers in the White Mountains in New Hampshire who froze to death instantly? One minute it was forty degrees near the top of Mount Washington, the next it was thirty-five below zero, and *that was it*. They didn't have a chance. Didn't know what hit them. Died instantly. Midsentence. Midthought."

I pictured the press photo of the hikers. It was taken from the back, shadowy and dark. Two men and a woman frozen to death in the act of climbing, the woman with her arm midreach, about to grasp at a tree branch along the trail. Beyond the three figures, Mount Washington's snowy peak loomed, a destination they would never reach.

"That was some kind of freak thing."

"It was *not* a freak thing, Val. I wish it was, but it's starting to happen all over. Look, katabatic winds are a temperature gradient thing. In Greenland, they're called piteraqs. They come down off the glaciers, hurricane strength, unbelievably cold, but no one lives on the glaciers, so not a lot of people know about them. Now, with climate change, they're starting to happen all over the world—"

"I haven't heard—"

"They're covering it up because they don't know how to stop it and they don't want people to panic!"

"'*They*'?"

"I'm not paranoid, Val." He ran a trembling hand through untamed hair. "I may be a fucking nut, but I'm not—"

"What does Wyatt want from you?"

"Another scientist in the room. Someone to verify his findings. Someone to bounce ideas off of."

"He has Jeanne. Isn't she a researcher too?"

"Jeanne's a grunt. She keeps the snowcat going, the pipes from freezing. She's not a scientist," he added with a touch of Chesterfield arrogance.

"How long will you be there?"

"As long as it takes."

"As long as it takes for what, exactly?"

"To verify his findings. To get the proof we need."

I started to feel queasy. "But, Andy, in a few weeks, it's going to be nearly impossible to get out of there. Remember when that happened to Dad when we were kids? He went to Antarctica and the weather turned and—"

"This is the Arctic, it's different."

"He had to winter over. Eighty degrees below zero and dark for six months. Mom almost left him." I fingered the soft leather of my briefcase, itching to leave.

"Be serious. Mom would never have—"

"Come on, Andy, don't do this."

"Dad wants me to go."

"Fine. Did you tell *him* what this is really about? You know, everything you're not telling me?"

Andy shrugged, picked at a scab on his arm, then lifted and let drop his torn sleeve as if just noticing it. "He trusts me when I say this is going to make a difference for mankind."

Of course Dad approved of the trip. Some groundbreaking scientific discovery might make the Chesterfield name go down in history after all. Old, babyish sibling rivalry leered at me from the usual painful places. "I gotta go home," I said, getting to my feet again.

He looked up at me hopefully, almost puppyish, like I'd changed my mind about him crashing on my couch.

"Go home," I said. "Apologize to Sasha. Get a grip."

He pushed himself from the chair, his face blank. "Cool. I get it. I'll figure something out."

Before I could stop him, he was out the door and down the stairs, banging through the swinging doors of the lobby to the quad. I watched him from my window, his hair scorched-looking under the sodium lights, ripped sleeve flapping. He crossed the soccer field at a clip, almost running, as if attempting to escape some inner beast while trying to stay calm at the same time. I stepped outside my office into the hallway; the place was deserted.

In my current fantasy, the one where I let him stay with me—just a small, sisterly act of kindness—everything would have turned out differently, but that night a horrible emptiness echoed in the shadowy corridors and cold marble floors. My heart was lodged in my throat with dread, and it was all I could do to take a full breath.

four

Nine long, sleepless hours later, Nora, Raj, and I stood among dozens of others dressed to our teeth facing the cargo door, packs at our sides. People looked tired, even bored. *How could they be?* Some switch flipped, setting the hatch to clanking and groaning as it unmeshed from the cabin floor and hauled itself upward.

A gray dome of sky met a flat expanse of snow and ice an incalculable distance away. To the west, a pure white, flat-topped mountain rose starkly out of a navy blue sea, distant waves disintegrating into foggy smoke. Just in front of us, a dozen or so squat, modern-looking buildings sat arranged in intersecting rows like words on a Scrabble board. The Thule base. Nothing else man-made in sight.

We stepped out into a world of white. Drugs long worn off, I narrowed my eyes against rising nausea. Focused on my giant orange boots. *You are still on the earth,* I told myself, *just a different part of it.* I turned, squinting into the gust. Shrank back into my parka to minimize every inch of exposed skin as fine snow in a bitter wind stabbed at my face.

Diesel hit my nostrils. Exhaust pluming white from the rear, a boxy military bus rolled up to the plane—chained tires as tall as we were—our ride to one of the buildings, where we were directed to make sure we were carrying no more than forty-three pounds of personal belongings. An unsmiling marine manned a set of scales next to the door that led to the runway for our second flight, our final leg to Tarrarmiut, another three hundred miles north. Our four-seater ski plane idled, its propellers turning slowly in the frigid air. In the cockpit sat Pitak, the local pilot from Qaanaaq who I recognized right away from Wyatt's description. We were handed a hot wrap—our lunch, fried eggs rolled in pancake-thin bread—and instructed to pare down.

Altogether my bags weighed fifty-one pounds; I reddened as I dragged them off the scale and to one corner of the cement floor to do my culling.

Nora, whose bag clocked in at a sleek thirty-nine pounds, approached my mess. "Need some help?" Nodding, I scrambled to contain a sheaf of drawings that had spilled from my bag. Nora picked them up. "Wow, did you make these?"

I reached to take them back, but she was already leafing through them. Watching her touch them was physically painful. "No, my brother Andy drew those."

Small, gorgeous watercolors of nature: landscapes, animals, and plants alternated with unnervingly accurate pencil portraits of our parents and other relatives. He even drew himself in caricature: the big features, wide mouth, auburn mop of hair. Above his face, elaborate thought balloons filled with his tiny script floated by. These drawings were meant to make me laugh—and they had—but also to catch me up on his day or week. I had boxes of them at home but wanted to bring some with me, for luck, to keep him nearby. He had loved yakking on the phone, too, though his favorite way to drive me nuts was showing up unannounced. God, I missed that.

Nora held up one of the drawings. "What an amazing artist he is! This one should be in a gallery or something."

My heart ached when I saw which one she was admiring. Once, when Andy'd been hospitalized, he'd assured me he would never do such a stupid thing as take his own life. Told me he was more worried about what I'd do on one of my bad days. So we made a pact: we would never hurt ourselves. A few days after I spoke to him, I received the drawing Nora held now.

In colored pencil: Andy, sporting a silly grin, held a gun to his temple. Apparently he'd fired, because out the other side of his head flowered a lush cornucopia of beautiful things: a strutting peacock, an elegantly wrought elephant, fistfuls of ripely blooming peonies, a naked siren of a woman reclining in a bed of her own raven tresses; she looked a lot like Sasha. I snatched the paper from Nora just as she was turning it over to the other side, where the billowing contents of his head continued but darker: gargoyles, a crowd of naked, emaciated people clawing at each other for a crust of bread, a blackened forest, the earth in flames . . .

"He's not around anymore, I'm afraid, my brother," I said, tucking the drawing under the others. "We were twins."

"Oh dear, Val. I'm so sorry to hear that. Raj has a twin, Sanjit. They're inseparable."

She looked genuinely shocked. So I told her the story, or at least what I thought was the story. "Wyatt didn't tell you?"

"No, nothing." She glanced around at the crew readying the plane. "So, this is going to be hard for you—being where it happened."

"It's hard no matter where I am."

"I can only imagine."

I tucked the drawing back in my bag, guiltily. As if it were some sort of evidence that I should have known what he was going to do, and I didn't stop him.

"Well, the drawings are light, so they shouldn't be an issue," she said with a touch of relief. At least this was a solvable problem.

I hefted a stack of picture books. "It's these books, for the girl . . . it kills me to leave them behind."

"Let's put them in my carry-on, at least a couple of kilos' worth, right?" she said with a bright smile.

"Yes, thank you, and the drawing pad and the markers, too, if you really don't mind. I've got to have those."

She complied, loading her bag with the books and supplies. "So, do you think you'll be able to suss out what she's saying?"

"I have no idea."

Nora tucked her hair under her hat, a wool one with the braided strings hanging down on either side that looked adorable on her. "Well, I think you'll be brilliant. I just hope Raj and I can get our work done before we have to get out of here. We have three months of work to do and half that much time to do it." She glanced outside. Raj stood next to the plane, waving at us. "The wind's died down—I guess this is our window to get out of here. Anyway, they're waiting for us."

QUICKLY I GROKKED the particular terror of small planes: the lawn mower engine, the thin metal skin the only thing between you and your erasure once the earth yawns beneath you. An iceberg several stories high and miles long filled our view from the front of the plane, an immense white wall striated with blue cracks like ancient porcelain. No one spoke or took a breath until we cleared it; then the frozen landscape opened up. Across an infinite horizon, in countless shades of blue and white, land became indistinguishable from sky. We were in it now: what I privately referred to as *the Enormity*, an emotional or physical place so overwhelming I couldn't face it without drugs or alcohol. We buzzed like a tiny silver bee over a backbone of slate-black massifs. Stomach-dropping cliffs plummeted to indigo fjords dotted with icebergs many times larger than our plane. I could almost hear Andy saying, *Val, there is no God, but God is here.*

Beneath us, a wedge of brown darkened a massive promontory of sea ice. Nora caught sight of it and tapped Pitak on the shoulder. He nodded, and we veered sharply away.

"What's wrong?" I called out over the deafening engine.

"Walrus," Nora yelled back to me. "Big herd. Thousands probably. They spook at any loud sound and stampede. The young ones get trampled. It can get pretty bad."

I nodded, in no mood to pursue details.

An hour and a half later, we dropped down through sleety bands of clouds, skidding onto rough ice before catching a smooth section and sliding for what felt like miles before shuddering to stillness in a cloud of snow. Three yellow buildings huddled together several dozen yards away. In the distance, out on the bay on sea ice, a bright yellow dome-shaped structure flashed between blasts of snow.

A figure burst from the orange door of the longest building— two industrial trailers joined end to end—and made its way toward us. I'd only seen him maybe a half dozen times, but I knew that slightly bowlegged gait, that hurry-up-and-get-it-done stride. Skullcap pulled low over his brow, Wyatt leaned into the wind dragging a metal sled behind him, his unzipped parka flapping over quilted overalls and a thermal shirt. Behind him, the orange door banged open again, and another figure emerged wearing a knee-length red parka, hood cinched tight. Nora, Raj, and I got ourselves out of the plane, a bitter gust buffeting us as we tried to get our bearings.

Wyatt engulfed me in a quick hug; even that brief intimacy startled and disturbed me, perhaps because he was probably the last person to see Andy alive. I exhaled, tried to smile.

"You look good, Val, you look good. You okay? Trip okay?"

"It was long. We're pretty wiped out—"

"Nora? Rajeev?" He shook their mittened hands, lingering a bit on Nora, as if he wasn't expecting such a beautiful woman.

"Call me Raj," he said, one arm slipping around Nora: a statement, for sure. We all introduced ourselves to Jeanne, a heavyset woman hard in her forties, ruddy-cheeked and moonfaced, brown silver-streaked hair escaping her hood and whipping in the breeze. She mumbled her hellos, staring at each of us in turn as if her eyes were ravenous for new faces.

"You guys hungry?" Wyatt gestured at the ugly yellow building. "Jeanne's been working her magic all afternoon."

"I think we could all use some food, right?" Raj said, heaving a box of supplies onto the sled. "That egg thing back in Thule was a joke."

Jeanne's forehead furrowed a bit; she said, "You're not a vegetarian, are you?" as if somehow a rumor to that effect had been going around.

"Why, do I look like one?" he said with a smile.

"You'd starve to death around here if you were," she said without a shred of humor. With a huff, she bent down to help Pitak unload a case of canned goods from the belly of the plane. Scrappy, lithe, with a windburned face, handsome despite missing a few teeth, he moved at twice her pace, all the while trying to jolly her up, smiling and joking with her. Any returned smiles were rare and unenthused.

"So, this weather! Crazy, right?" Pitak called to Wyatt. "Summer forgot Greenland this year."

"It was bizarre!" Wyatt said. "Two weeks in the fifties, a little melt, then boom, back to this."

"When this happens," Pitak said, "when there is no summer, we say the winters are like two dogs fucking."

Wyatt smiled as he balanced a crate of eggs on a wooden box of fresh fruit. "Thanks for that, Pitak."

He raised his gloved hands as if trying to erase his words. "Sorry, ladies."

Nora laughed. "We've heard the word before."

Pitak turned back to Wyatt, his face serious. "The girl is okay?"

Wyatt nodded. "My friend Val here's going to help us out with her."

"She a doctor? From America?"

"Sort of," Wyatt said, clearly interested in changing the subject. He sidled up to Pitak. "So, did you get them?"

"Oh, man, I almost forgot." Pitak hopped back up into the cabin of the plane. Grinning, he tossed Wyatt a plastic bag tied at the top. Wyatt caught it and tore at the sack, cursing the knot. Three avocados, perhaps the only green objects in hundreds of miles, fell onto his orange boots, rolling a yard or so across the ice.

Wyatt dove down, stuffing them in his pockets as if they were bricks of heroin and we were the DEA. "Damn it, Pitak," he said, laughing, "I owe you my life, man. My fucking life."

Smiling, the pilot climbed back into the plane. "Eat them slowly, friend. See you in seven weeks."

Seven weeks.

Wyatt, Jeanne, Nora, and Raj headed toward the bleak buildings, all of them banana yellow, doors painted orange, like children's toys dropped in a sea of white. Andy had told me the bright colors made the buildings easier to spot during a blizzard. I wondered which orange door he'd come out of that terribly cold night just five months ago. Would we be walking through it with all the gear, talking and laughing and getting to know one another just yards from where he had lain his head for the very last time? Tripping across the hallowed ground where he'd taken his last breath, hopefully past all pain? Maybe he was at peace; how could I know? Maybe he was in ecstasy that he'd finally taken the step he'd been mulling for so long, drifting off where none of us who loved him wanted him to go.

The wind froze tears to my cheeks; I leaned into it and headed toward the blur of yellow and orange and the sound of human voices.

five

Wyatt cracked open the door, motioning for me to hurry up, so I slipped in behind everyone else. For a minute or two we all crowded together awkwardly in the drab hallway, shedding our parkas and stomping the snow off our boots as we coughed the dry, cold air from our lungs.

Powerfully built through the shoulders and arms and well over six feet, Wyatt towered over all of us, but his gait—a tendency to walk along the outer edges of his feet—brought an odd delicacy to how he entered a room. According to Andy, most of the little toes on each foot had been lost to frostbite during an assignment manning a weather station in Antarctica. Still, he wore the ruggedly handsome face of a man who spent most of his six decades outside; he was bearded, black hair salted with white, dark eyes under heavy brows, a strong chin, and a good set of teeth.

"Let me give you the nickel tour so you can settle in," he said, ushering us past a wall covered with hooks that held axes, knives, rope, and a couple of rifles. We hesitated at the first room on the right, the largest in the building. "This is where I try to get work done." He gestured at one corner, where a few old Macs as well as a sleek new PC battled for space on a long table strewn with files and papers. Metal cabinets flanked another beat-up wooden table crowded with microscopes, Bunsen burners, and test tubes. The room's one long picture window looked out over the lapis water of an inlet packed with drift ice as tall as ships.

"And this is where we chill," he said, half-heartedly picking up some old magazines—*Journal of Glaciology, National Geographic, Scientific American*—and arranging them in a pile. A chocolate-brown L-shaped couch so pummeled by time it looked almost comfortable took up most of the rest of the room. In the air: onions, sweat, chicken soup, and a sulfuric smell—*formaldehyde?* I couldn't place it. Above us, tube-shaped fluorescent lights buzzed and snapped. An ancient television slouched under a well-used dartboard, its rabbit ears broken off. A plastic bowl of Cheez-Its teetered on the TV stand next to a half-eaten vanilla Hostess cupcake and an empty Wild Turkey bottle. So, there was alcohol here: *Thank God for that.* The floors were covered with cheap rugs, one over the other, the walls a noxious green.

"You've been here how long, Wyatt, a year?" Raj asked.

"Closer to two." He turned toward the hall. "Let's keep our voices down. The girl is sleeping."

We all nodded and followed along behind him like ducklings, except for Jeanne, who clomped off to the kitchen, its floor-to-ceiling open shelves crammed with nuts, dried fruits, canned goods, all manner of grains and flours as well as a stunning cornucopia of junk food. Wyatt's room was first: dark paneling, bed unmade, books, notebooks, papers, and magazines in teetering piles.

He knelt down. Peered at a pure white arctic mouse in a wire cage. "Here's a guy you all need to meet. This is Odin."

"Like the Norse god?" Raj said.

Narrow-eyed, Wyatt tilted his head up toward Raj. "What are you, some kind of wiseass?"

For a few seconds, no one said a word. Odin skittered up onto his hind legs, stretching his surprisingly long body upward—as if greeting Wyatt—scratching at the wire mesh.

"I know my Norse mythology," Raj said, folding his arms across his chest, clearly trying to read Wyatt. "What, is that going to be a problem here?"

"Could be." Wyatt pushed himself to his full height, which was quite a bit taller and easily fifty pounds heavier than Raj. His expression—or lack of one—remained, and I wondered if he was conscious of it, or if being stone-faced or on edge was the result of isolation in this place for years on end.

Wyatt burst out a sudden, forced-sounding laugh. Smacked Raj a little too hard on his back. "Kidding, my friend, just fucking with ya. But for the others here, who maybe aren't up on this sort of thing, Odin was the god who killed himself to gain knowledge about the realm of the dead." He reached down to the cage, unlatched the lid, and lifted up the mouse; after a bit of scrabbling, the creature seemed content to cuddle in his palm. Wyatt held him at eye level, studying him. "When I found this guy, over a year ago now, he was in the Dome, frozen solid. But now look at him."

"Well, *that's* impossible," Raj said with an exasperated exhale.

"Really?" Wyatt said.

"Cells burst when they freeze—"

Nora took his arm and tugged at it. "Come on, darling, he said it happened." She took off her hat; her shining hair fell all around her shoulders. "Look, we're all exhausted—"

"Who do you think is sleeping in the other room?" Wyatt said.

Raj lifted his fine-boned hands in an appeal for a truce. "You know what? Fine. I'm here to do my research and go home."

"That was my understanding too." Wyatt settled Odin back into his cage with great gentleness as the mouse's eraser-pink nose poked between his wind-chapped fingers. Without another word, Wyatt stepped between us, and we trailed him in silence past another open door.

"Jeanne's room is here."

Jeanne's narrow bed was neatly made with a handmade quilt, its pattern of mismatched squares of birds and flowers bleached almost completely white. Half a dozen dolls sat propped against the pillows; these, too, were beat-up and grubby, hair ratty, eyes lazy in their heads, chubby little hands in a half grip in the air; next to them a couple of disturbingly real-looking doll babies in doll diapers cuddled one another. We all paused, Nora and Raj exchanging *what the fuck* glances, but Wyatt kept the tour on a clip and motioned us to the bathroom: a sad, beige affair with a beige porcelain toilet and plastic shower, narrow as a coffin, its mold-dotted beige curtain barely covering the stall.

"Facilities," he said. "No tub, I'm afraid, but otherwise she flushes up to thirty below outside. Colder than that, we make other arrangements. But you'll all be long gone before then."

Wyatt gestured at a closed door across from the bathroom. "The girl's room." Shivering, I drifted my hand over the doorknob as I passed. I could hear her vocalizations in my mind, sounds I had committed to memory.

Wyatt paused at the door across from Jeanne's room. "Val, this is your little piece of paradise."

The room was the same dreary shade as the hallway, but a mural covered one wall. A trio of badly drawn palm trees sulked over what I guessed was a beach; coconuts strewn around, happy grinning fish popping between frothy waves. Perhaps some tropics-craving climate scientist felt like indulging his artistic side. Definitely not Andy's work. Wyatt clicked on a tube light. It swayed back and forth, illuminating a twin bed with a red sleeping bag unzipped over it under a small window. A bed table with a reading lamp cozied up to the bed; next to that, a simple bureau, desk, and chair. The rest of the room was stacked floor to ceiling with boxes.

"We had to improvise a little with the girl here and all, sorry. Your room's also the storeroom—well, one of them."

"It's fine," I said. "Which was Andy's room?"

For the first time, Wyatt looked uncomfortable in his skin. "Well, I took it over, I figured—"

"I just wanted to know. I'm fine here."

He gave me an efficient nod. "Now, Nora and Raj, I thought you could crash on the couch tonight, since it's too late to get you settled in the Dome, okay?"

They agreed, and we all shadowed Wyatt back to the office/living room. Outside, the wind whipped the snow sideways; it stuttered rat-a-tat at the wide picture window. "So, we're in the main building now, which we call the Shack. Jeanne does her repair work in the Shed. We heat it, but not as much as home base here. Behind the Shed is the Cube, where we store the snowcat and snowmobile, like a garage. Out in the bay is the Dome, but you knew that. Now, some ground rules." Wyatt paused near a whiteboard scribbled over with calculations. "We've had a strange summer here, as you know. Barely a summer at all. Lots of storms, temps closer to fall than summer, in the teens in the daytime; ten, fifteen below at night. So, listen up. Anyone, that includes me and Jeanne, goes *anywhere*, you sign here on this log sheet." He held out a clipboard chained to the wall, tapping it with a Sharpie as he spoke. "Mark the time you go out and why. You bring your walkie-talkie everywhere when you're out there, got it? No exceptions. It's part of your body."

He handed each of us one of the blocky, old-fashioned things. It was heavier than I thought it was going to be, but also cheap, like a toy. I thought, *So this is going to save me?*

"Everybody, turn yours on."

We all did so.

"Super simple to use. It's your responsibility to make sure the batteries are working. I've just put fresh ones in. Jeanne can give you more, ask her where they are when you need them.

"I've rated the storms one, two, and three. Level one: up to 25 mph winds, windchill to twenty below. You go outside with my permission only. Level two: 25 to 35 mph winds, windchills to minus thirty. Raj, Nora: the Dome can't handle that in terms of heat, so we all work and sleep here. Permission to leave granted from me on an emergency basis only, and no one goes out alone, understood? Level three storm: 35-plus mph winds, windchills minus thirty or below, no one leaves under any circumstances. You'll find that there are ropes connecting all the buildings. Crucial for getting from place to place if you're caught in a whiteout. Look, I know all this sounds like common sense, who would go out in a blizzard with thirty-below winds? But these are close quarters. Storms can last for days. It gets boring when we can't do our work—for me, too, okay? So, the temptation is to push the limits and say fuck it and go out anyway, but that won't work here.

"All right, then," he said, glancing at each of us as though we were a set of problems it was his job to solve, and he wasn't looking forward to it. "Let's eat."

FIFTEEN FEET LONG from tail to tooth-filled snarl, a massive polar bear pelt covered one wall of the kitchen. I ran my hand over it; even in death, each hair of its fur felt thick and strong, glinting with a yellowish tinge, like straw. I remembered reading that a polar bear's fur wasn't really white; it was actually clear and only reflected the light around it. It felt surreal to be touching the body of this beast, once so ferociously alive and so at home in all the vast reaches of the Enormity.

"Did you kill this?" I asked Wyatt.

He smirked. "I'm no hunter. That's from the mainland. Pitak and a couple other hunters took it down last year just north of Qaanaaq. Here," he said, gesturing at a chair. "Have a seat."

In the center of the table sat a bowl of peaches, apples, oranges, and grapes, all fresh from the plane. Wyatt snatched up an orange and held it to his nose, smiling and inhaling deeply before peeling it. The avocados were nowhere in sight.

Cornstarch-thick beef stew and white bread—a dense block of it cut thickly and spread with margarine that tasted a little off. Jelly-jar glasses of boxed wine that I deeply appreciated. Everyone chatted about their work, the strange weather, the trip, as if there weren't a young girl in the other room who had thawed from the ice alive, or as if we were all sitting around buying this fantastical story. The lunacy of what I'd done—*traveled a thousand miles from my safe apartment to a frozen wasteland with a bunch of near strangers*—hit me just as I felt my meds slack off. My hands shook as I buttered a slice of bread; Wyatt noticed, and I flushed. He had a certain appeal, even at twenty years my senior, but more than that—at the time—I wanted him to like me, admire me, as much as he'd liked Andy, if I was going to be honest about it.

Jeanne, who hadn't taken her eyes off Nora since she sat down, said, "So, how will you two be keeping busy out in the Dome?"

"I'll be diving quite a lot," Nora said, digging cheerfully into her bowl of stew. "On the lookout for fin whale and humpback, narwhal, beluga. Tracking how the changing sea ice here has affected their range and communication, see if or how their vocalizations have changed since the last study was done here. Darling?" She took a healthy swig of wine, draping an affectionate arm across Raj's back.

"I'll be sampling various kelps for changes since the last survey was done a couple of years ago: health, type, range. Even doing some studies on it as a potential packaging material. But who cares about that?" He turned to Wyatt. "What I want to know is where you found this girl. I mean—where you *really* found her." He eyed Nora and me in turn, as if seeking backup. "Sure you didn't just fly her over from the mainland as some sort of stunt?" he said, cutting himself a thick wedge of bread.

Wyatt paused, stew-laden spoon in the air, to consider Raj. "Maybe you should stick with seaweed."

Raj made a small noise of exasperation, picked up his plate, and headed to the sink. Nora followed suit, Wyatt side-eyeing her ass as she went.

She rinsed her dishes, folded her arms, and leaned against the kitchen counter. "Okay, so tell us. The day you found her, what was that like?"

Wyatt kept at his stew, heavy forearms guarding his plate, eyes on his food. "Not sure this is the right time—"

"It was just a regular day," Jeanne said, her voice dreamy thick. Head tilted, a rusty barrette barely holding back her shaggy shoulder-length hair, she seemed to address the center of the table. "We were headed out to Glacier 35B to get the rest of the samples. Remember, Wyatt?"

"Two weeks ago," Wyatt added quietly.

Jeanne said, "Five months after Andy passed, to the day."

I stiffened. We all did. Raj and Nora stood silently by the sink, listening.

Wyatt pushed his food away, face weary. "We'd finished drilling cores in the northeast quadrant, and we were heading back across the ice lake—what we call the section of the glacier near the Osvald Fjord. Overnight a fissure had opened halfway across, maybe thirty yards long, split sheer down a thousand feet, God knows how far, really. We saw it from the cat, and we started going real slow parallel to it, a couple yards from it, because now of course we didn't dare cross the lake and take the route we'd planned, and we were shitting ourselves wondering what was going to open up next. That's when something caught my eye a couple of yards down the far wall of the crevasse. This crescent-shaped flesh-colored thing, a color you never see out here, not like that. It was a child's foot, from the side, from the heel down to the little toe. It was like, I don't know, seeing a tarantula in my cereal bowl. Totally crazy. It was only by chance I was even looking in the right direction. We got out to look, but it was getting late, so we had to come back the next day with some equipment. Jeanne did this ingenious setup with a pulley and a ladder and a swing, got me down there just fine to have a look." Jeanne cast her eyes at the greasy tablecloth, stirring her stew. *Was she blushing?* "So I'm dangling there, just my ass in this sling over this bottomless pit, trying to make out where the rest of her might be. It took a while to figure out if she was standing, or lying down, or what. And even then, it was a guess."

"So, was she standing?" Raj asked.

"It looked like she was running."

"Was she alone?" Nora asked.

"As far as we could tell," he said with a heavy sigh, as if he didn't want to be sharing this much information, but part of him was relieved to be doing so. "We took a day or two to scope out a big area, a couple of kilometers around us. Absolutely nothing out there. Nothing we could see, anyway. So we went back with this battery-powered saw, but I had to be real careful. Didn't want to hurt her. But we did it. Cut around her and hitched this big block of ice to the cat. Towed it back here."

"But this island has never been inhabited," Raj said. "The literature, the history, all the charts say—"

"Look, here's the going theory," Wyatt said, lifting his eyes to Raj. "Last year, there was a major caribou migration change, maybe because of all the warmer summers we've been having—except for this one, anyway. Thousands of animals were coming through here.

There's a village a dozen miles south of Qaanaaq. Just across the water on the mainland. Very isolated. They'd been suffering a few really bad hunting seasons. Bearded seal population down by half, no narwhal, no polar bear. Even the fishing was bad. So a couple families pulled up stakes and came out here for the season."

"What happened, do you think?" Nora asked.

"We got a lot of sleet that year. Coated the lichen, just encased it in an inch of ice. The theory is the caribou starved to death. No one ever heard from the families again."

"Why not just return the girl to her village," Raj said, "if that's where you think she's from?"

"It'll happen soon enough."

Raj shook his head. "So what does Pitak think of all this?"

"Remind me, Raj, why that is your concern?"

Raj took off his glasses, wiped the shining circles with the tail of his flannel shirt. His eyes big and vulnerable-looking without his spectacles. "Child of color, taken by a white man, it's not like it's a new—"

"Aren't you listening, man? Nobody *took* her, we *found* her—"

Raj looped the wires of his glasses back over his ears, face hardening. Nora leaned into him a bit with her shoulder, but he ignored her. "It's not right to keep the girl from her family, her community—"

Wyatt raised his voice a notch. "Nothing's been proven. If she was with her family, then where are they? They would have fallen down the same crevasse, been nearby."

"They could be anywhere—"

"People from this village, if that's even where she's from, speak the same dialect as in Qaanaaq, but Pitak couldn't understand any of the sound bites I played for him. Why is that? We just don't know her story. And don't forget, he doesn't know she thawed from the ice, only that I found her and she's alive." He took a big bite of a brownie, chewed. "People talk."

Everyone stayed quiet. The cold violet light of the Arctic sunset poured over us, turning our faces bloodless and pale. My head pounded with exhaustion.

"What's she like?" I asked quietly.

"What's she like?" Wyatt shook his head. "The first day, all she did was scream. She was terrified of us, of everything. She smashed plates, lamps, dumped out all the kitchen drawers, but now, now . . . it's like all the air's gone out of her. We try, but truth is, she's freaked-out and confused. Inconsolable."

"Looks like you've got your work cut out for you," Nora said to me.

I nodded, my heart thrumming in my chest. *Inconsolable. How could I possibly comfort her?* Everyone seemed wrapped up in their own thoughts. I inhaled air tainted with our breath and congealing beef stew, felt our human closeness in the cramped room, the weight of our isolation, the unsaid. I thought of the level one storm that had delayed our flight from Thule, recalled Pitak saying that even a rescue flight was at the mercy of the weather. Pictured a little girl dropped into a new world, one with complete strangers babbling nonsense words. I'd break a few things too.

Jeanne fingered a saltshaker shaped like a happy cartoon whale, absently dumping a tiny mountain of salt in the palm of her hand, then pouring it onto her plate. "I heard her crying outside my window all winter long. I kept telling Wyatt—I don't know how many times—but he just said—"

The color rose in Wyatt's face. "Not now, Jeanne."

"That voice . . . it was like I knew her all along—"

Wyatt shoved himself from the table; the cracked plates rattled. "Knock it off, Jeanne," he hissed under his breath. "We've talked and talked about this."

Jeanne looked around, searching for a sympathetic face; perhaps that was mine, because her gaze rested there. Wide set and gray, her eyes contained an emptiness that chilled me, a toxic agony that echoed my own. "She was calling for help, but Wyatt, he wouldn't let me go out and find her, wouldn't let me go out and let her in—"

"I'm supposed to let you head out for a stroll when it's seventy degrees below zero?" Wyatt said evenly. "To what, chase some phantom?"

She smiled eerily at me. "Well, she's here now, isn't she?"

Wyatt got to his feet, slammed his chair into the table. Outside, the wind voiced its rage, the building rattling like a toy.

I felt a presence in the doorway and turned to look. A pitifully small Inuit girl hovered in the shadows. High, wide cheekbones under bottomless black eyes, ruddy skin that glowed with the heat of the room. Above her quivering upper lip, a drop of clear snot trembled from her nose. Her ink-black hair looked as if a mad person had cut it. Her body was lost in an enormous Christmas sweater featuring Santa's sleigh and eight reindeer flying up over one shoulder. Its hem swept the floor—it had to be Jeanne's or Wyatt's. As she scanned the room, taking in the three newcomers, her eyebrows met in an upside-down V of concern. Slowly, evenly, I got to my feet and said, "Hello, I'm Val," in West Greenlandic.

The girl let out a scream, pivoted, and bulleted down the dark hallway.

six

A cold, sharp light filtered through my frost-rimed window at just past six, bringing the weird palm trees and grinning coconuts into focus. Already I missed my cramped, lonely apartment. I missed warmth and plants and trees and couldn't imagine Andy or anyone else loving this brutal, desolate place, but he had.

The smell of coffee drew me from my room. Jeanne's door stood ajar, bed made tight, creepy dolls neatly arranged sitting against the pillows and staring straight ahead. Raj and Nora were nowhere to be seen.

Bearded like a pirate, salt-and-pepper hair escaping his cap, Wyatt hunched over his computer, mousing over a map on the screen.

"Right there," he said as I approached with my coffee, pointing to a tiny black dot on a vast glacier. "That's where we found her."

It looked impossible. A little girl alone, frozen in place ten feet down the wall of a crevasse. To truly understand her—the realization hit me viscerally—I had to go to this place, no matter how doped up I needed to be.

"I'd like you to take me there. Can you?" My hands rang with pain at the thought of venturing into this white void.

"Your job is to be here, with the girl. It's not like we have time to waste—"

"My job is to figure out her language, but part of that is knowing as much as possible what happened to her. At least see where she came from."

He took a bite of a waffle smeared with Nutella and tossed it back down on his plate. "I'll think about it."

"Do you buy the story about those caribou hunters who disappeared?"

He looked relieved by the change of topic. I tried to focus on the screen, not on his stockinged feet, especially the empty pouches where his toes were supposed to be. Without boots for support, his walk was shuffling, awkward, though he didn't seem the least bit self-conscious about it.

"It's just . . . where did everyone else go? Why was she alone?" He shook his head. "I am honestly fucking mystified. I'm not sure I believe the story. News gets pretty diluted around here. People don't keep track of things very well. And it's a good twenty miles to the mainland. Would they really come here for some caribou, the numbers of which could have been exaggerated? And why would they bring their families? Why wouldn't just the men go?" He dosed his coffee with a splash of fresh cream Jeanne had swooned over when she unpacked it the evening before. "But, you know, crazier things have happened here, that's for sure. Those people had nothing, they were desperate. And I know the route the hunters would have taken—but with everything going on, I haven't had the chance to go out there and really search."

He zoomed in to the featureless expanse, as if by staring long enough, the mystery of the girl in the glacier would reveal itself. The screen turned pure white, the dot a faint smudge.

"When did she eat last?"

"Yesterday morning, and it wasn't much. Maybe she's on a food strike to get what she wants, whatever that is. She likes fish and beef, especially raw hamburger." He went to a low refrigerator along one wall of the kitchen, opened it. "Pitak got us a whole shipment for her. Plus some seal." He unwrapped a package of ground meat, spooned some into a cereal bowl, and gave it to me. "She uses her hands."

I took the bowl and a glass of water to her door, knocked softly. "Hello," I said in Danish. "Hello, girl, I'm not here to hurt you. I'm here to help you."

The creak of a mattress, the thud of a bed shoved against the door.

"I have food," I said in West Greenlandic, a language I didn't know as well by a long shot. The word for *meat* escaped me. "Some beef. Not cooked. You are hungry?" I grabbed the doorknob and turned. The thump of her small body against the hollow door. "Be calm, young girl. Here is beef, and a glass of water, right here, here for you." I rolled my eyes at my pitiful command of the language as I set down the food and water.

Silence.

Wyatt lingered at the other end of the hall, a heavy, watchful presence. "Is that her language?"

"No idea. Does she use the toilet?"

"She's terrified of it. She shits in a coffee can I gave her. Makes sure to leave that out for me every morning."

"What about her clothes? What was she wearing when you found her?"

"Caribou skin coat, polar bear pants, and one sealskin boot. The usual outfit for indigenous folks around here in super-remote settlements, as far as I know. Don't know why only the one boot."

"Where are they, the clothes?"

"We had to cut them off of her. I threw them away. But I asked Pitak to send me some girls' clothes with the supplies we got in yesterday. They're over there." He gestured at a cardboard box near the door.

"What's with the Christmas sweater?"

"It's the only thing she'll wear. We gave her a pile of our clothes, and she grabbed that. Hasn't taken it off since she laid eyes on it."

I walked by him to sort through the box. Felt his eyes on me in a way I couldn't translate. Not sexual, exactly. More an estimation of some kind. A shot of cold shivered up my neck as I sorted through Hello Kitty pajamas, a hot-pink parka, down overalls, underwear, socks, and a pair of deerskin boots decorated with fringe and beads. Still, his eyes on me.

"I'll leave you to it," he said, finally, wandering off toward the kitchen in his odd shuffle walk.

I exhaled.

FOR TWO HOURS, all I did was talk to her through her door, occasionally nudging it open a crack, but she wasn't having it. Still, I could feel her just behind it, breathing, listening. Wyatt paced, observing my every move, until something seemed to snap in him. He thumped his way over to the door and rapped hard, his shadow monstrous under the hall light.

"Hey, girl," he said. "You know, we're trying to help you."

"Please watch your tone of voice," I said from my seat on the floor.

So he poured on the honey. "Come on, sweetie pie, you gotta be starving by now. How come all the sudden you don't like old Wyatt?"

I got to my feet, faced him. He towered over me; I took a step back, said, "Could be she's overwhelmed by all these new faces. Maybe you could leave us alone for a while?"

"I didn't do anything to her, you know. Never once raised my voice. She smashed some of my slides and half my test tubes, and I was cool as a cuke."

"I'm sure you were."

He gave me a look I couldn't parse, but there was no warmth in it. "Enjoy your girl talk. See you in a couple hours." He threw on his parka, pulled his hat down over his ears, and left.

When I turned back to the girl's door, the bowl of hamburger and glass of water were gone. In its place was a coffee can half filled with urine. I carried it to the bathroom and flushed the contents.

As I passed Jeanne's room, I detoured to her bed, grabbed a doll, and returned to the girl's room. An empty bowl and water glass had been set outside the door. I didn't know the Greenlandic or even the Danish word for *doll*. I knocked softly and said, "I have little baby." Slid down to my usual position and said again, "I have little baby for you. Want to see it?" I leaned into the door, put my shoulder into it. Suddenly it gave a few inches, enough for me to slide the doll in. The door slammed shut.

Seconds later, it was wrenched open and the doll sailed over my head, smacking against the wall opposite, its ceramic face shattering in pieces on the floor.

Guess she didn't like the doll.

In a salad of languages including Old Norse, I chattered through her door, filibustering at her about anything I could think of: how I wished she could have met Andy, the things I liked to do when I was her age, even Greenlandic history. I asked her what had happened to her, who her family was, what was the last thing she remembered. All the while I stared down the hall at Wyatt's screen saver, a narwhal floating in outer space.

Maybe it was only to get me to stop talking, but after an hour, the door creaked open. I smelled her before I saw her. A rank, acrid taste—unwashed hair and skin, the memory of leather—filled my mouth. Her clotted breath came rough in her throat as if her nose was stuffed up. Had she been crying? It all broke my heart a little bit. As tall as I was crouched on the floor, she stood inches from me, a small, somber-faced child backlit by morning sun.

Very softly she whispered, "Stahndala," and again, "stahndala."

I pointed at her. "Are you Stahndala?" I said in English. "My name is Val. *Val.*"

Her face screwed up in confusion.

I motioned for her to come out. Fear in her eyes, wild black hair sticking up every which way, she took a few steps into the hall, glancing both ways. Santa's reindeer led by Rudolph, his nose a puffy red ball sewn onto the loose knit, flew diagonally up the sweater. Her tiny toes, blackened with grime, poked from under the ragged hem.

"*Stahndala*," she whispered hoarsely.

She looked at me with such pleading in her dark eyes; I simply wasn't ready for it. The frank reality of her, this girl from ice. Just a child, but from what world, and how could I possibly enter it? *Who are you, dear child?* I drew in a sharp breath, uttering a little cry. *What should I do?* I had no children, no nieces or nephews. Sure, if you were eighteen and wanted to major in Latin or Greek, I could handle it, but *this*?

Maybe—*the toys*. I'd brought some, but they were in the front room and I'd have to walk past her to get them and she would run, I could see it. Very slowly, repeating the word she'd said to me, *stahndala*—which I now know was the exact wrong thing to say to her—I ventured a few paces toward the front room. Which is when I remembered I'd stored them in my bedroom. But she hadn't budged. Stood like a ghost of a girl. I sat in Wyatt's swiveling desk chair, glanced furtively around. Grabbed one of those stupid get-rid-of-tension rubber balls next to his computer.

I held it up and said in Danish, "Let's play." Rolled the ball to her. It bumped along the rug.

She watched until it came to a stop at her feet. Looked up at me. I motioned for her to roll it back. Her face said, *Why are you doing this weird thing?* Desperate, I took a pen and rolled it over to her. Then another. Tears welled in her eyes.

Bit by bit, so as not to startle her, I reached down toward the pile of her new clothes, holding them up one by one, but the tears kept coming, with little gasps for air now as she began to sob. I got down on the floor and upended the box, praying Wyatt had snagged some toys, too. Of course not. I tossed the deerskin boots on the floor.

She stopped crying and said something. Three words. Said them again.

"The boots?" I whispered. They were real deerskin, not the fake awful crap. "You want the *kamiks*?" The Inuit word for skin boots. I held them up.

She hazarded a few steps toward me, then ran and ripped them out of my hands before fleeing back to her room. But she did not slam her door shut.

Cautiously I approached her room.

She faced her window wearing the boots, shoulders shaking, hands flat against the icy pane.

"Hey," I said. "Hey," and sat down on her bed. "It's all right. It's going to be all right."

She whipped around and spouted several long sentences, each word polysyllabic and complex. *What is this language?* It was so eerie and beautiful it gave me chills; it was more like Greenlandic Norse than anything, but with a modulation, like Mandarin or Japanese. She wiped her eyes and plopped down on the tattered rug as if giving up on me, on everything. Stretching the cheap sweater over her knees, she dropped her chin between them, sullenly playing with Rudolph's red nose.

I approached her with slow, measured movements. She stiffened and glared up at me but didn't run. With zero plan at the ready, I sat down cross-legged in front of her. She watched my every move, scooting back toward the wall behind her. I made small noises of comfort.

When she had settled, I pointed to myself and said, "Val." Then I pointed at her with a questioning look.

She narrowed her eyes but said nothing.

"Val," I said, somewhat more forcefully, then gestured at her again.

She screwed up her face into a look of distrust, backing away from my pointing finger. Wiped her eyes and nose on the sweater and glowered at me.

I reached out my hand, gingerly touched one of the reindeer on her sweater. In English, I said, "Reindeer."

She repeated the word in her lilting cadence. "Rane-dar?"

I broke into a sweat, thrilling at the sound of English from her mouth. "Yes, *reindeer*."

She shook her head. Stuck her finger square in the reindeer's face. *"Kannisiak."*

I did my best to repeat the word.

She actually rolled her eyes. Tenting the sweater away from her body, she stabbed her finger at each reindeer in turn. *"Kannisiak."*

She seemed to silently count the rest, before announcing, *"Venseeth kannisiak."*

Caribou. Eight caribou.

Of course that was why she loved that sweater.

I laughed and had to stop myself from hugging her. My whole body seemed to melt with relief. *Eight numbers and a noun in just one session! What had I been so worried about?* I sat back, grinning goofily at her. At that pace, I'd have the basics of her language mapped out in a week.

seven

Eyes obscured by mirrored glacier glasses, Wyatt shifted the snowcat into neutral. We faced a final white wall: the tongue of the glacier that split the mountain range.

"Have to say," he said, chewing a thick wad of spearmint gum, the cloying smell filling the small space, "I'm still not clear on how this little trek is going to help you with the girl."

Not waiting for an answer, he shifted gears, the engine screaming until the metal teeth of the tracks nipped into sheer blue ice and propelled us up and over the bank. Before us: a mile-long descent onto a vast ice field; beyond it, black mountains jutted up against the horizon like cresting waves frozen in place.

"I need to see where she came from," I managed to say, though I doubt he heard me over the motor. Though cotton-headed from my drugs, anxiety had taken root; I fumbled for my sunglasses with fat-fingered gloves, trying to recall my shrink's advice. *Take in a little at a time. Look just below the horizon, or focus in one direction, or on one object at a time.* But it was like staring into a fire and trying to look at just one flame. I tried fixating on the control panel, my lap, my boots, then—daringly—a narrow hallway of tumbled ice that led down to the ice lake. But a panorama aches to be seen, so now and then I would let myself look, take in the Enormity, willing myself not to throw up in the cat.

"You okay?" Wyatt asked.

"Yeah. Doing good."

He downshifted and we rolled forward, snow and ice crunching beneath us.

"I appreciate you taking me out here," I added, squeezing Andy's lead heart, hot in the palm of my right glove.

"Anytime."

We crawled across the ice for several minutes of awkward silence until he turned to me with a blazing smile, white teeth flashing in his leathery face. "So, Val, how are you with secrets?"

"Are you asking if I'm trustworthy?"

"I'm asking if you can keep a secret." We banked down onto the windswept lake. It felt like we were flying.

"Depends on the secret."

"Wow." He grinned. "Complicated lady."

Was he flirting?

"Why don't you just try me?"

Was I?

"Here's the deal," he said over the roar of the motor. "You could learn a lot of important information out here, with that girl. Sensitive stuff. And whatever you learn, you need to share with me and only me. You and I, well, we'll work out later how we'll deal with whatever we find out." He cut the motor, and we slid to a stop on the frozen expanse. In the lull that followed, he flipped up his glasses and turned to look at me, full on. Acne scars, squinting eyes, a raptor-ish focus. It felt intimate and aggressive in the tight space. A steady wind scoured snow pellets off the lake and gunned them at the windshield, rocking the snowcat. I wondered how quickly I would freeze to death if he left me out here. Hours? Minutes? He stuffed another dusty strip of spearmint gum in his mouth, big jaw working. "So, we're partners, understand?"

"Of course. Sure." My voice a touch too high.

He sighed and turned back to the ice, mountains and sky doubling in the glasses that rested on his forehead. Perhaps feigning a stretch to get closer, or perhaps he genuinely needed to move in the cramped space, he eased his arm around the back of my seat—never touching me—the fingers of his Polartec glove inches from my shoulder. I half closed my eyes and took in a narrow band of silver-blue lake.

"You're so much like me, Val. I can feel it."

"Not sure what you mean."

"You're passionate about what you do. You're beyond curious. You've cracked the code on languages no one's been able to before. You've got a rare sort of mind. Your brother was in awe of you. I hope you know that."

At the mention of Andy, we both quieted a moment.

"He told me everything about you, Val."

Everything? I shifted the tiniest bit away from him, my right arm pressing against the metal door, cold even through my parka.

"I'm glad he had a mentor like you." I couldn't think of anything else to say.

"Look, Val, it's been a few days with the girl. She seems pretty calm around you, which is a good first step. But what are your thoughts? Do you think you can figure out what she's saying?"

"I need time alone with her, uninterrupted. A week, or at least a few days."

"Learn anything yet?"

"Not a word." Did my face betray my lie? I looked down, examined my gloves.

"We've only got a matter of weeks here. It's the middle of September. We lose an hour of sunlight every couple of days. True night—polar night—is coming. By the end of October, it's dark twenty-fours a day, for four months. Temps get to sixty below, colder."

"That happened to my dad once, in Antarctica. He stayed too long."

Wyatt's arm stiffened behind me; he removed it and studiously cleaned his glasses with the end of his scarf. "How's your dad doing? Such a brilliant guy. I still reference his work in my classes."

His change of tone knocked me off my tenuous balance. I suddenly felt claustrophobic; the air thick and too warm in the close cabin, the stink of spearmint nauseating. "He was fascinated by the story of the girl."

He snapped his gum. "Thought we agreed we keep quiet about all that."

Sweat prickled my armpits, dripped down between my breasts. "I left out the part about thawing out alive."

"You sure, Val?"

"He would never have believed it anyway. He thought coming here would be great for my career." Above us, dozens of big white birds with black-and-orange beaks circled, shrieking. Scat blotched the windshield. Thankful for the distraction, I said, "What are those birds?"

"Arctic tern. If we were out walking? They'd dive-bomb our heads."

"Why?"

He peered up at them. "We're on their turf. Actually, they consider the entire Arctic their turf. They're just protecting themselves." He folded his arms. "What's life like for you back home? Anyone else missing you right now besides your dad?"

I turned to him, his face still too close to mine. "Can you show me where you found the girl now?"

"It's your party, Val," he said, starting up the cat. "But I'm telling you, you're not going to learn a thing."

BIT BY BIT, a deep blue line came into focus. It widened into a fissure nearly six feet across, zigzagging across the ice and out of sight. We came within a dozen yards of it before Wyatt turned off the machine. He leaned his forearms on the wheel, as if remembering. Silence filled the space between us like another person.

"How deep is this lake?"

"Could be more than a mile in places. It's glacial ice. Thousands of years old."

The sun shone diamond bright on the ice, reflecting sharply in the rearview mirror. Wyatt hooked his rifle over one shoulder, creaked open the door, and hopped out. Bitter cold filled the cabin in seconds.

"Coming?"

The temperature gauge on the control panel read ten below; a brisk breeze snapped at the small American flag on the hood. I willed my gloved hand toward the door, watched it grab the handle, observed myself step out and down. Wyatt hadn't waited—already he was yards away. Wind came hooting down off the glacier. I cinched my hood tight over my face as I followed him, concentrating on his boots and his boots only as they crunched along in their rocking gait. The ice screeched under my feet; I took small bites of frigid air into my lungs. Eyes still lowered, I walked a bit past him, until the brilliant blue fissure came into view.

"Val, that's close enough."

Wyatt's admonition brought back what my high school ballet teacher said to me ages ago, her face pained after watching me "dance" for several weeks in class: *You don't seem to be enjoying yourself here. Have you thought of something else, maybe . . . swimming?* I have never had any sense of where my body is in space, which can be dangerous.

Stance rigid, arms tight to my sides, I peered over the edge. The fissure was shockingly wider than I'd first understood—closer to fifteen feet across, the inner slopes pale blue at the top, intensifying to turquoise, indigo, then black as a grave down and down to unspeakable depths. An eight-by-ten-foot block of ice had been cut cleanly out of the wall opposite; the new ice walls gleamed and sparkled.

The girl had been trapped in this? How was it possible?

"What do you think she was running from?"

He took off his wool cap, scratched his oily hair, slipped it back on. "Don't know, but whatever it was, she was plenty scared. Her expression, man, it was like she was running for her life."

I got down to my knees, took off my glove, and placed my hand on the ice, as if I could detect its slowly beating heart. *To be encased in this glacial prison, eyes frozen open in terror, how long had she been like that?* I had a feeling we were in a sacred place, that we were being watched, that there was more life around us than we knew.

"What are you doing?"

"I don't know." I took my hand away, almost missing the cold as I wrestled my glove back on. Turned and faced him. "So, what's the deal with Jeanne and those dolls?"

He shifted his weight, squinted into the sun. "She lost her husband and daughter in a car crash. Daughter was only seven. Never really got over it, as you can tell. Those were her daughter's dolls. Jeanne's a good person. A good worker, knows what she's doing. Anyway, we should get back."

I followed him to the cat. My legs heavy, my big orange boots kicking up little tornados of snow with every step.

Wyatt opened my door for me. "I'm sure it's pretty obvious by now. Nobody normal comes here. This place is just natural selection for people who want to leap off the edge of the world."

THE SUN HAD dipped behind the mountains by the time the cluster of yellow buildings came into view. I was glad to see them. Wyatt toured me through the Cube and the Shed, all the while droning on about Jeanne's prowess repairing you name it, how she'd saved their asses in more than one dicey situation, and how she could practically throw a cake together out of cocoa powder and dust. I couldn't concentrate on a word of it.

Ignoring Wyatt's monologue, I stopped a few yards from the Shack, the questions I'd been yearning to ask tunneling up my throat. Above us hung a nearly full moon, luminous among beating stars, its beams freezing us where we stood.

"Which door did Andy leave from that night, do you think?"

Wyatt looked exhausted, even a touch annoyed by my question. "You really want to get into that right now, Val?"

"Where did you find his body?"

He hooked his sunglasses through the zipper pull of his parka and spun away from me. "Come on." Shoulders slumped, he rounded the building, stopping at a nondescript hillock of snow and ice. He couldn't seem to look at me. "Here."

"Was he on his back? His front?"

"Val," he said quietly, "don't make me . . . you saw the pictures."

"Tell me how you found him."

"He was on his side, sort of curled up."

In my mind, there he was, clear as day. A bear of a man made childish in striped boxers, his big feet frozen solid but somehow still tender. On his side, knees up, arms folded against his chest as if to keep himself warm, all the shivering over and done with, a statue now, snow already building in little slopes against his prone body. I looked away from his glowing afterimage and back to Wyatt.

"Which door?"

"How could I know that, Val?"

I approached the closest one and was about to turn away, when something caught my eye. Moonlight revealed a series of scratches, metal glinting silver where the orange paint had been scraped off. I ran my gloved hand over them.

"What are these?"

Wyatt approached, folded his arms. "Those've been there for a couple of years."

I rattled the doorknob, pretended I was my brother, frantically trying to get back in.

"We think a polar bear did it. They're starving, you know. They come here sometimes."

"A *polar bear*?" I turned to face him.

"Why do you think I've got a rifle with me every second I'm outside?"

I didn't answer.

"Look," he said, placing his hand over the scratches and widening his fingers. "No man's hand is that big."

I brushed his hand away and placed mine there, stretching my fingers as far apart as I could. It was true, the spread of the scratches was huge, but a man freezing to death, out of his mind with panic, desperately trying to get back in? *Wasn't anything possible then?*

"Val, I'm sorry, but who knows?" Wyatt shivered as the moon-dark shadow of the building slid over us. "Maybe he changed his mind."

I blinked, gutted by this new possibility of suffering. Rattling the handle, I yelled, "Let me in, let me in, *let me in*!"

Dizzy, I rested my forehead against the freezing metal, then went at the door again, banging and calling.

Wyatt stood away from me, hugging himself, as if ashamed.

Jeanne appeared around the side of the building clutching a length of pipe, her face as pale and gray as the barren slope behind her. "What's going on? Is everything all right? Wyatt?"

"Yeah, Jeanne," Wyatt said. "We're just . . . it's fine."

She gave me a dark look, searched Wyatt's face.

I wrenched myself around. "You wouldn't have heard that, Wyatt?" I hissed. "You're telling me you wouldn't have heard my brother beating at the door to get back in? *Did you hear him?*" My voice cracked. I knew I was accusing him of something horrendous, but at that moment I would have done anything for a story rather than the one I still couldn't accept.

He took me by my shoulders and shook me quiet. I felt bantam in his grip; I didn't like it. He said, "No, Val. I heard nothing that night. I wish I had. I'd have come, kiddo."

My breath was ragged, and I could feel the hate and blame in my face, but his expression was surprisingly calm, surprisingly kind. It disarmed and confused me. He reached out to hug me, and I let him. It felt so good to let myself sink into someone else, if only for a few brief seconds.

"Come on, Val, come on," he said gently as we pulled away from each other, both of us looking slightly sheepish. "I know it's hard, I do. I'm a fucking wreck about it. I just process it the way I process it. And you have to do the same, I can see that." He took a step back. "But you don't want to scare the girl, do you? So let's go inside, let's get you a drink, some food. It's been a long day."

We turned back to the main door. Crossed with shadows in the deepening dusk, Jeanne stood staring at us, lead pipe dangling from one hand.

eight

I got my wish: two uninterrupted days with the girl. The bitch of it was, she turned away from me each time I tried to speak to her, as if she'd given up on me, as if I had already failed her.

All day long she planted herself on Wyatt's desk under the picture window, tracing circle after circle on the sweating pane as she chanted some lilting song. She drew three rows of eight rings: *Why eight?* The last circle she rubbed hard with her palm, as if trying to obliterate something. Hour after hour I pointed at the circles, counting one to twenty-four, my little recorder on to catch every sound she made, until finally she began to count in her language—at least I thought that's what she was doing. I thrilled at the new numbers but couldn't seem to progress from there. When I pushed her to move on to basics—my name, hers, simple nouns—she banged at the shining rings until I thought the glass would shatter, then ran to her room to bury herself under her bed in her fortress of blankets and pillows.

The hours-long twilights set me on edge: days that wouldn't quite end; true darkness that refused to arrive. Outside, a miserly palette of grays, whites, and blues. Thunderous crashes of icebergs calving in the bay—Wyatt called it Arctic white noise—rendered me jittery and anxious. I began to tap a fifth of vodka from the fridge during the day, just to take the edge off, watering it down to cover it up, like I was a teenager. I had to parse out my pills; I had enough to last until I was home—not one day more.

I barely saw Raj or Nora except for meals; they ate quickly, as if anxious to get out of the stifling, steamy kitchen and back out to the Dome on the frozen bay. I envied their privacy, their ability to move around, the fact that they were making progress with their projects while I was nearly stalled with mine. Except mine was no project; she was a living, breathing, miraculous girl.

DAY THREE. FOUR thirty in the morning. Small, hard fists banged on my door, blasting me from sleep. I flung open the door. The girl stood in her boots, drowning in a sweater of Jeanne's over her Christmas sweater, my hat engulfing her small skull, Wyatt's muffler that said "Ice Rocks" wrapped around her neck. Only her burning black eyes showed. She stole my hand and yanked me down the hallway. Seized the doorknob of the front door and rattled it, shouting in her language.

"Hey, calm down," I said in West Greenlandic, reaching for her shoulders. She pushed me away, her hysteria rising as she pummeled the door.

Ignoring our skirmish, Jeanne padded past us in her men's wool robe and stockinged feet. She lit the range and started the coffee.

"You can't go out. It's not safe out there," I said to the girl in English.

"She wants to go home," Jeanne said over the girl's screams, reaching into the fridge for our last pint of cream. After that was gone, it was powder only. "She wants her real family."

The girl turned and slid down into a teary puddle, repeating one word over and over.

Tahtaksah.

What did it mean? Was this the word for mother? *Or* father?

"Tahtaksah," I repeated to her. "Tahtaksah?"

Frustration filled her face. I'd gotten it wrong. Again. She wailed.

Wyatt's door flew open. He thundered out of his room, pounding down the hallway. "What the hell's going on out here?"

"She's having a meltdown," I said. My hand grazed her shoulder in an instinctual attempt to get her as far from him as possible; strangely, she let the gesture pass. I looked forward to the day we could get her to take a bath.

"Sometimes I think being in the ice messed with her brain," he growled. "Maybe she's just not right in the head, you know?"

"You're not right in the head till you have some coffee, Wyatt, ever think of that?" Jeanne said, setting a mug on his desk.

Whispering a barely audible *fuck you*, he jammed his stockinged feet into slippers, pulled a sweatshirt over his long johns, and tapped his PC alive.

Jeanne and I exchanged a glance, but I couldn't read her. I'd told her days ago I was sorry about the doll, but even though she'd accepted my apology, she still seemed miffed. The smell of frying eggs—the kind poured from a box—filled the air. Another pan crackled with spitting bacon. Jeanne flipped on her CD player. She favored the crooners: Frank Sinatra, Mel Tormé, Nat King Cole, Bing Crosby. The syrupy music—played day in and day out every second she was in the Shack—was wearing on me, but I had no intention of saying anything. Wyatt didn't seem to care; I doubt he even heard it anymore.

"Motherfucker . . ." he hissed under his breath. "You been reading about these ice winds, Val? Two more people died in Nova Scotia yesterday. Near Halifax. Tourists. Froze to death in seconds."

"Those poor people," Jeanne said. "I hope they didn't suffer."

"Doesn't look like it," he said, scrolling. "Looks like it was instantaneous." He sat back, as if stunned by a dawning realization.

"It's like these piteraqs—which are completely normal here—are starting to show up around the world. On steroids."

"The temperature gradients, do you think?" Jeanne said.

"Absolutely. These massive jumps and drops . . ." He became lost in thought.

"Piteraq," I said, finally recognizing the term. "That's Inuit for *that which will attack you.*"

"Sure will," Wyatt said. "Years ago, one was clocked at close to two hundred miles an hour in Tasiilaq. In East Greenland."

The girl continued to sob, but softer now, as if wrung out. I sat next to her on the floor, clueless and wretched. Played that word, *tahtaksah*, over and over in my head.

Wyatt's chair squealed as he swiveled around to face me. "So, kiddo, what's the deal with you guys? Any progress?"

I kept my eyes on the girl's back, listening to her gasps for breath as she sleep-cried. "It's slow going. Maybe she needs to feel more safe, comforted somehow before learning even feels important to her, if that makes any sense. . . ."

Jeanne brought over a plate of eggs and bacon to Wyatt, who nodded his thanks, not taking his eyes off the screen. "Have you learned any more of her language? Or has she learned any English?"

"No." I sighed. *Why am I continuing to lie about this?* Some bone-deep instinct told me to, but it didn't come naturally, and my stomach jumped every time I did it. *Better keep track . . .*

"Seriously?" He shook his head. "Jesus, Val, you've had almost a week with the kid."

"Look, I've been trying. It's just that . . ." I shifted on the floor, my body aching. "I don't even know the syntax I'm dealing with. Is it like English: subject-verb-object, or like a dialect of Greenlandic, where the word order is more complex, or something else entirely?"

"You're the pro, Val."

"But there's more to it than that. I can feel it. I don't know what's happened to her, what her culture is like, her family . . ." The truth was—unlike Andy, who children adored and followed around like the Pied Piper—I'd always struck out with kids. They could smell my discomfort, and it put them off.

"Maybe you're just not a kid person."

"Hey," I said, "I don't deserve that."

He burst out laughing, the yellow of the scrambled eggs jiggling in the back of his mouth. "Val, I'm just fucking with you, come on."

I reddened. *What is my deal?* Did I have a thing for charismatic, slightly mean scientists, preferably on the older side? I did and I didn't. Wyatt switched from collegial to cruel faster than I could clock. Jeanne noisily scrubbed the egg pan, humming along to "That's Amore." I was grateful for the noise.

He got up, trudged into his bedroom, and returned carrying a large, foil-wrapped bar. "I know what'll work the magic." He loomed over me and the girl, unwrapping a jumbo-sized chocolate bar studded with almonds. Broke off a piece.

"That might not be good for her," I said.

Ignoring me, he knelt and gently turned the girl toward him. I think she was too startled to protest. "Hey, kid," he said. "I think you understand more than you're letting on. Ya got me?"

Bizarrely, she nodded, her face solemn and serious.

He held the dark square under her nose. She sniffed it. Her eyes widened and she reached for it, but he jerked his hand away, brandishing the treat above his head.

"No," he said with a wide smile. "You know what *no* means, right?"

She nodded again. What the fuck. She sat up, at full attention, wiped her face with her hands.

"You want this?" He dangled the square of chocolate close to her. "You want to try this?"

She jumped up shockingly fast. He fake-tried to keep the piece of candy from her, but she nabbed it, shoved it in her mouth, and chewed—eyes closed—face in ecstasy.

"Not bad, huh," Wyatt said.

She opened her eyes and reached out her hand.

"Want some more, kiddo?"

She nodded.

"Then you have to understand what we're doing here, sweet-heart. We need to know what you ate to thaw out alive. Do you understand? What you ate"—he gestured at his mouth, then hers—"to thaw out alive. What your family ate. But mostly, what *you* ate. So you need to talk"—he pointed at me, at himself, at Jeanne—"to *us*." He snapped up a picture book, stabbed at the illustrations with his finger. "Polar bear. Walrus. Iceberg. Learn these words." He pointed at me. "With this very patient, very nice woman here, all right?"

Big-eyed, she nodded at him.

"You think about that, if you want more of this." He rattled the candy bar in front of her; she snatched it from his grasp and rocketed down the hallway. Tripping on the double sweaters she still wore, she skidded into her room and slammed the door. We all chased her, but she'd disappeared under her bed deep into her sanctuary of pillows and blankets, the crying replaced by sounds of paper and foil tearing and little noises of pleasure. Jeanne stood in the doorway, arms crossed, mouth a straight line.

"We can't let her eat all that!" I said. "She'll be sick."

Wyatt mumbled, "That was the last of my stash." The three of us lifted up the bed and placed it down on the other side of the room. She sat in a ball, her hands, mouth, and much of her face smeared with chocolate, the wrapper empty in front of her.

"Fuck," Wyatt said. *"Fuck."*

The girl smiled, elaborately licking her fingers before her face went rigid. She threw off her covers, lurched a few steps forward, and vomited against the wall. Face flushed, she turned toward us with a look of embarrassment and stumbled out of the room.

Jeanne sighed and wandered off to the kitchen, returning with a bucket of hot water and some towels.

"Nice one, Wyatt," I said.

"Hey, scientific method. She responds to chocolate."

"Violently."

"Hey, at least I tried something."

"Like I haven't been trying?"

He put a hand through his hair and blinked. "Maybe so. But you need to try a little harder, my friend. We're running out of time."

THAT NIGHT I dreamed I stood on the deck of a ship at sea surrounded by stories-high icebergs, each a sculpture carved by a madman. Creaking and groaning, they floated in a shimmering ectoplasm of their own vapor. Cold wafted off them; the air popping with the taste of carbon dioxide. A cathedral-shaped berg, awash in the golden glow of Arctic twilight, turned regally toward me, its wake foaming against the hull of the ship. As its flying buttresses rose and sank, something flesh-colored caught my eye, an eerily familiar shape. I ran to the bow of the boat, frantic for the apparition to reappear. The great berg swayed, its massive base jutting leagues beneath it in the jade-green sea, so much larger than what was visible above the waves, and I was reminded of something Andy used to say: *Icebergs are like people, you only ever really know twenty percent of them.*

The berg groaned, dipped, then torqued its new face toward me until I saw myself, naked and motionless in my aquamarine cage, frozen-open eyes staring out at the hissing salt spray. My body tilted side to side with the berg as it wobbled like a giant children's toy in a tub, until the ocean seethed beneath it and spun it away.

nine

Scribbling notes in my journal at dawn the next morning, I paused to gaze out my lone window at a carpet of drift ice that clogged the bay, the silence so complete I thought for a second I'd lost my hearing. Coughed to prove to myself I hadn't. Something white on the floor caught my eye. A sheet of notebook paper had been slipped under my door. In Wyatt's sideways scrawl: "Had to get an early start. Nora and Raj at the Dome. Jeanne with me. Good luck with the kid. See you at dinner."

I wandered to the living room, nearly tripping over a pile of blankets and pillows at the front door, which turned out to be the girl hibernating. For two nights she'd refused to sleep anywhere but curled up next to it, as if trying to breathe whatever glacial air made its way to her. I sipped my coffee and gnawed at a piece of toast, determination crystallizing. We—this girl and I—were going to have a breakthrough *today*. It was day nine. Already the ten hours of daylight we enjoyed the day I arrived had slipped to just under seven and was dropping fast.

I bent down and said in my sweetest voice, "Good morning, time to get up." No movement. "Hello," I said to the clump of blankets. "I've got fish here. Meat. Whatever you want."

She poked her head out—expression comically cranky—evicted her blankets, and got to her feet, my unknowable girl in her fraying sweater-dress, most of the knitted reindeer stretched out beyond recognition. She flew down the hallway and returned with her special coffee can, now half-full, handing it to me with zero embarrassment. After emptying the contents, I found her sitting cross-legged on Wyatt's desk, chewing on a piece of raw halibut. She'd obviously figured out the refrigerator. I cleared a space next to her on the desk and spread out the picture books, coloring books, toys, paper, markers.

"So, let's try this again." I pointed to myself. "My name is Val. Can you say Val?" I patted my breastbone. *"Val."*

Nothing.

I pointed at her. "You are . . ."

She snatched the remaining morsel from its paper wrapper as if I might steal it from her and crammed it in her mouth. That's when I saw her molars; they were almost completely worn down. My breath caught in my throat. From what I'd read, starting girls early in the tradition of chewing caribou hides to soften them enough to cut and sew for clothes was archaic, a custom no longer practiced except perhaps in isolated villages.

She swallowed the last piece and turned toward the picture window.

"Today, we're going to learn the names of things."

She reached up to the pane, squeaking clear a little circle with her finger. I clicked on my recorder I kept in my shirt pocket. She drew another circle, each time saying what might have been a number. Two rows of eight rings, the third row only seven, the last of which she rubbed out hard. Again and again she performed this ritual. *Is it the act of counting that's important, the circles themselves, the rubbing out of the last one, or all of it?* Beyond her small hand, the sun rested on the horizon, swept with dove-gray streaks in the purplish light.

I noisily dumped out the markers and crayons, flipped open the picture books, cleared my throat. "Okay, you need to look at me, honey. You need to look over here." As gently as I could, I took hold of her narrow shoulders and turned her toward me.

She tore out of my grip, punching down with her fishy hands, scattering the books and toys to the floor. Let loose a high-pitched shriek and pounded on the desk.

A flame of fury and frustration shot through me, so strong it frightened me. I paced the chaotic space, picking my way among the anarchy. *Why won't she just try? What is wrong with me that she won't respond at all?*

I went to the front door, banged on it once. "Is this what you want? You want to go outside? Say it: *outside*. Or you're not going anywhere."

Her eyes widened. She slid her legs off the desk and let them dangle there. Though the sight of her grimy little calves and feet aggrieved me, I never grew tired of looking at her: this child who had lived a life worlds apart from mine. Her expressive face, capable of conveying humor, sarcasm, pain, delight, fear, and maybe even love, her miles-long words and sentences, her bursts of laughter, even her fits of tears were as much a wonder to me as her refusal to learn confounded me.

"Do you want to go outside?" I gestured at the door.

She nodded, not taking her eyes off me as if I might change my mind.

"Say, outside. *Outside*."

"Ou-sigh . . ."

She slid her agile body to the floor with a thud and padded over to me, her sweater catching on and dragging a piece of a Lego set across the rug behind her. She reached up and rattled the doorknob, brow furrowed as she burned a *you promised* look into me.

What was I doing? Was this insane? Maybe, maybe not. I'd been running around after her for a week up and down the halls of this place; surely I could keep up with her outdoors for a few minutes.

"Then we have to get dressed, do you understand?" I grabbed her boots and set them next to her. She jammed her bare feet in them as I brandished her socks in front of her. "With socks." She whipped off the boots and hurried on the socks. I started to layer up too. Every article of clothing I laid before her she dutifully put on.

We stood at the door, parka'd, snow-panted, mittened, and muffled. It never occurred to me to sign the log. "Are you ready?"

She nodded, pulling her hat down halfway over her eyes.

"Say *outside*."

She smiled a little. *"Ou-sigh."*

"Are you going to stay with me? *Walk with me?*"

A slow nod.

"Hold my hand? Not run away?" I held out my hand. She took it. "Be a good girl?"

She nodded *yesyesyesyesyesyesyes*.

"Do you love me?" I asked, smiling.

She actually smiled back. Nodded once more. Of course it wasn't real, but it felt good all the same.

Gripping her hand tightly in mine, I opened the door.

She jerked her hand free and charged away from me like a scruffy little rocket, sending me tripping and stumbling forward onto hard-packed snow, the air bitter in my lungs. Behind us, the rime-powdered beach. Black dots—bullet-shaped seal heads—bobbed in the rich blue water. Before us, the glacier that led to the ice lake snaked up the mountainside, disappearing in the pass that cut through the peaks.

Which is where she was headed. Quickly she grew smaller and smaller in all the terrible white. I looked down: I still clutched her mitten.

I ran screaming for her to come back, my eyes tearing, glazing my cheeks.

My oversized snow pants and parka slowed me, binding my limbs. Snot froze and cracked in my nostrils as my steps shortened, stalling in the mounting drifts. The slope steepened. Undaunted, the girl flew higher and higher.

"Girl! *Girl, come back!*"

The dot turned to look at me, then went back to running, but began to lose steam, alternating brief rests with short spurts up the slope. Still, she would not stop. She was like a train chugging up a track, whipping up billowing clouds that obscured, then revealed her bright red parka. I called out to her again, my voice splintering in the brittle air. Gasping, I rested my hands on my knees—my lungs felt a third their normal size—thought how the StairMaster had failed me so completely, *what a waste!* I couldn't catch this girl, and at that moment she felt like the only person on this earth who meant anything to me.

"Stop!" I pleaded. "You've got to *stop!*"

She slowed to a walk but seemed to make just as much progress. Still, I began to close the gap between us. I cursed my stupidity, the huge risk I had taken. Remembered what Wyatt had said about polar bears: *Why do you think I've got a rifle with me every second I'm outside?*

The girl scrambled along the lip of the glacier as if looking for a foothold, then disappeared into a funnel of snow. My heart spun in my chest. Had she fallen into a crevasse?

Wind swept the ice clean; she had dropped to her knees.

I pitched toward her, collapsing next to her; her tiny form lost in Jeanne's spare parka. "Girl, are you all right? *Girl?*"

"Tahtaksah," she cried as she gazed up at the break between the cliffs. She reached up her one bare hand—purple with cold—moaning two words over and over. They sounded vaguely like West Greenlandic for mother and father, but—*tahtaksah*—the word felt like pure emotion. *Does it mean longing? Grief?* I knelt on the ice and touched her shoulder; she didn't push me away. "What are you doing? Where are you going?"

But, of course, I knew where she was going.

"Come on," I said. "We can't do this alone, we have to go back."

She wrenched herself around to look at me. That face: forlorn, bereft, but also determined—I'll never forget it—so much older than her age. I reached down for her bare hand, but she pulled it away and began a run-walk sort of totter down the hill. I followed at a respectful distance, thanking the gods of the Arctic for her acquiescence. She trundled along in the vague direction of the Shack, but soon it was clear that wasn't her destination. I thought to stop her but could see the fight had left her, so why not let her have her time outdoors? She was headed to the beach, where a gang of big bergs battled for position along the horizon.

I broke into a trot, suddenly a little queasy about her new plan. Desk-sized floes lined the shore, creaking as they ground into each other, jockeying for space. Long, shallow waves rolled under them, nudging them forward. Driftwood like dinosaur bones gleamed silver on a stretch of dark pebbles. A hundred yards out on a larger floe, a half dozen harp seals luxuriated in the sunshine, charcoal eyes and noses nestled in glistening fur. At our approach, gulls took to the sky as ravens shadowed us, scolding.

The girl casually picked her way among the rubble as if we were out for a stroll. Small but powerful waves offered up flattened bergs onto the bank before sucking them back to the seething dark sea. She turned and shot me a mischievous grin, all her previous sadness seemingly passed, before hopping onto one of the icy rafts, squatting as if it were a surfboard. Her weight had no effect; the disk of ice continued its ebb and flow until the waves subtly picked up speed and might and—bit by bit—floated her farther out, past the first line of bergs.

"No! No, get back here!" I jogged alongside her little craft—only a yard or so from me now, but utterly out of reach. Waves leathery with cold nudged her berg shoreward before sucking it back twice as far, the denim-blue sea like stained glass surrounding it, its broader base turquoise under the water. As if claiming her, the ocean drew her in, until an army of bergs five-deep separated us.

I speed-walked alongside her, begging her to get back to shore, somewhere in my brain aware that all I did was beg her: to talk, to stop crying, to pay attention. She laughed like I was the funniest thing she'd seen in years.

"Come on, please, come back here. . . ."

The waves lifted her, lowered her with slow, peaceful movements. Grinning, she squatted on the cake of ice. She looked calm, happier than I'd ever seen her. Only ten yards beyond her, one of the seals wriggled across its berg and slipped into the water with a slight splash.

The girl pointed to herself and said, "Sigrid."

Stunned, I stopped short. "*Sigrid*? Your name is Sigrid?"

"Sigrid," she repeated, patting her chest. She pointed at me and said, "Bahl."

"Yes!" I said, joyous even as I huffed along again, barely keeping up. "I'm Val."

"Bahl," she said, as if correcting me. She stood up, perfectly at ease on her raft.

"Sigrid, get off the ice, will you?"

She laughed. Loving the hopscotch, she jumped to another berg a bit farther out; it rocked slightly under her weight, but her balance was faultless. She motioned for me to join her, chanting my name in a singsong way. "Bahl, Bahl-y Bahl, Bahllalala Bahl . . ."

A disk of ice twice the size of hers sailed onto shore, delivered there by a rogue brawny wave. I considered it, attempting to calculate what might support my weight. I stepped onto it, falling immediately to my knees. A wave bloomed beneath me, lifting, then belching me forward. Like a slow, sick carnival ride, it sucked me away from shore, smashing and grinding its way among the smaller disks. I clawed my gloved hands into the ice and held on. Felt the telltale signs of my daily dose wearing off: colors turned migraine bright; bergs screamed as they bashed into one another, the sound stabbing behind my eyes.

Sigrid laughed, clapping and hopping all around me on the neighboring disks, until even she realized we were drifting steadily away from shore. I remained in precisely the same crouch I'd landed in; I couldn't bring myself to sit, or stand, or move. Chatting away, she leapt onto my little island, briefly patting my back—was this a game of tag?—before hopping berg to berg to shore. Underneath me, the great blue ocean tongue lolled, hoisting, then dropping me down, but always dragging me farther toward the open sea.

"Bahl!" Sigrid called from the bank, alarm tinging her voice as she sprinted alongside the shore as I had done, waving her arms. But I just floated, paralyzed, stomach heaving with every roll of the sea. I couldn't find my voice; all my languages had burrowed deep into the cavern of my body. Panic in her face, Sigrid turned toward the cluster of three buildings, then the bay where the Dome shimmered banana yellow on its plate of sea ice.

"Bahl," she cried in frustration.

"Sigrid, go get help, please!" I tore one hand off the ice to point at the Dome.

For a long, terrible minute she ran along the bank, calling my name, until finally she turned and bulleted off toward the Dome.

A choppy sea rocked the loose floes around me. Gulls landed on nearby bergs, eyeing me as they waddle-walked on the ice. One held a slender fish down with a webbed foot and tore it open with its hooked beak. I was just twenty feet from shore, but it may as well have been a mile. I couldn't stand. I knew that if I did, I would slip into the ocean, so I stayed in my crouch.

I began to lose feeling in my hands and feet. *Where are my words*, I thought, *which one can save me?* Blinking tears into my eyes so they wouldn't freeze open, I conjured the Japanese word *zanshin*, a state of relaxed mental alertness martial artists strive for when facing an opponent. Fears of losing, winning, even dying are set aside; muscles are relaxed and ready to fight.

As the floe rocked beneath me, splashing icy seawater on stiffened limbs, I breathed *zanshin* over and over until it thrummed in my head, until ice and sea disappeared and only the word remained.

ten

I t took all of thirty seconds for Nora to tow me to shore.

Sigrid had been able to communicate my distress—*so she could make herself understood if she wanted to*—and Nora had come running from the Dome and tossed me a rope. Now we sat on a wooden bench under the sunshiny glow of saffron canvas, Sigrid bundled in a fur blanket drinking hot chocolate cooled by ice chips.

Nora squatted near the four-by-eight-foot hole in the ice floor where she and Raj set off for their dives into the polar sea. The temperature inside the Dome hovered at forty degrees.

"He should be up any second," she said, checking a gauge on a piece of equipment nearby.

"Thanks for coming to get me. I'd still be out there—" I shivered.

"It's okay," she said, her concentration full on the slushy blue hole. It eyed me like the deep well of my subconscious mind, a terrible place to go. Raj was swimming somewhere under us, submerged in freezing water.

Suspended from one of the curved metal struts that held up the Dome and kept its shape, like the ribs of a whale, was a laminated placard entitled "Diving Checklist," a twenty-five-step-long agenda to be checked off in preparation for a dive. A spare diving suit hung like a dead man from a large hook over the specimen table.

Nora paced in front of the hole, eyeing the timer as it clicked from fifty-nine minutes to an hour. "Okay, Raj, anytime now would be good—"

Raj fairly exploded out of the water, his tank and gear clanking against the icy walls of the diving hole.

In alarm and surprise, Sigrid flung her cup of chocolate up in the air. The liquid sizzled onto the ice as she bolted for the door, but I caught her arm and forced her to stay. She looked equally fearful, bewildered, and strangely delighted, repeating the same two words over and over.

Nora seized Raj by his armpits, heaving him up and out of the hole and onto his stomach. He slid a yard or so across the floor. Rolled over and yanked out his mouth gear, slipped off his tank, and lifted his goggles from his eyes, shuddering.

Nora laughed as she helped him wrestle off his tight-fitting neoprene headgear. "Poor girl's freaking out! Could she think he's some kind of seal-man?" Smiling, she handed him his spectacles.

Maybe that's what she's saying, I thought. *Seal man.*

"This is Sigrid," I said, taking her firmly by the arm and escorting her over to Raj.

He sat up and smiled, held out his hand. "Nice to meet you, Sigrid. I'm Raj. I mean, Seal Man."

She didn't take his hand but, grinning with astonishment, reached up to touch his forehead gently, then his rubber-encased shoulder. Said, "Seal Man."

"How was it, darling?" Nora asked as she helped unzip the many crisscrossed zippers on the front and back of his suit.

"Perfect. I was able to plant it about forty feet down. Got the coordinate, took a shot of it. We're good, I think."

"Brilliant," Nora said, freeing him from the rest of his suit. "Well done, my love." Shivering in his long johns, Raj hopped into layer after layer of clothing that had been laid out for him across the specimen table. Sigrid couldn't take her eyes off him.

Nora poured Raj some chocolate, which he took gladly. Stomping his feet and rubbing his hands between sips, he reached into a dry bag and extracted a shrunken, sad-looking orange. Nora slid him a questioning look.

"Yes, I stole it from Wyatt's stash," he said, biting at the peel. "Guy needs to learn to share."

"He's been on the ice over a year," Nora said. "We just got here."

"He'll live," Raj said, digging in to the fruit.

"How's it been going with her?" Nora asked me.

"Slow. She's probably speaking some West Greenlandic dialect, I'm not sure yet."

"Wyatt pushing you?"

"Every day," I said. "How is it out here for you? Don't you get cold?"

"We're used to it. We love the quiet."

"She does," Raj said. "I'm not sure I like it. Sometimes it's so quiet I can hear my own heart beating. Spooks me."

"Some days I forget we're standing on the sea," Nora said. "That there are seals and humpbacks and belugas floating under us, giving birth, fighting, dying . . ."

"Do you want to listen to them?" Raj asked. "We have a very low-tech way."

"Sure." Sigrid's hand in mine, we followed Nora and Raj out of the Dome. Stood together in the rigid pristine air. Endless twilight burnished the sky; the bergs looked plated with gold. Nora was right: The silence was profound. Our footsteps squeaking along the ice were the only sound. Sigrid wasn't pulling away, but I drew her to me and said, "You stay with me, understand? No running. Okay, Sigrid?"

She shook her head solemnly, said, "No."

Sigrid, no, mother, father, seal man. Six words in one day. I was ecstatic.

"You can actually feel the sounds through the bottoms of your feet, but it's better to do this." A few yards from the Dome, Nora got to her hands and knees on the ice, then lay down on her side, her ear pressed to it. Raj did the same. "Come on," he said. "Listen."

I copied them, holding my ear a centimeter from the ice, which steamed cold into my head. Sigrid, watching us, lay down next to me, her face inches from mine.

Right away, I heard it—a Martian language of clicks, pings, squeaks, pocks, chirps, and staccato thumps. Even though I was losing feeling in my ear, I didn't want to stop listening. Would have given anything to understand this language, or languages: a seal calling to her pup, warning of a polar bear nearby? A fin whale singing to his mate? I pictured white belugas rising like enormous drowned ghosts beneath us. Just how close would they come to us as we lay on the ice?

Nora sat up, brushed herself off. "We can also make or record sounds into a hydrophone. Come on, I'll show you."

Back in the Dome, she shuffled around in a dry bag, extricating a digital recorder and two microphones attached to it with cords. One she dropped into the hole, feeding it down several yards. The other she flipped on and spoke into. Her amplified voice filled the Dome.

"Hello down there, brilliant sea creatures—"

Sigrid reached up for the microphone.

"Should I give it to her?" Nora asked me.

But Sigrid had already swiped it from Nora's grip. She made noises into the machine, similar to the squeaks and chirps we'd heard on the ice.

"Listen to that," Raj said. "She's quite good."

Sigrid squatted at the edge of the hole, ignoring us as she kept up her calls.

A long white spear poked out. *What in hell?* The adults jumped back from the hole, Raj knocking over a specimen bucket. Seaweed and half a dozen silverfish slid across the ice floor as the spear thrashed at the brash ice, rapping at the glassy sides of the opening. Sigrid didn't budge; a proud smile stretched across her face as she glanced at each of us, drew a breath, and—with even greater gusto—renewed her uncanny whistling and clicking.

"Sigrid," I said, approaching her, as if I got closer, or touched her, I might absorb some of her wizardry. "What are you—"

"Holy fuck," Raj breathed. "It's a narwhal."

She kept calling.

The length of twisted bone lifted eerily higher, then turned toward us as if sensing us there. Two more horns broke the surface, each approaching six feet, each fighting for room in the narrow space. One of the creatures lifted its dark gray head from the water. A blast of fishy-smelling air burst from its blowhole as the muscular flap opened and closed.

"She's called them—those are male narwhals," Nora said.

Sigrid was reaching across species, across worlds! *She* was the linguist. Never had I felt such wonder, this delightful urge to cry and laugh at the same time.

"Get the camera—Raj?" Nora said in a whisper, unable to take her eyes off the rubbery gray heads and waving spears.

But he couldn't look away either. "It's in the dry bag."

Cursing, she scrambled in the bag and pulled out her phone.

The unicorn tusks waved, as if trying to feel their way around in the strange air of the hut—*What is this place?*—before clacking together one last time and sinking down and out of sight. The steel-blue water closed over them, shushing against the sides of the hole.

Now silent, Sigrid sat back, as if spent.

"Did you record that, Nora?" Raj said in a hushed voice.

"It happened too fast. I've never seen anything like that in my life."

"That was . . . that was *yūgen*," I said.

"*Yūgen?*"

"It's a Japanese word for something that gives rise to feelings there are no words for . . ."

"That was *yūgen* all right," Raj said. "Just incredible."

We all watched the water settle, as if waiting—or hoping—for another appearance of these fantastical creatures. But this moment was over forever.

"If I were an opportunist of the Wyatt variety, I'd say *this* is the road to fame and big bucks. Forget the thawed girl fairy tale."

"Raj, come on," Nora said, cleaning up the detritus from the specimen bucket. "Wyatt doesn't deserve that."

"Oh, no? Honestly, Nora, you *believe* him?"

She tilted her head, her opalescent skin reflecting the cool ice floor. "Of course not—"

"He found her wandering on the ice somewhere, her family fallen into a crevasse or through thin ice, or who knows, maybe they're out there looking for her? Look, we both know he hasn't written a research piece in years. And have you checked out who's been assigned to head the new Arctic research base? The one they're going to build after they tear this place down next year? It's not him. He's not even on staff."

"Andy was being considered for that post, wasn't he?" I asked.

"He was, Val, but . . . well, I wasn't going to mention it."

"It's okay, Raj." I hugged myself, the frigid air suddenly penetrating my every layer.

"Raj," Nora said, "we're not here to investigate Wyatt. We need all of our energy, all of our concentration just to get this project done."

He tossed his goggles and flippers in a pile along with the rest of his diving suit. "Someday I'd like to get a peek at that journal he's always scribbling in. Or check out those slides he's got locked away like they're state secrets."

"Slides?" I asked.

"The ones he can't stop staring at. Arranging. Rearranging. Locking up in the spec fridge."

"Listen, Val," Nora said. "Maybe it is a good idea we keep this, um, narwhal thing to ourselves. Sound good?"

"Sure. I'm here to learn her language," I said. "That's it." I felt my stomach twist. Another secret to keep from Wyatt. On top of that, I wasn't exactly being straight with Nora. Of course I wanted to decipher Sigrid's language, but more than anything I wanted the truth about Andy, and now, Sigrid.

I had to find that journal.

IT WAS JUST past three in the morning. Swathed in a veil of silver twilight, I hovered in the hallway at Wyatt's closed door. I felt unreal, vampiric. Inhaling slow, measured breaths, I listened. Just the sound of Wyatt's snoring, the whine of the wind.

I tiptoed to the kitchen.

A cone of light shone down from the hood of the oven; the rest of the room malingered shadowy and vague, cast in somber blue by the gloaming outside the window. I crept into the main room. Every inch of Wyatt's desk swam with files and papers, but I knew what Raj had been talking about. A ragged eggplant-colored leather journal, held together by thick black elastic. Centimeter by centimeter—listening for his snoring—I creaked open the top drawer of his desk, then all the ones below. Old calendars, batteries, rusted razors, junk. No journal.

I was about to slink back to bed, defeated, when I noticed that the spec fridge, just a small cube plugged in behind his PC, was unlocked. *Slides . . . locked away like they're state secrets . . .* I froze, every cell on high alert. Still he rumbled on.

The fridge opened with a little pop of suction.

On the left side, a dozen metal rings held test tubes filled with what looked like blood, each vial and its corresponding ring labeled in Wyatt's slanted scrawl. One metal ring was empty. On the right side, several dozen slides were stacked in wire racks. Each was labeled, but there wasn't enough light to read them. Slowly I turned the little fridge toward the garish light from the window. With trembling hands, I removed a stack of slides.

The first one read ODIN, MUSCLE.

Then: ODIN, BLOOD.

Three more slides were labeled ODIN, STOMACH.

The sixth one said *Gynaephora groenlandica*. Latin for Arctic woolly bear moth. Again: MUSCLE, BLOOD, STOMACH.

The next label read *Tenebrionidae*, which roughly translated as "dark beetle." MUSCLE, BLOOD, STOMACH.

I reached for the next slide and froze. *What am I doing here?* I didn't even know what I was looking for. Blood like a rush of wind in my ears.

The tinkling of an alarm, distant.

The snoring stopped.

My hand shook.

I stopped breathing.

Listened.

Just the buzz of the light over the stove, the malevolent silence from the boundless waste outside the window.

Head pounding, sweating in the chilly room, I put the slides back in reverse order, praying I'd gotten it right. My hand hovered over the test tubes of blood—*That empty ring*—I couldn't quite think straight—*had I removed a test tube and put it somewhere?*

Closing my eyes, I mentally sequenced what I'd just done, praying it was right. Shut the fridge. Padded down the hall, pausing in the shadow of Wyatt's door. Caught in a triangle of light cast by his lamp, wearing a ragged T-shirt and sweats, Wyatt sat on his bed facing his window, one arm tied off with a length of rubber cord. Poised at the crook of his elbow, he held a needle, plunger at the ready. Perhaps he sensed me there, because his leonine head had begun to turn just as I slipped away and out of sight.

eleven

Sparks flew between Jeanne's hands as she welded two pieces of metal shelving together, unaware I had come in until the wintry blast from the open door of the Shed hit her. She cut the power and flipped back the face guard of her helmet. She didn't smile.

"Where's the kid?" She slipped off her welding gloves and tossed them on the workbench.

"Sleeping. Is this a good time to do this?"

"Good as any. Just about done repairing these shelves," she added with a touch of pride as she stashed her tools in cubbies above a long worktable truncated at one end by a circular saw. A floor-to-ceiling walk-in freezer took up nearly a third of the space, its door padlocked. *Why lock a freezer?* I knew the ice cores were stored there, but what else might be?

The thought occurred to me—unbidden—that I had never seen Andy's body. I'd been too upset to identify it. Dad had taken care of that horrific task. Andy had been cremated, because he'd always told me he wanted his ashes to be scattered over the ocean. He'd said, *If I ever die out here, don't waste a minute grieving for me. Grieve for this dying world of ours*, a request I could not seem to fulfill.

My breath bloomed white in the frosted air. Shivering, I wrapped my scarf a little more snugly around my neck. I was there because of Wyatt's latest dictum: Everyone on-site needed to know how to use all the vehicles. That morning he had run me through the basics of operating the snowmobile, but directed Jeanne to school me on the ins and outs of the snowcat.

And I was praying for a quick lesson. Jeanne put me on edge; something about her was a cautionary tale I hadn't yet deciphered. The chronic anxiety in her face, her downcast eyes, as if some Sisyphean task consumed her. In fact, she never stopped moving. First to rise, last in bed, she was forever cooking, cleaning, sweeping, hauling, repairing gear, clearing snow. If there was nothing left to do, she'd manufacture a task: flush out the snowmobile lines, fortify the struts in the Dome, rearrange the dry goods in the pantry. She'd even repaired the doll Sigrid had smashed, gluing back together every ceramic shard of its flush-cheeked face. It sat on a high shelf glaring down at us, red lips frozen in its Chiclet-toothed smile, pigtails retied tight.

WITH A GUST of canvas and machine oil, Jeanne creaked open the passenger door of the cat and heaved herself up next to me. The sun, rallying at its highest point of the day—just cresting the horizon—seemed to be beam cold down on us. A brisk wind rattled the machine as we sat on the glinting ice field. Once I got the hang of remembering to raise and lower the ice blade and rev the motor just so, I had us—after a few clumsy fits and starts—rolling across the tundra toward the frozen bay.

"What brought you here, Jeanne?" I asked after a few nearly companionable minutes.

She didn't answer right away, and I began to wonder just how awkward this trip would get. But after she knocked around in the glove compartment, slipped on a pair of glacier glasses, and handed me a pair, she cleared her throat to speak. "Not big on being around people, but you could probably tell about that. I'm one of eight kids, the only girl. The only way I could see my dad was to hang out in his garage, and I turned out a better mechanic than any of my brothers. My mom was a pastry chef for this Italian bakery. Cute place. Lots of real whipped cream. She taught me all her secrets too, so in those ways I was blessed."

"So you're from . . . Minnesota? Duluth area?"

"Now *that's* spooky."

"It's those long *o*'s. The flat *a*'s. Bit of a lilt. It's charming, actually."

She turned to me, unsmiling. "But you, Val. You're blessed in a way. Your talent with words and all. Wish I could have been the one to help with the girl, but I guess high school dropouts don't fit the bill. Wyatt wanted you up here in the worst way." She withdrew a flask from under her seat and took a pull. "Whiskey?"

"Sure, thanks," I said. I hated whiskey, but not nearly enough not to drink it.

"You asked why I came here, though. My husband and daughter were killed by a drunk driver a couple years ago. Wyatt tell you about that?"

"Just that it happened. I'm sorry."

She nodded but kept her eyes on the glistening ice field. "Everything I was living for—gone, just like that." She flipped the flask up, took a long swallow. "Best not to linger on it. Few months later, I see this ad for a cook-slash-mechanic way up north, middle of nowhere, and I think—that's for me. I can fix anything, cook anything, and I love the cold."

"And you have Wyatt, so you're not totally alone."

She shrugged. Ice crystals flashed in her mirrored frames. "He's my boss. Had tons of them, some better, some worse. He's not perfect, but he leaves me alone in the ways I need to be left alone." She gestured with the bottle at the blip of yellow on the stretch of luminous sea ice before us. "Why don't you head over to the Dome? We can do a circle around it and head on back." I did as she asked; the machine juddered as I made the turn—too sharp—then fell into the task. "So, you got somebody back home?"

"I'm recently divorced."

She nodded. "You use those, what are they, dating apps they're called? Swipe right and all a that?"

I laughed. "I've swiped right a few times. No luck, though."

"I see." She shifted in her seat, offered me another sip from the flask. "So, the girl, uh, Sigrid—got her figured out yet?"

"Not exactly." The whiskey burned down my throat. I could feel it joining forces with my meds, making me brave. "Can you tell me what it was like, thawing her out?" I asked as casually as I could.

"That day, that was something," she said almost wistfully. She freed a beat-up pack of Marlboros from the pocket of her parka, lit one. I drove slowly so as not to distract her, give her as much time as possible to tell the story. "First of all, day we found her, there was no doubt we were gonna cut her out, bring her back. Wyatt'd already froze and thawed out Odin a couple times, and he had some confidence in that regard. Anyway, the first couple days we kept her in the Shed. The ice around her was more'n a couple feet thick in places. But when it got close, maybe a couple inches or so, we brought her into the Shack. Laid her out on a tarp on the kitchen table and just blasted the heat and never left her. Put towels around her to soak up the melt. It started to smell weird in there, like sulfur, but also like flesh, or rotted leather, or mud. I thought of my daughter in the morgue, you know, and I almost couldn't take it, another dead girl in front of me. I even said to Wyatt 'Why are we doing this? I can't go through with this,' especially after everything that happened with Andy. I mean, a mouse is one thing, but a girl . . ."

I felt her watching me but kept my eyes on the yellow Dome, stalwart and solitary in the dead white vista. We crept along in the lowest gear, the steering wheel rattling in my grip, the smell of diesel leaking into the cabin.

"But Wyatt, he always has things under control. He's got his reasons for things, for what he does. Like I said, he's been a good boss, and I felt like I owed him a little faith, you know? So we watched her till most of the ice was gone. And she became—she was just a little girl lying on the table in a rotted caribou anorak and polar bear pants and one boot, eyes open, and she looked so scared. Then we cut off her clothes real slow, real careful. You think she's dirty now, but so much of that is stain from those wet skins. We covered her with a couple of blankets, like she was sleeping. It was crazy, what we were doing. Fucked-up for sure. I even said to Wyatt, when we found her, 'Why not leave her? Why make a mess of things?' But he wouldn't have it. She was coming out of that ice. So, there she was. A human being cut out of a glacier lying on the kitchen table. I touched her hand. Her skin was so cold, but not hard anymore. It was softening by the minute, but we had to give her time, because you know things thaw from the outside in, so we were patient. But soon we checked for breathing or a pulse and of course there was nothing, so I was getting nervous. I couldn't believe we were disrespecting a body like this, a body that had been at peace in the ice. What were we going to do now? If she was dead, and it sure looked like it, how would we bury her in the frozen ground?"

She blew a lungful of smoke out a crack in the window. We sat just beyond the Dome in a world of white, the low sun spearing us with icy late-afternoon beams. "Why don't you cut the motor? You need to practice starting her up a few times anyways."

Nodding, I turned off the ignition, cutting the heat, the glow of the dials; stilling the shaking joystick. Immediately I missed the reassuring hum of the motor. In seconds, the temperature plummeted in the cab, the vicious cold slipping through every crack in metal or glass. My blood grew gelid in my veins as I clutched the wheel.

"Then her left hand twitched under the blanket. We both yelped and jumped back. After a while, I thought we both imagined it. But then her jaw dropped, and her mouth opened and closed, so we checked for a heartbeat—nothing. So: boom—right away, Wyatt was on her with the defibrillator. Just about bounced her off the table she's so small, but he did it again and nothing. She wasn't breathing. Eyes still glazed over, both hands still—like what we'd seen was just some side effect of a body thawing—and I begged him to stop, but he wouldn't. I begged him in Frances's honor—Frances was my daughter—to *stop*. I said, 'Wyatt, maybe this is some rigor mortis thing setting in, just leave her be.'"

Her voice had broken a little. I didn't dare start the machine and break the spell. A searing breath of icy air whooshed up my spine, encircled my legs and feet in a frigid vise. Hatless, gloveless, Jeanne seemed oblivious to the cold; it seemed to enliven her.

"I smelled flesh burning, but he kept at it long after I would have, you know, given up. But that's not Wyatt. That's just not him. He *willed* that girl alive. I was in the corner in a pile sobbing, 'Oh, I'm so sorry, forgive us this unholy thing,' to whatever gods this girl prayed to. I was begging him, *begging* him to stop, Val, you understand?"

I nodded, teeth chattering, but she wasn't looking at me; she was gazing out at all the white, deep in thrall of the Enormity, which seemed to be drawing the tale out of her. "Must have been the tenth try, something changed. You could feel it in the room; this crackling energy filled it up. He was looking down at her, smiling. From where I sat, I saw her hand shoot up and sort of smack his arm, and I screamed and jumped up and ran over. The girl was coughing and gagging, threw up all over the floor but she was breathing! *She was breathing.* Wyatt, I mean, he was spattered with puke but he had this look of rapture, like he was in his own sorta church. Standing next to him like that, watching her try to catch her breath, this little filthy, naked child, hair in knots, I was trying to understand where on God's earth she had come from and what had happened to her. And I felt like, in a weird way, *we* were her parents, or her second set of parents, you know what I'm saying? I mean, he started her little heart, but we worked together to bring her out of the ice, to bring her alive. Think about that."

She reached under the dash and withdrew a dog-eared photo, handed it to me. A younger, thinner version of Jeanne, fresh-faced and quite pretty, almost delicate-looking, her eyes not buried in thick flesh and sadness, pushed a young girl on a swing. A tall man in a flannel shirt stood in the background, hands stuffed casually in baggy jeans, smiling as he watched. "That's my husband, Adam. My daughter, Frances."

"I'm so sorry for your loss. She was beautiful, what a great smile."

She took back the photo, passed her rough thumbs over her husband and daughter's image. Said, "Pitak thinks God saved Sigrid because killing all her family and all the hunters who were going after those herds of caribou was too much of a punishment. It was this act of mercy, you know?"

"Could be."

She turned to me. "I'm sorry you were punished. To lose your brother like that. Your twin, even."

My fingers stiffened with cold; I forced myself to move them. "Tell me what it was like, Jeanne, to find my brother that day." The gates seemed open, so I had to try. I steeled myself for her answer.

She took another sip of whiskey; her face closed down. I wondered if we'd be able to start the motor again, or if the cold would knock it out. "Wyatt found him, not me."

"What happened the night before?"

"Come on, you . . . Wyatt must have told you everything by now."

"He told me his version."

"Well, I don't know what you're getting at," she said testily. "There's only one version." She pushed herself up in her seat, capped the flask. "But all right, if you need to hear about it so bad. Him and Wyatt had some contest going on for months about trying to find out what made Odin thaw out alive. They messed around with everything: shellfish, moss, lichens, flowers, even pollen—every kind of combination of stuff. That night they were drinking, laughing a lot. Drunk. Or maybe they were arguing, it was none of my business. They were the best of friends, they didn't need me around." She flicked her half-smoked cigarette out the window; the wind sucked it away. "Well, that's half-true. Wyatt still needed me for day-to-day stuff 'cause Andy wasn't great at the nitty-gritty, you know, he wasn't great at doing the kind of homework you gotta do around here to stay alive: scouting glaciers for the safest routes, keeping track of equipment. You got to be Johnny-on-the-spot with this stuff, it's life-and-death. Don't get me wrong, I liked him, he was a good man—"

"He was a dreamer, I know."

"Right, scattered. Point is, he made things a little more compli-cated around here. In ways that weren't always good. Times it felt like Wyatt'd forget the important stuff, like how he still needed good ole Jeanne around to get him in and out of a crevasse alive because she brings along the right harnesses and ropes, collects his weather monitors safely, keeps him on track with logistics and all. I mean, those two could yabber on about science till the cows came home, but talk won't save you out there." She sighed mightily, as if lifting herself out of some bottomless thought chasm. "Anyway, that night I left them to their carousing and headed off to the Shed. Had an ice drill to fix. Went to bed after that—assumed they had too. It was real late. Woke up the next morning and he'd found Andy. Wyatt was destroyed. Never seen him like that. I felt sick about it."

I clutched the wheel, willing the image out of my brain. "Just tell me one thing, Jeanne. Were all the doors locked the morning Wyatt found him?"

"Locked?" She grimaced, leaning over me to turn the cat's key. I nearly cried to feel the blast of heat on my face, see the friendly glare of the dashboard. "Have a look around. No locks on any of the outside doors. Locks freeze out here, they're a pain in the ass. I got rid of them. Besides, who would we be locking out? Polar bears can't turn doorknobs. Look, Andy went out there, God knows why, but he could have come back in if he wanted to. Whatever he did, Val, he did it on purpose."

twelve

It was nearly midnight. We'd all stayed up drinking shitty wine, getting into heated theories about Sigrid, before Jeanne turned in and Nora and Raj trudged off to the Dome in haunted blue twilight.

"So, Wyatt," I asked, "what's next for you, after this place?" I sat on the rug with Sigrid, who—newly entranced with markers—scribbled on page after page of drawing paper. She'd refused to go to sleep that night, hadn't eaten much, and had barely spoken all day.

He tossed the dregs of his wine in the sink, whipped around to face me. "Ah, come on, Val," he said with derision. "Don't be coy. You must have googled me by now."

I reddened. "Guess I missed something."

He exhaled. "I was"—finger quotes—"*inappropriate* with a student back home. Grad student. She came at me, she was all over me, it was . . . mutual. For months. Then she blew the whistle. I should have known. Anyway, the powers that be are letting me finish my time here. Then they want me gone. They probably figure, what harm can I do? No nubile nymphets running around *this* place, that's for sure." He tugged at his scraggly beard and snapped at his spearmint gum. On his PC, a time-lapse animated field of glaciers melted and reformed, over and over. "So this is my last dance. Fuck knows where I'll end up after this."

"I have a feeling you'll land on your feet."

He strolled over to me, reached down, and traced his rough finger along the side of my face, gently lifting my chin to look him in the eye. I was stunned, but didn't stop him. When was the last time a man had touched me like this? Even I didn't know. His gesture felt intimate, sexual, but also spontaneous. Still, the flip from aggression to seduction unnerved me, and I felt my expression tightening. Sigrid had stopped drawing and watched his every move.

"You think less of me now, don't you?" he said, stroking my hair.

Shivering, I drew back, and he pulled away. I felt relieved but also mourned the loss of his touch, of any touch. "Look, Wyatt, it's none of my business how you deal with—"

"Val, I mean well. That's what people don't understand. Yeah, I've made bad decisions. Done things out of passion that just aren't right. Things I'll never forgive myself for." He gave me a searching look—seemed vulnerable for the first time in memory—and might have kissed me. I would have let him, even in front of Sigrid. But he didn't, and the moment passed. "Here's the thing. I'm not the worst guy. I call my mom—she's ninety—every Wednesday morning, nine o'clock sharp. Right here, on the sat phone. And hey, I've got some arthritis, some other old age bullshit, but I'm not completely washed-up. I'm sixty-one, which is a crime in America, to be over thirty—"

I laughed and nodded, and he finally smiled. I thought about the exquisite Japanese word, *shibui*, the beauty of aging, a concept that doesn't exist in American culture in any real way.

Wyatt got comfortable at his desk; Sigrid returned to her scribbling. "I've never been more passionate about what I'm doing." He leaned forward, his face half in shadow. "I'm not just curious about stuff. I *have to know*. Those odd striations a mile down in the ice, what's the explanation? *How does the world work?* It's almost like sexual frustration, which is pretty much my constant state anyway." He laughed ruefully. "It's like I'm a little pissed off all the time that I don't have the answers to my questions right away. But if I had them, what would be left for me to care about?"

He lowered his voice. "And, Val, listen. I loved Andy—you know that—but I care about all my students. So many of them are going to go on to change the world. They're doing it now. I'm very proud . . ." He rubbed his forehead, exhaustion plain in the deep creases of his face. "So what's left? I've got these cores, this fifteen-year body of work, which I'm damned proud of. But now, *now*? It's the girl. The girl is everything. The reality of her, the science of her, the *why* of her. Let me show you something."

He lifted the top off a long, low freezer in the kitchen. A fog of dry ice billowed into the stale air of the room. Slipping on canvas gloves, he reached in and gingerly lifted out a tube of ice four inches in diameter and a yard long: an ice core.

"See this? Pulled it out of Glacier 27G this morning. I've got dozens of these. This is going in the walk-in freezer in the Shed tonight—they degrade if they're not kept in super-cold conditions. It's fifty-three below in there. Anyway, I've sent hundreds of these back to the states, which is, in total, hundreds of thousands of years of data." He held up the steaming rod. It glistened in the light that flowed like violet-colored syrup from the window. "You're looking at a couple decades of climate information—hydrogen and oxygen isotopes, levels of CO_2—all compressed into a few centimeters a year. I could spend years reading all of these, trying to understand what was happening during different time periods. It's like a book written on fine paper. A really, *really* long book. A puzzle with a million pieces. The difficulty is seeing the whole thing, the patterns among all the clues about temperature, precipitation, volcanic activity— even wind speed and direction—but it all drives me crazy some days, you know? The most sophisticated computers in the world work on this data, and still we have more questions than answers." He slipped on a pair of magnifying-lens glasses and peered at the core. "Is that what it's like with Sigrid, Val? Too many puzzle pieces?"

Hearing her name, Sigrid lifted her head and watched us, wary.

I sipped at the dregs of my red wine, dreading my answer. "Her language isn't rooted in any known language. Certain words are similar enough to West Greenlandic to be loanwords—"

"It's been more than two weeks." His tone shifted, chilled. "Closer to three."

"Look, I'm making progress." My hand trembled; the skin painfully cracked and raw. Wine shuddered in my cup. "She's coming along in her own way."

But I was lying. Again. Sigrid was clamming up, wanting only to wander around outside, watch Nora and Raj do their dives, sit on the counter as Jeanne cooked or hang out with her in the Shed. She was fretful, fidgety, and distracted. Something felt off.

Wyatt nestled the ice core in its wooden sleeve and tucked it back into the freezer. "Fine. I've got some homework for her, right here." He plunged his hands deep into the icy fog and lifted out a shoebox-sized terrarium, its base scattered with what looked like thumb-length orange and black furry turds. Sigrid squinted at the glass box.

"See these little guys?"

I got to my feet and looked down into the clear case.

"Very special creatures. Orange things are Arctic caterpillars. Black guys are *Upis* beetles. Frozen solid. For weeks now." He shook them a bit in the glass box; they rattled against its sides. I thought of his slides: *muscle, blood, stomach*. "These insects can survive any kind of cold, as much as a hundred degrees below zero. Indefinitely."

In bare feet, Sigrid stepped on her pile of drawings as she made her way to us. Wyatt seemed unable to hide a look of satisfaction. He winked at her. Set the terrarium on the coffee table, its upped edge at her eye level. I sat next to her. She remained expressionless, but he seemed oblivious or simply without fear of acting the fool with children. "So, what happens in nature, when winter comes," he said, getting all ginned up, sidling up to me like a coconspirator, "is that the caterpillar's heart will completely stop beating. Then its gut will freeze, followed by its blood. Then the remainder of its body will freeze. It survives all this by producing a cryoprotectant in its tissues. It's a kind of sugar that protects the cells from the damage freezing does."

Sigrid rested her elbow on my knee and said softly, "Bahl." She hadn't learned Wyatt's name yet, or if she had, she wouldn't say it.

He set the terrarium on the rug next to her, smiled down at her. "You know these creatures, Sigrid?"

She glanced at the terrarium, then away, shifted her weight to her other foot, absentmindedly picking her nose. Wyatt reached down toward her shoulder. She snapped to attention and backed away.

"Come on over here, kiddo. Have yourself a better look."

But she'd utterly lost interest; she kicked a toy walrus across the floor as she wandered toward the kitchen and a plate of just-baked sugar cookies Jeanne had left on the counter.

"Hey, Sigrid, watch this." Wyatt snatched up the terrarium and set it down tight to the long, low heater that ran the length of the wall. "You have to see this, Sigrid. It's magic. Can't you call her over, Val? Maybe she'll come if you—"

I joined Wyatt by the glowing coils of the heater. "Sigrid, come over here for a second," I said in mashed-up West Greenlandic and Danish. She turned to me, gnawing on a cookie, fat crumbs falling to the floor. I gestured and patted my knee. She wandered over to us.

Heat blasted at the sides of the case, steaming it up. With a cloth, Wyatt steadily wiped away the condensation. Nothing was happening. The furry caterpillar blobs stayed blobs; the curled, brittle beetles stayed curled, brittle beetles. Sigrid wandered away, distracted by the animated bergs on Wyatt's screen.

"Hey, Sigrid," he said, rotating the terrarium, exposing each side to the warmth, the glass squeaking as he wiped it. "Don't give up so fast." I stared at the sad little frozen dead things, suppressing images of Andy, trying to stay present.

I yawned, only closing my eyes for an instant.

I saw it the second I opened them. At first I thought, *This is some trick of light and shadow*. But it happened again. One of the beetles' legs jerked as if kicking a tiny foe, then trembled in the humid air of its cage.

"Sigrid," Wyatt said gruffly. "Get back here."

She turned, gave me a questioning look.

"It's okay," I said. But she stayed where she was.

A few of the insect's other legs shuddered, as if a current of electricity was passing through, then it grew still, and I thought, *It's just thawing out; things shift and move as they thaw, don't they?* Long seconds passed with no movement, but I couldn't look away from the warmed-over black lump.

Suddenly its antennae stiffened from their drooping pose, straightened as if stretching, before slowly helicoptering. The two appendages then worked together, dropping down to probe the floor of the terrarium, then a neighboring beetle. Other beetles had already rolled off their backs, taking tentative steps with a stiff, rocking gait. A dung-colored caterpillar unfurled centimeter by centimeter, extending itself luxuriantly. It took a few sips of air before trundling its many legs along the pebbles at the bottom of the tank. Sigrid, picking up on our rapt attention, made her way over and squatted, chin level with the top of the tank.

Cross-legged on the floor, Wyatt joined her, attempting to get his head in line with hers. "You know these bugs, Sigrid?" he asked with unconcealed excitement. "Have you eaten these? Ask her, Val."

I did.

She continued gnawing on her cookie as she observed the crawling insects, all of them now quite lively, scrambling over one another and venturing up the sides as they scouted an escape. I asked her again, pointed, *Have you eaten these?* She shoved the rest of the cookie in her mouth, swallowed thoughtfully.

Nodded.

Wyatt sprang to his full height, paced around us in his droopy-toed socks. "She said yes, right? Good God, she said yes." He smacked his forehead. "Can you ask her, how does she eat them—cooked? Raw?"

I pointed at my mouth as I asked her. "Do you eat them just like this?" I gestured at the insects and made little walking motions with my fingers.

She nodded again, quite somberly.

"I think she's saying she eats them raw, but who knows," I said.

"Makes sense," he said. "Makes total sense." He stopped, thought a few seconds. "But I need to see her do it." He reached into the terrarium and plucked up a beetle, caging it in one hand. "Here you go, kiddo." He held out his closed fist. "Have at it." He took her hand and opened his over her small one, folding her fingers around the bug. The beetle dropped and scrabbled around on her palm. With a yelp of shock and surprise, she shook it off; it scuttled under the couch. She clutched my knee; a flood of words pouring from her.

"You scared the shit out of her."

"All right, I got this. We're going to try something else." Wyatt lifted a frying pan off a hook over the sink, splashed some oil into it, snapped on the burner. He picked up the terrarium and shook the insects into the pan, gathering the errant ones with his hands and slamming on the lid. Sigrid watched me wide-eyed, cheeks flushed with the heat, a death grip on my sweatpants. In seconds, an acrid smoke seeped from under the lid. Wyatt shook the pan from side to side like a gourmet chef perfecting an omelet, then grabbed a plate and slid the now genuinely dead creatures onto it.

Sigrid's body pushed harder into me as he set the plate of sizzling bugs on the coffee table. "What do you think now, kiddo? They look pretty tasty to me."

Her fingernails dug into my flesh through my pants.

With a thick finger, Wyatt nudged one of the beetles around on the plate. "Maybe a little salt." He ran for the shaker, salted them; they sizzled and shrank into themselves, the caterpillars melting into a furry paste. "Come on, Sigrid, you just said you ate these. Well, here they are. Let's go." He picked up a beetle and popped it in his mouth, crunching, his face a blank mask. "See? Mmm, delicious, right? Now, you," he said, opening his mouth and pointing. A few spindly black beetle legs remained on his tongue. He closed his mouth, swallowed, and edged the plate closer to her, up against her chest now. She shuddered, recoiling. "Come on," he said. "Just try one."

He picked up a fried beetle and held it to her lips. She jerked away, her mouth opening in a wail as she sent the plate flying, scattering the bugs across the floor. She thrust herself away from me and bolted from the room.

"Nice, Wyatt," I said, jumping to my feet. "You really found the way to her heart."

"Fuck." He grabbed a broom and began sweeping up the bugs. "She said she ate them. You saw her! She nodded when you asked."

Feeling his eyes burn into me, I retrieved the plate and brought it to the sink. "I'm going to talk to her."

I EXPECTED TO find her where she usually escaped: burrowed deep in her refuge of blankets and pillows under her bed, tearful. But she was sitting on top of it, facing the window, bare legs dangling, a pad of paper on her lap. It was full dark outside now, and she drew by lamplight with great concentration. Her forehead shone with sweat.

"Hey, Sigrid," I said softly as I approached her, hoping the tenuous trust between us would hold, until I settled next to her, watching her draw. Carefully I lifted my hand, easing it around her until I rested my palm on her forehead just beneath her hairline. She didn't react in any way; just kept sketching furiously, mumbling under her breath. I could feel her heart beating in her temples, her soft flesh pulsing with too much heat.

On the page, outlined in black emerged what looked like strips of seaweed, or like snakes or worms, sometimes separate, at others in squiggly piles. A wide-winged bird soared over the odd shapes. She carefully colored the seaweed strips dark purple; the bird—very simply drawn—stayed white with a black head and long, red beak. When she was done, she smoothed her hands over the drawing, as if ensuring it was dry or safe somehow, and with abundant ceremony, spread it across my lap.

"Thanks, Sigrid."

She put her hand on my arm and looked up at me with trust in her eyes. The damp heat of her palm radiated through the sleeve of my wool shirt. I clicked on the recorder hidden in my pocket. Pointed at her drawings.

"What are these animals, or plants, can you tell me about them?"

For several minutes she spoke to me in the strangest way: patiently, slowly, as if I were the child and she were the adult and I'd better pay attention because *this was important*.

She began most sentences with one of seven words—I'd been tracking this much at least. But now she spun off into some kind of explanation, gesturing, pointing at the bird, then the squiggly lines, back to the bird. I repeated the words she used for seaweed or snake and bird back to her, "*Sahndaluuk, kahdayglu*," and she got very excited, more excited than maybe I'd ever seen her.

She jabbed her dirt-encrusted nail over and over at the snake and bird, then carefully tore the piece of paper from the pad. Folding it into the smallest possible square, she tucked it into my palm, closing my fingers around it. She reached up with both hands for my face—it took me a second to understand—I lowered my head to hers, and she rubbed her forehead on mine, like a forehead kiss. I'd read that this was how Greenlandic Inuit greeted each other sometimes; they leaned in to each other, touched foreheads, and smelled each other briefly. I wondered how I smelled to her; I'd grown used to her essence: earth, skin oils, fish, wet leather, so I breathed her in and for several seconds we relaxed like that. I wanted to ask more questions, but that was her good night, her benediction. She dropped to the floor and disappeared in her hideout.

LATER THAT NIGHT, I crawled into my own bed and unfolded the drawing under the glow of my desk lamp. *What the hell is she trying to tell me?* Squiggly lines and birds; clearly, these things were both meaningful and a secret. I played back snatches of her speech along with samples of every dialect of Greenlandic I could find. No correlation. *If this girl is Greenlandic, why doesn't she speak any of the dialects?*

The seven words that preceded each sentence, phonetically, were *stahndala, tahtaksah, oosahmtara, mahkeensaht, sahsahnaht, neneesaht,* and *verohnsaht.*

The mystery haunted me: *What in the world are there seven of that she needs to refer to each time she speaks?* Days of the week, the seven deadly sins, the seven seas, wonders of the world—none made any sense at all.

I WOKE TO a rustling sound; I'd been kicking something. Dozens of white packets. Like palm-sized sailboats, meticulously folded pieces of paper dotted the blue wool blanket at the foot of my bed. I

opened them. They were all the same: laboriously rendered drawings of the same snake and bird. I pictured her up at dawn, churning out more of these. *Why?* It reminded me of something I'd read
once: *Repetition is the mute language of the abused child.* I wasn't
speculating abuse, but I had to acknowledge repetition as a desperate attempt to communicate.

As I gathered the drawings, I felt—in my body, like a little flame—
her budding faith in me, and my growing determination to help her.
Nothing else seemed to matter. I tucked the scraps of paper in an
envelope and slipped it inside one of my books—there seemed no
better place to hide them.

thirteen

The second week of October, a blizzard swept down off the mountains so fast and so fierce, no one was prepared for it. Fifty-mile-per-hour winds boomed down from the glacial pass as snow pelted the Shack, swiftly building into man-high drifts. Blinded by the whiteout, Nora and Raj had to use the rope—hand over hand—to battle their way from the Dome to the Shack. Wyatt raced back from the glacier, his eyelashes and beard caked with snow, shaken that his GPS had quit so all he'd had to guide him were glimpses of the yellow flags flying over our three buildings. Only Sigrid, Jeanne, and I had been safely in the Shack when the storm hit.

Two days later, the blizzard showed no signs of letting up. It became hard to imagine any reality other than howling, snow-filled darkness. We'd gone through most of the card and board games, and a good deal of alcohol. We were running low on conversation. I felt walled in, jumpy, trapped.

With the exception of Jeanne constantly rummaging in the kitchen, we all hibernated in the living room on the broken-down couches and chairs, Raj and Nora sprawled on the rug under a sleeping bag, her head on his lap. We watched old black-and-white science fiction movies on DVD, like *The Thing*, *Godzilla*, and *The War of the Worlds*. Sigrid, agitated, sat on Wyatt's desk with her sweater stretched over her knees, rocking as she stared out the picture window, the view a smear of bruised silver and white, like living inside a thunderhead.

The air inside was heavy with the smell of human bodies; until we could get outside again, all water was for drinking and cooking. I could have closed my eyes and identified each of us by our particular bouquets. Wyatt was all acrid tang, spearmint, and tobacco; Raj smelled like rubber and neoprene; Jeanne: wood shavings, metal, biscuit; Nora like citrus perfume barely masking a musky bite. Neither I nor Sigrid helped the situation, of course. Worst of all, Jeanne had disconnected the toilet so the pipes wouldn't freeze. Everyone got their own bucket.

Lounging on the couch in his pit-stained long johns and down boot liners, Wyatt gestured at the TV with a can of beer. Some sort of worm was crawling out of a man's eye. "Check out that monster parasite."

"Reminds me of what I see under the microscope every day," Raj said, tucking his sleeping bag closer around him. "You want to know horror, just look at what hangs around on kelp. There's this parasitic worm that lives in the anus of a certain species of krill. Worse thing I've ever seen."

"Thanks for the nightmares, darling," Nora said sleepily.

The credits rolled, and Raj wrangled himself to his stockinged feet. Bored to distraction, he wandered to Wyatt's desk, tossing stale peanuts one by one into his mouth from a much-recycled ziplock bag. Odin rustled in his wood shavings, his pink nose pushing through the mesh of the cage. "How's the research? Heard it didn't go too well with the bugs."

Wyatt shifted in his seat. "I'll get there. It's just a matter of time."

"What have you tried?"

"Why do you ask?"

Raj peered out at the never-ending storm, the snow so heavy it was like the sky falling to the earth. "So I can steal your fucking ideas."

Wyatt let the comment slide, as if it were beneath him to react. "I've worked with Arctic char, cod, flounder—they can all survive temps below freezing—all kinds of Arctic shellfish, some amphibians, lichens, moss. You know there are lichens that stay frozen for years and thaw out just fine?" Wyatt jumped to his feet and withdrew a glass tray from under a heat lamp. Tiny green shoots poked from what looked like a thin mat of black dirt. "This stuff's been locked in the ice for hundreds of years. Put it under a heat lamp and bam, it sprouts."

"Fine, but what's your process? How do you study the why and how of all this?"

Wyatt considered Raj, said, "I test for cryoproteins, or other cryoprotectants, isolate them, then try them on their own, or combine them in every possible way."

Raj listlessly tossed the bag of peanuts on Wyatt's desk. Plopped down on the couch and folded his arms behind his head, glasses flashing in the dim light. "What do you mean, *try them*?"

"Raj," Nora said from her sprawled-out position on the rug. "Can you get me some tea?"

"In a minute."

Wyatt said, "I worked with lemmings at first. Put them on special diets, injected them, froze them, but so far . . ."

"Just a bunch of dead lemmings?"

Wyatt swirled his can of beer, knocked the rest of it back. "I think I need to be working with larger mammalian subjects. You up for it?"

Raj scoffed, got up and poured himself some wine, Nora her tea, and sat back down next to her. "You're wasting your time, man."

"I'm wrong until I'm right."

"With all due respect, Wyatt, this is crackpot science. There's no methodology. You know it, and I know it."

Wyatt crushed the beer can in his hand and tossed it in the trash. "Tell you what I know. Odin exists. Three times in a year he's thawed alive."

"Where'd you find him?"

"In the Dome. What difference does it make? Sigrid's alive. And people all over the world are freezing to death in these ice winds. Five, six, a dozen people at a time, wiped out. And it's going to get a lot worse. You think knowing what kept Sigrid from dying won't help the human race?"

"So that's what you're doing?"

"Beats making kelp sandwich bags."

Sigrid turned to Raj from her perch on Wyatt's desk, a smile dimpling her cheeks. She said, "Seal Man."

"That's me, darling," Raj said to Sigrid with pride. "Seal Man." He hopped to his feet and went to her as if to give her a hug—it looked like he could have used one—but she withdrew, smile fading, so he only stood awkwardly close to her and took the time to have a good look at her. "You know, she looks a little peaked. She okay, you think? Can we at least try to give her a bath?"

"She won't do it," I said. "We heat up the water, but she won't go near it."

"So, Raj, you two seem tight," Wyatt said. "She say anything else to you besides 'Seal Man'?"

"Oh, for sure. We chat all day long, don't we, Sigrid? She's told Seal Man all her secrets, every last one of them."

"I see." Wyatt got up, brushing past Raj on his way to the kitchen, where he extracted another beer from the fridge. "Gotta say, she's not looking a hundred percent to me. You know what I'd like to do? Get a blood sample from her."

Sigrid drew her circles in the condensation, one after the other in neat rows, before rubbing them away, the wailing wind the only sound in the room.

I thought, *It's impossible to escape this place, no matter how bad this gets. . . .*

"Wyatt, no, seriously?" I sat forward, clutching the arm of the couch.

"Bad idea," Raj said.

"Why would you do that?" Nora pushed herself up to one elbow.

I got to my feet. "Wyatt, come on. You can't do that to her. You're just going to ruin any progress I've made."

"Any *progress* you've made?" Wyatt snorted.

I boiled inside but said nothing.

Wyatt kept his eyes on me, said, "Hey, Jeanne, got a second?"

Jeanne set aside some bread dough she'd been working and dutifully came into the living room.

"So, guys, it's simple. I need a blood sample. Raj is right, look at her. Something's up with her."

Sigrid, reading the room, dropped down off Wyatt's desk and wandered over to me, her sweater fanning out on the rug behind her.

"Nora?" Wyatt said. "Help me out?"

She turned to Raj. "Maybe it is a good idea. Poor kid. She can't tell us how she's feeling."

Raj put his hands on his narrow hips and paced. "I can't be a part of this. She won't understand."

Wyatt rooted around in a drawer, pulled out a box with a red cross on it. "It'll just take a second. She may need antibiotics. Val, come on, help us out. Try to do . . . whatever you do. Explain it to her somehow."

All eyes drilled into me.

My knees went wobbly as weakness flooded me; I leaned on the back of the couch. In my effort to conserve my stash, I'd gone a few days without a pill. I rued that decision as heat flashed up my neck and shoulders. It was as if I was standing at the edge of the crevasse, its blue jaws open, beckoning me down.

"Can you just give me a minute?"

"Of course," Raj said.

"You stay with Seal Man and Nora," I said to Sigrid. "I'll be right back."

I ran to the bathroom and threw up. The walls rippled and throbbed as they closed in. *I just need a pill*, I thought, *then I'll be able to deal with this.*

I staggered down the hall toward my bedroom, craving the chemical balm on my nerves even as I chided myself for needing it.

I jerked open my sock drawer, venturing with a trembling hand beneath the bright knots of cotton and wool to the back right corner. Anticipated the comforting heft of the plastic pill bottle in my hand, the reassuring rattle of the dozen or so pills I knew were left.

Nothing.

Only socks.

Had I moved the bottle to the other side by accident? My heart did its fight-or-flight dance. I checked the left side. Just cheap old pegboard, rough with splinters.

I wrenched out the drawer and dumped the contents onto my bed. Just socks, a couple of pairs of underwear, a scarf. A safety pin.

Where the fuck are my pills?

I emptied each drawer on the bed. Nothing. Rummaged through every pocket of my pants and sweaters, all the while knowing good and goddamned well I would have never been so cavalier with them. Someone had taken them. *Or am I just losing my mind?* I sat on my piles of clothes on my saggy bed, quaking as I tried to keep my breathing under control. Gripping my thighs with my hands, I stared at my broken-open skin, rife with pain no creams or potions could ease.

No pills, no pills, my mind echoed endlessly.

How would I ever go out on the ice again? How would I ever get home?

Screams from the living room shocked me to my feet. I bolted down the hallway. Their faces ghostly by the TV's shifting light, Jeanne held Sigrid down while Wyatt took vial after vial of blood from her arm. Nora and Raj stood back while Sigrid shrieked, her eyes never leaving mine.

I ran at them. "Get off of her—let her *go*!"

"Stand back!" Wyatt growled, intent on his task. "Or she's going to get hurt."

Wyatt was right, all I could do was watch as the tubes filled with her dark blood, until Jeanne finally released her and she ran cater-wauling by me to her room.

fourteen

The storm ended at dawn. We all took shifts shoveling out the main door, heads down, exchanging minimal good-mornings, as if each of us—in our own way—was the guilty party. I felt sick at heart about what had happened, furious at Wyatt and Jeanne, frustrated that we—me, Raj, and Nora—seemed to constantly bend under Wyatt's will. *What was wrong with us?*

Around noon, I ventured outside to relieve Raj. I found an eerie and terrifying sight. Snow flowed over the tops of the buildings, the Dome now just a blip of yellow in the alabaster bay. We'd practically been erased from the landscape.

The severity of the storm had forced Wyatt to abandon the snowcat several yards from the Cube. Now, cursing and metal-on-ice chopping sounds came from it; I wandered over to investigate. Raj was bent double inside the cabin, chipping away. The wind had been so powerful that snow and ice had tunneled through the narrowest cracks between the windows and doors, caking the interior like thick white mold.

"How's it going?"

He gave me a look, like, *Really?* and kept on banging at the ice with a hammer and chisel. "It's just swell in here," he said, eyes on his task. "I've been out here three hours, and this is how far I've gotten." He stopped to wipe the fog from his glasses, looking like a polar explorer in his cave of rime and blue ice.

"Can you turn it on, heat it up?"

"If I ever reach the controls. How's Sigrid?"

"Hard to tell. She's doing her old push-the-bed-against-the-door thing."

"Look, Val, I feel terrible about last night. It happened so fast. They had her pinned and that needle in before either of us could move."

"Hey, I abandoned her too."

He started to speak, stopped himself. Slipped his glasses back on and had a good look at me. "Maybe it's a good thing. He's got his sample. It's over."

"You really believe that?"

"I believe we have to get through the next couple weeks the best we can." He banged at a thick covering of ice over the ignition; it cracked and fell away. He inserted the key and fired up the machine; I nearly swooned at the whoosh of heat. "Let's just survive it. Agreed?"

EVEN AS OUR meager afternoon light began to fade into velvet black, Sigrid refused to leave her room. I left a dinner of fried fish and canned black beans—her new favorite—outside her door.

The next morning, the dish sat cold and untouched.

"Hey, Sigrid." I stood outside her room sipping a cup of coffee. Knocked a few times. "It's me, Bahl. I'm coming in."

The door was unlocked, bed back under the window that faced the Dome. Sketch pad on her lap, Sigrid sat cross-legged on the floor, her slight back bent, a child island in a sea of drawings.

She didn't acknowledge me. The air tasted static with her manic energy, her helter-skelter tufts of wild blue-black hair tipped by lush morning light, her ripe smell so familiar to me now I barely noticed it. I approached her, my slippers noiseless on the thick rug. Her scruffy bloodstained bandage—apparently there'd been a struggle to get the needle in—sat balled up next to her. It hit me in the chest how much I cared about this child, and how dangerous caring was, because of how quickly people can be taken away. I took a breath into lungs that felt stingy and small. I tried not to spin off into dread, to bring myself back into the room, focus on the things that brought me to sanity—the small things, the practical things: getting her fed, getting her to talk, getting her to comprehend the danger of not making herself understood.

I knelt to examine her drawings, expecting more squiggles and birds, but no. Each was the same: She'd traced seven circles per sheet of paper. Every circle drawn with a black marker and left blank in the middle except for the very last one. On the first few drawings, she'd neatly filled the final ring with red ink, painstakingly coloring inside the lines, but with each subsequent drawing her work on the last circle turned more and more frantic, out of control, until agitated red marks burst through its boundaries, the violence extending across the page.

Her breathing was labored.

"Sigrid."

She looked up at me, fist clutching the marker midair. Bald fear in her eyes. Clearly I'd interrupted some nightmarish reverie, some memory no child should have. She grabbed my pant leg and pulled me toward her, whispering, "Bahl, Bahl."

"Yes, I'm coming." I sat cross-legged beside her. She ripped a fresh sheet from the pad, smoothed it on the rug.

"I'm sorry about what happened. Is your arm okay?"

No answer.

As if she were afraid my attention might lag, she raced through another drawing, each circle more sloppily drawn, until she came to the last one. Tossing the black marker aside, she seized the red one and attacked the final circle with it, tearing through the paper, not stopping even as she stabbed at the rug, staining it, crying in a helpless way before hurling the marker at the wall. She rocked in place, holding herself, panting.

"Hey, Sigrid, hey." I reached out and touched her shoulder, but she swatted my hand away. Jumped up and whirled around to face me. A crescent-shaped knife glinted in her fist. "Whoa, put that down," I choked out, hands up in surrender. "I'm not going to hurt you. Now give me the knife." I held out my hand.

She circled me, knife held high. Through choking cries of rage and disappointment, she rambled on in her language, "Bahl" interspersed between phrases. I kept my eyes front, inhaled the fusty rug smell, focused on the Dome, a blip of banana-yellow cheer in the bleak landscape.

"I'm so sorry I let that happen to you. I'll never let them touch you again."

She stood behind me now, crying and talking at the same time, the knife hovering at my neck; its silver face mirrored in the window, glimmering. I closed my eyes. Felt her hot breath on me. *Is she really going to try to hurt me? Does she feel no one can help her now? What can I say to calm her down?*

She lay the tip of the knife at the base of my neck below my left ear. I stiffened at the touch of shocking cold metal. Held my breath.

Of all the words in all the languages I knew, not one rose to the surface of my consciousness to help me.

Chanting in her singsong voice, she dragged the white cold tip along the base of my neck. I pictured her plunging it into my jugular, my spine. Braced for the pain, for blood to pour down my back. I could have reached back and grabbed the knife but would have been too late to stop her from cutting me.

"Sigrid . . ." I breathed.

She rested the point of the knife on the other side of my neck.

My skin vibrated where the edge of the knife had traveled. I couldn't tell if she had cut me shallowly or my flesh was merely remembering the blade's touch.

"They think you're sick, so they needed to look at your blood," I whispered. "So we can help you."

The knife lifted from my flesh. She began to sob; in the corner of my eye, the blade still quavered, flashing. Slowly I turned to face her. Blinded by tears, she held the knife high, thin arm quaking.

I whispered the seven words that prefaced her sentences: "*Stahndala, tahtaksah, oosahmtara, mahkeensaht, sahsahnaht, neneesaht, verohnsaht . . .*"

She lowered her arm and hiccuped; her face breaking into a confused smile. I repeated the words as I reached up to take the knife from her. She took a step back. "Bahl," she said, wagging her head no at me as if I were a child being silly.

I lunged for the knife, but she was faster and scuttled under her bed with it. Moments later she emerged, smile erased by a look of exhaustion.

"Can I have the knife, Sigrid?" I made a slicing motion with my hand.

She gave me a blank look as if she didn't understand. I didn't buy it. Slowly, evenly, I reached back and touched my neck.

No blood.

I exhaled. "Jeanne'll be looking for it. It's not safe for you to have it."

Cheeks ruddy with emotion, she gazed at me with the oldest eyes in the world, as if not understanding why I still didn't understand. *Keep the knife*, I thought, *if it makes you feel better.*

The drawings frightened me more than the fact that she was collecting knives. I picked up her final one, the one she seemed to draw especially for me, and flattened it with my hands. "What does this mean?" I sighed, running my fingers over the bloodred hole she'd made. "What are these circles?" I repeated, as always, in Danish, West Greenlandic, English.

She went around gathering up all the drawings, piled them in my lap. Maybe because I'd been listening to her cry, I began to cry quietly myself as she stacked the peculiar pictures on my knees. Her efforts felt so passionate, so full of her own urgent needs.

She pointed at the red circle. Took my hand and pressed it on the gouged-out drawing.

I searched her dark eyes. "You haven't eaten in a couple of days. Aren't you hungry?" I pointed at her mouth, rubbed my belly.

With a cry of frustration, she swept the drawings off my lap and disappeared under her bed. Tiring of the game, I dove down onto my belly and wormed my way toward her.

"Come on, Sigrid, don't do this. Everyone is sorry. *I'm* sorry." For several minutes I rattled on about nothing, trying every bribe imaginable to get her to come out. She knew the words *fish, hamburger, seal, caribou, beans, cookie*. Even *outside*. I slung them all at her. No effect. Then I remembered Raj's plan to go diving that day. Impossible to forget her look of unmitigated joy as she watched Raj burst out of the water after his dive.

"What about going to the Dome? We can watch Seal Man."

From her nest of pillows came Sigrid's faint voice, "Seal Man?"

"They're doing a dive today." I went to the door. Made sure I made a lot of noise creaking it open. "I'm going to go watch them, want to come?"

A scuffling sound, then silence.

"I'm going to go get dressed. See you outside for Seal Man."

WYATT SAT GAZING thoughtfully at a dead Arctic lemming in a plastic container, desultorily reaching in with his pencil and poking at it, slowly rolling it onto its back. Vials and test tubes sat in their stands surrounded by a few of the slides I'd sneaked a look at.

"How is she?" he asked, not looking up from the motionless rodent.

"Better."

"She put a turd in my bed this morning."

"Guess I don't have to translate *that* for you." I gathered my snow gear and began to suit up.

"Where are you going?"

"The Dome. With Sigrid."

"Where is she?"

"She's on her way."

He gave me a look that said, *So where is she?* then placed a slide under the microscope. Adjusted the machine, peered down.

I slipped on my boots. "Find anything?"

"What do you mean?"

"In Sigrid's blood."

"Her white blood cell count is a little high."

"What does that mean?"

"Could have an infection. Could also be stress. Emotional, physical."

"What should we—"

He turned to me. "You know, Val, *you're* the one who made this into a traumatic shit show. We didn't need all that drama the other night. Totally unnecessary. She was looking at you for cues, and all you did was freak her out."

"You got what you wanted. Isn't that the important thing, Wyatt?"

He gave me a raw look, removed the slide, and fished out another, dialing down the scope. "You okay to head over to the Dome without me or Jeanne?"

"Of course."

"So sign out. You haven't been doing that. I'm not clear on why. I'm just trying to keep everyone safe."

I approached him, sweating in my parka in the hot, close room. The smell of burned coffee and stale blueberry Pop-Tarts lingered in the air. "I know you took my pills," I said in a furious whisper, my rage surprising me.

"What pills?" he said, not looking up from the scope.

I forced myself to take a breath. "Don't forget, Wyatt, you still need me here."

"Not sure what that has to do with your pills. Sure you didn't lose them?"

Perspiration dripped between my shoulder blades; I was dressed for ten-below-zero winds. I could feel our two hours of daylight ticking away. "*Lose* them?" I gestured around the room, a half-mad Michelin woman. "Where would I lose them in this place?"

He gestured at his desk, a cacophony of papers, files, specimen boxes, old computers, half-eaten Ring Dings. "I lose things all the time. I spend half my time just looking for shit—"

"Well, I'm not *like* you, Wyatt." I struggled to keep my voice calm, though my limbs quaked under layers of wool and down. "I'm *different*."

He lifted an eyebrow. "Andy did mention—"

"I'm *organized*. I'm in control of, of . . . *my belongings*."

He laughed. "That must be nice. Look, I won't go through your stuff if you don't go through mine, deal?"

Heat flushed up my neck, setting my cheeks aflame. I looked at the rug. "Someone helped themselves to my medication."

He leaned back in his chair, clicked a pencil against his teeth. "Maybe you're better off without that stuff, ever think of that? Could be you'll have a clearer head, especially when you're trying to work with the kid."

The fact that he may have had a point infuriated me. "Those pills help me do my job."

"Good to know."

"So maybe you better take the time to find them," I stuttered, "if you want me to be helpful."

He gave me a long look, straightened out one leg so he could reach deep in the pocket of his overalls. "Speaking of finding things, maybe you can tell me about these." He took out several wads of paper. One by one, he unfolded them: Sigrid's snake and bird drawings.

"Where did you find those?"

"Jeanne was doing laundry. They were in your pants pockets."

But I didn't remember putting them there . . . *I'd stashed them in an envelope and tucked them in a book . . . hadn't I?* I reddened. "Why didn't she give them back to me?"

He shrugged. "I'm sure she was going to. They were lying on the counter. I happened to be walking by."

I approached his desk. The drawings looked personal, private, a little girl's secrets raw and vulnerable under his bright specimen lamp. I pictured the curve of Sigrid's small back as she drew them, her concentration unbreakable.

I held out my hand. "Give them back to me. Please."

He patted a stool near his desk, dragged it close to him. "Come here, Val. Just sit a second."

I didn't want to. But I did as he said.

He rested his elbows on his knees, head close to mine. "I thought we had an agreement. But times like these, finding these little drawings lying around, makes me think you're holding back on me. And I don't know why."

"I was going to show them to you."

He unfolded one of the drawings, flattened it with his hand. "What does this mean, do you think?"

"I wish I could tell you."

"These spirals, this tern, they don't mean anything?"

"I'm sure it means something—"

"But you don't know what it is. Okay, fine." He shoved the drawings in my direction. Jabbed his finger at them. Lowered his voice to a growl. "From now on you tell me every goddamned thing about this girl. Every word you've translated. Everything she does. You show me every drawing, got it? *When* she draws it. You tell me what you think it means, every guess, no matter how crazy you think it sounds."

"Sure." I reached out to gather the drawings. He grabbed my wrist, yanked me in tight, my face kissing close. "No more games, understand?"

We locked eyes in the airless room. My wrist felt like a twig in his grip.

"Bahl," came Sigrid's soft voice. I jerked my arm free.

She stood at the door, bundled head to toe in her ersatz polar gear. *How long had she been standing there?*

"You ready?" I said, injecting levity into my voice.

Unsmiling, she looked from me to Wyatt, then back to me, before nodding her head. Wrist aching, I signed us out on the register, Wyatt's eyes burning holes into me until I hauled the door shut behind us.

fifteen

Watching Raj prepare to dive was like witnessing a holy ritual. With solemn quiet, by the unearthly blue light of the Dome, he unhooked the red-and-black dry suit that hung from the ceiling, its alien-like red gloves dangling from the sleeves. He sat on a folding chair, flopping the suit out in front of him. Starting with the legs, he worked the rubber fabric over two layers of long underwear. Nora helped him with each step, double-checking every snap and hook until finally assisting him with the long zipper that crossed his chest from hip to shoulder. The gaping blue hole where he would soon disappear leered up at us like a deathly eye; it seemed the way to every subconscious horror, the place where nightmares lived and multiplied, laughing among themselves in icy delight, yet that's where he was headed, with intent, reverence, and apparent interest. I couldn't have admired him more.

Though clearly he and Nora had memorized each step, Nora consulted the illustrated, bulleted list. She whispered her way through every zip and valve, each adjustment and setting. Raj may as well have been on his way to the moon.

Bug-eyed, Sigrid sat next to me on a bench watching the transformation. Suited up for the most part, Raj paused in his preparation and excused himself, crossing to a corner of the Dome where a towel-sized, colorful mat had been laid out. Facing away from us, he got down on his knees and prayed quietly to himself, occasionally resting his forehead on its vibrant weave. Nora laid out the rest of the gear on a rubber mat: air tank, weight belt, fins, goggles, headgear, short-handled knife, flashlight.

Satisfied with her work, she lifted a kettle off a Coleman stove and poured water into a couple of cups. "Want some cocoa?" She glanced over at Sigrid, who nodded with her whole body.

Sigrid chugged the chocolate, handing Nora back the cup as if fully expecting a refill. Nora laughed and gave her one.

Raj finished his prayers and poured himself some cocoa, his face distorted by the tight rubber headpiece.

Sigrid wiped her mouth, said, "Seal Man." No smile or laughter this time. More like awe.

Raj squeaked on his swimming fins and slapped the few steps to the edge of the hole, where he sat on a metal stool. Nora circled him, adjusting his headgear before heaving the tank from the ice floor and hooking it over his shoulders.

Sigrid jumped from her seat, caught my elbow, and led me over to one of the remaining two dry suits suspended from hooks attached to the ceiling supports. She took my hand and placed it on one of the sleeves.

"You want *me* to dive?" I laughed.

Nora smiled. "That spare suit would fit you perfectly."

"No," I said to Sigrid. I pointed to Raj. "*Seal Man*. Not Seal Bahl."

She shook her head and reached into one of her mittens, unfolding a scrap of paper; she had torn the snake image from one of her drawings. She squirreled it into my hand and closed my fingers around it.

"No, I could never—"

She squeezed my fingers tight around the crumpled paper, said, "*Taimagiakaman*."

I knew this word. . . . I gasped and got down to my knees to be at her eye level.

"Sigrid." My hand trembled as I drew back wisps of hair from her face. "Listen to me. Say that word again, please, Sigrid."

She drew me into a huddle, brought her forehead close to mine, touched my hair thoughtfully with cocoa-sticky fingers. Face full of anticipation, she whispered the word to me again, syllable by syllable as if to say, *Really, you finally understand?* Pointed at the beat-up image on the paper.

Translated literally, the word meant "the necessity of understanding nature—in all its complexity—to stay alive," but it was also shorthand for *Let's find the things we need to stay alive*, or, *These are the sacrifices we need to make to stay alive.*

Somehow this Inuit word was a part of her lexicon. I felt like a person emerging from a dark cave, granted a glimpse of sun.

"You need this to stay alive"—I pointed at the paper—"this seaweedy thing, is that right?"

She gestured at the spare suit.

"You want me to . . ." I glanced at the hole.

She nodded vigorously.

"You guys ready?" Nora called over to us. "He's all set."

I knelt and looked Sigrid in the eye, her sweet face glowing with excitement and impatience. "Sigrid, thanks for saying that word. I can't put the suit on right now, but I will. I promise, okay? Let's go watch Seal Man."

I pointed at Raj, and she looked disappointed but followed me to the hole. Slushy water sluiced against its sides.

"How cold is it?" I asked.

"Barely above freezing." Raj made final adjustments to his face mask, shook out his arms, quivered his legs. "Honestly? You're never exactly cozy down there. It's always a borderline situation, staying warm. Quick dives, always keep moving, that's the key."

"Darling, are you ready?" Nora said with quiet intimacy, checking his gear a final time.

Below us, the dull cry of the ice, the screech of the Dome's supporting poles as they scraped against it. The place felt so barren—just folding chairs, a few tables, some movable shelves, a heater strapped to supporting poles a few feet off the floor, and a couple of cots pushed together—surprisingly little attention paid to any comforts at all, Raj's mat the only splash of warmth in the place. I suddenly missed trees, the way they shelter you, the way they wrap you in their arms even though they never touch you.

"All set," Raj said. "I love you."

"I love you too," Nora said.

He got down to the rubber mats that covered most of the ice floor and scooted over to the hole. Dropped his flippered feet and legs into the water. Wasting no time, he folded his arms across his chest and slipped in with a small splash. He bobbed there a second or two, tank pinging against the sides of the hole. Without another word, he fit in his mouthpiece, gave Nora a thumbs-up, and dropped down into the cold blue eye.

"How long will he . . ."

"This is an eight-minute dive," Nora said, staring down after him. "Ten max."

"It's not possible that I would ever do this," I said.

"The worst part is going to oxygen," she said thoughtfully. "After that, the biggest danger is getting so blown away by the beauty or weirdness of everything down there you lose track of time."

An old-fashioned kitchen timer with a big second hand ticked off the numbers on the dial. Nora clicked on the mic. "Raj, how's it going?"

His voice was garbled. "Good. Twenty-three feet. Murky. Out."

"Roger that," she said into the mic.

A thud. A dragging sound. Sigrid had climbed to the table from a chair and knocked the heavy diving suit from its hook. She hopped to the floor, grabbed the suit by one creepy red glove, and hitched it bit by bit across the mats. Dropped the cumbersome pile of rubber at my feet. One of its neoprene hands lay with a loose grip at my ankle, like a dying man crawling across a desert grabbing at me for a glass of water.

"Guess she wants you to dive," Nora said with a laugh.

"Sigrid," I said as gently as I could, stepping away from the suit. "I'm no seal woman. No, okay?"

Undaunted, she seized my hand and led me to the stool Raj had sat on to prepare. I let her push me down into it, amused as she wrestled with one of the floppy legs of the suit, trying to ease it over my boot.

"Really, Sigrid?"

"Maybe just put it on," Nora said. "Make her happy. You don't have to dive. But we can go through the steps for fun."

I kicked off my boots, wriggled my toes and smiled. Sigrid struggled to fit the heavy, awkward fabric over my socks.

"It's okay," Nora said to Sigrid, getting down on the floor with her. "We're going to get Val sorted in no time."

Finally, Sigrid smiled.

"If I do this, if I dive, will you take a bath?" I motioned washing myself.

She nodded. It was fun asking her questions when she was in this mood, knowing she would say yes.

"Is she doing okay?" Nora helped Sigrid ease the other leg of the suit over my pants. "That was rough the other night with Wyatt."

"I think so." Warmed by Sigrid's smile, I felt like a parent who would do anything to make her child happy. "Do you guys want kids someday?"

Nora yanked a zipper across my thigh a little too hard. She took a few seconds to answer. "We had a son, but he died. It's all we want—or it's all *I* want, anyway—to try again, but it's been a year and, you know, nothing." Her face pale against her dark hair, her features tight, she wouldn't meet my eye. "So, there. We've already done five steps on the chart, see here?" She pointed to each item for Sigrid's benefit.

The clock read three minutes, thirty-three seconds. I still couldn't believe a human being had dropped down into the ocean beneath us and now swam among narwhals, seals, walrus, belugas.

"I'm so sorry."

She clicked on the mic. "Raj, darling, how's it going?"

"Fine. Forty-three feet. Clearer now. Out."

"Roger that."

She clicked off the mic. "His name was Charlie. He was only two months old. He was born with a heart defect. They tried surgery, but he died during the operation. Can you imagine? Seven doctors huddled around our tiny baby, and none of them could . . ." She glanced at the clock.

Four minutes, twenty seconds.

"You don't have to do this now," I said. "Get me geared up, I mean."

"It's okay, I want to."

I stretched my arms back so she could jigger the sleeves up to my shoulders. "Sigrid looks so happy, watching us get you geared up," Nora said with a wistful smile. She worked the hood over my head, showed us on the chart where we were: step fifteen. "Raj hasn't been able to put himself back together at all, really. He's got some heart issues himself, blames himself even though that makes no sense; the defect wasn't inherited. Sometimes I think grief affects everything, I mean, maybe his body at some level is saying no to mine."

"How did you two meet?" My attempt to ease off the subject.

"In grad school. Doing a research project at Woods Hole. I came from London, he transferred from New Delhi."

"Was it a *coup de foudre*?"

"Coup de *what*?"

"It's French for love at first sight. Literally means a bolt of lightning."

"Yes!" She smiled, finally. "Straightaway we were mad for each other. Still are. How did you guess?"

"It's . . . the way you talk to each other, the way you are with each other."

"Has that ever happened to you, Val—a bolt of lightning?"

"No. I don't leave my house enough for that sort of magic to ever happen."

"Well, you sure left it this time." Nora hauled the big zipper across my chest and took a step back. "Look at that, you're already at step eighteen, see?"

I felt like a sausage in the dry suit, which reeked of old rubber.

She turned back to the clock. Six minutes had passed.

"How many times has he been down there?"

"Oh, we've dived hundreds of times. All kinds of conditions." She clicked on the mic. "Raj, how's it going?"

His mic snapped on, but only static came through.

Nora tried again.

More hissing and clicking.

"Bloody thing." She rubbed her forehead, her eyes beautiful without a trace of makeup. "Sometimes, when it's this cold, we get crystals in the mic and this happens."

Me half-amphibian, we sat on stools next to the slushy blue pit, watching the second hand tick into seven minutes. Sigrid sat cross-legged next to me on the floor, occasionally grinning up at me or hugging my rubber-encased calves. I wanted to keep talking to Nora, learn more about what it was like to be in love like she and Raj were, but it felt wrong, as if that would distract from our unacknowledged prayers that Raj's voice would ring clear from the mic or that he would burst to the surface. Nora got up and paced around the hole, then back the other way, never taking her eyes off it. She smoothed back her gleaming black hair and tied it in a hasty ponytail; seconds later she yanked out the rubber band, jammed on her hat, and knelt at the pit, staring down into it as if she could will him up.

By seven minutes, forty-seven seconds I had already imagined her a widow, dumbstruck, floating senseless through a year of grief before being swept up in a new love, even more tainted by the ever-present possibility of loss.

The second hand swept cruelly around the face of the clock. We were staring down nine minutes. The struts of the dome rattled with a sudden blast of wind; the canvas walls bellied in and out with the gusts. I shivered in the suit, hands numb, as if I were already in the water.

Nora clicked on the mic. "Raj, are you on your way up? Over."

Continuous static grated the air, spitting and crackling.

Nine minutes, fifty-seven seconds.

"Raj, can you confirm—"

He exploded from the water, shards of ice flowing off his black-hooded head. I nearly fell backward off my stool, while Sigrid clapped and laughed. He bobbed for a moment, goggles clouded, before nudging out his mouthpiece with a pop. Nora caught him by the straps that secured the tank to his shoulders and with shocking strength hauled him halfway out of the water. We each took an arm and slid him the rest of the way. She got down on the ice and helped him sit up.

"Couldn't you hear me?" he sputtered.

"Couldn't you hear *me*?"

"Sure! I responded but—"

"Something's up with the mics." She cradled him, one hand over his heart. "All we heard was static for the last four minutes. Nearly five."

He coughed a bit, shook his head, and peeled off his rubber hood with a wet smack. "It's probably the valve again. You weren't worried, I hope. I was fine—"

Nora hugged him, soaking herself. For a few moments they breathed together, then he pulled away, aware of the audience.

"Everything went perfectly. It was a ten-minute dive exactly, right? Didn't I say it would be? Down to the second almost." He held out one red rubber hand, a lidded plastic bucket half filled with pearly sand dripping from it. "Got the sample."

Nora nodded and put a smile on her face.

Raj looked me up and down in the spare suit and laughed. "So, you're going to give it a try?"

Which is when I made my decision—I could at least drop in with my head above water—show Sigrid I hadn't put the suit on for nothing.

"Just going for a quick dip." Making sure Sigrid had her eyes on me, I got on my ass and scooted over to the hole, dropped one finned foot in, then the other. Snakes of cold encircled my calves. "I'm not going under, just to be clear."

"Val, that's brilliant!" Nora said. "She'll love you for it."

"We got you," Raj said. They gathered around, took me under the arms, and helped lower me down. Sigrid did a little happy dance, clapping her hands and chattering away. I focused on her as cold swept up my legs, shocking my torso and chest. I thought I'd lasted a good minute, but later Raj broke it to me that it had been only fifteen seconds before they hauled me out.

When it became clear I wasn't actually going to dive, Sigrid turned away, refusing to look at me. Dripping, I stood over her like a swamp monster. Apologized as I unzipped and unpeeled the gear. She kept repeating that word, about the snake being necessary for her to stay alive. It cut me to feel the limits of what I could do for her—for anyone, including myself—just as it began to register with a flash of joy that I had, in fact—unmedicated—dangled my body in the great polar Enormity.

sixteen

Steaming water sloshed in the massive pot as Jeanne heaved it from the stove. Bracing it against the pocked metal basin, she poured in the third and last round of hot bathwater. The tub was nearly full, but with enough room for a little girl's body. I'd scared up a few slivers of lavender soap, laid them on a clean washcloth next to the tub. Anything to tempt Sigrid into taking a bath.

"What do you think, Sigrid? Give it a try?" I called over to her.

She got up from the couch with her chin high, gave me a look that said, *Please, have you forgotten about our deal? You chickened out on the dive, so no bath for me,* and ambled down the hallway toward her bedroom, sweater dragging behind her as if she were a deranged bride.

"There's your answer," Jeanne said, not without satisfaction. She folded her arms across her gray, stained sweatshirt, an Arctic wolf's face distorted across her voluminous chest. Her hair a lusterless brown under harsh kitchen lights, her face puffy and red after several early-evening glasses of wine. I thought, *She's me, in some fun-house way.* She's absolutely me if I really gave it all up, let grief dictate all: *How close am I to this?* We weren't as far apart as I pretended.

"Sigrid's stubborn," Jeanne continued, wiping down the perfectly clean counter for the umpteenth time. "She's got her own mind. Just like my Frances did."

We both watched the water settle in the basin. I opened my mouth—keen to share my recent progress with Sigrid—but flashed on the vicious determination on Jeanne's face as she'd wrestled the little girl to stillness, Wyatt jabbing the needle in her blood-spattered arm. I swallowed and said, "Just have to keep on trying with her."

On her cutting board, Jeanne arranged a shank of red meat attached to a jagged length of bone.

"What's that?" I asked.

"Caribou."

"What's it taste like?"

"You should know." She rummaged around deep in the low kitchen freezer. Emerging with a bag of frozen peas, she tossed it on the counter. "You've been eating it for weeks. In the stew."

"I didn't realize . . ." The meat was heavily marbled, one rib cracked and sticking out at an odd angle, as if that was where the animal had been shot. "Where do we get it?"

"In the regular deliveries from Pitak or the other hunters in Qaanaaq. Really helps them out to sell to us."

"Guess I thought I was eating beef."

She selected a cleaver from the knife rack.

"Listen, Jeanne, I was wondering . . . I think I've misplaced some of my medicine, these pills I take, have you seen an orange bottle around?"

She brought the knife down on the caribou shank, cutting cleanly through the shattered rib. The wine-red meat glistened under the sterile lights. "Check all your pants pockets?"

"Yes."

She hammered the cleaver down again, severing another generous portion. "They should be in there. Found them when I was washing up. Put 'em back when your pants were dry."

"But I've . . . I've checked all my pockets—coats, shirts, everything."

She peeled off a stray knot of gristle, flicked it in the trash. "Well, to be honest, I wouldn't put it past Wyatt to chuck them." She arranged the slab of meat for another hit of her knife. Gave me a sidelong glance. "He's very antidrug, you know."

Whack.

"I didn't know that. But he says he didn't touch them."

"Well, have you asked Raj or Nora? Raj seems to be having a bit of a rough time, if you ask me—"

I took a step closer to her, keeping the big kitchen table between us. "So, you read the label—"

She waved the cleaver in the air, as if she'd forgotten she was holding it. "Well, they were right in front of me—"

"You should have just come and found me. You should have come and handed them to me."

Jeanne wiped the sweat off her forehead with a sleeve, a look of profound exhaustion dragging her heavy features down until she looked like an old man. I was one more pain in the ass on top of all her pains in the ass—the broken snowcat motor, the nonfunctioning heater in the Dome, the never-clean-enough counter . . .

"What am I, your servant? You were somewhere with the girl. Making her your best friend." She stabbed the cleaver into the meat; it stuck there. "Listen, I got enough I gotta take care of, never mind making sure you got your pills—"

"Okay, I believe you. Never mind." But I didn't believe her. I would never put my pills in my pocket, for one thing.

"Maybe it's a sign."

"Sign?"

"Maybe this isn't the place for you."

I glanced outside. The picture window framed a crystalline land-scape soaked in bruise-colored light. My stomach tightened down.

"Maybe you're in a little over your head. Ever think of that?" She worked the cleaver free, laid it down on the soft wood of the cutting board with a strange reverence. "You know, everything was so peaceful here before Andy came. Wyatt and me, we had these long, quiet days, just getting work done. None of this high drama."

"I'll expect my pills back by breakfast," I said, my voice higher and breathier than I'd intended. "In my room. No questions asked."

"Val, I didn't take your precious pills." She turned to face me, wiping her meat-stained hands on a rag. "And speaking of missing things, I'm down a knife. My crescent knife. Have you seen it?"

"No," I said, my face hot.

She opened the oven door; the aroma of baking cornbread flowed out. Suddenly I was dizzy with hunger. "You know," she said, "Andy lost things all the time."

The mention of his name a shot of pain between my eyes.

She took out the hot bread and set it on the rack. "Every day, we're looking for his spikes, his headlamp, his knife, his gloves."

"Well, I'm not like him. I don't misplace things. People assume twins are the same—"

"He was a pretty mellow guy, when he was in a good mood. When he wasn't freaking out about the end of the world. Loved to cook. Loved to bake. I even let him, and you know I don't like any-body in my kitchen."

Memories of Andy flooded me; he did love to bake! It relaxed him. He always made our birthday cake. Even when we were kids, he let me choose from our two favorites: chocolate and coconut, often compromising with chocolate cake and coconut frosting.

"What did he bake here?"

"These great mocha brownies. Just killer. I had to hand it to him. And Rice Krispie squares."

"With chocolate chips?"

"When we had 'em. Plus he played practical jokes on us all the time. Used to put Wyatt's frozen specimens—you know, lemmings and so on, in his bed. Wyatt freaked out. But they were like brothers, those two. Never saw anybody crack Wyatt up like Andy could with his silly drawings and whatnot. And the way they talked? Couldn't get a word in edgewise."

I was quiet, hungry for more, but she misinterpreted me.

"Hey, I'm sorry. Yapping about all this stuff. Can't imagine how you must feel."

"It's okay."

"I mean, I get depressed too. I get down. I miss my husband, my Frances. They were everything to me. Every bit of light in the sky. But I'd never do it. I'd never end things like that. I'm not made that way. Point of pride. Sometimes it almost feels silly, because, you know, what do I really have here? What's left in this world for me, besides fixing the next thing that breaks, and the next, and the next? Guess I'm a stubborn old broad. I just hang on." She raised her mug of wine to me, drank it down, and set it on the counter with a flourish. "See you in an hour for supper?"

"Sure," I said, unable to repress an image of the cleaver toma-hawking into my back as I walked away.

seventeen

"Jeanne and I are headed back to Glacier 35A tomorrow," Wyatt announced as he sliced into his caribou steak. "We'll be back pretty late, so you're all on your own for dinner."

"Brilliant," Nora said, winking at Raj. "We'll get a curry."

Raj's face stayed serious. "What's going on out there? Why are you going back?"

"Just feel like there's more to learn about the girl out there."

I took a swallow of wine, said, "If it's about Sigrid, I need to go."

"Not a good idea." Wyatt's voice was flat.

"I'll be fine," I said, but as I pictured the Enormity, I quelled a rising nausea. The vastness would certainly suck me away, erase me. The heavy meal turned in my stomach.

"This is serious work," Wyatt said. "We can't be worrying about you—"

"Since when have—"

"I have to consider everyone's safety—"

"I won't even leave the cat."

He served himself some rice, not meeting my eye. "There's no reason for you to come. You need to watch the girl. Make some actual progress."

Just the sound of knives slicing across plates, glasses clinking. I cut into my caribou steak picturing a herd of them swimming across the icy waters of the fjord, antlered heads held high, slowly starving as they searched for lichen trapped under a glaze of ice.

"Sigrid can hang out with us," Nora said cautiously. "Seal Man would love it, right?"

Raj shrugged a yes, a bit oblivious as he buttered a piece of cornbread. "Sure. We'll keep an eye on her."

Wyatt swept a hand through an oily forelock. "We can talk about this in the morning."

"We don't have to talk about it anymore," I said. "What time should I be ready?"

Jeanne and Wyatt exchanged a glance I couldn't decipher.

"Maybe Val needs a little break, Wyatt," Nora said. "What she's doing with Sigrid isn't easy—"

A long, guttural ringtone purred from somewhere under the papers on Wyatt's desk. We all jumped. I'd never heard the sound before.

"The sat phone," Jeanne said, vaulting from the table, but Wyatt had already sprinted to his desk and begun sweeping away papers, magazines, books. Two more rings, and he found it.

"Wyatt Speeks, Tarrarmiut Station." He stared at me as he listened. "I'm good, sir, we're all good, how are you?" *Jesus, who is he sir-ing? Is he in trouble?* ". . . Yes, she's right here." He held the phone in my direction. "It's for you. It's your father."

I was gut-punched by my last image of my father: his stooped back as he turned away from me that broiling summer afternoon he dared me to come to this place. As I took the phone, I pictured him now, sparse white hair sticking up from his warty skull, angular body sunk in the wingback chair, visiting room walls garlanded with fake fall leaves and childish paper skeletons.

"Hey, Dad."

"Val, what's going on?"

I glanced around the room. Everyone was watching me, listening, until it kicked in how rude that was and they all got busy clearing dishes, went back to chatting, pretending they were no longer interested.

"Nothing. I mean, I'm fine," I said as quietly as I could.

"Glad to hear it. Any progress?"

"Some . . ."

"Sounds like you . . . Can you talk?"

I took a walk around the cluttered room. The second I stepped beyond a five-foot radius around Wyatt's desk, static roared in my ears. "Not really."

"No privacy?"

"No."

He sighed heavily.

"You okay, Dad? Everything all right?"

"Never better. Hadn't heard from you. I was getting concerned. So I'll ask the questions, you say yes or no. Do you think Wyatt killed your brother?"

I sat on the edge of the desk, gazing out at the skyline of majestic bergs in the bay. Recalled what Andy had said once about this frozen world: *What looks permanent will fall. We will fall.* "I don't have an answer for that."

"Jesus. Are you safe there now?"

"Pretty much."

"Answer me."

"Is anyone really safe?" I said louder than I'd intended.

"Val, I don't know how much news is getting to you, but there's been another incident, in Nova Scotia this time. Just outside of Halifax. A couple dozen people were hit by an ice wind. A wedding party, just leaving a church. Tragic. No one could do anything for them, understand?"

"I hadn't heard that. We . . . hadn't heard that. We lose the internet all the time."

"I want you to get out of there."

"Why?"

"You know why," he growled. "Look, I'm going to make some calls. Get cash to the right people, whatever it takes. What happened to Andy happened; I can't change it. But I can't lose you, too."

I pictured Sigrid's eager, trusting face as she drew me into a huddle in the Dome and whispered the word for *Let's find the things we need to stay alive.*

"That's not a good idea, Dad."

"I shouldn't have pushed you to go, Val. You're not up to the task."

Odin lumbered around his cage on Wyatt's desk. These days the mouse was logy, sleeping a lot, barely bothering to climb on his wheel for a spin.

"That's a shitty thing to say to me, Dad. I'm already here."

The phone crackled and buzzed and for a moment I thought he'd hung up, but then his voice blasted through loud and clear. "Listen to me. You're going to lose the sun pretty soon. Less than two weeks, full dark."

"I'm aware of that."

"I want you out of that place, Val. I've got connections in Thule. I'll wire some money over and they'll get a plane out to you in two days, weather permitting."

Raj and Nora set the last dish in the rack, Nora laughing at something he'd said.

"I won't get on it."

"Don't do this to me, Val."

"I'm doing what you wanted me to do."

A long pause. "You're not Andy, Val. I forgive you for that."

"Thanks a lot."

"There's no shame in coming home."

"Dad, listen to me. I'm not leaving until I finish what I started. You take care—"

"Don't you hang up on me, Val—"

"I'm not hanging up, I'm saying goodbye. There's a difference."

A frustrated silence. "I'm frightened for you," he said. "I was wrong to push you—I mean that. It wasn't right."

"It's okay, Dad, really. I'm going to be all right."

"The fact is, I'm—I'm fresh out of caramels. Can't get my hands on any damned sweets around here. You've got to get back here soon and bring me some, is that a deal?"

"Sure, Dad, I promise. Boxes of them."

"Goodbye, Val. Stay safe." A clumsy clunking sound as he hung up, then the vaguely disturbing, high-pitched dial tone.

Was I mistaken or had I felt him wanting to say he loved me? But that wasn't a word we'd ever exchanged, as far as I could remember. I didn't know if we would ever speak it to each other, but that was all right. I felt it in his voice. Felt it in my hands as I hung up the phone. And right then I decided to stop protecting my heart, to take my chances next time and be the first to say the word *love*.

eighteen

I woke with a jolt. My battery-powered alarm clock read 3:24 a.m., the minute the battery must have died. But it had to be much later than that. The air brimmed with the smell of coffee and pancakes. From beyond my thin walls, muffled conversation, the stomp of boots up and down the hall.

I dove into my clothes, working a brush through my hair as I hurried down the hallway. The day had broken gloomy and overcast; a pallid light leaked into the main room.

Wyatt, fully suited up, stood at the door. "Sleeping Beauty awakes."

"Where is everyone?"

"Girl's asleep. Jeanne's helping Nora and Raj fix some piece of dive equipment in the Dome. You're lucky for that. Otherwise we'd've been long gone." He zipped his parka and flipped the hood. "I've got to deice the cat. Soon as Jeanne's back, we leave."

"Fine," I said, gulping lukewarm coffee.

He left, a frosty blast of air in his wake.

I sat on the bottomed-out couch considering my options. Facing the Enormity without assistance wasn't one of them. I needed alcohol, something, anything to take the edge off. And I had to act fast.

I had a bad feeling about the wine; I checked around the kitchen. The boxes of red and white had been drained the night before; the empties sat by the door. *Had Wyatt planned this?* Maybe, maybe not. Normally only a red and white were kept in the Shack; the bulk of it was stored in the Shed, since the kitchen was so cramped.

Limbs quaking, I paced the room, viscerally craving the surge of calm from my daily pill. I mourned its powers of transformation: from a tiny white disk in a bottle to an elixir that soothed my monkey brain with its velvety embrace. But it wasn't to be: I was naked, a newborn under klieg lights. I looked around. The furniture no longer looked shabby but cozy, it looked shredded, as if some wild animal had attacked it; the vials of blood weren't science, they were ominous forebodings; the searing primary colors of the chipped breakfast plates stabbed at my retinas, vibrating me into migraine. Snow pellets gunned the windows, always wanting in. Dry heat thrummed from the radiator, but my back was cold; some part of me was always numb with cold, my hands, feet, the back of my neck.

Drug-free, I felt the ghosts of everyone in the room, could smell Wyatt's, Raj's, Nora's, Jeanne's sorrows, angers, their griefs, their regrets—all so apparent, so viciously raw. I balanced on a precipice with no shell, no fur, no feather, no human skin; I was an anemone on a dying reef helplessly siphoning oil from a spill, veins blackening. I couldn't last here like this.

I had to move. Find some alcohol. A pathetic Band-Aid, but a necessary one. Someone had to have a stash.

Listening for Wyatt's footsteps, I tiptoed to the low freezer on the kitchen floor and opened it. Frosted air ballooned up into my face as I gingerly lifted out package after plastic-wrapped package of hamburger, caribou, fish, hot dogs, chicken, vegetables, buffalo wings, and mozzarella sticks. I tried to keep things in order but soon got sloppy. The ends of my fingers lost all feeling.

Just food, no booze.

Fuck.

I had to try the Shed.

I slipped on my boots, threw on my parka, and left the building, keeping my eyes on the ground, a trick I'd learned. No horizons for me, just twilight-blue snow crunching beneath orange boots. A biting wind body-slammed me as I fumbled for the rope that connected the two buildings. Threaded my way hand over hand to the Shed, praying that Jeanne was still tied up at the Dome. As I pushed open the heavy door, I tried to conjure some excuse for barging in should I find her there.

"Jeanne? It's Val." My voice cracked in the thin, frigid air.

No answer.

Metal filings and dust motes danced in the weak light that streamed through the window; the rest of the room cowered in shadow. I snapped on the overhead bulb. It creaked, swinging slightly, protected by its Hannibal Lecter wire cage.

As always, the place made me want to run. The stench of crankcase oil; the circular saw hulking over the far end of the table, its shark's teeth still specked with sawdust; machinery guts exploded on the floor. Gaskets, tubing, pipes of all shapes and sizes, plastic jugs of mysterious liquids. The place vibrated with a latent violence, with the memory of Jeanne's constant movement, her restlessness, her compulsion to make something right that could never be right again.

A cursory check revealed no boxed wine, *damn*. The walk-in freezer was a remote possibility: it had a combination lock. I gave it a tug, hoping she'd forgotten to spin the dial. No luck. Got down to my knees next to the smaller, hassock-sized freezer, fully expecting to rattle the lock a bit, curse, give up, stay back, accept defeat, and sink, sink, sink into my maelstrom of fear. I couldn't face the Enormity stone-cold sober, full stop.

I yanked down on the lock; its two teeth disengaged from the round barrel.

She hadn't spun the dial.

The lid of the freezer resisted me at first, then let go with a snap of suction. Steam swirled up, momentarily blinding me. Through the mist, the faint outline of an animal. My first thought was: *Frida. The little mutt Andy and I had as kids.*

I blinked. Of course this wasn't Frida. But what was this thing? I'd only seen them in photos, but it had to be an Arctic fox. It was curled up as if sleeping or trying to stay warm: paws tucked under its chin, tail wrapped around its body, kohl-rimmed eyes shut tight. Lace-ice fans feathered out across its glistening white pelt. It was so beautiful I wondered if it was real, but its blood-stained muzzle—clearly it had enjoyed a meal just before death—cast a pall on its Disneyesque perfection. I touched its black nose: a frozen marble.

Next to it, tucked into ziplock bags: several frozen Arctic lemmings; small, thick-bodied rodents; an antediluvian-looking fish with flat eyes wide as quarters; and a puffin, its cartoon-orange beak and webbed feet bright even under the plastic. All in perfect condition, no marks, icebound. How much had they suffered, I wondered; how quickly had death come?

With great care, I slipped my hands under the fox. A filigree of ice crackled free, tinkling into the box. He was so light—a sparkling cloud of opalescent fur. Underneath him, the mother lode. Three full fifths of Smirnoff vodka. I carefully laid the fox on the sawdust-covered floor, picked up a bottle, unscrewed the cap, and drank.

Two swallows later, a wave of self-loathing crashed over me. *Why not do it? Why not just take Dad's offer and get out of here?* Have him call in that favor to his friends at Thule and go home. The world would happily close in around me again, and I'd welcome it; I'd hop on my Möbius strip of seeking safety and—not finding it—conclude I needed to make my circle smaller still, just tighten that noose . . .

The sputter of an engine firing up outside the Shed startled me back to the present moment. I squeezed my eyes shut. My head swam. *I'm a mess, but I'm all Sigrid's got.* Heart smashing against my rib cage, I tucked the bottle of vodka in my parka, wiped my mouth, and ran to the door. Wyatt and Jeanne were just turning the cat to face the glacier. I took off as fast as I could across the field of ice toward the idling machine.

nineteen

Buffeted by winds lashing down from the glacier, the snowcat rocked on the ice lake, its small, tattered American flag on the hood snapping crazily. I sat buckled in the back seat like a child left in a car waiting for her parents to finish shopping. Through half-closed eyes—my head swimmy but functional—I watched Wyatt and Jeanne drill ice core after ice core, loading the gray tubes on a metal sled. Each new drill site brought us closer to the crevasse where Sigrid had been found. It seemed wider that day, a deeper blue. Impossible to look at for more than a few seconds at a time without hyperventilating.

Through slitted eyes, I took in the sun, a sizzling fat ovoid resting on the horizon, set to lurk there for the next couple of hours before our three-hour "day" came to an end. I reached out my gloved finger, tracing its perimeter on the steamy glass, just as I'd seen Sigrid do countless times. Traced another, and another, until I'd drawn a row of circles. My finger hesitated on the glass. *The circles were suns! Days!*

The perimeter of the setting sun pulsed red. . . . *Why were the last circles Sigrid drew red? What would happen to her on the final day?*

I stopped drawing; my hand fell from the window. Sigrid drew a picture of suns every day, each day with one less sun. *She was counting down.*

WYATT LIFTED HIMSELF into the driver's seat with a blast of icy air. He unscrewed the cap on a thermos and filled it halfway with hot coffee, offered it to me. I shook my head. A few yards from the cat, Jeanne knelt on the ice, struggling to free a core from the corer with a plunger. Wyatt downed his coffee, rubbed and blew on his hands, slipped his gloves back on. "Last chance to see the crevasse up close. You change your mind?"

"I'm coming."

I flipped up my hood, tightened the drawstring around my face. Climbed down onto the ice. A barbarous wind whooshed up; I teetered, took a step. Kept my focus on the mottled blue-and-gray surface, following Wyatt's wide red back as he crunched across the snow in his rocking gait.

We stood only ten feet from the abyss. The fissure had indeed widened; the sharp edges around the block that had imprisoned Sigrid now softened from exposure to the sun; the deep blue of the ice had soaked in the heat. Now it looked hard and glassy, evil and grim.

"Why are you taking samples from here?" I called to him. "So near to where you found her?"

His glacier glasses repeated the serrated black peaks beyond, lonesome and windswept. "Question is, why did it take me so long to think of it?"

We followed Jeanne as she walked parallel to the chasm. In the distance, a herd of several dozen caribou picked their way down the glacial pass in a jagged black line.

"Val, keep way back from us. At least twenty feet, okay?"

I backed up awkwardly, away from the abyss, not having much of an idea what twenty feet felt like.

Jeanne, a smudge of red and black behind veils of fine falling snow, yanked at a cord on a small yellow engine. It started up like a lawn mower, its whine crashing into the silence. She and Wyatt hoisted a twelve-foot pole, the last five feet or so a bright red screw-shaped device. It was already turning fast. They struggled to hold the pole perpendicular to the ice—clearly they needed all their strength to keep it going straight down—then hauled it up bit by bit out of the ice. Working full tilt, they laid the corer down, gently bumping out into a wooden trough a perfectly cylindrical yards-long core that glistened blue and silver gray. Finally, they loaded the core and equipment on the sled we'd towed from the Shack for this purpose. I couldn't help admiring their coordination, their grunting efforts, this dance in which each knew precisely what steps to take and when.

The entire panorama—snowcat, Jeanne, Wyatt, sled—disappeared and reappeared through curtains of snow and blowing fog. I had a sense of unreality, or of shifting realities. Beneath me: creaking, pings, atonal twangs as—miles deep—the ice settled ancient scores with itself.

The crevasse, a jagged blue wound, lurked only yards away. It beckoned me. I crunched a few steps closer. It exhaled its deathly cold breath up at me, its green walls darkening to black as they plummeted to unknowable depths. How far would I fall? Would it be lights-out, or would I impale myself on some ice sword a hundred yards down, lingering in agony until I froze to death? I flirted with this ghastly yet seductive choice. It would be easy, so much easier than everything I'd been trying and failing at: discovering the truth about Andy, deciphering Sigrid, battling my grief and fear. For several long, frigid seconds, I was lost.

WYATT APPROACHED ME, squares and triangles of red and black flashing in the blowing snow. Painfully, I slammed back into my body. Made fists of my freezing fingers in my gloves, couldn't feel my feet at all. Sobriety edging closer, I extracted my bottle of vodka from an inside pocket and took a long pull. Instead of the soft release a pill usually granted me, the booze spun me off to a rageful, dark place: *How much had Andy suffered that dreadful night?*

"What are you doing, Val?" Wyatt gestured at the cat. "Come on, we have to get out of here." He'd seen me drinking; he knew that's why I raided the Shed; I didn't care.

"Why don't you tell me what really happened that night with Andy? You know I can't prove anything. You have nothing to lose by telling me the truth."

He stomped his boot on the ice and groaned. "Unbelievable."

"You haven't told me a damned thing—"

"Of course I have. Many times. Are you . . ."

Drunk? Crazy? "Not blow by blow, you haven't."

"You're too close."

I took a step toward the edge. Chunks of dirty gray ice dislodged under my boot, echoing as they ricocheted, plunging down to nothingness. "What was Andy working on? Where was Jeanne that night?"

"Val, you've been drinking—"

"Fucking tell me."

His face grew strained, mouth thinning into a grim line. Snow crystals lodged in his three-day beard. "Look, Val, I'm just saying I've told you—"

"Where was she?"

"She was there. The whole time. In the Shack."

"That's not what she said."

Wyatt turned toward Jeanne. She stood by the snowcat, far from earshot, watching us.

"Well, she's not remembering right." He pointed to his head as if to say *Jeanne's a little off, haven't you noticed?*

I ignored his bid for a wink and a nod. Waited. The alcohol like hot ice in my veins.

"Okay. Let's go over it again. Andy and me were working on our separate projects. I was cataloging the cores. He was . . . experimenting with different ideas about Odin. But he was pretty depressed. Nothing was working out for him. I know he was looking at some permafrost studies and getting freaked out by them. He was a gloom and doom kind of guy a lot of the time. Look . . ."

My voice rose to a fever pitch. "Jeanne said she heard you laughing, that you guys were having a great time. Such a great time she went off to work in the Shed, and—"

"Val, you've got to calm down, okay? Just calm—"

"I'm calm."

"You need to take a few steps away from that thing, come on, a few steps toward me. . . ."

"I'm fine where I am."

He hazarded a few paces closer, arm outstretched. "Just take my hand, okay?"

My body felt wooden with cold, molten with vodka and fury. The always-setting sun bled frozen gold beams across the expanse.

His expression shifted from one of concern to something darker, as if another possibility had opened up for him.

He let his hand drop to his side. "Val," he stage-whispered, as if someone was listening, "no matter how badly you may want it to, my story's not going to change just because you keep asking me the same damned questions over and over. It's not going to suddenly turn into some kind of fucking revelation for you, or for me, or for anybody, okay?" He took another step toward me, ice squeaking under his boots. Spitting distance away. "It's going to be the same horrible, sad, tragic story, I'm sorry to say. It could have been something as stupid as Andy going out for his chocolate. He was always hiding his stash from me. He liked it frozen, and he knew I'd find it in any of the freezers, so he probably had a place outside. Could have been something as stupid as that. Just that idiotic and simple. Him going out for his chocolate. Maybe he got turned around out there somehow, we'll never know."

"Andy hated frozen chocolate."

Wyatt took another step toward me, closing the gap between us. One push and I would go careening into hell.

"I got him to like it." His face so close I could see snowflakes landing on his eyelashes, smell the smoky wet wool of his hat.

"I don't believe—"

"I don't get you, Val. You're an enigma to me. I haul you all the way up here to do a job, something I was under the impression you were uniquely good at, by the way, and all you do is fuck me over. Andy's all you've been thinking about. I should have known. No wonder you've got nothing on the girl." His countenance took on an ugliness, as if he were making some terrible calculation; my own pale, small face reflected twice in his lenses. He glanced back at Jeanne, nodded. *A signal?* She turned away, busied herself with something on the sled.

"Has all this been a waste of time, Val?"

A fresh wind savaged my cheeks; in vain I tried to feel my fingers in my gloves, to feel the contours of Andy's lead heart. Cold shivered from the crevasse, calling me down.

"Because that's what we *should* be discussing here. Have I wasted four precious weeks? Would we all be better off without you? What do *you* think?"

He stood legs spread apart, spiked boots dug into the ice, a human wall. Behind his shoulders, mountains sliced black daggers up into the sky, dove gray in the purplish light.

"Enlighten me, Val," he said. "What the fuck do you want from me? Do you want to go home? Is that it? Because I can arrange that. I can get Pitak here in a day and a half—"

"I want to stay." My voice barely audible over the siren call of the fissure.

"I think—no, I *know* you know more than you're telling me about the girl. That's what concerns me. You keeping secrets from me."

I took a step away from the abyss and toward him, close enough to hug. He didn't budge. "I know this, Wyatt. You have zero chance with Sigrid without me."

Jeanne fired up the cat. Swung it in a tight circle away from us, idling as she faced toward home, as if whatever happened between us was something she didn't want to witness. Without a word, Wyatt turned and trudged across the bleak stretch of ice toward the cat. Each of his steps left me more alone in the Enormity, set me deeper into a bloodless blue-gray world, the light ominous over the shimmering expanse. He did not look back. Climbed into the cat next to Jeanne. All pride erased, I broke into a run, crying out to the both of them to wait for me, begging not to be left behind.

twenty

Wyatt ordered all of us to gather in the living room that evening at seven sharp. No word why. I took a seat on one end of the sofa, while Nora perched stiffly next to Raj on the other. Jeanne hummed as she cleared the dishes, her CD player churning out "Luck Be a Lady." Sigrid had gone to bed early, refusing dinner, refusing to talk. She'd been pouty—I theorized—because I'd left her alone with Nora and Raj all day. But in truth I didn't know whether to be touched that she'd missed me or worried that she wasn't feeling well. I held my revelation about Sigrid counting down days close to my chest, filled with dread as to what it might mean.

Wyatt blew in at the stroke of seven, a yard-long ice core encased in a wooden tube under one arm. Reverently he set it down on the coffee table, turned toward us, and unzipped his parka.

"Jeanne, would you turn that shit off and get in here, please?"

Wordlessly she snapped off the player, strolled into the main room, and took a seat between us.

"I've had a chance to look at the cores we drilled today." He glanced at Jeanne, then at each of us, as if to say, *Pay attention.* He lifted the wooden lid from the core. Twisted the business end of a gooseneck lamp directly on it. Frost smoke sizzled up, floating along the length of ancient ice. Hundreds of slim bands of alternating pale blue, gray-white, and murky storm-cloud colors glistened, even sparkled here and there. At about the midway point, a thin, coal-black ring encircled the tube. "Here," he said, pointing with the blade of a hunting knife. "Around the seven-hundred-year mark. See it?"

We all leaned forward to get a better look.

"Human remains."

"Christ," Nora breathed.

Raj knelt on the rug, peering at the black ring. "How do you know they're human?"

"I looked at the cells. Human bone cells are shaped differently from those of other mammals. They're like concentric rings. Animal bone cells look more like bricks. Want to have a look?" He gestured at the microscope behind him.

Raj didn't take his eyes off the black ring. "No."

Wyatt continued. "I don't believe Sigrid was encased in ice a few months ago, with her family chasing caribou. I think something happened to her between 1300 and 1400 or so, around the Little Ice Age. I think she's ancient."

We were all silenced, but the rightness of Wyatt's words slammed me in my gut, illuminating Sigrid's every mystery. This was why everything—from markers to beds to snowmobiles to heat flowing from a box—fascinated her. This was why modern Greenlandic was mostly noise to her. If she was alive in 1300, she could have been Dorset or from the culture that conquered them, the Thule.

"What's the Little Ice Age?" I asked Wyatt, breaking the spell of quietude.

"This was a cataclysmic, compressed, natural climate change event, where extreme changes—severe and dramatic cooling and warming events—happened in a matter of years or even months. From around AD 1300 to 1800."

Raj rocked back on his heels. "Okay. All right. This is getting—"

"Here's my theory. Could Sigrid have been caught in some naturally occurring piteraq in 1300, similar to what we're calling 'ice winds' today? Think about it. Around 1250, there's evidence that pack ice in Greenland had grown beyond what anyone had ever seen. Summers disappeared. Temperature fluctuations were crazy fast."

"This has nothing to do with—" Raj said.

"Just listen!" he snapped. I kept my eyes on the slim black band, lost in my own amazement. "These katabatic winds—these piteraqs shooting down off the glaciers—they can easily kick past a hundred miles an hour, hit seventy, eighty degrees below zero—the question is, are these being roiled up by insane temperature swings happening around the world right now?"

Raj folded his arms over his chest. "Sounds like a reach, sorry to say."

"What's your explanation?"

"Katabatic winds only happen on glaciers. They've never been recorded anywhere else on earth. Wyatt, these deaths, they've occurred everywhere *but* on glaciers—"

"Santa Ana winds are katabatic. Oroshi winds happen in Japan. Bora winds? Adriatic piteraqs, you could say. Williwaws, derechos, shall I go on?"

Raj sat back on the couch, smoothed a hand through wavy black hair. "All just semantics. You've gone from human remains in a core to some wacko theory about ice winds then and now? Tying it in with the whole Sigrid fantasy? This is *not* science—I don't know what it is, but it's not—"

"Last week." Stone-faced, Wyatt clicked his PC alive. "Saint-Eustache in Canada. Small town north of Montreal. Temperatures bouncing all week from fifty, sixty degrees to zero or below. Friday? Boat ride on the Saint Lawrence. Four people freeze to death. Why? How?" He clicked some more. "The week before. Amsterdam, ten p.m. A woman's walking her dog along the seacoast. Both found dead the next morning, frozen solid. You think nothing's going on out there? You think what I'm doing here with the girl isn't important? It might be the most important science on earth right now—"

"Why didn't you film it?" Raj said quietly.

"What?"

Raj crossed his slippered feet on the coffee table just next to the ice core. "Sigrid thawing out alive."

Sweat popped on Wyatt's brow. "We just didn't. We were too caught up in what was happening."

"You know, whenever I go to thaw a child from the ice, I set up my camera first thing."

"Get your fucking feet away from that core."

Raj didn't acquiesce; in fact, he settled in a bit. "You're telling me you didn't think of that? You weren't interested in proof?"

Wyatt swung his arm down. Punched Raj's feet, sending them—and a couple glasses of beer—flying off the table, just missing the core. The glasses shattered against the wall as Raj was knocked sideways. He sprang to his feet like a boxer, Nora at his side. I breathed the hoppy stink of beer as it soaked into the rug.

"All I'm asking is for you to goddamn listen," Wyatt said, face dark. "You think you can just hear me out?"

Raj shook his head in disgust, wandered over to the counter, and poured himself and Nora two more glasses of beer.

"This *is* science," Wyatt hissed. "It's messy. It's flawed. You know that. Look, the slightest wobble of the sun—"

"The sun *wobbles*?" Raj said.

"It can. It does. It's complicated, but the tiniest shifts can cause extremely fast freezing and thawing events. Big changes in the ice sheet can create its own weather, its own crazy swings. You know that. You can't deny that. They don't know what caused the Little Ice

Age, but I bet it did terrible things to people's lives. Decimated their food sources. Drift ice must have bottled up entrances to the fjords. Bowhead whales couldn't get through. It completely disrupted migration patterns for caribou, birds, seals, everything. It would have pitted people against each other for resources."

With great care, Wyatt picked up the core and placed it in the low kitchen freezer. "I mean, think about it! Those winds must have been nuts. People's number one priority—besides finding food— must have been protecting themselves from those goddamned piteraqs."

A tinny, mechanical sound quieted him. Sigrid's new favorite toy, a windup walking polar bear, marched into view from the hallway. It churned along in lockstep, face fixed in a perky bear-smile, until, slowly, it ran out of gas and stopped dead, one plastic foot midair.

I jumped up. "Sigrid?"

No answer.

I sprinted down the hall. She sat slouched with her back against her door, feet sticking out from her sweater, chin dropped onto her chest as if the weight of her head was too much. Listlessly she fidgeted with Rudolph's nose, now just a few red strings. "Bahl." She looked up at me with exhausted eyes.

I put my hand on her forehead—too hot—and picked her up. She didn't resist. I held her against me, the knotted cord of her spine heartbreakingly slight under my hand as I carried her into the living room.

Everyone spoke at once.

"She okay?" Raj said.

"Sigrid, sweetheart." Nora rushed over to us. "What are you doing up?"

"You hungry, kiddo?" Jeanne opened the fridge, pulled out a bowl of leftover fried fish.

"What's wrong?" Wyatt came toward us, hands on hips.

Sigrid moaned and turned her head away from the crowd of concerned faces, resting her chin on my shoulder. Nora touched her forehead, grazed her cheeks, said, "Shit."

"She sick?" Wyatt said.

"Maybe the flu or something," I said. "She's got no resistance, after all."

Raj approached her. "Hey, honey, it's Seal Man." At the sound of his voice, she turned toward him; her face brightening a bit. His gentleness moved me. "Not feeling so great, huh. Okay for me to just touch your forehead for a second?"

She nodded. He laid his hand across her temple. "Wow, oh wow. She's on fire. We've got to fly her out of here, get her to the mainland right away."

"Let me have a look at her," Wyatt said to me. To my surprise, she allowed him to touch her as well, even let him hold a thermometer briefly against her forehead. "Ah, okay. She's just shy of one hundred. Poor kid. I've got some antibiotics. We can crush them up in her food."

"You need to get her out of here, Wyatt." Raj squared his shoulders, faced him.

"She has the flu. Or some kind of bug. She'll be fine. Jeanne, get me some hamburger, and we'll—"

"And what if she's not?" Nora said, gathering her gear at the door.

"If there's no improvement by morning, I'll make a call, all right?"

Raj slipped on his boots and parka. "Those human remains from the core; I'd like to take a look at those cells."

Nora suited up with brisk, angry movements. "I understand, Wyatt. This isn't ideal for you, having us here. But, here we are. So maybe you should smarten up, remember you have witnesses to everything you're doing."

With a disgusted shake of his head, Wyatt bent to retrieve the ice core, as Raj began to set up the scope. I carried Sigrid back down the hallway, pausing as she deposited a balled-up slip of paper in my hand. Felt her intense gaze as I opened her present and examined the drawing: five circles, the last slashed red.

"Okay, Sigrid," I said. "I think I understand." With a soft whimper, she hugged me so tightly I could barely breathe.

twenty-one

I spent most of the night awake—*in thrall*—feeling, *knowing*, that Sigrid was ancient. Realizing that the Inuit words I'd recognized from her speech borrowed from *her* centuries-old language, not the other way around, and they were mostly concerned with elements of survival. A small, tantalizing window into the distant past.

The next morning, still lost in wonder, I passed Wyatt's desk, pausing by Odin's cage. He lay on his side in a sea of food pellets, his breathing rapid, exercise wheel still. I set down my coffee and had a closer look. "Hey, buddy." I poked a finger through the grate, stroked his white fur. "Why don't you eat?"

Wyatt whistled as he flipped pancakes in the kitchen.

"Your mouse doesn't seem to be feeling too well."

"Ah, he's fine," Wyatt said. "You check on the girl?"

The girl. As if she didn't have a name. "Still sleeping." After getting her to drink an antibiotic-laced cup of cocoa the night before, I'd put her to bed with a hot water bottle, which enchanted her. She'd dragged it under the bed with little cooing sounds.

Next to Wyatt's computer, a drawing in Andy's signature style peeked out from under a stack of file folders.

I stopped petting Odin midstroke.

The sweeping, skilled pen marks shouted from the page like a living presence. I freed the drawing from the pile. Caricatures: Jeanne, sporting her enigmatic smile, stood at the stove surrounded by boiling pots of stew, loaves of bread, cakes, pies; Wyatt waving and grinning as he zoomed over the frozen bay in the snowmobile.

"He made these here?" I asked, collapsing in a chair.

Wyatt finished rinsing a pan and joined me at his desk. "Seemed to calm him down." He sat next to me. A little too close. He looked handsome in his rugged-polar-explorer sort of way: wide shoulders in double flannel shirts tucked into thermal overalls, wild hair freshly tamed, combed back after his shower. Confusion reigned: was he a monster or just a cranky, lonely, horny misanthrope, a scientist desperate to solve a mystery?

Minute by minute, I changed my mind.

Ignoring his presence, I concentrated on Andy's artwork. There was a pen-and-ink depiction of me in my teaching clothes, but instead of placing me in the classroom, I stood in an ecstatically beautiful field of flowers. Only when you looked closely was it clear that the flowers and leaves were created with tiny words: I recognized Greek, Latin, French, German, Finnish.

A few tears surprised me. I brushed them away. "I've never seen this one."

"He was missing you when he drew that. It was a long year on the ice for him without you. He talked about you nonstop. I guess twins are like that." He pulled out another folder; other drawings spilled out: caribou crossing an ice field saturated with violet light, an Arctic hare leaping from a bank of soft snow, a polar bear dragging a bearded seal from a vent in the ice, snow splotched crimson. "I meant to give these to you," he said. "Just couldn't find the right time."

"You look at these sometimes?"

He cocked an eyebrow. "I can be sentimental, Val, not that I expect you to believe that. Your brother and me, we were like the *Wizard of Oz*, you know? Together we had enough heart, brains, and courage to figure this thing out, to understand how Odin survived the ice. But without him, I'm struggling. Anyway"—he tossed his hands in the air—"your brother had the biggest heart. I try every day to be more like him. Most days I fail."

"He couldn't have gotten through grad school without you, Wyatt. You know that."

"Maybe. You should just take these, okay?"

With some effort—gathering the drawings would have brought me even closer to Wyatt—I got to my feet and turned toward my pile of gear. "When I get back. I'm heading over to the Dome while Sigrid's still asleep." I began to suit up.

"Why?" he said.

"Just a change from my room. I've got some books on Thule culture I want to show—"

"That girl knows exactly how to survive the ice. You get that, don't you?" His affect changed: smile gone, warmth gone. He shuffled the drawings into a stack, so roughly a corner of one of them tore off.

I jammed on my hat, looked for my gloves. "It's logical that she would."

He laughed. "Let me tell you about badass. There was this hunter in a sealskin kayak. He's out in a fjord packed with sea ice. He's hunting seal, but his boat gets a tear from a berg. It's sinking, so he thinks fast. He harpoons a seal, brings it into the boat, guts it *through its mouth*, inflates its body with his breath, ties it off at the neck, and rides that fucking thing to shore while his boat sinks."

"That doesn't—"

"These people *survive*, Val. They know how to do that better than any of us, in the harshest environment on earth. And that girl?" He rose, tucking the drawings under one arm. "She's not helpless. She knows things. She's *seen* things." He came close, jabbed a finger in my face. "She's playing us."

Heart racing, I pulled on my snow pants, big orange boots, vest. "What do you want me to do, Wyatt?"

"What can you say in her language? Tell me."

"Man, woman, seal man, yes, no, outside, caribou, numbers up to twenty—"

He waved me away. "She understands far more than that. *Far* more. She doesn't seem to like me, is that the problem?"

"I—"

"Make me the bad guy. Whatever you have to do." He folded two sticks of spearmint gum into his mouth, chewed with vigor. "Tell her it's a secret between you two, what she did, what she took. I don't give a shit anymore, understand? We have days left here, not weeks."

I turned toward the door. "I'll be back in a couple of hours."

He expelled an exasperated sigh and held out the clipboard. I took it and wrote in my destination and when I was headed back, even though I thought it was ridiculous. He snatched it back from me and tossed it on his desk.

"You think you're special, Val? You think you're safe?"

"What do you mean?"

"From the ice winds. You think any of us is safe?"

He stood too close to me, blocking the door, his breath stinking of maple syrup, stale coffee, spearmint. I angled myself away from him but couldn't reach the doorknob. Seconds passed.

"Look, your anger is a bit much for me sometimes, Wyatt. It's counterproductive to any progress—"

"You mean my rage?"

"Your word, not mine."

He laughed. "My ex-wife? A yoga instructor. She used to tell me I carry my rage in my hips, that with enough fucking downward dogs I could set myself free, but you know what? I like my rage, right where it is, thank you very much."

"There isn't much light left. . . . Can I get by, please?"

He stepped back with a melodramatic "after you" gesture.

I opened the door. Cold rushed me.

"Listen."

I turned to him.

"Jeanne's been working on something to help us out at the site. We're headed back tomorrow, first thing. All of us. I need all hands on deck. The girl comes, too."

He closed the door, and I turned to face the glittering expanse.

twenty-two

Step by step, I made my way toward the Dome, eyes on the ice beneath my feet, rope gripped tight. A snorting, scuffling sound to either side of me brought me to a halt. I tried to quiet my banging heart. Stared straight down. In all the big wide world there were only bright orange boots on blinding white. I heard a sharp animal whine, stuttering grunts. Breathed a bracing lungful of *What is it?*

I'd smelled it before, an animal smell, like cows in a field, but this was gamier, sharper. Not horses, but. I touched my pocket. No walkie-talkie. I'd left that back in my room. Another rule broken. Great job, Val. I felt a wild presence on all sides. I felt: *assessed*. A shadow broke the sun on my face, hooves crunched brittle ice; I looked up.

A herd of caribou—a couple dozen at least—surrounded me, their breath snorting out dragon puffs through flared nostrils, antlered heads cutting black puzzle pieces into blue sky as they towered over me. Heavy gray flanks over spindly legs that clicked as they walked, shining brown eyes set deep in inky faces. They swayed their huge necks toward one another and back at me as if confirming, *She is nothing, no danger, keep moving.* The musk of their exhalations so close they moistened my cheeks. In a casual gallop, they threaded around me, leaving me in their wake to grapple with an inexplicable state of longing.

I BURST INTO the Dome, full of the story of the caribou. Nora and Raj made me hot tea, settling me in their "living room," the corner of the Dome nearest the heater where they'd thrown blankets and polar bear skins over several chairs. A propane lantern burned with a golden glow, sending around a little cheer; still, the dark blue hole in the ice opposite us exerted its own gravitational pull, and I tried not to look at it. After a few sips of tea, I brought out Sigrid's draw-ings of squiggles and birds, spreading them out on their worktable among microscopes, specimen jars, and lab notebooks.

Raj glanced at Nora as he pulled up a chair. "We should tell you, Sigrid's been giving us these drawings as well."

I sat back, nursing the faint hurt that perhaps Sigrid had given up on me. "When?"

He shrugged. "Over the past week or so. Whenever she thinks no one is looking."

"Mostly she gives them to him," Nora said. "She loves Seal Man, you know."

"What do you think of them?"

Raj drew his finger thoughtfully along the squiggly lines. "These could be a kind of seaweed, don't know. But that bird does look like an Arctic tern."

"Why would she want them, do you think?"

He got up and brought over a box of shortbread cookies: stale, processed, and delicious. "*Want them?* I have no idea."

I retrieved the drawings of "suns" I kept in one of my Greenland books. Flattened them on the desk. "What about these? I must have thirty of these pictures. What do they look like to you?"

"Like circles," Raj said. "Babe, what do you think?"

"Maybe she likes the shape."

"Could they be suns, do you think?" I asked. "Or moons?"

"I guess . . ." Raj said.

"Think about it," I said. "She could draw anything. Anything at all. And this is what she draws. *Why?* She's drawing squiggles, birds, and then circles, the last one red, and look how she colors it, see? Like it's, I don't know—" My voice quavered, the possibility of what it meant haunting me.

"Like it's what, Val?" Nora asked gently.

"Like those suns indicate days." I extracted one of the earlier drawings. "Look. Fifteen suns, the last one blotted out with red Magic Marker." I freed the next one in the pile. "This one, made three days later. Twelve circles. Twelfth circle colored red. But this one?" I held up one she'd drawn just days before. "Seven circles. Seventh circle, same thing." I scrambled in my pocket, hands shaking as I unfolded her latest drawing. "This one is from last night. *Five circles.* The last one, look what she did to it."

The red marker had torn the paper nearly in half.

"She's trying to tell us she has five days to live. Don't you see? She has *five days* unless we find her this snake and this tern. Otherwise she'll die." Hysteria rose in my chest, fluttering like a trapped bird. I clutched one hand with the other, trying to stop the quaking.

Nora and Raj exchanged a glance.

"Val," Nora said. "Would you fancy a little drink, maybe?"

"A *drink* drink?"

She nodded.

"You have *alcohol* here?"

Raj laughed, got up, and rummaged around in a box of supplies. "All we have is this revolting Icelandic liqueur called—"

"I'd love some."

Raj poured a shot of brown liquid into a metal coffee cup. It tasted like actual mud, but sweet. "You know, we've been a little worried about you, Val."

"Why?"

"You seem somewhat strung out. I mean, Wyatt told us you misplaced your pills—"

"He *stole* my fucking pills."

Another glance exchanged, like I was so bad off I couldn't notice these things.

"Like I said, we're just a bit concerned, that's all. Have you been sleeping?"

"I was up all night reading these books on ancient Inuit culture."

"Too stimulating," Raj said. He tossed me a copy of their diving checklist. "Read this. You need something boring and tedious. This will do it. I'm serious."

I stuffed the checklist in my pocket. "Can we talk about Sigrid now, please?"

"Has Wyatt seen the drawings?" Nora asked.

"Just the snake and bird ones, not the suns, I'm pretty sure."

"Because she showed him or you showed him?"

"Because he snoops around my room when I'm not there looking at my shit and stealing things from me—" I thought of the journal I'd started and abandoned after my pills disappeared, convinced he would find it. After that I spoke all my notes into my handheld recorder, kept it with me at all times.

Raj poured me another shot. I willed myself to sip it, not inhale it.

I said, "Do you realize how old this girl is? These people hunted seal, narwhal, walrus—even whales!—from flimsy sealskin boats. They made sleds out of whale jaws. Lived in sod houses. Four or more families to these cramped underground dwellings pieced together from earth and whale ribs and driftwood. Windows made out of stretched seal intestine that barely let light in, all winter, ten months at a time. They spoke some ancestral language, which evolved into Greenlandic but is incomprehensible to me. And she won't . . ." I dropped my head in my hands, struggled to lift it. "She refuses to try to communicate with me, to really learn, and I'm mystified, and terrified, because we've only got these five days. . . ."

Raj set his drink down. "That's one interpretation, Val, I can see that. But do you really believe she thawed from the ice alive? Much less that she's hundreds of years old?"

"Well, did you look at the cells?"

"They were human, but the leap from that to Sigrid being . . . Well, it's a bit rich. It really is. Wyatt's got some fame-and-fortune scheme cooked up, which would rankle me except he's going nowhere with it. He's flailing around with pseudoscience, with science fiction, really!" Face drawn tight, he leaned forward, one fist clasped in the other hand. "The thing that kills me is that this girl has been *taken* from somewhere, and—mark my words—the minute we wrap up here and get back to civilization, Wyatt is going to pay for this. We're going to get Sigrid back to her home and her family, and he is going to bloody pay."

"I agree with Raj, Val," Nora said. "He and I have talked a lot about this. When we first got here, all I said was let's report this, but now—and probably this is selfish—we want to stay and finish our study here. It won't be long. We never dreamed she'd get sick . . ."

"But her language," I said. "It isn't a living language."

"Aren't there obscure dialects few people speak anymore?"

"I've gone through all of them. Checked her vocalizations against every conceivable database. There's no other conclusion I can come to. Her language, to me, is proof that—"

"Look, Val," Raj said, regarding me with thin patience. "The minute I believe that girl woke up alive from seven-hundred-year-old ice will be the minute I believe she's trying to tell us she's dying. Otherwise, to me, she's just some confused kid stolen from her family by some greedy prick trying to game the system."

"Seems like you want to shut your eyes to every ounce of evidence that this girl is ancient, and that she's dying. Why is that? Your research—nobody's research—is more important than a child's life."

He flushed, threw a hand up in the air. "Let's not go there, Val—"

"Go where, Raj? I think sometimes people believe what's easiest for them to believe, and it sure is easier to think Wyatt found her on the ice. But nothing points to that, not the clothing she was found in, not her behavior, not her language, not her ground-down molars—have I told you about that?"

"Plenty of Inuit still work skins with their teeth—"

"Actually, that's completely false." I tossed my books on Greelandic history on the table. "Just look at these, will you, please? Keep an open mind?"

"Sure," Nora said with a polite smile, but I wasn't convinced. "You want company going back?"

"No," I said, suiting up. "I'll be fine."

HEAD DOWN AGAINST the bracing wind, I practically ran back to the Shack, furious and sad I hadn't been able to convince them of what I knew in my heart: Time was running out for Sigrid. And if I was alone in helping her, so be it. Alone was a place I knew well.

twenty-three

Two seventeen in the morning and I still felt three cups of coffee awake.

It was the circa-1906 photo of an eight- or nine-year-old Inuit girl that hooked me. I stared at it so long I felt I'd actually entered the sepia-toned shot. Smelled the blood of the freshly killed ringed seal that hung from a hook behind her, felt the sting of the glacial wind that tousled her hair and ruddied her cheeks. Dressed in a caribou anorak, polar bear pants, and sealskin boots, she wore a worried look, the same expression that seemed permanently imprinted on Sigrid's face. The girl stood next to her mother, who wore her hair in the topknot style of the time, a baby in a pouch on her back. They looked through the camera from this other century as if to say, *What is it you want from us?*

According to the book on ancient Nordic cultures balanced on my lap, the Dorset people dominated the north coast of Greenland from around 600 BC to AD 1300, but were decimated when the Thule arrived around AD 1200. Only a hundred years to wipe out a people. I had to wonder: Did the arrival of the Little Ice Age play a role in the friction between the Thule and the Dorset?

The human remains Wyatt found in the core dated to around AD 1300. . . .

Was Sigrid Thule or Dorset?

I flipped on my recorder, my voice rough with exhaustion. "Few artifacts remain to illuminate either culture. Author poses the theory that little changed technologically before the arrival of Europeans in the eighteenth century. This was a subsistence culture . . . hunting and fishing, following caribou, hunting sea mammals."

I paused at a 1901 photo of an Inuit hunter wearing a cavernous sealskin parka, so big he could squat in it—the idea being he could light a fire inside it to keep warm while waiting on the ice for a seal to emerge from a breathing hole. It reminded me of Sigrid and her obsession with the Christmas sweater.

I clicked on my recorder. "Eighty-five-year-old native hunter, 1955 interview. Reveals secrets of hunting whales in a sealskin boat. Said that since the whales weren't afraid of these meager boats, the trick was to get as close as possible . . . scout out a subtle pulsing movement under the skin below her spine—the door to her kidney. A spear was inserted quickly and quietly. Apparently no fight from the whale. Perhaps no awareness that she was bleeding to death. Hunters followed until she was dead."

Sigrid had done nothing like this as far as I knew, but she had called the narwhals up from the depths with her own voice. According to the text, narwhals were the filet mignon of sea mammals.

I read about all the brilliant ways Arctic people innovated with what few materials they had.

"Arctic rabbit skins were used for periods. Small bird skins turned inside out made baby booties. People lived on the knife edge of survival. Starvation was . . . not uncommon."

I thought of how Sigrid ate—so fast I thought she would choke, as if there would never be any more food.

I skipped to the pages on the role of women.

"Girls at a very early age were expected to prepare skins for clothing. To scrape, stretch, and soften the skin by chewing it. Then to cut and sew—with caribou sinew—the skin and make clothes."

I pictured Sigrid's ground-down molars.

"Women were tasked with preparing the dead for burial. They closed the mouth and eyes of the deceased, washed them, dressed them in a clean, new skin. Encircled their own eyes with soot to indicate a state of mourning. A day was reserved for grieving. Just one. After that, people were expected to get back to the business of survival."

I stopped cold at the photo of an *ulu*, known as a "women's knife."

My stomach flipped.

This ancient, crescent-shaped knife was the same size and shape— out of all the knives Jeanne possessed, and she had plenty—that Sigrid had chosen to steal.

Brain on overdrive, I forced myself to close the book, click off my recorder. Jittery, I went to the kitchen in search of wine. Midpour, I heard something. A dull thud.

I knew every creak and groan the building made. Even the distant thunder of icebergs calving was background noise by now.

This was different.

A living being made this dull *thump, thump, thump.*

I stole into the hall. Total darkness. Peeked in Sigrid's room— she was fast asleep. Wyatt snored steadily; Jeanne's door stood ajar. Moonlight swathed her in cerulean; the sad quilt rose and fell with her breathing.

Back in the kitchen, I crept past hanging pots, pans; knife-scored counters gleaming silver.

Another thud.

Where are these noises coming from? A dull bang, like wood on wood, or the heel of a boot against a door. I walked the length of the main room, past Wyatt's desk, past the couch lumbering in the shadows like a reclining beast.

At the picture window, I scanned the moonlit ice field. Nothing moved. I pictured the animals hunkering down in the cold and the dark. Then I heard it: a high, keening whine that could have been the wind, but wasn't.

Another cry—high-pitched, sinewy, sad. Clearly from outside the Shack.

The front door unlatched with a dull clunk. With my shoulder, I nudged it open a crack and hovered there, the great Arctic night slicing through my long johns as I closed my eyes and listened with every pore.

A *thud-thud-thud*, a scraping sound. A bang.

It sounded like it was coming from the Shed.

What is out there? Had something or someone—Raj or Nora—been locked in the Shed by accident? If so, why didn't they cry out?

But then, I did hear something. A long, drawn-out whimper. So very, very faint. *Am I imagining it?*

I heard it again. It sounded human. I shut the door, latched it. Tugged boots over my slippers, threw on my parka and gloves, yanked on my hat.

Feeling as if I'd lost my mind, I stepped out into the ferocious cold, pulling the door closed behind me. The air so raw my lungs gulped half portions. I squinted at the ramshackle silhouette of the Shed, a stark black cutout against the deep blue night sky. Blinking to keep moisture in my eyes, I felt along the wall of the Shack for the rope that joined the two buildings. Devilish gusts blew fine snow into my face, then swirled away in glittering funnels before disappearing like stardust.

From the Shed, more noises. A dull pounding, a mewl.

Someone was dying.

I walked faster, achieving a clumsy trot. Slipped and fell forward, sliding on my belly like a penguin, too frightened to let go of the rope to break my fall. Head down, eyes closed, I tasted the oxygen fog my hot breath made on the ice. Pulled myself to my knees and touched my forehead. Blood steamed, then froze to a shiny streak on my yellow glove. I blundered on.

The Shed was barely warmer inside than out, my footfalls heavy on the creaking slats. I clicked on the overhead lamp. Shadows leapt across the room. The air snapped with quiet.

"Hello?"

Nothing. I turned in a slow circle, my breath puffing out in small clouds.

"Is anyone here?"

The wind rattled the windows in their sashes, then stopped. Silence. Stillness. As if the Enormity was listening to me, waiting for my next move.

I thought: *I've got the wrong building. The sounds must have come from the Cube—*

Behind me, a dull scraping sound.

Spine rigid, I turned around.

Nothing. Just the walk-in freezer where the ice cores were stored.

"*Hello?*" I said, my voice thin and wheezy. "I'm here to—"

Another bang, like wood on metal. A pitiful dragging sound.

It was coming from inside the freezer.

A knock. Then another.

I approached the enormous metal box. The floor-to-ceiling steel door leached its own chilled fog.

"Hello? Is someone in there?" I pressed my gloved palm flat on the steaming surface.

Nothing.

"Answer me!" I banged on the door, kicked at it.

A dull scratching from inside. Andy was trapped in there, too cold to speak, and I was about to let him die all over again. I pounded on the door, grabbed the combination lock and yanked down on it. Didn't budge. Spun the dial, tugged at it again.

"Who's in there?"

A terrible lowing sound, from something or someone in unimaginable pain.

I spun around. Wrenches, saws, blowtorches, hammers. *Hammers.* I snatched up the heaviest one I could find—a sledgehammer—and turned toward the door.

I could barely lift it over my head, so brought it down full force but out of control. *Bang.* I missed the lock completely, denting the door.

A kicking sound, a howl.

"Hold on, I'm coming!" I tore off my gloves—I couldn't grip or feel the handle otherwise—and wound up again, coming at the lock sideways like a club. A colossal clang and the lock was damaged now, its metal arms cockeyed but still attached to the dial. Another windup and I bashed the thing further sideways.

Something big and heavy collapsed against the door; a pitiful yowl.

Breath ragged, I circled the damaged lock, assessing it. I needed to come at it from a different angle. Gripping the sledgehammer, I whispered Sigrid's seven words like an incantation. Spun a hard circle and came slamming at the lock from underneath. It broke off with a metal scream, the dial skittering off to the dark recesses of the room, the deformed upside-down U still holding the door fast. I dropped the sledgehammer at my feet and found a smaller hammer, banging at the remaining metal until it bent just enough for me to slip it off.

From behind the door: utter quiet.

I was too late.

I lifted the latch; the door opened with a smack of suction and swung wide.

For the first few seconds, ice smoke rolled out, obscuring my view, until, as if from a dream, a massive caribou filled the doorway. One side of his elegant set of antlers scraped the ceiling; the other had broken off and lay in pieces on the freezer floor. Dried, frozen blood, already sugared with frost, covered his hooves and forelocks. Sluggishly he scraped at the floor just once. With a human-sounding groan, he fell onto the knees of his forelegs before his haunches gave way and he dropped all the way down. He sank his long snout onto the steel floor, frosted black lips sputtering out a white foam before his eyes fluttered shut.

"Come on," I choked out. "Get up! You have to get up." I ran to the door of the Shed and flung it wide. The black cold roared in. "See? You can go. *Go!*"

But he lay like a broken statue, ice knitting around his closed eyes, cockeyed antlers motionless. I ran back to the freezer, stepped up onto the raised floor. Without thinking, I reached down to touch his long muzzle. He cracked open his frost-rimed brown eyes and lifted his tremendous head with a snarl, nostrils sputtering hot breath. I jumped backward and climbed out of the freezer.

Still collapsed on the floor, the creature snorted, huffing the night air, reading freedom. He lifted one front hoof and scraped it along the corrugated metal again and again, seeking traction of any kind. Somehow it caught in a groove between the interlocking metal sheets and he muscled himself up onto his forelegs, his backside still heartbreakingly inert. Nuggets of ice broke off his face and body like rock candy. For long, terrible moments he stayed that way: front half up, bottom half glued to the floor, until, with a harrowing cry, he unlocked his haunches and lifted himself all the way up to standing. He trembled so hard and so long in the steam of his cage I thought for sure he would fall to his knees again and simply die.

I heard voices.

Framed by the open door, the figures of Wyatt and Jeanne began to make their way up the hill toward the Shed.

"Come on," I said. "You've got to run." I backed up into the shadows of the room, trying to give the animal all the space he needed.

With a clop, the caribou tendered a leg out and down on the floor of the freezer. Took a wobbly, jerky step. Panted, snorted, shook his lopsided head. Banged another hoof down. One knee nearly buckled but he caught it, sticking the other leg out straight and commanding his body forward. He scrambled clear of the freezer and clattered down to the wooden floor of the Shed. Took a few confused steps—a half circle toward me, a half circle away—as if he'd lost the scent of the night and the way out.

"Go! Run!" I breathed the musky tang of his thick fur. For a moment he looked at me as if I had something he needed, some answer. "Bah!" I screamed, waving my arms, anything so he would move.

He skittered back, then pivoted—hooves screeching—toward the doorway, his big body and one antler filling it. Tilting his head sideways, he negotiated the opening, then launched himself full throttle across the snow. Jeanne and Wyatt, just yards from the door, reared back and out of his way, watching him leap toward the glacier as if witnessing something of the divine.

twenty-four

"That's unforgivable." From her seat on the floor, Nora nudged a plate of fried fish closer to Sigrid's bed, no doubt hoping hunger would lure her out. "What did they say to you?"

My head pounded from lack of sleep, adrenaline from the night before still pulsing through me. "That it was none of my business. That it was *science*. Said I was getting in the way."

Nora shook her head. "Look, Val, I would let it go. A few more days and we're out of here, all of us. We just have to hang on."

Sigrid crawled out from her lair and gave us both a shy smile; in no time she was tearing through her plate of food. She licked her fingers clean and handed me the crumbless plate, then climbed on the bed, where she leaned against her window—palms on the cold pane, breath clouding the glass—as if willing her body outside.

"She seems better," Nora said with a little laugh.

"Her fever's gone, but have you seen her eye?"

"No . . ."

"Sigrid." I got up and gingerly approached her. Nora followed. "Look at me."

She spun around as if she understood me, her face full of intelligence, soft brow furrowed. The outer corner of her left eye drooped and was tearing up. She shrank back but let us both have a brief look before getting fed up and turning toward the window.

"Has Wyatt seen this?" Nora asked.

"He says she's fine. Says kids get pink eye."

Nora walked around the bed for a closer look. "That's not pink eye. But it could be a kind of palsy that goes away when the cold goes away—"

"You really believe that, Nora?"

She sighed. "I don't know what to believe anymore."

Sigrid's door swung open; Wyatt's haggard face appeared. The sight of the two of us talking seemed to embarrass him slightly, but he recovered fast. "Raj and Jeanne and me are ready to go. Cats are loaded up. Think you can get her suited up in a couple of minutes?"

I said, "She's not well enough to go, Wyatt."

"I don't think it's a good idea either," Nora said.

He shifted his weight in the doorway, a rifle slung over one shoulder gleaming in the dimness. "We discussed this last night and we agreed, remember? I need all of you to help out. She can't stay here alone."

"Why don't I stay back—" Nora started.

"Her fever's gone," he said. "She won't even have to leave the cat. I've got blankets, hot chocolate. She'll be like a bug in a rug."

Neither of us said a word.

"Get her dressed," he said, pulling the door shut behind him.

THE SUN WAS a smear of yellow paste between the pearl-gray worlds of land and sky. Though the air was still, it nipped at the flesh. Wrapped in Jeanne's old red parka, Sigrid settled next to me in the back seat, occasionally drumming on the window with her fingers. Her fascination with glass was not lost on me; perhaps the last "window" she'd looked through was much less miraculous, affording her only light and shadow through lengths of stretched seal intestine.

As we approached the glacier, Sigrid gave off an air of mania, rambling to herself in low tones, not even attempting to make herself understood. Behind us, we towed a Dr. Seussian contraption Jeanne had built—its use a mystery—a circular plate as big as a garbage can lid she'd hooked up to a motor.

In the front seat—Jeanne riding shotgun—Wyatt motored on, inscrutable behind his mirrored glasses as we crawled along the rough, uneven ice toward the glacier that undulated over the mountain pass. To our left, the land sloped down to the beach. Slashes of red stained the gray and white brash ice.

Wyatt thrust the cat into neutral; behind us, Nora and Raj did the same in their snow machine. He cracked the window to help clear the steam; a horrendous smell leaked in. Three starved-looking polar bears, their ribs evident under loose, dull hides even from a distance, ripped at the beached body of a rotting beluga whale, the ocean heaving small bergs at them as they tried to drag it out onto shore and fight over it at the same time. All three bears halted their efforts and turned their bloody faces to us, as in: *Who else do we have to kill in order to eat our meal?* One lost interest in the whale entirely and started a huffing sort of run toward us, enormous black footpads flashing in all the white, leaving a trail of gore in the snow. Wyatt took us out of neutral fast, and soon the bear lost heart and turned back. Scoured by salt wind and mist, the red turned pink, then was erased, and all was blue gray again.

As we crawled up the glacier between gleaming ice cliffs, Sigrid broke out of her odd funk. She squirmed into the front seat and sat on Jeanne's lap, eking a rare laugh out of her. Jeanne's device clanking and banging, we coasted a few yards across the ice side by side toward the glacial lake, until we stopped and all was silent. Already the shadows of the cats stretched nearly halfway across the lake as the sun flattened on the horizon. More than ever, a desperate loneliness seemed to dwell in this place.

Wyatt broke the silence. "Val, you and Sigrid stay in the cat." He unlatched the door and jumped out onto the ice, Jeanne right behind him. But there was no keeping Sigrid in that cab. She grabbed the door handle and swung herself out and down to the ice, glancing back at the sled where Wyatt, Jeanne, Nora, and Raj gathered around the ungainly piece of equipment.

"Bahl," she said, reaching toward me. *"Bahl."*

"Coming." I stepped down to the ice, but she had already raced off. Her voluminous red parka flapped in the wind as she skirted far too close to the crevasse, which had widened by several yards. Its wine-dark walls pulsed in the eerie light as if blue blood coursed through inky veins just beneath.

"I said stay in the cat," Wyatt called over.

"Sigrid," I shouted, holding my hand out to her. "You're too close!"

Chin thrust out, she marched along the fissure as if to show me she understood the tone of my words but had no intention of heeding them. I caught up to her, and we walked together in silence, arriving at the gouged-out place where she had been freed from the ice. She paused there but said nothing. The edges were even softer now, molten-looking, an odd cave-like hole along one wall. Some decision made, Sigrid spun on her heel and jogged toward the mountains. I took off after her, feet heavy in my boots, but I caught her, or she let me. She pulled me along with surprising strength, chattering, pointing, and smiling as if she knew where she was going. I skidded along with her on the sun-goldened ice, ignoring Wyatt's shouts.

Pausing, she squinted at the snow-swept, barren peaks, said in her language, "Mother, father."

"Your mother and father are here?"

She nodded. Freshly inspired, she jerked me in another direction, and we were running again. I clung to her hand. Once more she stopped, looking disappointed by her choice. She wiped her nose, her too-big hat falling down over her eyes as she constantly shoved it back. Behind us, Nora, Raj, Wyatt, and Jeanne, now toy-sized figures on the ice, struggled to drag the strange contraption across the frozen lake.

I knelt down. Her eye looked worse, red, oozing, sagging down in one corner as if dragged by some singular force of gravity. It hurt to look at.

"We have to go back, Sigrid."

She pointed to the mountains, their brittle black teeth jutting up into the violet sky. Under our boots, a deep-throated groaning sound, followed by a drawn-out, dull creak. *Is another crevasse preparing to open and swallow us?*

"Mother, father," she pleaded.

"We can't—"

A gunshot split the air. Wyatt was making his way toward us, shouting and waving his arms. Even at a distance, I could tell how pissed he was. I didn't blame him.

I knelt to get close to her. "We've got to head back, honey, I'm so sorry. I promise we'll come back for mother, father, okay?"

Sigrid's face crumpled with disappointment. She looked on the verge of bolting, but I took hold of her arm, half dragging her at first until she realized I meant business and kept pace with me.

NORA KNELT ON the ice, arms wrapped around the bright yellow motor that whined and vibrated as if it wanted to dance away with her. The cord looped across a few yards of ice to Wyatt and Jeanne, who gripped either side of the T of the ice-core-drilling machine, its massive screw replaced with the heated metal plate that—rigged to the motor—spun against the ice. Raj leaned into the plate, using his body weight to try to guide it across the surface, but it wouldn't budge. Steam rose up, quickly erased by frigid air. Momentarily exhausted, Raj sat on the ice to catch his breath.

"Turn it off!" Wyatt called over the motor.

Nora shut it down.

Wyatt lifted the plate out of the shallow depression, pushing it aside in disgust. It had burned a circular hole a yard across and a few inches deep. A light snow had begun, quickly covering the perfect circle of polished ice.

Raj got to his feet. "Are you sure this is where you took the cores?"

"Of course I'm sure," Wyatt said.

"We're going to have to do this a little at a time," Jeanne said, circumnavigating her invention. "It's a pain in the ass, but we can't slide it. We're going to have to keep making circles."

She got down to her knees, casually brushing snow off the ice ring. Her gloved hand froze midsweep. She sat back on her haunches. "Wyatt," she breathed. "Nora, Raj. You have to see this. Val, keep Sigrid back."

twenty-five

Once they got the hang of it, they worked fast, burnishing contiguous rings until they'd covered an area the circumference of a good-sized room, all the while gesticulating, talking animatedly to each other. As if worn out from her jaunt on the ice field, Sigrid nodded off as soon as we settled in the cat, head resting on my lap, whistling softly through her stuffy nose. I couldn't hear a word over the cat's motor. My only thought was, *What had they discovered that Sigrid wasn't allowed to see?*

She woke as soon as Wyatt opened the door, squinting at him from under her hat.

He looked stricken. "Val, you should come and see this. Leave her here."

But Sigrid had already wriggled out of my arms and vaulted from the cab. I jumped out after her, but she was sprinting toward the weird pattern of shining circles that gleamed like giant ice lily pads. Raj, his face closed and dark, knelt with his camera, snapping shot after shot. In a rare moment of stillness, Jeanne rested against her ice-polishing invention, staring down into the depths. Nora sat back on her heels next to a gleaming ring, occasionally reaching down to brush the snow away.

When Nora caught sight of Sigrid, she sprang to her feet, darting toward the girl with a cry. Nora caught her and swung her up in her arms, facing her away from the site.

"Val, she can't see this, I'm telling you!"

Dread coursed through me; the looks on their faces chilled my blood.

Sigrid, more shocked than anything else, let herself be carried toward the cat until she saw me and started to struggle. Nora lost control of her, and she slipped free. Wyatt made a grab for her, but she shot her arms up fast and twisted cunningly out of his grasp, bulleting toward the shining ice.

She came to an abrupt halt at the edge. Far above us, seabirds rode the updrafts, carving graceful arcs across a silver sky. Snow lightly patterned Sigrid's slouching hat and baggy coat. *What is she looking at? Why is everyone so quiet, their faces turned away?* The faint buzz from the morning splash of vodka in my coffee was no more, my body gone brittle with the cold, as if had I tried to move, some part of me would snap off. I wanted to run back to the cat, to anywhere that felt safe, but how could I not bear witness? The air an ache in my lungs, I made my feet move to stand next to her.

She didn't budge.

She was a child in a state of wonder, of horror, of understanding.

Beneath us, a scene of utter devastation. A couple of yards under our boots, a ghastly diorama: several dozen Inuit people frozen in place in the midst of fighting, spears and knives drawn. Dressed in polar bear leggings, sealskin anoraks and boots. Many had terrible wounds, their necks gashed, arms severed, bellies disemboweled. Men, women, children. Some were twisted in impossible positions; others looked stunned into icy suspended animation. Like lunging statues, a half dozen sled dogs were caught on their hind legs, snarling, paws midchurn.

Sigrid dropped to her hands and knees and began to crawl,

clawing at the ice with bare hands. She stopped directly over a woman—a few yards beneath the ice—who had collapsed face-down across a man who lay on his back, a pool of blood under his head. A knife jutted from her lower back. Crying, Sigrid repeated one of her seven words, "*Tahtaksah*," then, in her language, "Mother, father."

Raj relaxed his grip on his camera; it hung limply around his neck. "We need to get her out of here."

"No," Jeanne said. "She deserves to see."

Wyatt walked the perimeter of the polished ice, eyes never leaving Sigrid.

"Why did you bring her here . . . ?" Nora murmured.

"I didn't know it would be like this. . . ." Wyatt's voice trailed off.

I got down on my knees next to Sigrid. The snow had ceased, as if in respect for the ravaged scene beneath us. She swept off the last delicate flakes. "Tahtaksah," she breathed. "Mother, father."

"You're sad," I said. "For your mother, and for your father. I'm so sorry." And that's when I understood, kneeling with Sigrid just yards above the seven-hundred-year-old bodies of her parents, what *tahtaksah* meant. Seven words used constantly . . . *Where had I read about the seven basic emotions? The Book of Rites*, a first-century Chinese encyclopedia, named the "feelings of men": fear, sadness, contempt, surprise, disgust, anger, and joy.

An attempt to categorize emotions. *Tahtaksah*. It had to mean sad, grief-stricken.

She was telling me how she felt before telling me what she thought. I finally understood: in her language, every sentence began with an emotion. What a compassionate, gentle way to communicate: prioritizing feelings over facts.

"What is she saying to you?" Wyatt crouched at the edge of the gleaming ice a few yards away.

"That she's sad. That her mother and father are beneath us."

"Let's get out of here," Nora said. "What good is this doing anybody?"

Raj wandered to the far side of the cleared area as if scouting a better angle for photos. He came to an abrupt halt. Got down on his hands and knees, set aside his camera, and polished one of the circles with a gloved hand. "Guys, you have to come see this."

Nora joined her husband, kneeling beside him. A strangled yelp escaped her. She clutched his arm. Wyatt and Jeanne quickly made their way to stand behind them.

Wyatt let out a low whistle. "Better get over here, Val."

Sigrid had sunk into a state of melancholy. I'm not sure she felt or noticed the kiss I placed on her head before reluctantly leaving her side to join the others.

I gazed down into the dim, blue otherworld. A baby boy, perfectly preserved, floated a few feet below the surface, his body partially wrapped in a dun-colored rag that seemed to flutter in an eternal wind. His dark eyes were open, and he looked alert, one chubby hand reaching out as if to touch his mother's face or pick a flower off a stem.

"My God, Raj," Nora breathed. "Look at him."

He gripped her arm, consumed by the sight.

"How did he get here," Nora said, "so far away from all the others?"

Wyatt knelt next to her. "Maybe he was swept up in the same gust that took Sigrid, who knows? Look where she was found. Just yards from here."

We all squinted at the azure depression on the other side of the crevasse, piecing together the weirdly plausible explanation.

"Perhaps they tried to place the children away from danger," Raj said softly. "But the wind had other plans."

"He looks just like Charlie, doesn't he?" Nora hugged herself, eyes glittering.

"Come on, babe," Raj said, peering out at the brooding mountains, their black cliffs crosshatched with ice. "Keep it together."

Her voice rose. "It's the truth, and you know it. Look at him. His smile, his eyes . . ."

Raj wrapped his arm around her waist and pulled her to her feet, tried to lead her away. "This isn't good for you—"

She brushed him aside. *Just let me look at him!*"

"I say we cut him out of there," Wyatt said. "He looks in good shape, not like the rest of them."

Raj stepped briskly to his camera, snatched it up, and slipped the strap around his neck. "You've finally lost your fucking mind."

Wyatt smiled and tipped his head to Jeanne, who was already on her way back to the sled and the ice saw.

Raj got up into Wyatt's face. "This sick little sideshow cannot go on," he growled. "I will not let it. Your game with Sigrid. Even if she did thaw out alive, you've still got no idea why or how, even after all your screwing around. This place"—he gesticulated at the shining circles beneath us, the vast lake with its jagged blue scar, the peaks beyond—"is sacred. This is a grave site. We should leave these poor people in peace."

Head down against the wind, Jeanne dragged the ice saw behind her.

"If it'll really offend you that much to watch us cut him out," Wyatt said, "why don't you head back?"

Raj stood over the baby, arms folded tight. "I won't let you do it. This is obscene."

Jeanne, out of breath, laid down the saw at Wyatt's feet.

"That's not very democratic of you, Raj. Maybe we should ask around. Take a vote. Nora?"

"I . . ." She wiped her eyes, looked at her husband imploringly. "I— *Look at him.* I can't just leave him here. Not if . . . Raj, I'm sorry."

He said, "Then what about everybody else down there? Why don't we thaw out the whole lot? What have we got to lose?"

"Look at them, Raj," Nora said. "They're all—"

"Dead?"

She dropped her head, as if ashamed. "Maybe. But we can start with the boy."

Wyatt turned to me. "Val?"

Raj stepped away from the cleared ice. I got on all fours to look. The baby was near enough for me to reach down and scoop up in my arms. He wore the slightest smile, as if seconds ago something had delighted him. I couldn't get close enough to him. *What if this little boy did thaw out alive?* It would be a kind of murder to leave him in ice forever.

I knew that Sigrid would die unless we could finally under-stand each other. She had days to live; she had told me as much in every way she could. What hope would I have communicating with a baby? I could barely grasp what an eight-year-old was trying to tell me. Was Wyatt close to the answer, with his frozen foxes, caribou, lichen, beetles, bugs? Would this boy be the final clue to understanding how to survive the ice winds? Was I even thinking clearly? *Andy, what would you do?* I got closer, peering at the boy's flushed cheeks, bow lips, toothless smile. *Darling boy, is your little heart ready to beat again?* How could I know? How could any of us know?

Now that we've found you, how can we leave you here?

"Val, your vote?"

Sigrid tugged at my pant leg, nudging me away from my posi-tion over the boy. I got to my feet. I felt a hundred years old. "Okay."

"Cut him out?"

I nodded.

Sigrid rubbed her hot palms on the ice, making it clear as glass. Her face somber as she looked at each of us in turn. With surprising strength, she seized the handle of the ice saw and began to drag it toward the cat. I ran after her, grabbed her by the shoulders, and turned her toward me.

She dropped the ice saw and I hugged her tight, kissed her cold cheeks, stroked her hair from her face, which shone with tears. "Tahtaksah," she said. *Sad*. "Mother, father."

"I know, my darling, I'm so sorry."

"What's the problem over there?" Wyatt called over.

"Looks like we've got a 'no' vote," Raj said.

"Just give me a minute, will you?"

Wyatt shook his head, said something to Jeanne the wind blew away.

I pulled Sigrid close. "We're going to leave your mother and father," I whispered. She winced at the words *mother, father*. "We're going to cut the baby free." I pointed to the place where he lay.

"*Stahndala*," she said.

By now, I knew this word.

It meant "fear."

twenty-six

That night, Sigrid seemed to have just one goal, and that was to drag from under the sink the giant metal basin Jeanne used to make her vats of stew or to wash clothes. I bent down to meet her eye. "Really?" I made scrubbing motions on my body, on hers. "You want to take a bath?"

She nodded.

We had just finished a remarkably congenial dinner of Arctic char, reconstituted dried potatoes, and peas, an event made surreal by the proximity of a baby frozen in a trunk-sized slab of ice on the counter. Wyatt and Jeanne had cut ample space around him, over a foot on all sides, so it wasn't clear how long the process would take. Nora, cheeks flaming with the heat of the room and her third glass of boxed red, not that I was counting, stood next to the block, occasionally sliding her fingers across the ice, as if she could already touch the boy. Raj gazed up at her from his seat, eyes blazing with love and worry.

"Jeanne, you up for this bath thing?" We'd been through this a few times.

"Sure. Gotta heat up some water to do the dishes anyway."

"This could be the big night," Wyatt said with a wink.

Raj smiled slightly and sipped his tea. "It's a day of discoveries."

Wyatt shrugged. "That's what we're here for. But I have to take a moment to thank the person who made it all possible." He gestured at the block of ice with his cup of wine. "And that's Jeanne. Without her crazy brilliant ice-polishing gizmo, we'd have come home with nothing today." He gave her a brief round of applause; we all joined in with varying levels of enthusiasm. Up to her elbows in dishwater, Jeanne—blushing hard—nodded her acknowledgment, but by the time she gave Wyatt a shy smile, he'd turned away and was on to other things. "In fact, I'd like to declare tomorrow a day of celebration. We've all been working hard, and besides, tomorrow is a certain person's birthday, or so I've been informed. . . ." Wyatt smiled at Nora, who rolled her eyes and laughed.

"Yes, I'm turning twenty-one," she said. "Or wait, maybe it's more like . . . thirty-three."

"Forecast for tomorrow is actually pretty balmy for late October," Wyatt continued. "Three hours of sunshine, three hours of twilight on either side, highs in the teens. I'm thinking a tropical theme. Jimmy Buffett on the CD player. Hawaiian shirts. Fruity drinks. Anybody? Raj?"

Raj caught Nora's eye; she nodded, smiling.

A thud, another thud. Two small boots landed halfway across the room.

Sigrid stood naked next to the tub, arms by her sides, clothes in a haphazard pile nearby. A mirage of a girl from another age. She was even slighter than she'd seemed, delicate ribs visible above her taut belly, little knobs for knees, impossibly tiny hips. She looked at us as if to say, *When are you going to stop talking and pour my hot water?*

IT TOOK AN hour of soaking and scrubbing to make any progress. She took it stoically. We replaced the water at least twice. Her nails had what seemed like tar underneath them, and she lost patience with me there. I worked her over with shampoo and soap until she'd had enough and made that clear by throwing the washcloth across the room and climbing out of the tub. I'd laid out some clean clothes and one of my sweaters, but she opted for her filthy leggings and Christmas sweater, now an abomination of its former self—unraveling, missing half a sleeve as well as Rudolph's nose.

When I approached with a comb, she climbed on a chair—all obedience—and sat facing the block of ice. Serious, somber. In front of us, the baby flew sideways through the ice, a cherub escaped from Michelangelo's ceiling. I relished the feel of Sigrid's small, wet head, the slow but steady progress the comb made through her soft, shining hair. Her wet-leather smell replaced by that of cheap shampoo. She reached up and touched her hair, whispered something I didn't catch. I wanted to give her a trim but knew that would be pushing it. The ice made dull popping sounds as it melted. I smelled carbon, tar, an earthy musk. When I was mostly done, she knocked my hand and the comb away and climbed down off the chair.

I thought she would run off to her room as she always did in the evenings, but this night was different. She headed to the corner of the living room where I kept the picture books, drawing paper, and markers and gathered them all up in her arms. Tromped down the hallway.

Not to her room, but to mine. I followed.

She heaved everything helter-skelter on my bed. Crawled into the chaos. Opened one of the picture books and pointed at a bird. Praying this mood wouldn't vanish, I grabbed my digital recorder and tucked myself into bed next to her.

"Bird," I said.

"Bird." She reached up into the air as if grabbing a bird and pulled the phantom creature toward her.

"You need a bird. You want a bird. *Sigrid want bird?*"

She said, "Sigrid want bird. Sigrid want bird." She flipped madly through the book as if searching for something. Frustrated, she shoved it to the floor.

I opened the book on the history of Greenland. Pointed to a young Inuit girl around her age, circa 1888, standing in a swirling snowstorm. "Snow," I said, pointing to it. "Sigrid, say *snow*."

"Suh-no."

I had an idea. "Wait here, please, Sigrid." I ran to the kitchen, got a glass of water and a piece of ice, brought them back. Set the ice a few inches from the water on a sheet of notebook paper on my desk. Curious, she slipped out of bed, stood eye level with the display.

"Ice," I said, touching the chip.

She repeated, "*Ice*."

I pointed to the glass. "Water."

"Water."

Giddy with excitement, I drew a line on the paper with little arrows from the ice chip to the water and said, slowly, "Thaw."

She let me take her finger and touch the ice, trace the arrows, then touch the glass of water. "Thaw," I repeated.

She smiled and said, "Taw."

"Yes! Thaw."

"*Taw.*"

"Okay, good. Now watch." I drew another line with arrows, this time from the water to the ice. "Freeze," I said, with great drama. Touching the glass of water, arrow, and ice, then reversing the order, and back again, I said, "Water, freeze, ice. Ice, thaw, water. Now you do it." I took her hand and she let me touch the items with her finger one by one.

"Ice. Taw. *Wah*ter," she said. "*Wah*ter. Feeze. Ice. *Feeze!*" she repeated, giggling. The word *freeze* seemed to crack her up.

"Good job, Sigrid." I went back to the snow scene and pointed at the young girl. "Girl."

"Guhl."

"Girl."

"Grlll."

She learned so fast. Through repetition, goofy pantomime, picture books, and drawing, she mastered *yes, no, freeze, thaw, baby, eat, drink, hungry, wake, sleep, walk, fish, dog, talk, hair, eye, snow, water, ice, ice bear, seal, walrus, dead, alive,* and *fly,* everything caught on my recorder. For one versus many, I emptied a bag of marbles on the bed. With her weeping, drooping eye, she learned the concept of hurt, of sick. I think I even got across the word *sorry,* after spilling a bit of water on her by accident and repeating the word a few times. Abstract verbs were tougher. Want versus love, for example.

Pointing to her and then the picture of the bird, I said, "Sigrid wants bird."

She nodded, said, "Yes."

I was so thrilled by her progress I hugged her, surprising her slightly. "Val loves Sigrid," I said in an exulted tone. Then I let her go and hugged myself, an enraptured expression on my face. Pointed at her. Repeated, "Val loves Sigrid."

She thought this was hilarious. She hugged herself, saying, "Love, love, love Sigrid," before bursting into her own language, which—I had to continually remind myself—was most likely liberated from English's choke hold of subject-verb-object. A simple sentence such as *I like fish* might be translated as something like: *happy, delicious, love, want, the kind of fish, the time of year it is caught, likes it the way her grandfather used to make it, burnt at the edges and roasted over stones, wants the fish now, thanks the spirit of the fish, misses her grandfather.*

Sigrid rattled on, distracted by the toys on the bed, conversing mostly with her windup "ice bear" and stuffed narwhal. After my initial excitement, I was feeling somewhat screwed. *How would I ever grasp her stream of consciousness answers to simple questions, much less those to complex ones?* I got out of bed, opened my bottom drawer, and retrieved the bottle of stolen vodka.

I sighed and took a swig. "Val wants drink."

"Sigrid want drink."

"No, you don't. Sigrid wants bird, and that"—I rubbed my forehead—"snake thing."

Sigrid reached for the bottle.

"No, honey. Not for you."

I sat on the bed next to her. The room was so overheated in contrast to the frozen world outside, the painted palm trees on the wall looked almost right. "Listen to me, Sigrid. Bahl is *tahtaksah*. Sad."

Her face betrayed a mixture of delight and worry, perhaps from hearing a word in her language combined with a concern for what it meant. She reached out and touched my cheek. "Bahl?"

"Yes, I am *sad*." I let the vodka warm me. "Bahl is tahtaksah because she is worried *Sigrid dead*. Bahl is afraid, she feels *stahndala*, okay? She feels *fear*. And she's good at that. Fear. She feels fear for you, for herself, for the world, fear of the ice winds. Sigrid, you know the secret for thawing out alive, but you're not telling Bahl. You can't tell Bahl, but why? Bahl knows you're getting sicker." I pointed to her eye. "Hurt?"

"Yes."

"This looks worse by the hour. Stahndala, okay? Fear. Oh, sometimes Bahl is so tired of Bahl. For being so useless."

With her newly clean hand, Sigrid patted mine. "Bahl," she said. "Tahtaksah." *Sad*. She reached for the Inuit picture book—the real one, not the kiddie version—pointed at a photo of a hunter standing next to a woman.

"Mother, father," I said in her language, then in English.

"Mother, father," she repeated in English.

"Very good, Sigrid. Great job."

She uncapped a red marker and crossed out their faces, then

their bodies. Her hand shook slightly, *Is she cold?* I held it briefly; it was warm but continued shaking. "Mother, father . . ."

"Dead," I whispered.

"Dead," she said, solemn faced. "Mother, father, dead." She pointed at herself, said, "Sigrid, dead."

"No," I said. "Sigrid is *alive*." I pointed to myself. "Val is *alive*."

"A*ligh*," she said.

"Yes, *alive*."

Gesturing at herself, she said, "Stahndala." *Afraid.* Then, slowly, "Sigrid dead a*ligh*." She indicated the baby in the photo, a small face peering out from a papoose strapped to the mother's back.

"Baby," I said.

"Baby," she said thoughtfully.

"Is baby dead alive, Sigrid?"

She looked at me soulfully, said, "Stahndala." *Afraid.* She slipped out of bed and padded out of the room, and I was worried I'd gone too far with my questions, but she appeared moments later with the crescent knife she'd stolen from Jeanne, the *ulu*. She placed it on the bedside table and got back in bed with me, facing me. She said, as far as I could understand, "Joy, Val, seals, many, love, want, joy." She smiled, eyes nearly closing above her high cheekbones, gleaming black hair cascading over her shoulders. She put her forehead on mine and breathed me in, and I breathed her in: Ivory soap, strawberry shampoo, a little-girl smell, snow. She pulled away, said again, "Joy, Val, seals, many, love, want, joy." It reminded me of an old Inuit saying, "May your life be rich in seals." *Is this what she was saying to me, a kind of blessing?*

Looking into her eyes, I said, "Joy, Sigrid, seals, many, love, want, joy." She smiled with intense pleasure and turned, backing her body up into mine, a tiny hot ball.

She was asleep in seconds.

twenty-seven

Jeanne bustled around me as I rinsed my coffee cup in the sink, her sweatshirt dusted with flour and powdered sugar. Dirty pots and pans teetered on the counter, an uncharacteristic disorder. Above us, a clattering of boots on the roof, muted laughter, a wolf whistle, the tinny twang of canned Jimmy Buffett. Nora's party was already in full swing at eleven in the morning, just before the break of "day." By four, it would be full dark.

"Sure I can't help, Jeanne?" I asked.

"You can grab those crackers and cheese," she said, lugging a six-pack of beer out the door.

"Got it," I said to her departing figure. The tray of crackers and steaming Velveeta cheese dip—which kept well perennially frozen, I was told—sat next to the block of ice, now covered by Raj's beautiful prayer rug. He must have placed it there sometime after we gave Sigrid her bath. I gently drew back the rug, now heavy with melt and stuck to the tacky surface, letting my fingers glide over the smooth cold surface that was thawing in gentle waves. Overnight, the block had shrunk to half its original size. Only inches remained between the child and the stuffy kitchen air. In places, the baby's body was clearer than ever: the tiny fingers, nails a dull gray, his wide, flat nose and cracks for nostrils, the eyebrows just a brush of fine black hair.

After checking on Sigrid—she'd shown little interest in getting out of bed that morning—I suited up and headed outdoors with the cheese dip, feeling like a waiter who'd forgotten where her section was. The sky was a soft faint lavender, the sun a yellow sheen at the horizon. The air felt raw but nothing like the usual blast of bitter misery. Nora's cry made me turn toward the distant beach. She was running away from us, looking back and laughing. Raj, jogging toward her, called out, *Go long!* He popped a toy-sized football from hand to hand, feinted a throw, then lobbed it hard. The ball sailed over her head. Nora howled something like *No fair!* as she sprinted toward the beach and open sea where icebergs yawed and swayed like ghost shipwrecks. She snagged the ball and kept on going until she was a dot, until Raj took up a fast trot toward her, imploring her to come back.

Wyatt strummed an unplugged electric guitar with a tuneless *dud-dud-dud-dud* as he belted out "Margaritaville" along with the CD player. Under his down vest, he wore a Hawaiian shirt that strained over long underwear, skullcap cockeyed on his head. A cigar consumed itself in a petri dish, smoke fading skyward. He sat on one of several blankets spread out over the metal roof, heels of his orange boots dug into the joinery to keep from sliding down. Palm trees fashioned out of paper towel rolls tufted with cleverly cut green paper for leaves had been taped haphazardly around the roof. Nearby, Jeanne struggled to balance a few glasses on a tray next to a bowl that contained exactly one orange, one lime, and a fake banana. A ladder led the way to the party.

Wyatt gestured magnanimously at the spread. "Join us, won't you? The water's fine."

Balancing my tray, I started up the ladder. Nora and Raj, arms slung around each other, made their way toward us across the pale expanse. I set the cheese next to the drinks tray. A bottle of tequila—

Where has that been hiding?—cozied up to a pitcher of Kool-Aid. I made myself a strong one.

"Jeanne and I here were just discussing what we missed the most about, I don't know, real life, whatever that is. Jeanne?"

"Cheese. Fresh milk. Cream," Jeanne said. "And French bread. Fresh crusty bread with real salted butter and jam in the morning. It would almost be worth going home for. Almost."

Wyatt plucked at the strings of his guitar, gazing off through his glacier glasses at the bergs, majestic as they floated in their ice kingdom. "For me," he said, "it's the smell of fresh-cut grass. And actual *trees*. The color *green*. That organic smell. Farm smell. Dirt, tomatoes hot on the vine."

Nora was chasing after Raj now, who had sprinted off to try to catch an errant fly ball. She tackled him, and they rolled a bit on the icy ground, laughing.

"Ah, young love," Wyatt said, flipping his glasses up on his head. "I remember the day. Sort of." He turned to Jeanne, who handed him a "margarita" and a chipped ceramic bowl of peanuts. He took the snacks and said, "Why, thank you, Jeanne, for arranging this lovely party. I'm sure Nora will remember it forever."

She said, "You're very welcome," as she arranged ham sandwiches and cups of tomato soup on a tray.

The football came crashing down between us, flipping the cheese tray. Hot Velveeta coagulated in the air and showered down in hard yellow droplets; tomato soup sprayed all around us, landing in gelatinous piles of gore.

"Whoa, sorry guys!" Nora came clambering up the ladder. "Sorry, Jeanne! Are you okay? Raj can't throw to save his life. Anyway, I think I won the game."

"Of course you did, it's your birthday!" Wyatt shoved some couch cushions in Nora's direction as she helped Jeanne clean up the mess. "Come on, have a seat."

Leaving Jeanne to it, Nora plopped down on the cushions, letting herself fall onto her back, releasing her arms out behind her with a rapturous sigh. "What a brilliant way to spend a birthday," she said as Raj scooted up next to her. "Sunbathing in the Arctic."

"I don't know about that," Raj said. "Sanjit got married this morning, remember?" He scrambled a beer from the six-pack.

"Oh, that's right!" Nora said, reaching out to stroke his back. "That must have been so beautiful. So sorry we couldn't be there."

Raj took a swig. "My brother married his longtime love today," he explained. "Couple hundred people dancing and eating for days. Incredible live music and singing. Lavish gifts. Thousands of flowers everywhere. You've been to one yourself, I think." He winked at Nora.

"You miss a lot on these assignments," Wyatt said. "Weddings, funerals, birthdays. Just the name of the game out here. Missing big family moments is something you have to live with."

Nora mixed herself a Kool-Aid margarita. "But you have to make sacrifices to get anywhere, especially for what we do. And we've collected a lot of great data, haven't we, Raj?" She sat up, tucking her knees tight to her body. "And now, this amazing thing is happening inside our kitchen, this miraculous moment is coming. . . ."

Raj put his arm around her, squeezed her shoulders. "Nora, take it easy."

She smiled, but shrank a bit from his touch. "Come on, Raj, think about it! Maybe it's not just *my* birthday today, you know?"

He shook his head and gazed out at the desolate horizon, his glasses reflecting the golden light like two more suns.

Nora said, "What good does it do to be negative? I've been praying for him. I've been praying for him since the second I saw him."

"So have I, love."

Jeanne appeared below us with a new tray of soup. Peanut butter sandwiches this time.

"Jeanne, you are incredible, and I'm a klutz," Nora said. "Thank you for this beautiful spread."

"No worries," she said.

Raj and I jumped up to grab the tray out of Jeanne's hands so she could climb the ladder.

Wyatt watched the proceedings with a kingly air. "I see no reason why we shouldn't all be hopeful. It happened once. It can happen again. I've got some new data, from blood work, from Sigrid and Odin, too, that's taking me in a new direction with my research. I feel like I'm *this close* to the answer, you know?" He took another swig from his jelly jar. "Like"—he swept his hand across the boundless vista—"all this was meant to be. Fate. Us. All of us. Sitting on this roof, just like this, in the middle of nowhere, on the cusp of something so remarkable, so life changing. *World* changing. Friggin' teamwork, man, that's what it's all about, right, Jeanne?"

She chuckled and clicked the top off a beer, sat down for a rare break. "Whatever you say, Wyatt."

"All I know is, that ice in the kitchen is melting fast. I'd say eight, nine hours tops. We're going to have to be paying attention." He turned his beneficence in my direction. "So tell us, Val, how's the young lady doing this morning?"

I washed down a bite of dry peanut butter sandwich with my margarita, said, "She's got a bad headache, I think. Otherwise she's better. No fever."

"Could have sworn I heard you two talking last night," Jeanne said. "You guys making progress?"

I swirled my drink in my cup. "Here and there. I was listening to recordings. Old Norse, West Greenlandic. Dialects. That sort of thing."

Wyatt set his guitar aside. Picked up the tequila bottle and had a taste. "You seem like best buds to me these days. No new words to report?"

Heat flushed up my neck, sweat gathering at my hairline under my hat. "No, sorry to say."

"Well, *there's* a terrible shame, don't you think? For me, for you"—he swung the bottle around—"for all of us. I get it, Val. You're putting the time in, but— Hey, you know, doesn't matter. Because—that little boy in the kitchen? He's the missing piece, as far as I'm concerned."

"I'm going to go check on Sigrid," I said.

Nora said, "I'll come with you."

As I bent to pick up a plate, I glanced down at the hummock of snow where Andy had been found. He lay in the fetal position, dressed in the tuxedo he wore to my wedding, his bare feet black with frostbite.

I blinked, and he was gone; just elongated shadows marked the place his body had been.

THE LUMP UNDER the blankets didn't move. In the air, an acidic, greasy tang. Nora walked around the bed, knelt down to a small, glistening pile.

"Looks like the poor thing's been sick."

"Oh no." I gently folded the covers back; Sigrid yanked them over her head with a growl.

Nora went to the kitchen, returned with a wet towel, and got busy cleaning up the mess. "That was you talking last night, wasn't it?"

"Yes," I said, relieved to spill the truth. "Last night she completely turned around with me, Nora. She wanted to communicate. She learned a couple dozen words, easily! And concepts, too, because language is learned in chunks. It's how a toddler learns."

"That's brilliant, Val."

"But why now? I can't stop wondering. Why did it take weeks for her to open up?"

Nora shrugged. "Maybe she realizes her family really is all gone. You're it for her now."

Why hadn't that occurred to me? Maybe Sigrid *had* been hanging on to the fantasy that her family would be found alive, but seeing them mortally wounded under the ice put an end to that.

Nora sat next to me on the bed and inhaled deeply. "She smells so good now. I almost miss my stinky girl."

I laughed. "No, you don't."

"It's great she's making progress."

"Look, Nora, you've got to keep this on the down low, okay? That she's finally talking to me?"

Jeanne rapped on the open door, startling us. "Hey, birthday girl," she said to Nora, unsmiling. "Mind going outside to wait for your cake?" Not waiting for an answer, she disappeared from view.

FROM BEYOND THE open door, peals of laughter from Wyatt mingled with the muffled sounds of Nora and Raj talking. Jeanne rifled through a drawer next to a tall, round cake festooned with swirls of canned chocolate frosting, extracting a beat-up box of birthday candles and matches.

"You have *birthday candles* here?"

"People have birthdays in the Arctic. We did it up for Andy last spring." She poked half a dozen candles in a circle on the cake. "Mine was last week."

"Why didn't you tell us?"

She waved me away, concentrating on her decorations. "Never liked my birthday. Happens to fall on a really bad anniversary, if you want the truth about it. Wyatt never remembers it anyway."

I opened the door wide in preparation to march outside with the cake. The thunk of the football on the roof, another bout of laughter from the party.

Jeanne struck a match and lit the first candle; the flame glowed against the rough skin of her hand. She lit the next one before her match burned out.

Wyatt spoke in a stage whisper. "Well, you'd think that after a year with just my fist I'd screw anything . . ."

The wick of the third candle sputtered and drew the match's flame, igniting. Her hand shaking slightly, Jeanne moved to the next one.

". . . and then I think, well, Jeanne's not *that* bad . . . I mean, she is female, after all . . ."

The fourth wick caught, but the match was used up. Something clattered on the roof, a plate or silverware, maybe. A bitter gust shunted down into the kitchen from the open door, sucking all warmth from the room. Jeanne struck another match.

". . . but the same thing always happens. I have a really good look at her, and I'm back to my fist."

Jeanne's hand shook badly now, the match's flame not catching at the wick for the longest time until it singed her flesh as she lit the final candle. She threw the match in the sink, where it sizzled on a gob of frosting.

"Ready?" she said, meeting my eye, her face so tired-looking, so pinched and hard and sad, before picking up the cake and starting for the door. I felt punched in the gut—as if he'd been talking about me instead of Jeanne—but cleared my throat to try to belt out my best "Happy Birthday."

twenty-eight

I t was just past four o'clock in the morning. Under blinking fluorescent lights, we all crowded around the industrial sink, bleary-eyed and thrumming with energy. The baby, with his inscrutable smile, soft rise of belly, and fat-dimpled knees, rested in a shallow lake of warm water. Though stiff as a porcelain statue, he had nearly melted free of his ice block. Only a millimeter-thick coat of ice remained on his body, as if he had been dipped in glass or varnished to a high glaze. From the picture window, the black polar night gazed down on us, fat-mooned, clear, windless, stars sparking with their unspeakable knowing. Sigrid, hair mussed with sleep, stood on a chair next to me clutching the rim of the sink. We were all silent; the mood was reverent.

We'd prepared the defibrillator, dialed down to its lowest charge; the syringes of atropine and adrenaline filled to the proper dosage placed side by side; cloths and blankets set out. But like any birth, there came the time when all anybody could do was wait. For several more hours we'd done just that, sleeping sitting up in chairs, or our heads resting on folded arms on the table, until Wyatt nudged us awake.

We gathered at the basin in such quietude the air seemed to vibrate. Raj, face haggard, broke away from the group, wandering into the living room. Instinctively, we closed ranks tight around the baby, listening to Raj pray, a low muttering chant. Wyatt looked annoyed by his departure, and at some level it bothered me, too. It was as if the baby needed all of our energy in the room in real time to live.

"Okay, let's get started," Wyatt said. "Like we talked about."

I was the first to touch him. I was terrified but slid my hands into the lukewarm water and under his tiny buttocks and shoulder blades as instructed and held him. His skin softened slightly at my touch as I gently settled him back down. Jeanne carefully poured more warm water into the tub as Nora, cooing, massaged his shoulders, arms, and fingers, cracking off what was now just a patina of ice from his tender baby flesh. The rag that had partially covered him, perhaps the remains of some ancient diaper, disintegrated in our hands like slimy brown seaweed; we wiped it off him with a clean cloth and dropped the remnants in a bowl. A whiff of wet leather, iron, stones, an earthy tang. Wyatt, in wonder, stroked the baby's face, massaging him where flashes of ice held on stubbornly—under his fingernails and behind his ears.

"Jeanne, are you ready to turn him? We'll need to clear his lungs."

"I can turn him," Nora said.

"No," he said gruffly. "Stick to the plan we agreed on. Val, you with us?"

"I'm here," I said.

Raj's prayers grew louder, more insistent.

"Raj, get in here, man!"

Clearing his throat wetly, Raj quieted and came to stand between Nora and me.

Using a coffee cup, Nora scooped warm water from the basin and dripped it over the baby's forehead, kneading the thawing wisps of black hair.

"What do you need me to do?" Raj said.

"Give him some love," Wyatt said. "Like we talked about."

With his long, graceful fingers, Raj reached into the sink and stroked the child's stomach; it seemed to give at his touch, a pearl of ice escaping from the wink of his belly button. I rubbed my thumb along the child's nose and across his forehead. Flecks of ice slid off his fat cheeks, dissolving in the bathwater.

His flesh had real give now, though it was still so terribly cold. Nora tenderly laid her thumbs on the two petite frozen ponds over his eyes; in moments they slid away. Only a small cap of ice covered his slightly parted lips. With the handle of a knife, Wyatt tapped at the clear chunk; it broke up, and he brushed it away. He dislodged the ice plugs at the baby's nostrils with a toothpick. Reached into his mouth, swiped it with his little finger. The baby's jaw dropped down—we all gasped—Wyatt held it open and peered down his throat with a flashlight.

"His throat is clear."

Supporting his head, Wyatt lifted the baby out of the water, which coursed off his little body, splashing down into the tub. His tiny shoulders slumped, his arms and legs hanging limply while his open eyes seemed to gaze into mine. Hurriedly, Jeanne drained the sink, plugged it and poured in a fresh round. Wyatt gently laid the baby back down in the new bathwater.

"Come on, guys, it's time," he said. "Jeanne, take him."

Jeanne took a step back, hands dripping onto the tiles. She looked momentarily stunned.

"*Jeanne.*"

She snapped out of it, reached in, and lifted up the child. One foot resting on a chair, she swiftly and carefully turned him over so he lay facedown along her arm, which rested on her thigh. With the heel of her hand, she rapped him on his back. His arms juddered forward with the force of her blow.

He lay motionless as if he had fallen from a great height, his flesh glistening in the glare. She gave him another firm rap. Nothing.

"Again, Jeanne, come *on*!"

She clapped him a third time, a fourth; we all leaned toward them, listening for the cough, the grab for breath, the miraculous cry. She rapped at the space between his shoulder blades three more times in quick succession. Each time his body jumped at her touch, then stilled. I had to remind myself to breathe. Sigrid, her face solemn, broke away from the scene, drifting into the living room where she sat on the floor with her drawing supplies. We all felt the loss of her spirit in the room.

"Bring him here," Wyatt said. Jeanne settled him on his back on a bed of towels piled on the kitchen table. He tilted the baby's head back, dropped his ear close to his mouth. Shook his head, face dark. "Nora, ready?"

She nodded, positioning herself at the baby's head. With two fingers, Wyatt pushed rapidly down on the baby's chest, pausing for Nora as she put her mouth over the baby's nose and mouth and exhaled two short breaths. Each time, the little chest rose and fell. He looked like a doll, his skin losing, not gaining color.

"Raj, the injections."

Raj flicked the needle and a drop rolled out. Wyatt stopped the CPR, and Nora stood back, the baby limp on his cradle of towels. Raj lay the needle alongside the baby's chest. Angled it down and punctured the skin, injecting into the child's heart.

We waited.

No sound, no movement.

Unbearable stillness.

Nora cried out but covered her mouth. Regained her composure. The silence in the room rushed back, much more terrible than her cry.

"Jeanne," Wyatt said. "Come on, get him ready."

She brought over two small pads that had been cut down from the adult size, and spaced them diagonally across his tiny chest. Wyatt flipped on the machine, said, "Stand back."

We did.

His small frame bucked with the shock.

Wyatt checked for signs of life.

Nothing.

Another shock. A third.

"Nora, *let's go*!"

Eyes shining, Nora tilted the baby's head back and blew into him. I felt numb, outside my body, as if I were watching from an enormous distance. Helpless. I thought of Sigrid's small body enduring all of this, but there she was, doodling on the sketch pad on the living room floor.

After three more rounds of compressions and rescue breathing, the baby lay inert on his pallet of towels.

Jeanne readied the defibrillator and zapped his little body once, twice, three times, checking for breathing or a heartbeat at every turn. Wyatt stood undeterred, pads in hand, ready for a fourth round.

Raj staggered a step back from the table, sweat slicking his forehead as if he'd been running laps. "He's gone. Let's stop this."

Wyatt shocked the child, checked for signs, peeled off the pads, and turned to Raj.

"Nothing's different than what we did last time. This is what it takes. Another injection, let's go."

"No, man, it's been eleven minutes. Nearly twelve. I'm not—"

Wyatt lunged for the needle and bottle of adrenaline, sucked up the fluid and injected the child again, deep into his heart. No reaction.

"Nora, come on, the CPR."

"But, Wyatt, nothing's . . ." She turned away and stumbled out of the kitchen. Raj followed her, wrapped his arms around her.

"His lungs are clear!" Wyatt roared. Nobody moved. "Are you all fucking insane? Jeanne, help me."

Jeanne dutifully tilted the child's head back. For close to five more minutes, they tried to pump his heart alive, to breathe life into that tiny body, into lungs that rose and fell with Jeanne's breath. But there was no independent movement, no pulse, no heartbeat.

Finally, the counting stopped.

No child's cries. No exultations. No miracles.

Nora extracted herself from Raj's embrace and lurched back to the kitchen. The baby lay still on his dais of towels, elfin arms splayed back, perfect hands and fingers fixed in a gentle curl. Wyatt and Jeanne had turned their backs to him, conferring in a huddle by the sink, as if they couldn't bear the sight.

Nora went to the baby, who was bathed in moonglow. Cradling his head, she gathered him up and swaddled him in a towel.

"Wyatt, please, you did it with *her*." Nodding in Sigrid's direction, she stroked his fine black hair, jounced the baby as if comforting him. "Why couldn't you make it work for him? You told us you knew what you were doing." Her voice broke into a choking sob.

"Nora, please." He faced away from her, leaning heavily on the sink. "We're all disappointed."

"*Disappointed?*" she cried with reddened eyes. She bounced the baby harder. His head lolled back horribly; she held him tighter. "I'm *disappointed* when my train's late. When I don't get any birthday cards. When my hairdresser fucks up my hair. I'm holding a dead baby. *Disappointed . . .*" She paced. "You're the one who said you knew how. You're the one who said he would *live*—"

"Guess you weren't listening very well, Nora. That wasn't—"

Raj approached her, reached out for her. "Come on, darling—"

She spun away from him and marched over to Wyatt, who now sat slumped in a kitchen chair, elbows planted on his knees, big hands hanging down uselessly. "You *knew* he was dead, didn't you?"

"You need to calm down." He stared at the floor. "Take care of your woman, Raj."

Cursing Wyatt, Raj once again reached out for Nora. "Babe, come on, just take a breath—"

"Don't touch me." She backed up against the far wall under the hanging pots and pans, eyes flashing in the dimness. Held her nose to the baby's head and inhaled his scent. "Oh, God, why does he smell so good? That shouldn't be. He smells like he's alive. I just can't believe that he's . . . Are you sure he's gone?"

Raj got a little closer. She allowed it. Sigrid shoved aside her drawing and wandered into the kitchen to Nora's side.

"He's dead, sweetheart," Raj said. "He died seven hundred years ago."

Rocking him in her arms, Nora collapsed into the child, sobbing. Her grief pushed everything else from the room. Sigrid stretched upward and wrapped her arms around Nora's waist. Momentarily startled out of her hell, Nora reached down and stroked Sigrid's hair.

With a groan, Wyatt got to his feet, face pallid in the bleak light, beard scraggly and unkempt. He held his arms out to Nora. "Give him to me."

"Go fuck yourself."

"Come on, it's time to . . . to take care of him."

She gripped the baby tighter, broke away from Sigrid, and darted into the living room. "Oh, no. You've had your chance with him. You're not fit to touch him again."

Wyatt followed her in his awkward, yet eerily fast, stocking-footed gait. "Look, you're exhausted. I'm exhausted. We're all wiped out. Nobody wanted this to happen. But the reality is, he's gone, and we've got to—"

The whites of her eyes shone. "What are you going to do with him?"

"Learn from him."

"What, you're going to *cut him up*?"

"He's dead, Nora. Maybe . . . if I take some samples, I can understand why Sigrid lived and he didn't. Find out what he ate, how he lived . . ."

"You knew there was no hope. You just wanted his body."

Wyatt reached out again; she slapped him away.

"You keep your filthy hands off this baby—"

His face turned hard. "Nora, do you know how many people froze to death in an ice wind off the Oregon coast yesterday?" he hissed. "*Fifty-seven.* Fifty-seven people who—if they'd had access to whatever protected Sigrid—would be alive right now. And you—*a fellow scientist*—stand there telling me to look away, to *squander* clues that are literally in our lap?"

Raj stepped between them. "Let's . . . let's calm down. Why don't we take the baby to the Dome for the night? Get some sleep. Talk in the morning."

"Fine," Wyatt said. "But the baby stays here. In fact, it's too late to go to the Dome. No one's going anywhere tonight."

twenty-nine

I n the dream, I stood on the ice lake, a fine snow falling like silt all around me. Just beyond the orange toes of my boot, where the polished rings had been, a cavernous hole gaped. At the bottom of the pit, bodies lay scattered just as they had when beneath the ice, the now-soft snow beneath them soaked in blood. Moaning echoed from shadowy corners. Here and there, the twitch of an arm, the rasp of breath in ancient lungs. A woman dragged herself free and staggered to her feet, eyes wild the moment she caught sight of me. Clawing at the ice wall, she cried, *My baby, where is my baby?* I wanted to tell her how sorry I was, that we should have left her child in peace, but couldn't open my mouth to speak. With a scream, she lunged at my ankles. Jagged ice tore at my face as I tumbled into the pit.

I JOLTED AWAKE, the laminated dive instructions I'd used to fall asleep cutting into my cheek. In disgust, I tossed the sheet on the floor. The room was infused with gauzy gray light. It was eight o'clock in the morning, only two hours since we'd gone to bed.

I rolled over, expecting to find Sigrid buried in her usual pile of pillows, but I was alone. Maybe she was getting something to eat; maybe she couldn't sleep. Quite possibly she missed her refuge under her own bed and had retreated there. Exhaustion steamrolled over me; every cell in my body cried out for rest.

So go back to sleep, I told myself.

But I couldn't.

Something felt off.

I slipped on my clothes and padded down the hall. My stomach dropped at the idea of going into the kitchen. The night before, after we'd all agreed to do nothing with the baby for the moment, Wyatt suggested putting him in the refrigerator, which caused Nora another round of hysteria. The compromise was to leave him where he was for the night: on the kitchen table, covered by a towel. As I shuffled into the kitchen, I couldn't bring myself to look at him, even concealed, so kept my eyes averted from the table as I made my coffee, then settled on the couch near the picture window.

Eyes glazed with fatigue, I scanned the snowfield, luminous under turquoise skies. *What was that?* Something was advancing, slowly, steadily down to the brash ice at the shore. Hot coffee lingered in my throat, burning me. I swallowed, slamming the cup down. Bolted to the window. The red dot bobbed along, the only movement on the icy slope.

Sigrid.

What the hell was she doing?

I whipped around, scouring the kitchen. Yelped.

The baby was gone. Even the towels were gone.

I glanced back out the window. Sigrid was a red speck now. I suited up fast and woke Nora and Raj as quietly as I could.

WE PLUNGED THROUGH the violet half-light, the snow oddly soft under our boots. Even as I ran, I wondered, *What is different?* I whipped off my hat and stuffed it in the pocket of my parka, real-izing I was too warm with it on. The air felt above freezing, full of moisture, even with the strong wind bearing down off the glacier. Our boots sank to our ankles in the snowpack.

Massive bergs floated on the horizon, an eerie Arctic skyline. My ears rang as distant blocks split and calved, exploding in the swells. Closer to us, along the beach, several dozen walruses dozed, a wide brown wedge along the line of foaming surf.

We called out to Sigrid. She ignored us. In the middle distance, she paused at a small, dun-colored lump, knelt down briefly as if to examine it, then tore off again toward the beach. Nora and Raj approached it, slowed, stopped.

From a few yards away, I realized it was a baby walrus, pulling itself along by its flippers, its old-man mustached face low to the ice; leathery wrinkled skin shuddering at our approach. It whimpered softly as if in pain. I ventured a few steps closer.

"Val, stay back," Nora said. "He's probably sick."

Sigrid stopped at a relatively calm stretch of beach. Just beyond her, waves broke in a slurry of foam over chunks of ice that ground against one another with raucous squeaks and groans. Permeating the air, an overpowering fish smell from the walrus herd.

Exchanging looks, we slowed as we approached so as not to spook her. Finally, she turned to look at us. Nora uttered a little gasp. Sig-rid had blackened the area around her eyes—she must have used the charcoal pencils from my box of markers and crayons. Her droopy eye looked terrible, its inflammation emphasized by the black.

"Tahtaksah," she said. *Sad*. "Baby dead."

She removed the knapsack—mine, I now realized—and laid it gently on a scattering of ice-glazed pebbles. Kneeling, she loosened the drawstring of the main compartment and eased out the towel-swathed body of the little boy. He wore a pink doll's hat from one of the dolls she'd never played with.

Raj got down to help her, but she pushed him away. He held up his hands in defense, said, "Okay, Sigrid. Okay."

"Don't take it personally," I said. "Women are the last to touch a body in her culture."

Several yards from us, a thousand-pound bull walrus grunted and barked, eyes bulging from his regal head. He jacked himself up on his front flippers, broke from his herd, and began to waddle toward us, his bulk rolling and quaking.

"Keep your voice down," Nora whispered. "You don't want to startle them. Any loud noise and they'll charge."

I nodded. The animal paused, lowering his great muzzle to the snow as if to size up the level of threat, before wrenching his colossal bulk back in the direction of the brood.

Stumbling slightly, Sigrid made her way to the nearest floe and lay the baby down facing the great purple dome of sky. Even as she retreated from the beach, a wave, lead-colored and syrupy with cold, skulked under the berg, lifting and sucking it back among its brethren. In his pale green towel and pink hat, the child looked like a doll that had fallen from the sky. In seconds, a stronger, angrier wave lifted and swept him out several dozen yards. No one could reach him now. We all stepped back as though the ocean might take us, too.

On his floe, the baby drifted and twirled, bobbing with the ebb and flow of the swell until, one last time, he dipped down and out of sight, and all was a wash of blue and white again.

Without a word, Sigrid trudged toward the baby walrus, which had stopped moving. We rushed to join her there. It had rolled onto its side, closed eyes black slits, mud-colored flesh motionless under a dusting of fresh snow.

Sigrid dropped to her knees, excavated her crescent knife from deep inside her parka, and without hesitation sliced open the walrus's belly. I think we were all too stunned to come near; we only watched as she plunged her bare hands into the steaming cavity and removed the purple slab of liver, tossing it onto the snow. Shrieking, an Arctic tern shot down out of the sky and snatched it up, flying away with his prize. While a dozen more circled above, screaming and caw-ing with excitement, she cut into the stomach, withdrawing several blood-slicked pieces of plastic: a toothpaste cap, a tampon inserter, cellophane sandwich wrapping, a length of tangled dental floss, and last of all, a tiny troll, the size of a toy in a kid's fast-food lunch. This she took and wiped clean in the snow, peering with fascination at its buggy eyes and bubble-gum-pink hair before pocketing it.

While we adults stood silently, she cut deeper into the walrus's abdomen, carving out chunks of meat and blubber and throwing them onto the snow. The big birds folded their wings like fans and plummeted from the sky, diving at the entrails, screeching as they carried long strings up and away. Sigrid took off her parka. In no time, most of the meat was gone, until—in a battle for the last shred—three birds dive-bombed at once. An explosion of feathers, beaks, claws. They fought one another so viciously they paid no at-tention to Sigrid as she pounced over them using her coat as a net. Two escaped easily, but the third struggled under the parka, its beak caught up somehow in her sleeve. She lay on top of it and reached down under the hood; the snap of its neck a dull reality.

We all exhaled, none of us with a clue as to what she might do next. Very sweetly, with imploring, blackened eyes and blood-slippery hands, she held out the dead bird to me, said, "Sigrid want bird."

I knelt, eye to eye with her and the limp creature in her arms. There was no mistaking her pride and satisfaction. "You finally got your bird, Sigrid. Verohnsaht." *Joy.*

She said, "Sigrid want sahndaluuk." She looked from Nora to Raj and back to me. *"Sahndaluuk."*

"The drawings," Nora said. "Of the snakes and birds. I just thought of something. Let's go to the Dome, and I'll show you."

thirty

Sigrid crouched on the floor of the Dome with the dead tern. Charcoal-saddened eyes intent, she studiously severed one of its wings. Picking two of the hollow, straw-like feathers clean, she sliced one of them on the diagonal, creating a sharp point, inserting the thinner feather into the larger one, like a plunger.

Nora pulled down several glossy magazines from a high shelf wired to the struts of the Dome. On the cover of *Marine Invertebrates*, an octopus wrapped its many arms around a barnacle-encrusted anchor. She flipped the magazine open to a spread featuring different kinds of eels. Brought it to Sigrid.

"Here, sweetheart. Have a look at this."

Crying out excitedly, Sigrid dropped the feathers and wrested the magazine from Nora's grip. She pointed to one of the eels.

"That's an ice eel," Raj said.

Sigrid ran to me with the magazine, jabbing at the eel and talking fast.

I said, "*Sahndaluuk?*"

Yes, she nodded. *Yesyesyes.*

Of course, the word meant "eel"!

"They're not as common as they used to be," Nora said. "But—Raj, we haven't sorted through yesterday's specimen bucket."

Raj hauled a sloshing plastic bucket from the far end of the Dome and the diving hole to where we were gathered on the fur-covered chairs under the heater. "We drag for specimens every day," he said. "This was at ten meters down."

Sigrid peered into the bucket. In the frigid seawater wriggled a baby octopus, a bright orange-and-black jellyfish, several small slender fish, and a nearly transparent eel about a foot long. "Bahl," she said, pointing at it.

"Get it out of the bucket, Raj, can you?" I said.

He reached in with a sieve-like tool. The eel squirmed in the contraption, seeking an exit. "Looks like a juvenile, nearly dead, I'm afraid." He lay the sieve on the floor; the eel zigzagged out onto the ice, looking much more alive than it had appeared in the bucket.

Sigrid brought her knife down, slicing its head off neatly. As black blood spurted from the headless creature, Sigrid held the tip of her hollow, sharpened feather at the artery, where lines of blood mapped the eel's translucent length. She shoved the sleeve of her parka up her arm and inserted the sharp tip into the crook of her elbow, working the tapered feather into the larger one, injecting herself until what little eel blood the feather held was gone. Uttering something unintelligible, she stumbled a few paces, then scrambled along the ice as she tried to catch the eel. Even headless, it wriggled with eerie vitality, its blood quickly draining out. Practically transparent except for its black veins, it nearly disappeared where it lay on the ice, lifeless.

"My God, that's what she's been asking us for all this time," I said. "A bird and an eel, not a snake. Not seaweed."

Sigrid scrambled to her feet and grabbed my pants, resting her weight against me. "*Sahndaluuk*," she moaned.

"Are there any more?"

Nora dumped the bucket over; the contents sluiced out. The little octopus rippled across the ice, sliding into the diving hole with a plop. Raj nudged the rest of the fish into the opening with the toe of his boot, but there were no more eels.

Stricken, Sigrid squatted at the edge of the hole, said, "Sigrid ice alive." As if coming to terms with the fact of just the one eel, she wandered back to me and held out her arms. *"Taimagiakaman."*

"What is she saying?" Raj asked.

I lifted her onto my lap; she collapsed into me, the black kohl from her eyes smudging into the orange of my parka. "It's an Inuit word that means the necessity of staying alive through knowledge of the natural world. That means all traditional wisdom—the caribou migration patterns, where the good fishing holes are, and for her, surviving the ice winds by injecting blood from this eel." Sigrid burrowed into me, moaning the word for *eel* over and over. "But look at her. This one eel—it can't be enough. How can we get more?"

"They used to be everywhere. Very common species." Nora knelt next to us, stroking Sigrid's hair. "But the climate's probably pushed them farther north. They need very cold water to survive. They used to hang out just under the ice, but now?" She turned to Raj. "What do you think? Could be they're near the ocean floor."

"We don't have the equipment to dive that deep," Raj said, taking a seat on the upturned bucket.

"But maybe . . . the traps," Nora said. "We could drop them much deeper, to the seabed."

"We'd have to dive down and anchor them." He shook his head as if to say, *Not a good idea.*

Sigrid excavated from the pocket of her parka a balled-up piece of paper, took my hand and wrapped my fingers around it.

"What's this, Sigrid?" I smoothed the picture out over my knee.

"She was drawing that last night," Raj said. "While we were with the baby."

I could make out a rough depiction of two sets of people, barely more than stick figures, facing each other and holding arrows. A child's rendition of what we'd all seen in the flesh from the surface of the ice lake. Between the two groups she'd drawn a vertical line, dividing them.

"Sigrid, are you in this picture somewhere?" I pointed at the drawing. "Where is Sigrid?"

She put her finger on a diminutive figure in the crowd on the left side. "Sigrid," she said softly.

I traced my finger across the figures near her, on the left side of the vertical line. "Is this your village? Your family? *Mother, father?*"

She nodded.

"And the baby? Where is the *baby* in the picture, Sigrid?"

She moved her finger to an oval shape near the feet of the people on the right side of the picture. A look like shame passed over her face, and she snatched the sketch from me.

"What, Sigrid?"

I stretched out my arm toward the drawing. "Sigrid? Please?"

With a good deal of reluctance, she handed it back, resting her finger on a squiggly shape just above the drawing of herself. The same snakelike image she'd been churning out for weeks. An ice eel.

"So your family, *you, Sigrid,* and your mother, father, here," I said, touching the people to the left of the line, "had the ice eels, had *sahndaluuk,* but these people"—I ran my fingers over the stick-drawn figures on the right, "had no *sahndaluuk?*"

"Tahtaksah." *Sad.* "No ice alive."

"Good God," Raj said. "People were killing each other for these eels."

Nora sat down heavily next to us, head in her hands. "And the other village didn't have the eels, which is why the baby died in the ice wind, and why we couldn't revive him."

Raj flipped through the magazine to the spread featuring eels of the Arctic. "Maybe there was some secret about where the ice eels were, or how to get them," he said. "Maybe they were scarce and people were fighting over that knowledge."

I turned Sigrid's face to mine. Already her eye was drooping less severely. I said, "Ice alive. *Tukisilitainnaqtuq*." The word meant "the sensation of seeing or understanding a thing for the very first time."

Smiling, she repeated the word back to me. My heart fell open. Here was another loanword, an expression from her language that had persisted across all these centuries.

Raj took the drawing and flattened it on the specimen table. "I never would have believed this if I hadn't seen it with my own eyes. I mean, look at her. She's shaking less, her color's better. And her eye . . . It's incredible."

Sigrid slid off my lap, went to the table, and turned her drawing over. Drew two circles. Scribbled over the second one and handed it to me.

I said, "She has two days, maybe just one."

The walkie-talkie on the table crackled to life. Wyatt's voice was low and raw. "You need to get your asses back here right now."

We all looked at one another.

"Fuck him," Raj said. "Nora and me—we're going to get cracking on these traps. Figure out how to get them as far down as we can."

A surge of hope rang through my body as I suited up to head back to the Shack, a sense of being so much less alone, so much closer to understanding how to save Sigrid. I prayed she felt this as well, but all kinds of exhaustion had flooded back into her face, and her hand felt limp and lifeless in mine as we made our way across the ice.

thirty-one

In the spectral gloom of the Arctic twilight, Wyatt sat hunched over his desk, the beam of his headlamp lasering a spotlight into Odin's dissected body. Paws pinned in four directions on a rubber mat, the mouse lay spread-eagled on his back, his tiny intestines piled in a glossy knot.

I slipped off my parka. Sigrid took one look at Wyatt and the dead mouse and vanished down the hall, slamming the door of my room behind her.

"You let this happen," Wyatt said, not looking up from his project.

I dropped down on the couch and took off my boots. "She was already at the beach by the time I noticed she was gone—"

"You're telling me you couldn't catch up with an eight-year-old?" He spun around; I squinted into the burning light. "Why couldn't you bring the body back?"

Beyond him, framed by the window, mountainous bergs limned in black shadow loomed in the bay. I pictured the tiny boy, a dash of pink and green floating in an incomprehensible Enormity, under towering ice arches, past bergs shaped like mosques, dragons, monsters, gods.

"It was impossible. She'd already put him on the floe."

"I see."

He kept the blinding light in my face until I dropped my gaze down toward the ratty braided rug, rubbing my hands together. Warmth melted into my fingers. "It's what she wanted to do, Wyatt."

He turned back to his work. With a needle-nose tweezer, he extruded something gristly from the body cavity, draped it over a slide. "Like that's some sort of respectful burial. Some polar bear's having himself a tasty snack right about now, I'll bet."

"She did what was traditional in her culture." My shoulders slumped. Fatigue pummeled me. "I'm going to get some sleep."

"Where are the lovebirds?"

"They've got things to do. What happened to Odin?"

He flipped the light up on his head, rubbed his eyes. "He died last night. Must have happened while we were busy with the boy."

"He wasn't looking too well, I noticed."

Wyatt pulled off his headlamp and tossed it on the desk. "His eye was drooping and he was starting to stumble around, starting to get clumsy. He was just a fucking mouse but he was my pet, too. Loved the little guy."

What was I supposed to say—*sorry for your loss*? I gathered myself to leave. In full view were contents of his small refrigerator; slides and test tubes covered every available space. For the first time I noticed the slides weren't just labeled by content. A few had been turned over, revealing a date scrawled on a piece of masking tape attached to the other side.

The door burst open; Jeanne blustered through. "You ready to head out?"

"Give me a minute," he said.

"What's going on?" I asked.

"Something's wacko with the weather equipment," Jeanne said. "We got some real weird readings, these really high temps. I mean crazy high. Then no readings at all." She poured herself a glass of juice and knocked it back. "I think a bear took it down, but I don't know. We've got to check it out."

"Yeah, haven't you noticed?" Wyatt said. "It must be forty degrees out there. And it's gone up a few degrees just in the past hour. Something screwy is going on." Quickly he assembled the slides and tubes back into the fridge and began suiting up, signing off in the log with a flourish. "We might be a while. I wouldn't wait up."

I nearly crawled back to my room, the lack of sleep finally taking over. Sigrid, still in her hat and parka, sat in bed surrounded by drawing pads and books on ancient Greenlandic cultures. She moved over to let me in. Took my hand—ravaged by eczema—and turned it over in hers. From the pocket of her parka, she removed a fist-sized gray cube of walrus blubber she'd secreted away and warmed it between her palms. Chanting "Bahl" in her singsongy way, she rubbed the cube into the skin of my hands, wrists, and forearms. The smell wasn't bad, like almonds or walnuts. The heat of my skin released a thin sheen of oil from the cube.

"Sigrid, thank you."

She kept swirling the slab of blubber over my skin, happily jabbering away.

"Verohnsaht," I said. *Happy*. "But, Sigrid." I stayed her hand, lifting up her chin to look at me, her floppy wool hat half obscuring her eyes. "Stahndala." *I'm afraid.*

I took the block of cool, greasy fat from her, set it on the night table. Her face was wiped clean of the charcoal, but her eye drooped again, worse than ever. She wore a look of indelible sadness, as if she knew she was going to die, that it was simply too late. It devastated me.

"Where are the ice eels, Sigrid?" With a Sharpie I drew my best ice eel on the sketch pad. "You must know. Your family knew. That's why you're alive. *Ice alive.*"

I drew two circles. The second I crossed out with a red marker until she stilled my hand. Her movements slow and deliberate, she tore off a clean sheet of paper. The perspective flat but recognizable, she traced the particular outline of the mountain range, the pass where the tongue of the glacier poured through, and the glacial lake where she'd been found, a zigzag line for the crevasse. She looked up at me, eyes pleading, *Do you understand?*

"Yes, I know what you're drawing. Keep going, Sigrid."

She traced smaller circles—*footprints?*—stepping off the ice lake and marching over what looked like another mountain range. Flipped the paper over and carefully sketched more footsteps as if this was a continuation of her map. Then she began to lose me. She drew three piles of flattened circles, connecting them with lines. From the last cluster of circles, she drew her little tracks to a set of waves—a beach?—and with great concentration, a pile of ice eels.

"What are these, Sigrid?" I pointed to the piles of squashed circles. She gazed up at me as if to say, *How much more do I have to explain to you?* She looked so weary. I flipped through the Greenland book to the thick section of photographs in the middle. We pored over pages and pages of them. Engraved onto whalebone: elaborate drawings of whale hunts, teams of sled dogs sledging, snow shelters, a caribou shedding the velvet from its antlers for winter.

On the last page of photographs, Sigrid slammed her hand down, yelped with excitement. She yanked the book from me, pointing to a picture of cairns. *Inuksuit.* Ominous-looking piles of rocks, seven, ten feet high, created as graves or to mark good hunting grounds. Sometimes vaguely in the shape of humans, often used as silent messengers. The stones might be arranged to warn of thin ice, or to frighten caribou in the direction of hunters. These were decorated with seagull wings, bone, or long strands of seaweed that blew in the wind, a kind of scarecrow. I imagined ribs and antlers clicking and clacking against one another in an otherwise soundless landscape.

I struggled to understand how Sigrid's three cairns were related to one another, *Why can't I just go straight to the ice eels that—according to her drawing—are at a beach?* And what about distances? We couldn't seem to get anywhere with how close the cairns were to one another, much less how far away the eels were.

We both had to give up on it after a while: I was loath to end on a note of frustration after all her valiant efforts, but she could barely keep her eyes open. I folded the drawing and zipped it into the side pocket of my sweater for safekeeping. Even as I hugged her good night, she began to doze. In minutes I followed suit. It was during those odd, between-worlds minutes of drifting off, brain cycling and stuttering through the wild images of the day, when I saw the numbers flicker by.

The month, day, and year I knew so well.

I sat up as if a demon were hurtling toward me from the dark corner of the room.

Where had I seen them?

Sigrid barely budged, curling deeper into my hip like a cashew. Heat radiated from her, eyes darting under her lids in a fevered dream. Gently I peeled off the heavy sleeping bag.

Crept down the hall to the main room.

Are Wyatt and Jeanne still out fixing the weather equipment?

I heard no snoring. They had to be gone.

Indigo light draped across the room. A bloated moon ogled the glittering landscape.

Wyatt's specimen fridge opened with a soft popping sound. I slid out the first few racks. Ran shaking fingers across the slides and tubes: mosses, pollens, shellfish, seaweeds, each with its Latin name and—on the reverse—the date the sample was taken.

Gynaephora groenlandica. I remembered this one: the Greenlandic moth. Two slides: BLOOD, STOMACH. Flipped it over, read: 2/5/23.

Tenebrionidae, "dark beetle." Two slides: BLOOD, STOMACH. Date: 2/9/23.

Cladonia borealis, a kind of lichen. One slide, 2/11/23.

Vulpes lagopus, "Arctic fox," a test tube and two slides: BLOOD, MUSCLE, STOMACH, 2/13/23.

Carefully I replaced each slide and tube where I'd found it, but this was all going too slowly. I had to move. I had to find the date I'd seen—*unless I'd imagined it*—when Wyatt was dissecting Odin. Forced myself to concentrate. Scanned every specimen—dozens of them—from February 2023 right through March . . .

Listened for the snowmobile. Silence roared in my head.

All the dates meaningless.

Until I saw them.

Two test tubes, one filled only halfway: BLOOD. Two slides: MUSCLE, STOMACH. All marked: 3/21/23.

The date of Andy's death.

I flipped over the slides, turned the test tubes. Read: *Dilectus meus discipulus.*

"My beloved student."

I picked up the full test tube of blood, terribly cold in my warm hand. As if rejecting the knowledge of what they held, my fingers opened. The vial dropped from my hand, shattering against the sharp corner of the metal desk. Shards of glass exploded, blood spattering everywhere—the specimens, the rug, my shirt, Wyatt's keyboard.

The next few minutes are fuzzy. I know I went to the kitchen—hands slick with my brother's blood. Drained what was left of the box of red wine into a tall glass and drank it. Slid down onto the tile floor, tipped over onto my side, and curled into a quivering ball for who knows how long. I remember the heavy iron tang of Andy's blood in my nostrils as I pressed my knuckles to my mouth to keep from screaming. *What did he do to you I will kill you Wyatt.* Began to hyperventilate. Repeated Sigrid's words for emotions: *Contempt, fear, sadness, disgust, anger; contempt, fear, sadness, disgust, anger,* until the distant but unmistakable buzz of the snowmobile entered my consciousness.

Heart thumping, I forced myself upright, jumped to my feet. Flipped on the overhead lights. Spatters of red on tile, cupboards, sink, faucet! *How could just one test tube of blood end up everywhere?* Terrorized, I frantically got to work, even as I knew it would be impossible to clean every stain.

thirty-two

Minutes later, heavy boots clattered on the roof. Above us, Jeanne's and Wyatt's unintelligible shouts. I rested my fingers on Sigrid's forehead. Too hot. Her pulse pounded in her velvet temples, her breath shallow and fast.

Fully suited up, I bent down to her. "Come on, Sigrid, you have to get up."

She spun away, tunneling into the sleeping bag.

"Let's go watch Seal Man and Nora look for ice eels. *Sahndaluuk.*"

With a moan, she rolled toward me. "Bahl," she said, eyes still closed. "Stahndala." *Fear.*

"I know you're afraid, Sigrid."

She patted her forehead, said, "Pain, pain."

"And your head hurts, but I need you to wake up—"

"No, Bahl," she groaned. Said, "Ionanut."

"What did you say?"

"Ionanut!"

The Inuit word for *It cannot be helped.*

"No, we're going to get you ice eels, no ionanut!"

"Sigrid dead. Sorry."

"No, no, Sigrid *alive.*" I gently but firmly pulled her to a seated position, the sleeping bag falling away as she hugged her pillow tight. "Seal Man. Ice eels. Sigrid alive, come on, now."

Head lolling forward, she mumbled nonsense words as I hurriedly dressed her.

Above us, the whir of an electric drill.

"Sigrid, can you walk?" I lifted her off the bed and set her down. She wobbled, pitching forward and landing on her hands and knees as if I'd set her on a steep hill.

"You can't. It's okay." I scooped her up, sat her back on the bed, and turned away from her. Crouching down, I said, "Climb on my back, okay? I'll give you a ride. It'll be fun." She lay her cheek against my back and might have dozed off, but I grabbed her arms, looped them around my neck, and stood. She wrapped her legs around me, and I huffed her up a bit higher on my back. She barely weighed anything. As I passed Wyatt's desk, I stole one of his syringes, zipping it into an inner pocket of my parka.

I stepped outside. Twilight. A dense fog shrouded everything, the fuzzy outline of the Shack barely visible an arm's length away. Facing away from us, the cottony silhouettes of Wyatt and Jeanne in work pants and shirtsleeves balanced on the slanted tin. I caught snatches of their conversation: they were bickering about the best way to repair the satellite dish that had toppled over, its supporting strut snapped in half.

Clutching the rope that joined the two buildings, I took off toward the bay and the Dome through veils of shimmering ice crystals. Chilly vapor snaked off the crusty snow, encircling my waist. It had to be close to sixty degrees. Unable to see my feet, I unzipped my jacket and took up an awkward run. Sigrid's arms stayed tight around my neck, her small body bouncing against my back.

I unzipped the heavy canvas of the Dome and burst inside.

Curly hair sticking up crazily, Raj faced the diving hole as he struggled to work the thick rubber sleeves of his diving suit up his arms. He whipped around to face me.

"Val, help me with this!"

A sick, electric panic vibrated in the moisture-laden air. Raj grappled with the many zippers, unable to get a grip with his shaking hands. I slid Sigrid into a chair, where she slumped into unconsciousness, tossed a blanket over her, and ran to him.

"Where's Nora?"

"Oh God, Val! We built this special weighted trap and sent it down—the line broke, so she dove down to check on it. Her line's been cut, or it's caught on something. She's not answering—*help me with this!*"

I wrestled with the main zipper; it was tangled in the fabric it was sewn to.

"Just force it—"

"I don't want to tear it—"

"Christ, she's down there—"

With a yelp, I unzipped it with all my strength—freeing it—then zipped it all the way across his chest. He grabbed his hood and snapped it over his head. "Put on the emergency suit, Val, I'll need—"

"I can't dive—"

"Put it on!" He clutched my arm, fixed me with bloodshot eyes. "You don't have to dive, just get the suit on." He jammed on his flippers with two loud thwaps. "I need someone to shine a light for me when I'm down there. Keep your head above water."

"Why don't I just shine the light—"

He unhooked the suit from the struts and threw it to the floor. It looked like a dead sea creature. *"Put it on!"*

"But, Raj—"

"Nora's going to die, do you understand? *Put it on!"* He heaved his oxygen tank over his shoulders.

Feet first, I battled with the bottom half of the suit, breathlessly reciting the diving steps as each was completed, methodically and too slowly, until Raj took over and we raced through them, ending with the heavy tank, which nearly knocked me backward. For a moment, we stared at each other through our goggles, absolute terror in his eyes. I felt numb.

He dropped into the hole, then bobbed up, reaching to grab a blocky flashlight that emitted a strong beam of blinking red light. "There's just forty minutes left in the tanks. Watch my safety line. As soon as I go under, get in and hold this light down as deep as you can. Don't move until I get back, understand?"

Without waiting for an answer, he sank down into the fizzing blue hole. Bubbles belched up; the surface flattened. His safety line, a neon-orange rubber cord, jerked from slack to taut. I fit the regulator in my mouth and practiced breathing through it as I watched the seconds tick down. Removed it.

I sat at the edge of the hole, legs dangling in the icy slush. Gave Sigrid one last glance—she'd curled into a tight ball on her chair—and pushed off.

Instant oblivion.

Weighed down by the tank, my head and shoulders dropped underwater—not my plan. A numbing blast smacked my face, the merest bite of oxygen in my lungs barely kept there by pursed lips. My legs like two logs as I tried to kick my way to the surface, red rubber hands grappling for the edge of the ice hole. The lamp above it a smear of rippling yellow.

I caught hold of Raj's line and popped my head and shoulders clear of the water with a shout.

Scrambling for the blinking flashlight, I plunged it into the depths and held it as steady as I could, now fighting my own buoyancy. Cold sank its teeth into the flesh of my legs, crawled up my arms, crushed my chest.

At the three-minute-and-twenty-second mark, Raj's safety line suddenly took on a life of its own, snapping from one side of the hole to the other as if it were a fishing line hooked with an immense fish. As if something had gotten hold of him.

I screamed his name.

Back and forth his line lurched. *What is happening to him? What is pulling him away?* But there was no time to wonder. Some force of equilibrium breached and the stretched-thin cord set in motion, in fits and starts, the heavy box of diving equipment it was tied to, dragging the box across the ice toward me. The metal trunk gathered speed and momentum, shrieking across the ice floor while I could only watch. With a boom, it butted up against one of the struts that supported the building, just a yard from my head.

The strut bent, but held.

Bobbing in the slushy blue hole, I took a breath, closed my eyes, prayed, opened them. Sigrid slept on.

Raj's line slackened. I couldn't tell which was worse—the taut line or the alarmingly flaccid one. I roped in a yard or so, no resistance. This was too much. I had to put my head down in the water, see what was going on. I was useless just dangling there like fish bait.

I fit the goggles tighter over my eyes, the regulator in my mouth, and dropped my face in the brine. It was as if I'd plunged it into a bowl of ice shards. To calm myself, I visualized the final step on the laminated dive sheet: *Practice breathing for several minutes before you commit to a dive. It will feel strange to picture oxygen being pumped into your lungs, but at some point, you need to trust, to let go and breathe . . .*

I sucked in a mouthful of manufactured oxygen. It tasted like rubber, but I filled my lungs with it and consciously blew it out. I devoured another, and another, the sound of my breath roaring in my ears. Pale green digits glowed on my diving watch: 35:03. Already nearly five minutes had ticked by. Arm aching, I shone the blinking flashlight—three seconds on, two of utter blackness—down into the depths, following Raj's orange line—tight again—

until it disappeared in the murk. He was nowhere in sight, but as far as I could tell, the light gave up at around ten feet down. I tilted it up, sweeping its plum-colored gaze across the underbelly of the ice, a tumbling panorama of ghostly green caves.

Raj's line jumped again. Danced back and forth across my sleeve, then slid to the sharp edge of the ice hole, as if whatever had him changed direction, the line so stressed it trembled like a guitar string until it snapped loose, its new tail fluttering in the violet beam.

I swept the flashing light in an arc beneath me. A thin, zebra-striped fish eyed me, then shivered past. No Raj. I had to stay calm. Breathe correctly. Keep hold of the light. Not leave my body. My heart banged in my rubber chest. A frigid vise tightened around my rib cage. Again and again, I shone the light across the gloom, until it lit up a human shape. A dark silhouette.

Nora floated facedown in the shadows, her arms out to either side like an angel's, body undulating in the current. Her bright yellow tank and flippers glowed neon in the light. A diving rope tied around her waist kept her in place, as if she were a kite maneuvered by a sea creature on the ocean floor. I screamed into my mask, deafening myself.

I lifted my head out of the water, popped out my regulator, and gasped for air. Snatched up Raj's line, held it up close. It had been cut at an angle, clean and straight across. *What could have done this?* Twenty-nine minutes, seven seconds of air remained. Raj was not in my sights, but I could still help Nora. I angled the regulator back in my mouth. Again, dropped my head down beneath the slurry of ice and brine, flipping my headlamp on as I had seen Raj do. This time I left the flashlight behind.

I gripped the edge of the hole and thrust myself down into the frigid blue depths, keeping my focus on Nora, whose arms drifted like seaweed. Above me lurked ornate ice caverns, silent emerald-green cathedrals, and whatever had taken Raj. My body colder than it had ever been, I opened and closed my fists as I swam; a head-sized jellyfish approached and belched itself away.

Fighting a constant current, I swam down to Nora and then beneath her as if I were flying in slow motion. Now I could see: a makeshift trap rested on the seafloor between two sharp-edged rocks. *Could her safety line have been cut as she'd tried to pull it up? Was Raj's line slashed as he tried to free her?* I seized her arm and shook her; she was limp. Framed by her black mask, her beautiful face glowed alabaster, but her eyes were closed, mouth slightly open, lips blanched. She looked dead. I maneuvered myself above her. Untied the rope around her waist, meaning to bring her up. The moment the knot came free she shot up, banging into me, momentarily stunning me. Her body turned with the current, traveling sideways.

I kicked out after her, caught hold of her flipper but couldn't keep my grip, and she slipped free. Her body rotated with dream-slowness once, twice, before she began to fade into cerulean depths, the black of her suit meshing with the fathomless void that was sucking her away, until only the twin yellow flippers and bright yellow tank glowed, and in seconds those were gone too.

Watching Nora fade into the shadows, I couldn't muster the will to move. For those moments, it was as if the connections from my brain to my limbs had been severed. I almost abandoned myself. I almost pulled out my regulator and drank my fill. But I couldn't. Didn't.

The numbers on my dive watch pulsed *nineteen minutes, eleven seconds* of oxygen left—but that fact did not set me in motion. Above my listless body leered a pockmarked ice beast, its twisted spinal column spinning off into the gloom, its massive jawbone glittering with fantastical teeth. Beyond the monster, stretching out into eternity, the ice ceiling dripped with blue and green stalactites. Forget above the ice, *this is the Enormity*, the truth no one talks about, the other earth, the fifth dimension, the underbelly of dreams, the inverse mountain, all of it unbearably exquisite and strange.

I couldn't take my eyes off it. This astonishing ice metropolis. In my head Nora's voice came: *The biggest danger is getting so blown away by the beauty or weirdness of everything down there you lose track of time. . . .*

A muffled explosion as a berg split and crashed nearby. My ears banged; water shuddered around me. I opened and closed my jaw. A ringing silence followed; had I lost my hearing? I kicked and waved my arms like a newborn, rotating my body in the murk until I had no idea which way was up.

Seven minutes, twenty-five seconds of oxygen left. I stopped struggling. Floated. Breathed my rubbery air. Found my way to up: the glowing ice; down was the shadowy seabed.

I couldn't let go of the thought *I have to swim after Nora.*

Precious seconds passed, indecision paralyzing me.

Five minutes, twelve seconds.

But of course I knew: Nora was gone.

I had to get the eels, or Sigrid would be gone too.

I focused on the trap.

Kicked down to it. Trapped behind the slats of the box and fine red netting: a boiling knot of eels. The bone-white rope drifted in the current. I caught it, tied it around my waist as it had been around Nora's. Avoiding the serrated rocks, I swam parallel to the seafloor. The trap jerked me backward as if it were nailed down. In despair, I circled back to it. Sand and grit had drifted into the trap, weighing it down. I clawed it loose from the seabed, momentarily lost in a cloud of swirling sand.

Two minutes, thirty-five seconds.

I charged upward, grabbing at the frigid water and dragging it behind me with frenzied strokes. Still roped to me, the trap popped free from the seafloor, its drag like a body chained behind me.

Frantically I flashed my dim headlight up toward the underbelly of the ice. Green rings glowed everywhere.

But which is the diving hole?

I pictured it: a long oval shape, like a bathtub. Caught sight of it. Clawing at the water, scissoring sluggish legs, I made slow progress toward the glimmering beacon. The trap jerked along beneath me, yanking me back down with every upward thrust, the rope cutting into my waist.

Finally, I reached the pale green pellucid circle. Thrust my red rubber hand up, expecting air. Solid mass greeted me. Eagerly I felt around the surface. *Had it frozen over? Impossible.* . . . Eyes leaking tears inside my goggles, I balled my hands into fists and came up hard with my knuckles. Only ice, several inches thick.

This wasn't the hole! Only a thinning of the ice where some light shone through. The trap bumped up against my back, then floated past my face, eels churning.

Fifty-nine seconds.

Pushing up against the solid ice, I sent myself back down a yard or so. Had to see the geography of my underworld. I twisted my neck, trying to comprehend what I was looking at.

There were dozens of these glowing circles, these false holes.

It was only then that it hit me. *The ice sheet above me was slowly creeping along, like a sky full of clouds in a swift wind.*

That explosion was no calving berg. The Dome had broken away on its own ice floe.

And it was moving.

I kicked myself down a few more feet, dragging the wretched crate behind me like everything I'd ever dragged in my life, the great weight of my fears and phobias and grief and all I could not solve.

Forty seconds.

What is special about the diving hole? What makes it different from all these other rings of thinning ice? For Christ's sake, Val, what?

I craned my head back, knowing I couldn't wish any of the green circles to be the hole; all I could do was scan the rippling ceiling of ice for some sort of clue. Shockingly far away, a faint lavender light blinked on and off, on and off.

The flashlight I'd abandoned near the edge of the hole.

I thought, *It's too far away.*

I'm going to die down here.

I kicked off toward the smudge of winking purple, the horrendous trap jerking me back half a stroke for each one I took.

You have to let it go, Val. Untie yourself and let it go.

Twenty-seven seconds.

Could I make it to the hole with this trap chained to me? I pictured Nora's body rolling lifelessly in the blue hell, Raj's corpse butted up against the soapy underbelly of some pitiless berg. The light flashed in the distance, and I loved its battery-powered heart with all of mine, but for every kick, the crate reeled me in, oxygen already thinner in my lungs.

I had to let the eels go.

Sigrid will die without them.

I will die with them.

Thirteen seconds.

I felt for the rope at my waist, begging a god I didn't believe in for forgiveness. My clumsy rubber fingers grappled at the knot, but to my horror the force of my swimming had tightened it to something I didn't have the strength, dexterity, or time to loosen. I had no knife. I was wedded to this cargo. I yelped in my mask, contorting my body in a vain attempt to free myself. Priceless seconds wasted.

Two seconds. One.

Blinking red zeros.

With a low hiss the pump of oxygen slowed. My head felt gaseous, like a balloon. I stopped fighting the rope and became still. I felt high. I was an astronaut severed from the ship. The purple beam swept across my retina, flashing deep into my brain. Jump-starting some primal life force.

Flippered feet churning, I reached up and hauled the water behind me, the trap like a boat I was towing. Sipping at the wisp of air that remained, I pictured my body free of anchors and slim as a knife. The purple caress of light bloomed as inky curtains fell darkly on either side of my vision and began to knit together. A violet radiance filled my head. So *this* was God, had been God all along, *How could I have doubted?*

But as I was blacking out, that revelation fell away. I forgot why the light mattered. *What did it mean, this bright pulsing marvel above me, this tender neon angel?* Oxygen-starved weakness rippled through me, ironing me flat. All I knew was to go up, to touch that sweet glow. I was aquatic; I was a sea creature; I was something about light.

What is it? I'm supposed to want light.

Want light.

thirty-three

I shuddered awake. Among the clink of dishes and scrape of silverware, Wyatt and Jeanne spoke in hushed tones, their slippered feet hissing back and forth. I squeezed my eyes shut. Could still feel their rough grip as they hoisted me from the freezing water, hear my oxygen tank bang against the sides of the hole, taste my first sweet shot of heavenly air.

I inhaled the odors of brewing coffee, fried fish, wet wool steaming over the heater, musty couch stink as I gathered blankets tighter around my shoulders. Every muscle and bone of my body ached, my mouth sandpaper dry. I didn't dare lift my head, only hazarded a peek at the rug—I'd done a fair job cleaning the bloodstains, but how soon would he learn about the broken test tube, *did he already know?*

I recoiled at the screech of Wyatt's chair as he dragged it close. Slitted my eyes open and coughed but otherwise stayed quiet. He worked a hand through the graying stubble of his beard as he examined me, something like concern on his face, or was it curiosity? Jeanne bustled around a minute longer, finally landing in the blown-out recliner next to him. Deep blue twilight lent their faces a deathly pallor.

"Where's Sigrid?" I managed.

"She's fine," Wyatt said. "She's sleeping."

I shed the blankets. Got myself to a sitting position. Gulped down in one go a glass of water Jeanne set down in front of me. Tried to put together what had happened. Remembered; saw everything. My gut hollow as I choked out a sob. "Raj, he—then Nora . . ."

They let me cry for quite a while before saying a word; I thought that was strange even as it was happening.

"What happened out there, Val?" Wyatt said calmly, sipping his coffee.

I took a deep breath, tried to oxygenate my brain, keep my cool. "You two were up on the roof fixing something. Sigrid wanted to see Raj, see Seal Man, you know, so we went out there—"

"I saw you. I called. You didn't answer—"

"Raj—he was about to dive because Nora, she was down there . . . she was in trouble."

"What happened to Nora?"

"She was diving, and her line got cut, so—"

"What were they diving for, Val?"

"Specimens . . ."

"What kind of specimens?"

I drew the blanket back over my lap, suddenly cold again. "How should I know? Raj asked me to suit up, so I did. He dove to look for her, then I dove to look for him, but then his line started acting—"

"How do you know how to dive, Val?"

"I read the dive checklist when I can't sleep. I memorized it. And I've watched them dive a bunch of times—"

He leaned back in his chair, laced his fingers in his lap, contemplated the space above my head. "So many talents I knew nothing about."

Jeanne poured a cup of coffee and brought it to me. I thanked her with a nod. Blanket slung like a cape over my shoulders, I wandered to the window in stockinged feet. Lit azure by evening light, heavy snow fell from a pastel sky. On the rug, a curved shard of glass, tipped with red. I nudged it under the desk with my toe. Felt their eyes on me.

"What time is it? How long have I been asleep?"

"Around seven. Eighteen hours or so. Temps have gone way down. It's about five degrees out there now. Snow's supposed to quit soon, but it's going to blow pretty bad out there all night. Jeanne's radioed for help, but we're stuck here. No one's coming till the wind dies down."

I turned to face them. "How did you get to the Dome?"

"The floe it sits on broke away, but it butted up against that long spit of land that juts out. Otherwise you'd be out in the middle of the ocean by now. You're a lucky woman."

I flashed on Nora and Raj, forever entombed in the haunted blue grottos under the ice. Glanced furtively at Wyatt's specimen fridge—I hadn't returned it exactly flush to the wall where he always kept it. Heat rose in my face. "Have you been able to reach their families?"

"No."

"Why not?"

He got up and paced in his floppy-toed socks. "Haven't tried. Wanted to talk to you first."

"Well, they should know. You should try. I'll talk to them."

"Relax. Eat something."

Jeanne brought over a plate of fried fish and potatoes. I sat, but didn't touch it. "What about the crate?"

He crossed his arms and leaned against the kitchen table. Stark light cast bruise-colored circles under his eyes, deepened the creases in his face. "We have it."

"Where is it?"

"Why do you want to know?"

"Because it had . . . it had—"

"What, Val?"

"Their specimens." My hands balled into fists, fingernails cutting me.

Wyatt popped a scrap of potato from the pan into his mouth, licked the salt off his fingers. "No, it didn't."

"Of course it did, I was hauling it up and it—"

"The trap was empty, Val."

"That's impossible."

"The netting was torn when we pulled it up."

"I thought—"

"Maybe you have something to tell me, Val. About that crate."

"Who cares about the crate? Nora and Raj—"

"I care about the crate. I care *a lot* about the crate. Clearly, so do you. So does Jeanne, don't you, Jeanne?"

Jeanne gazed out at the swirling snow. "Gotta say, I'm curious about it."

"*Curious*, that's the word. About what Nora and Raj were so frantically searching for. Why you risked your life to bring it up. Yeah, we're wondering."

I set my coffee down, tightened the blanket around my shoulders. "I'm going to go see Sigrid."

"Don't be rude," Wyatt said. "You haven't answered the question."

The hair on the back of my neck stood up. The words, *Dilectus meus discipulus, My beloved student*, paraded across my mind. I focused on the scene outside the window, the veils of white shimmering across the stark landscape, the Enormity, this time—somehow—calling instead of repelling me.

Wyatt watched me closely. "We want to save that girl as badly as you do, don't you get it, Val? What good to us is she dead?"

We're stuck here. No one's coming till the wind dies down.

I threw up my hands. Let the blanket fall to the floor. "Ice eels."

I looked from Wyatt to Jeanne, both stone-cold poker-faced. "That's how she survived the ice. She needs the blood of ice eels to live. Periodic injections. She used a hollow bird feather to inject herself—"

"Oh, come on, Val, why are you feeding me this horseshit?" Wyatt massaged his forehead. "You're gonna make me do something I don't want to do. And the irony is, I like you, Val. I really am fond of you. I think you could always feel that, right? Maybe even liked me, too, just a little bit, if only on my better days?"

I clutched the back of his chair, suddenly dizzy with fear. "There were no eels in the crate?"

Wyatt poured himself a jelly jar of wine. Took a sip, warmed the glass between his hands. "Did you know that I'm dying, Val? I've got ball cancer. Just a few people know." He tipped his drink, set it down. "Jeanne knows."

Jeanne reddened, kept her eyes on the carpet.

"I got maybe a year, two if I actually take care of myself. So, make a dying man happy. Tell me the goddammed truth about the crate."

"It was full of ice eels—they must have gotten out—"

"*There was nothing in the crate!*"

"Wyatt, I'm *telling* you—"

"But it doesn't matter, does it? Whether they were there or not. Because that's the wrong answer, Val. *That's the wrong answer.*"

Sweat needled my brow. "I *saw* her—"

"Ice eels." He whipped a fork into the sink; it banged against the metal. "They were the *first* thing I tried! God knows how long ago. Had to be—before Andy got here, over a year now, right, Jeanne?"

"Well, nothing's worked so far, so—"

"Total failure. Complete waste of time. Kind of like asking you to come here and talk to the kid." He sought out another chunk of potato, chewed it thoughtfully. "So that's it, Val? That's your final answer?"

"Final answer?"
"She's dying, Val."
"Look, Wyatt, I can prove it—"
"Jeanne?" Wyatt said.
She turned to him.
"Let's get this done."

thirty-four

Jeanne tossed my parka and snow pants on the couch next to me.
"Put these on." Her tone set every fiber of my being on edge.
She turned away to slip on her own gear, as if ashamed.

"Why? I'm not—"

"You need to put them on."

"What the fuck, Jeanne—"

But she wouldn't look at me. She unhooked the rifle from the wall and slung it over her shoulder. "Plenty of time for questions later."

I dropped my gaze, focusing on the task of pulling on my snow gear as slowly as possible while my mind lunged for some sort of plan. *But what's theirs? Is the rifle for protection or for something else?* Wyatt scuffled down the dim hallway, returning moments later half dragging Sigrid. Her appearance shocked me. Both her eyes drooped. She limped along, whimpering with every step, as if it hurt to move.

He gave her a mean little shove in my direction. She tripped on the carpet, landing in a scruffy pile at my feet. "Get her dressed."

I pulled her toward me. "Sleep," she moaned. "Sleep, Bahl."

"I know, Sigrid wants sleep, but first we have to get dressed," I said, forcing cheer into my voice as I worked her snow pants over her leggings and threaded her arms through the sleeves of her parka, her body rag-doll limp.

With obvious effort, Sigrid lifted her head to Wyatt's dark face, read it, and whispered, "Stahndala." *Fear.* She crawled into my lap.

"What did she say?"

"That she's afraid."

Wyatt ambled into the kitchen, extricated a caribou steak from the freezer, and dropped it in a pan already sizzling with oil. "I don't get any satisfaction from this, I really don't." He stabbed at the rock-hard hunk of meat with a fork. "It's not how I pictured things turning out."

"For the love of God, Wyatt," I said. "What are you talking about?"

Jeanne hovered at the door, hood cinched tight, gloved hand on the knob. "Let's get moving, you two."

CARRYING SIGRID, I plowed through knee-deep snow to the Shed, Jeanne at my heels. She knocked the door open with the butt of her rifle. A blast of snow ushering us in, we clattered onto the wooden floor, the stark room barely warmer than the air outside. She snapped on the light, slapped off her hat and gloves. Lay the gun on the waist-high worktable, barrel pointed in our direction. Clomping around the dimly lit room, she took down some dusty jelly-jar glasses from a high shelf.

"What's going on, Jeanne?"

She held her palm out flat toward me as if my voice or my question pained her. Popping open the lid of the low freezer, she liberated a bottle of vodka and filled the two glasses, sliding one toward me. "Sorry," she said. "Don't have anything for the girl. Been meaning to get some kind of hot plate in here for cocoa and whatnot."

Still holding Sigrid tight to my chest—she'd begun to doze on my shoulder—I drank the vodka down in a few gulps. Elbows on the woodshop table, forehead furrowed, Jeanne sipped hers, sucking the liquid between her teeth as if she was new at this hard-alcohol thing. Wiped her mouth with the back of her hand, then folded her arms over her barrel chest. Harsh overhead light cast a long, gun-shaped shadow toward Sigrid; I imagined the weapon could easily blow her small body in half.

"You know, I'm not big on saving the world and all that." Jeanne swept a few filings and flecks of stray sawdust from her otherwise spotless worktable. "Not because I don't think it's a good idea. Course it is. I just don't think the world is a place that can be saved. Not with us stupid human fuckers running this particular shit show. So it's not where I look for my, you know, satisfaction." She poured us both another shot of vodka. Sipped, smacked her lips. "I'm good at a handful of stuff. Baking. Following orders. Keeping things running smooth. Nothing fancy. Nothing sparkly." She swept her fingers along the barrel of the gun with one long, sensuous stroke. "You don't notice us, but the world keeps spinning because of people like me."

Sigrid stirred, whispering in my ear. I couldn't concentrate on her words. Suddenly restless, she pushed herself away from me and I set her down.

"What did he ask you to do, Jeanne?"

She smiled crookedly, as if half her face wanted to and the other hadn't been informed of her intent. "Well, how did he put it?" She chuckled. "God, he's got a way with words. 'The girl will have to thaw out at a more convenient time.' Something like that."

She coughed and shifted her weight; the boards creaked under her. She dropped her eyes, as if suddenly shy. "But then, push comes to shove . . ." She knocked back the rest of her vodka, shook her head, set the glass down hard. "Gotta say, it's harder than I thought. Then again, everything's harder than you expect. Don't you think?"

"Jeanne, I don't know what we're doing here."

She poured us out two more shots. Thoughtfully capped the bottle before approaching the walk-in freezer. "Good thing I had a spare lock for this puppy. You sure beat the shit out of the last one." She spun the dial in both directions a few times, mumbling to herself as she peered down at the numbers. Quietly I lifted a ball-peen hammer from a hook on the wall and dropped it in one of the roomy inside pockets of my coat. The tumblers aligned; she swung the door wide. A wave of frost smoke rolled out, swirling at our ankles.

Jeanne crossed to the table, snatched up the rifle, and shouldered it. "Get in. Both of you."

"You can't be serious."

She smiled, tilted her head. "I 'can't be serious.' You academics all talk like assholes, you know that? Tell you what, if you'd actually done what Wyatt brought you up here to do, learn Sigrid's language and such, we wouldn't be standing here like this. We'd be in the clear. He'd have the answer. We could save her. Now, I've got to do what I've got to do. What choice do we have? She's dying—"

"She needs the ice eels, I've told you. And even if— Jeanne, *look at her*! She's so weak, she'll never thaw out alive again—"

Sigrid reached her arms up to me; I swept her up again. She buried her face in the hood of my parka, mumbling into the down.

"I thought you liked this girl, maybe even *loved* her—" Jeanne scoffed.

"I *do* love her!" I clutched Sigrid closer to me, her breath hot on my neck. "Of course I love her. And you do too, Jeanne, I know you do—"

She shifted the gun to waist height. Jerked it toward the freezer. "Get in."

"You're insane."

She took on an exasperated expression, as if I was merely being childish. "It'll take ten minutes. It's almost a mercy. The pain goes away fast, and then you're warm."

"*No!*"

She raised the gun and squinted down the barrel at me, then at Sigrid. Cocked it. "Get the fuck in the freezer."

I set Sigrid down, unzipped my coat, lifted her up again, and zipped her in close to my body. Faced the steaming cold metal box. The thermometer inside the door read forty-eight degrees below zero. Deep in its recesses, under a glowing tube of fluorescent light, the ice cores in their wooden cradles were stacked in neat rows from floor to ceiling, the walls and door dented where the caribou had kicked it.

I faced Jeanne and the long muzzle of the gun. "First tell me what happened to Andy."

"Good try. You know all that."

"Do I?"

"Some things just don't matter anymore."

"I found the blood samples Wyatt took from Andy's body."

She lowered the gun, looked me in the eye. Blinked. "He was already dead. It was all for . . . science."

"Jeanne, I'm going to die in there. You have nothing to lose." I shook so hard I feared Sigrid would fall, but she held tight.

Bit by bit, the gun dipped until it scraped the floor. Jeanne wiped her nose, looked down and away from us. I squeezed the handle of the hammer in my pocket *I have to hit her.* But I held back. She could have lifted the gun and fired before I freed the weapon from my parka.

"I'm going to tell you this 'cause—okay—you deserve to know. Not for any other reason you say. Only 'cause I got brothers back home and I get it. Andy, he wanted to make this discovery in the worst way, bad as Wyatt. What Odin took or whatever to thaw out alive. So one night they fought pretty bad. Next morning me and Wyatt found Andy outside, frozen. He'd left us a note, said, *Thaw me out* in so many words. And so we did, and well, he woke up alive, that son of a bitch. Man, he had it figured, whatever it was."

"He *woke up alive*?"

Jeanne shifted her weight, set the gun down on her worktable—still aimed at us—and sat on a stool. Her face had gone slack and pale, lost its determination. "Yeah."

I took a step toward her. Clutched the handle of the hammer, now warm in my pocket. *Hit her hit her hit her.* But I couldn't. I had to know. "How did he die?"

"You stay back," she hissed, fingering the trigger.

I complied.

"It was like this," she said, entering a kind of reverie. "Wyatt grilled him hard, but Andy? He was tough. He would not let on about what he injected. Just flat-out refused. It was this power thing with those two. But your brother, he . . . he really got it wrong. Wyatt's temper, I mean. He should have just spilled the beans. I mean, he was real weak when he came out of it—Andy was—and Wyatt hurt him, he—he *cut* him, but your brother, he just smiled and smiled like he had the world by the tail—"

I took a step toward her, the hammer half out of my pocket.

She seized the gun and I stumbled backward, the hammer dropping into the recesses of my coat as I struggled to keep Sigrid in my grip. "*You get back!*" she cried, her voice hoarse with emotion.

She waved the barrel of the gun in my face, forcing me closer to the freezer. Phantoms of cold sank into my back as Sigrid whimpered in my ear. This was her last day, the final circle on all her drawings, torn and bloodied with red ink.

"You have no idea about that morning. You couldn't imagine it. It was— Everything happened so fast. I couldn't stop him. I tried, but he just, he lost it. He—he grabbed a cushion and held it over Andy's face, and I couldn't—and then he put him back outside, just like we found him. Only he was really dead then. Wyatt said I was part of the whole thing, that I was guilty too."

"That makes no sense—"

"But it does," she said, wiping away tears of rage or shame. "When Andy thawed out alive, Wyatt said to get out. Leave them alone. He didn't want me to know things I wasn't supposed to know. But I wouldn't do it, I *refused*, because I had a bad feeling about what Wyatt was gonna do, and I was right, so you see, if I'd left like he asked me to, maybe he wouldn't have—"

"Wyatt murders my brother, and you do his dirty business out here with us. Why's that, Jeanne?"

"Enough." She shook off any emotional residue and lifted the gun. "You, you get the hell in there."

"Just let us go, Jeanne."

"Go?" she snorted. "Where ya gonna go? This is for the best. The *best*."

"We could try to find the eels." I eyed the keys to the snowmobile hanging just over the worktable. "You could help us! Or just let us—"

"Shut your trap."

"Anything for Wyatt, right? Doesn't matter what he asks you to do, you just do it—"

"*Get in the fucking freezer!*"

Every shred of humanity leached from her face as she charged me, poking the barrel of the gun into my belly. I backed away, but she was relentless, jabbing me in the gut over and over, eyes halfmad. I staggered backward, stepping up onto the steel platform of the walk-in, Sigrid's arms so tight around my neck I was close to choking. The ice cores in their neat rows glittered in the bleached light. Before I could draw a breath, the heavy door slammed shut and the bulb snapped off.

thirty-five

Complete and utter darkness.
  Unfathomable cold.
  Hell.
Instinctually, I narrowed my eyes, blinking fast to keep them from freezing open or shut. Let barely enough air in my lungs to breathe—I simply couldn't warm it with my body. I knew I had a handful of minutes before my fingers froze. Blindly, I unzipped my jacket. Sigrid had welded herself to my torso; I peeled her arms and legs from me, forcing her to the floor of the freezer. She cried out pitifully.

"Sigrid." I bent down to her in the blackness, both of us gasping at the stinging air. "Brave girl, strong girl." I pulled her parka tighter around her, flipped up her hood and cinched it, all by feel. Her cheeks icy, her hot, quick breath in my face. She mewled, clutching at my snow pants. Tried to monkey her way up my legs, but I hauled her away. "Stay by the door." I lifted her and set her down facing it, or where I remembered it to be. "Sit here. Stay still."

I stepped away from her, into the center of the terrible cold black box. From the darkness she cried out, "Bahl!" I heard her crawling toward me.

"No, Sigrid, no!" I groped for her, found her hood, gripped her shoulders tight. "Don't move. Taimagiakaman, okay? Taimagiakaman." *The necessity of staying alive.* I half led, half dragged her back to the door; this time she let me. "Sigrid. Wait for me. Here."

The moment I was convinced she had understood me, I grappled my way along the door, along the side wall of the cube, to the cache of cores stacked in their wooden cradles. Stopped, listened. The skin of my face stiffened as it froze. The blockade of ice rods radiated their own glacial breath. I could barely move my fingers anymore, my blood a frozen sludge, mind congealing.

Turning in a small circle, I called for Sigrid. Her answering moan oriented me in the space, but I couldn't waste another second. I pulled the ball-peen hammer from the deep inner pocket of my parka, wound up, and swung at the bank of cores. Ice daggers blasted at my pant legs, stabbed me in the cheek near my eye. Again and again I pounded at a thousand years of Arctic climate history. Fragments of wood and ice skidded across the floor. I shut my eyes and didn't stop. I might have been screaming.

The door swung open wide. Sigrid, who had been leaning against it, tumbled out onto the floor of the Shed just as the light above me snapped on, catching me half-crazed, breathless, midswing.

I stood in a sea of shattered cores and splintered wooden cradles.

Jeanne leapt up into the freezer with the gun, crying, "How dare you!"

She lunged for me. Lost her footing and coasted across the floor on a chunk of ice, smacking headlong into the wall of battered cores. The gun skittered away, lost in the icy detritus. Groggy, she made a play for my ankle, but I jumped over her and out of the icebox, slamming the door shut behind me. I scooped up Sigrid, scraped the keys from the wall, and sprinted to the door.

THE SNOWMOBILE ROARED to life, and we charged out into the polar night, the sky pulsing with stars. Even by moonlight, the way to the frozen lake was unmistakable, the streaks of moraine in the glacier marking a dark path over the mountain pass. Tucked inside my coat, hooded head down against the vicious wind, Sigrid nestled close as we climbed steadily upward, snow churning behind us.

I paused at the apex of the pass. Surveyed the vast lake beneath us, thinking to cross a section of it, *but who knew how thick the ice was now?* The crevasse where Sigrid had been found, a crooked toothless smile, nearly divided it in two. I heard water flowing but couldn't place where the sound was coming from. How far down was this river of meltwater? Adrenaline surged through me.

I cut the motor; I had to stop and think. I gathered Sigrid closer, but she barely moved and made no sound. I had to harness my breathing, ease my shocked heart. My goggles had fogged—*here was a simple task*—I took them off, blew hot breath on a skin of ice that had formed, wiped the lenses clear.

I snapped off the headlight. Our lonely cone of light disappeared. Diesel fumes swirled up and away. Polar night rushed in and erased us. We were nothing in the terrible blue expanse. The wind swept us clean, then covered us in sugar-fine sheets of crystalline snow. Something huge seemed to be listening to us.

All I could see was Jeanne frozen to death in the walk-in, but I couldn't face it. *It'll take ten minutes. . . . The pain goes away fast, and then you're warm.* My mind blocked the image. I hadn't meant to kill her. *Don't think about it now, or we will die too. . . .*

The vodka had already burned through me; my mind was as clear as the night sky, achingly sharp. I bit off nips of slicing air. Cold turned the skin on my face hard as leather; I slapped my hands, my cheeks, just to feel something, beat the blood back to moving. Clutched Sigrid to me so hard she moaned and turned away. I eased up on her. Forced myself to look at my surroundings. Car-sized chunks of tumbled ice jutted up at odd intervals across the sparkling tundra.

"Sigrid," I whispered. I lifted her slightly, turned her to face me. Her eyes at half-mast under the slouchy hat, arms wet-noodle limp. "The cairns, Sigrid. *Inuksuit.* The first one. The map, please. Drawing. Help. Stahndala." *Fear.* In her language, I said, "*Rocks, many, ice eels, dead alive, paper, drawing, Bahl, want.*" No idea where I'd put the map. Felt like I had brain damage. *How could I lose such an important thing?*

Her mittened hand crept up the side of my sweater under my coat. Tried with no luck to grab the cunning zipper hidden in the seam. *Of course, that's where I put it, so I wouldn't lose it!* I took off my gloves and rescued the crumpled piece of notebook paper. The flesh of my fingers waxy in the moonlight. My heart sank at the sight of her crude crayon drawing of the Shack, the glacier that led through the pass, the frozen lake . . . *Good lord, where are we, where are we going?* Sigrid pointed to a craggy set of low mountains in the distance and the slender river of glacial ice between them.

"That way? Are you sure?"

She turned the paper over, where the drawing continued. Jabbed her finger at the three cairns.

I tucked her back into the folds of my coat and started the engine, which seemed to make all the available noise in the world. We threaded between waist-high and taller ice formations like waves frozen in place. Infinite shades of blue and gray continually tricked my eye: *Is that a depression, a shadow, an abyss?* The light too flat to judge. Always listening for another motor, the only other motor in hundreds of miles. The snowcat.

But we were alone.

We banged and growled up through the narrow pass, only slowing to ease past natural rock formations that rose like soldiers guarding the stygian night. Descending over ridges of rough, uneven ice, we rocked so hard I was sure the machine would break apart beneath us.

Spread out before us, a snow-swept plain met the black bowl of night an untold distance away. I jammed the machine into neutral. Listened. Just the wind fluting past.

"Where now, Sigrid?"

She gestured weakly at the icescape. Peered up at me as if to say, *Can't you see?* Her cheeks burnished red, smile like a Cheshire cat. She said, "Verohnsaht." *Joy.*

I scanned the desolate landscape. My pelvis felt frozen in place on the machine, legs stiff, shoulders locked, hands petrified on the controls. "Sigrid, I don't . . ."

But—there! There was something. Between snow-filled blasts gusting across the plain, a pea-sized black form took shape in the distance.

I shifted into gear and tore off. Quickly the mass grew taller, fatter, and vaguely man shaped, the absolute weirdest thing to find in a sea of nothingness. In minutes, I kicked off the motor. We glided the last several yards in white silence. The rock creature loomed over us, one stone "arm" raised as if in judgment, its jagged form blocking out the stars. Wide-set pillars served as stumpy legs, a thick slab capping them like a pelvis, a mammoth block as a torso. Two long flat stones rested on top—its shoulder girdle—a roundish boulder set squarely in the middle. A stone man who towered close to twelve feet tall. How long had this craggy monster existed, condemning everything that passed? A hundred years? Thousands? Wind and flying snow sheered across its unforgiving angles.

If only he could speak to us.

I climbed out of the machine, lifting the child to her feet. She swayed, unsteady.

"Sigrid, help me understand . . ." *What are we doing here?*

She reached her arms up to me; I carried her to the beast. Sapphire scarves of ice draped the length of its shoulder and pelvis stones, while a comical rounded cap of ice rested on its head. The cairn blocked the wind, and I was thankful for that; it had been a while since I could feel my toes or fingers.

Sigrid leaned out of my arms. Grabbing on to the ledge that was the shoulder stone, she pulled us closer to it, speaking a few words lost to the wind. I stumbled along where she led me, up close to the thing, my face almost touching its icy skin. It felt sentient in a quiet, slow way, like a tree.

Sigrid pointed to my eye, then toward a triangle-shaped hole created by the two shoulder rocks.

She said, "Eye. See."

I huffed her up higher in my arms, squinting through the fist-sized hole. Perfectly framed, perhaps miles away, there it was. Another blocky, vaguely man-shaped form.

The second cairn.

thirty-six

Increasingly reckless, I gunned the machine across ridges of snow and ice to the next rock man. This one stood even taller, but cockeyed, one massive leg a bit shorter than the other, pelvis and shoulder slabs tilted, one rock arm jauntily pointing skyward, the other down, like it was disco dancing. Four stacked oblong blocks made up its torso; the one placed where the belly might be looked like it'd been rescued from the sea. Waves had worn away a long shallow groove and a hole, like a belly button. It curled inward like the fossil of a snail shell or an ammonite, breaking through to the other side in a perfect quarter-sized peephole. Someone had had fun building these stone beings. I peered through the hole and sighted the third cairn, again perfectly framed by the contours of the opening. We were off.

We flew across rough, tumbled ice. The next cairn seemed to reach a rocky, beseeching hand to us. Up and over a shining blue hillock we sailed—I wasn't looking down—and landed hard, my brain banging against my skull. I comforted Sigrid as we thudded along, but I knew it was bad. Belching out an ugly blast of diesel, the motor breathed its last. We coasted across the slick surface in silence, until we stopped.

Were we one, five, ten miles away?

Impossible to tell.

Sigrid barely stirred.

I jerked the key from the ignition, cursed, jammed it back in, and turned. It made a clicking sound; clearly some crucial connection had been severed. I propped my forehead on the wheel, tried to calm my breathing. Lifted it up. The wind cuffed me. I smacked the side of the machine, kicked at the pedals, screamed into the void. Tried the key again: *tick, tick, tick* . . .

Silence.

Or was it?

A motor. Faint, but real. The snowcat. I would know it anywhere. *How long has it been tailing us?* Our own motor had deafened us to any other sound—*they could have been following us since the second cairn.*

"Sigrid." I shook her. "Do you hear? They're coming."

Her eyes glimmered open, and she nodded, exhausted, sad.

"We have to move, okay? We have to walk."

She closed her eyes and melted into me.

I got out of the machine. Set her down on the windswept ice. She listed, staggering a few paces, but remained upright. I ransacked the snowmobile in vain for anything we might use. By the time I raised my head from the guts of the machine, she had already commenced a stumbling walk in the direction of the cairn. Blowing snow revealed a blip of red, then obliterated her with a pure white canvas.

"Sigrid, wait!" I ran toward her, sick at heart to leave the machine even though it was useless.

We were really in it now. Alone in an astonishing country of snow and ice that was simply not of human scale. We pitched forward on the flat expanse. My heart beat weakly in the chilled rigid box of my body; I walked on feet I no longer felt. Looming in the incalculable distance, the last cairn cut a jagged black hole into a velvet sky matted with stars. I no longer felt the wind.

Sigrid tripped, fell forward, and didn't get up. I dropped down over her, lifted her, held my ear to her mouth—*Are you breathing?*

Her eyes were closed, her breath a weak heat against my cheek. Snow crystals gathered between her fine straight lashes, in her half-open mouth. A flash of the baby thawing; I pushed the thought away.

She didn't have enough life in her to hold on to my back, so I carried her in my arms. I don't know how far I walked. The whine of the motor grew neither louder nor fainter, but stayed a steady buzz in my head . . . *Have I lost my mind? Is it just the wind?*

But if it is them, can they see us?

I turned, scouring the circle of mile-high peaks, the pewter-gray glacial pass that led to the frozen lake. Nothing moved. I whipped back around, terrified to lose sight of the cairn. My breath raked across my throat. I thrust my limbs forward, robotic. We were freezing to death.

I spoke to Sigrid using all the words I knew in her language, about a hundred by then, to try to keep her awake and with me, but there was no answer. How useless was all this—was *I*—if I lost her. *I can't lose her.* But the Enormity didn't care what I wanted; it just stretched out and out, beyond all human understanding, its brutal blue jaws stretching ever wider. It would take her dear breath, her faint heartbeat, then mine, and we would become human statues, rock-hard in the snow, not even as useful as a cairn.

I careened toward what looked like a snow-dusted boulder. The massive body of a musk ox lay on its side, one curled horn anchoring it to the ice field. A meaty tongue lolled out stiffly from its regal head as a golf-ball-sized eye held me in its gaze. Its back like a wall covered with rough brown and black fur; half-shed tufts clung in ropy tangles, fluttering in the wind. Boxy hooves jutted skyward; legs gnawed to the bone.

I circled it, expecting to see the rest, but it was gutted. Just a shell articulated by a huge set of ribs, for the most part empty of viscera and flesh, yet a thin film of vapor rose off it, and its nose still glistened. Crouching, I stepped inside its oil-drum-sized body cavity, startling a couple of ravens snatching a few remaining strings of tissue from white fascia. They squawked their annoyance as they battled their way past us and out into the night. As I bent nearly double inside the chamber—teeth clacking, shuddering uncontrollably—it finally occurred to me to wonder *Where is the animal that did this?* Footprints next to mine said polar bear. Shaped like a man's footprint but wider, dinner-plate-sized, and deep; five toe prints, five claw marks. The bloody tracks led outside, erased by swirling snow.

I didn't care. It had to be twenty degrees warmer inside the tent of ribs and skin. I smelled meat, hide, blood, and offal. Under a shoulder blade the size of a snow shovel, a wedge of flesh still steamed. I lay Sigrid on the bloody snow, wrenched off my gloves, and clawed my hands between bone and skin, yelping as my blood turned from sludge back to liquid, from death back to life and all its agonies. With shaking, blood-slicked fingers I yanked Sigrid's mittens off her terrifyingly stiff hands and worked them into the hot tendon. Her eyes banged open, then fluttered closed; she moaned but didn't resist me.

"Sigrid. You have to tell me about the eels. You have to tell me what to do at the third cairn."

Pearly coat striped by the slatted rib fence, an Arctic fox wandered by. He caught a glimpse of us and froze, one paw raised. For several heartbeats, he appraised us—our huddled, wretched forms—before skittering off, the pads of his paws flashing charcoal in the great white waste before he was gone.

Hands still planted in the steaming flesh, Sigrid mumbled what sounded like an incantation. I let her spool out as long as I could bear it. "The cairn, Sigrid. Stones. Help, eels, dead alive, *alive*, please, now."

She pulled her hands free, eyes slipping into the back of her head. "Love, happy, Bahl. Walrus, bone, ice eels, dead alive, dead alive."

She lost consciousness. I rubbed and blew at her hands. Stuffed them back in her mittens. Gathered her up and abandoned our shelter in a run.

thirty-seven

I grew weaker. I could feel my energy waning as if a hole had been drilled into me, and my life was steadily leaking out. I was pure intention, pure will. I threw myself toward that petrified monolith like it was everything I'd ever wanted in this brief and miserable life.

I fell to my knees at the base of the rock beast, a penitent. Lifted my head. This one—taller than the others—looked the most human, one rock foot slightly forward of the other as if it were in the midst of taking a step. Its block-for-a-head had a mouth, an ear-to-chin gash in the stone; it looked as if it were trying to speak, or snarl, or curse. It had only one stone arm, a promontory of shale about five feet long that narrowed off like an attenuated hand, pointing to something it had been pointing to for millennia.

Holding the child close, I circled the creature, wind battering us as I searched for a hole, a pattern, anything. Ran my hands over what I could reach—pelvis, torso, monumental shoulders—but all the rocks fit together with no opening I could find.

Nothing to look through. My heart broke. We were lost.

The sound of the motor ramped up, a dull, constant roar, not my imagination. A loaded gun aimed at us.

"Sigrid," I yelled through the wind, though her face was inches from mine. "There's no peephole. . . ."

I pushed her hair off her face. Spoke her name over and over, but she was still.

From somewhere beneath us: grunts, barks, snorts; an appalling fishy smell. Ammoniac.

What is this?

Only then did I look down, along the sight line of the stone arm. The ice field descended sharply, plunging into a slender fjord that glistened like black oil in the moonlight. Low tide revealed a magnificent natural arch of ice over a pebbled beach. From the dark water, the lusty blow of a fin whale. On the far flank of the inlet, an immense herd of walrus, perhaps thousands.

The stone arm commanding me, I half fell down the steep slope toward the beach, glancing back at the immobile face of the cairn. Its leering mouth seemed to say, *Just look, what you're searching for is right there, I cannot be more clear.*

Something snapped under my boot, turning my ankle; I fell sideways onto my hip. A white wedge cut me through my pants, deep into the flesh of my calf. Sigrid spilled from my arms. I marveled at the shell-sized piece of bone stuck into me and pulled it out without thinking. Blood darkened my pants at the cut; it warmed my leg, but froze in seconds, the fabric of my pants crackling as I moved. I tossed the chunk of bone aside and looked around. I could see it now. A thousand walrus jaws—interlocking chevrons—had been arranged in a semicircle, a demarcation of something precious.

I gathered up Sigrid. Picked my way down the slope, past the ring of walrus jaws, toward the dark beach. Which seemed to be moving.

Love, happy, Bahl. Walrus, bone, ice eels, dead alive, dead alive.

Filling the shallow bay, countless gleaming ice eels twined around each other as if sleeping or in some sort of love embrace. The mat of twisting ropes shone under the moonlight, eminently peaceful, as if this was their homecoming, their great nature under the ice arch, like salmon that have battled untold miles upstream to spawn and die where they were born. In places, the eels moved gently with a slick sound, as if they were one creature with one brain.

A trace of diesel tainted the air.

The eel I stole from its brothers and sisters with my bare, blood-stained hands did not resist me; it contorted slowly as if cold stunned or moonstruck. Separate from its clan, it practically disappeared where I laid it on the snow; its nearly transparent flesh mapped by a fine netting of ebony veins. As if accepting its fate, it hardly moved as I prepared to cut off its head and gather the curative blood.

On the beach, just beyond the ice arch, the walruses grunted and snorted, flapping their flippers with a wet sound. The earth beneath us shook as they rolled and smacked against one another. I dropped down on the snow with the precious syringe, cradling Sigrid. I shook her, yelled her name. She was silent. Her head lolled, mouth slack; I thought, *She's already dead, what's the use?* I rolled back the sleeves of her parka and sweater, laid bare her thin arm. Found a tiny blue vein and did my best to inject her there. Drew her close, prayed out loud in her language, *Hope, love, Sigrid, alive, wake up, wake up, wake up,* as the rock hand pointed down at us as if to say, *What have you done? Given her too much? Too little?* Even for the minutes I held her there, the tide sneaked in a few feet, lapping at the shelf of eels already being subsumed by the frigid sea.

As the snowcat charged to the crest of the hill, she began to stir in my arms. Slowly at first, then with the vigor of a child wresting herself from a nightmare, ready to punch her way into consciousness. A surge of joy lit a fire in the base of my spine, warming me; if death came for me at that moment, how could there be sorrow? There could be no better thing I would do than what I had just done.

thirty-eight

Each squeal and slam of the snowcat doors—first the driver's, then the passenger side—seemed to strike me bodily. As if finally understanding where she was and what had happened, Sigrid settled in my grip. Her eyes still looked terrible, but she patted my cheek gaily and her voice was strong. "Bahl, verohnsaht!" *Joy.* "Love, thank, eel, ice alive, more, please—"

From the crest of the hill: low conversation, the crunch of boots on brittle snowpack.

"Okay, Sigrid," I whispered. "We'll do that later, I promise."

"Bahl, stahndala." *Fear.* "Sea, awake, big"—she threw her hands out wide—"wave, eat, eels, no!"

"The tide is coming in, the sea will eat the eels, I know. We'll gather the eels soon, okay?"

"*Bahl,*" she said, worrying the sleeve of my parka, unconvinced.

Two human shapes, Wyatt and Jeanne, stood framed between the stone monster's legs, Jeanne leaning slightly to one side, echoing the stance of the rock creature. Sigrid wriggled out of my arms and dropped to the snow.

"Get up here," Wyatt said.

Behind us, the herd of walruses had begun to move. They raised their yellow scimitar tusks and bellied along the edge of the inlet, their great bodies obscuring the bay of eels.

"What did you do to her?" Wyatt said.

I reached down to pick her up again; she let me. "It's the ice eels. They're down here, on the beach."

He shrugged his rifle off his shoulder. Casually aimed it at us. "No more, Val. You tell me what you gave her, and she lives. It's simple."

"I told you! They're here. . . ." I gestured at the crescent of black eels, but even from where we stood it was impossible to make them out. They could have been anything—seaweed, a scatter of rocks, lava. "There must be millions of them."

Her face featureless in the shadows, Jeanne stood as mute and still as the rock pile behind her.

"I've been telling you all along, Wyatt, it's the eels. I injected her and look at her, she's *better*—"

"I can see that. We can both see that, right, Jeanne?"

She shifted her weight. "Sure can."

"I can also see someone who's been fucking with me since day one."

"Go! Go look for yourself." I set Sigrid down, nudging her behind my legs. Found the syringe in my pocket and tossed it a couple yards up the hill. "See? I just dosed her."

Wyatt shifted slightly, his silhouette a black hole where all light had been devoured. Gun still trained on us, he said, "Jeanne, go down there and see what the hell they're talking about."

But Jeanne just gazed out at the sparkling midnight water. With dull creaks and sighs, the waves flattened as they morphed into thickening sheets of ice. Perhaps in the midst of working out some sort of dispute, the gang of walrus snorted and honked as they broke into two distinct groups, now flanking the nest of eels.

"*Jeanne?*"

"No."

His annoyance deepening, he half turned to her. "No, *what*?"

"No, I'm not going down there."

He jerked his gun toward the dark morass under the ice arch. "What the hell is wrong with you?" A tinge of embarrassment in his voice. "Get the fuck down there."

She stepped out of the shadow of the cairn. Moonlight cast a blue pall on her face; she looked oddly younger. "This is your game, Wyatt."

"My *game*?" He let the barrel of the gun drop. "There is no game. What's the matter with you?"

"I don't need to go down there. They're telling the truth."

"How do you know?"

"'Cause I do. And you should respect that."

"Respect . . ." He shook his head. "What the *Christ* are you talking about?" Spittle flew from his mouth. "Go the fuck down this *fucking* hill, and see what's down there!"

She was quiet, then said softly, "You heard me."

"Jeanne, she tried to kill you."

In the distance, miles deep, the dull white thunder of splitting ice. "Wyatt, why would she lie to you?"

"Why *wouldn't* she?" he fumed. "How do you know it's the eels, Jeanne? How are you so goddamned sure—"

"Because I know."

He turned to her. Their forms nearly merged under the great stone legs. "You've been running your own trials, is that it? Is that what you've been doing all this time? *Betraying me?*"

"No, Wyatt," she said, as if placating a child. "That's not it—"

"You've known all along what it is! *Goddammit*, why didn't I see this?" He smacked himself in the forehead, stomped a half circle in his heavy boots. "You in the Shed day and night with your endless repairs, your silly projects. Of course! I should have known."

"I wasn't running my own trials." She drew in a long breath, let it out slowly. "I was only . . . screwing up yours. Every single one of them," she added with a touch of pride. "I guess you call them double-blind, isn't that the scientific term?"

Wyatt hurled the gun on the ground; he was fairly dancing with rage. "What the hell is wrong with you?"

"It was pretty easy. I'm not stupid, you know. It's all just chemistry. It's like baking. You add an extra egg, a few more tablespoons of butter, and you've changed your cake. Texture, taste, density. The entire experience. People don't think about that."

"Mother of God, you and your fucking cakes."

"And Odin. You found him in the Dome after those other polar divers left. The ones before Nora and Raj. They brought up a ton of spec buckets. Dumped 'em out all over the place." She puffed up a bit. "What do think that mouse was eating in there?"

"But you—you were sabotaging my work. How the fuck would I know . . ." He injected calm into his voice. "Look, I thought we were friends. I thought you liked it here. We work together, Jeanne, we're a team. Why in fuck did you do this thing to me?"

Her voice turned breathy, reedy; I could barely make out her words over the walrus's snorts and grunts. "Because . . . because I didn't want you to—"

"*What?*"

"Leave this place. Leave me . . ."

Wyatt panted as if he'd been running. Tore off his skullcap and hurled it on the snow. "Oh no, please tell me *no*—"

"Those times we— I know. It was different for you, but I . . ." Her voice broke, and she became unintelligible.

His shoulders sagged. He gazed up at the answerless moon. "Oh, this is just: *no*. Somebody, please, *please* tell me this isn't happening." He spun around to face her. "So what *did* you actually learn? Something you can prove. Because I think that's the very fucking least you owe me after all of this—"

She squared her shoulders, lifted her chin, and said, "Honestly, Wyatt? I think we're even."

I didn't see it coming, what he did next. The explosion of sheer violence. He snatched up the gun by the muzzle, wound up hard, and whipped the butt across her face. Knocked sideways, she collapsed onto the ice, moaning as blood spurted from her nose and mouth.

"That's just a taste," Wyatt muttered, wiping the gore-stained gun on his thigh. "A tiny taste of what's coming to you."

Weeping into her gloved hands, Jeanne rolled onto her side on the unforgiving ice.

Wyatt ventured a couple of steps toward us. "You. Both of you. Get up here and stay up here. Wait for me."

Making the slowest possible progress, I clambered a few yards up the hill, dragging Sigrid behind me.

But Wyatt didn't wait. He sprinted past us like a mad bat, a jagged shadow hurtling down the bluff toward the ice arch and pool of eels beneath.

thirty-nine

Jeanne was so still on the snow I thought she was dead, that he had killed her with one blow, until I saw her parka rise and fall. I dropped down to where she lay in the moon-shadow of the cairn. Tried to lift her to her feet. She let me roll her to her hands and knees bit by bit, as if we were testing for broken parts. Tipsily, she rose up, coughed some blood, and turned toward me, her face a calamity. A couple of front teeth gone, nose pointed the wrong way, bottom lip split. She reeled away from us, staggering a few paces, only to crumple back down to her knees. I ran to her, grabbed her around the middle in an attempt to steady her. She lurched to her feet, knees wobbling. I wasn't strong enough to hold her long.

"Are you all right, Jeanne?"

She pushed me away with a grunt. With a couple of spastic steps, she listed toward the ridge as if following Wyatt down to the eels, but stopped. As his form threaded through the gap between the two bands of walrus, the mood seemed to shift among them. Mammoth flippers slapped ponderous backsides. Rumblings rippled through the two broods, snorts exchanged. First, just one massive bull forded the narrow pass between the two throngs; then the smaller females dragged themselves toward one another, as if recognizing family;

finally the infants—two, three hundred pounds—wriggled toward each other, until the mob had merged once again. Only Wyatt's head was visible beyond the herd as he crossed under the arch.

Still hunched over, Jeanne watched the roiling mass of flesh and blubber. In her face, I read longing, fear, then—something else. Her eyes hardened. Head down, chin set, decision made. Blood from her wounds staining the snow, she stomped past us to the cat, animated by whatever possessed her. Wrenched open the door, climbed in, and started the engine. Slammed it into gear.

She didn't have to go far.

Because what she'd wanted was already happening. The confusion, fright, and alarm clear in rounds of panicked barks and squeals. Halfway down the hill, she banged the machine into neutral. Revved it hard, the engine noise echoing between the steep banks of the fjord.

But she didn't need to do more, because the walruses had been on the move the moment the snowcat blasted to life. It wasn't like they steamrolled over Wyatt; their crushing charge didn't seem intentional. There was just no place for him to go as they climbed over one another in their stampede to reach the sea and safety, flippers smacking, whiskered faces shuddering with terror, yard-long tusks cracking together. Shoulders colliding like blubbery waves, they crushed their own infants in their exodus as they filled the bay en masse, Wyatt's cries barely audible over their grunts.

Sigrid stared at the scene in silence; I pulled her toward me. I didn't dare take my eyes off Jeanne.

For close to a minute, she sat unmoving in the snowcat, then reached down and switched off the motor. Just walruses bellowing; no more sounds from Wyatt. She fumbled at the door and climbed out of the machine. Took a few wobbly steps down the slope.

She dropped to her knees crying Wyatt's name. The grief in her voice stunned me, this raw pain loosed from some cavernous place inside her, like she was turning herself inside out. I thought to comfort her but couldn't seem to move my limbs. After a minute, her manner changed; she dropped her chin to her chest. Seemed cried out, drained of energy and purpose.

I assumed she would stay there, wedged in the snow like that, but no. Gravity helping, she found her footing. Bolted with stunning agility down the bank toward the undulating mass of walrus flesh. Two big noisy females turned to her, shocked quiet at the sight of this woman jumping into their midst. Jeanne climbed onto one of their backs, teetered crazily as she tried to leap from there, but lost her balance and slipped down between them. She screamed once and was silenced.

THERE WAS NOTHING Sigrid and I could do for anyone except ourselves. We gathered the dregs of the eels that remained in the bay— no trace of Wyatt or Jeanne—and drove the snowcat from cairn to cairn, back to the empty Shack. My first call was to Pitak, who told me the winds would be calm enough the next day for him to safely fly out to the station and bring us to Thule.

A few tries later, I reached my dad on the sat phone. At first there was only dead air as I spoke that terrifying word *love* to him; in fact, he was quiet for some moments after I'd finished telling him all that had happened.

When he finally spoke, his voice was full of so much tenderness, I hardly knew him.

"You've been through hell, Val. How can I express my . . ."

"It's okay, Dad. Are you doing all right?"

"Don't change the subject. I wish . . . I wish your brother could know somehow what you've done. That I could have taken Wyatt's life with my own hands . . . that I could have spoken with Andy one more time. Fantasies, all of them."

"I have them too, Dad."

"Mostly I wish I could tell you to get on that plane with Sigrid and come home right now. Order you to come back and see your old man—"

"I can't say what I'm going to—"

"I understand. You've got to see this through in your own way. But promise me one thing."

"Name it."

"When you do come back, I hope you'll tell me about yourself. Let me just be a dad for a little bit, for the time I'm here. It's like I hardly know you, Val, and that's my fault, I know. Here you are, bringing me my favorite candy every time you visit, and I—I haven't the faintest clue what you like."

"I like strawberry licorice."

He laughed. "Strawberry licorice it is. I'll get my hands on some. And I'll shut up this time. I'll listen. Just let me get to know you. That would be a gift."

forty

In the rock-strewn yards of simple, brightly painted wooden homes, caribou antlers lie in tangled heaps. Tied to wooden racks, strips of drying fish flutter in the wind as sled dogs yip and howl, one round stopping just as another begins. Polar bear pelts hang over porch railings, black claws grazing the frozen turf.

Nearly two months have passed since Sigrid and I flew from Thule to the town of Qaanaaq, population 627, on the northwest coast of Greenland. Old-fashioned Christmas lights festoon the simple town hall, which also serves as church, general store, and post office. We live in sixteen hours of hard dark followed by eight hours of soupy twilight; the sun won't return until February.

But we're finding our way. Already Sigrid has playmates, friends her age who understand her well enough to toss a ball around or sit on the swings together overlooking the iceberg-choked bay. In such a small community, it's as if everyone in town is already a mother, father, grandparent, aunt, uncle, or sibling for Sigrid. Pitak offered us the cozy in-law apartment attached to his home; he seems glad to have us here. Sigrid is learning the alphabet, working on writing down what she calls "talk marks." She can't quite grasp that paper comes from trees—she's never seen living ones!—and wonders why I won't come clean and tell her what animal-skin paper is made from.

There's talk of me staying and teaching the kids English, and I'm thinking about that. These days I feel less awkward around children. I think it has to do with feeling better about myself; funny how kids pick up on those things.

It's not that I'm planning to stay, it's just that I haven't left yet. Dad and I talk a few times a week, and I feel the pull to go home, but every day, I wake with the same thought: *How can I possibly leave her?*

The official story was that Sigrid was the only person found of the families who had trekked from the remote village to the island in search of caribou; that we at the research station had found her traumatized and were trying to bring her back to health when the tragedies occurred. She had no living relatives.

Meanwhile, the eels are being harvested and studied; much has been learned already. This particular ice eel cryoprotein was unknown until now, but it's a simple compound, one that can be made synthetically for pennies a dose. No need to eradicate the population of ice eels. Though cheap and easy to produce, it is—like any medicine—challenging to distribute, and the ice winds are hitting everywhere now. They're unstoppable. I know the story of these eels and how they'll change the world isn't over; it's just the end of my part in it, for now.

A COUPLE OF times in my life, I have felt transcendence. Once, years ago, when I was witness to a baby being born, and last night, with Sigrid. She insisted we watch the northern lights together, that we gather pillows and sleeping skins, as she calls them, and go lie on the town dock near the fishing boats.

It was past midnight when she waited at the door, dressed in her parka and boots. I'd put her off most of the evening, because, you know, the Enormity. It had been months since I'd taken a pill, much less had one to take, and alcohol was scarce here. So, there I was. Sober, but not as steady as I wanted to be.

"Bahl?" she said, clearly losing her patience.

"Stahndala," I said. *Fear.* "Big sky, night, dark, cold." I shivered melodramatically in my snow gear.

She said, with sarcasm, "Okay, come on, let's go," a phrase she'd heard me say countless times by this point—she knew it cracked me up coming from her—then marched over to our bureau, where she scrambled through the sock drawer. Grabbed Andy's heart-shaped lead piece, plopped it in my hand. Reached in her pocket and extracted the tiny troll she'd found in the walrus's belly. Waving it by its pitiful pink hair, she said, "Joy! Bahl, Sigrid, safe, night, magic, warm."

BATHED IN MOONLIGHT, we lay under caribou skins on the rickety dock. In the bay, a lone, truck-sized berg listed, creaking as it pitched over, seawater seething across its phosphorescent underbelly. Across the entire dome of night, the northern lights rippled green and purple, yellow and orange, each display morphing in the space of a breath. I'd never seen anything more beautiful.

Sigrid held my hand tight, said, "Excitement! Lights, sky, story, father, mother, child, true, Bahl, want?"

Pretty sure she was asking me if I wanted to hear some story about the northern lights.

"Yes. Tell me. Bahl want, true, lights, sky, story."

She said, "Childrens, dead, spirits, play, dance, sky, alive."

So there they were: eons of children's spirits swirling in ecstasy across the night sky. "Tahtaksah," I said. *Sad.* "Children, dead."

She got on one elbow, eyes sparking in the dark. "Come on, let's go, Bahl, verohnsaht!" *Joy.* "Dance, play, childrens, baby, spirit, always, mother see, father see, safe, night, love. Always. Okay?"

I understood. The spirits of the children were dancing happily, their mothers and fathers would always be able to see them, and they were safe up there.

I smiled, said, "Bahl, love, story, dancing, children, sky, night."

And so I dwelt in the Enormity and did not fall up into the sky, nor was I erased by my grief; I was wrapped in the arms of the world and the night and a precious girl.

JUST BEFORE BED that night, I talked to Sigrid about the ice winds around the world, and my worries that humans were destroying the earth. An adult conversation, but she could handle it. I lost my way when I tried to explain the word *hope*. But she told me about a word in her language for a particular kind of hope: the feeling a hunter has when he's waited all day at a breathing hole for a seal and one comes up but he misses with his harpoon, and even though the sun is going down and he's hungry and cold, he knows he'll try again tomorrow, and tomorrow he'll be successful. He has no doubt.

I love that word.

acknowledgments

I'd like to thank Jennifer Bergstrom, my publisher at Simon & Schuster, Gallery Books/Scout Press. You believed in me once again, and I feel incredibly fortunate to be one of your authors. Enormous gratitude to Kate Dresser and Jackie Cantor for imparting the finest possible editorial wisdom; to Molly Gregory and Andrew Nguyen, who both kept me happily on track; and to everyone on the stellar Gallery/Scout team—you make book magic happen every day.

As always, I am indebted to my brilliant agent, Erin Harris at Folio Literary Management. Thank you for your warmth, passion, patience, and insight. You are a life changer.

To research *The River at Night*, I embedded myself in Maine's Allagash Wilderness; for *Into the Jungle*, I spent weeks exploring the rainforests of Peru; for *Girl in Ice*, I was lucky enough to travel to Greenland in 2019 to help me understand the lay of the land. I can't say enough wonderful things about Natural Habitat Adventures and their trips, but I specifically wanted to thank my knowledgeable and fearless guides, Drew McCarthy and Rachel Sullivan-Lord, and the entire Greenland team for keeping me well fed—thank you, Shelley Paul!—safe, warm, and in awe. Back home, linguists Drita Protopapa and Bill Nelson proved incredibly helpful. Deep gratitude to Dr. Jason B. Strauss and Jamil, Sophia, and Selma Roshaan for your insights. Margrethe Heimer Mikaelsen and Kirstine Møller: I can't thank you enough for your wisdom on all topics Greenlandic. As always, I'm so grateful for GrubStreet's wonderful writing community.

I read dozens of books about Greenland and the Arctic, but the works of Norman Hallendy and Lawrence Millman proved the most rigorous, illuminating, and moving.

Without the pivotal guidance of readers for initial drafts, I am lost. For this book, incalculable gratitude to: Anne B. McGrail, Andrew Mozina, Katrin Schumann, Mary E. Mitchell, Betsy Fitzgerald-Campbell, Sandra A. Miller, Linda Werbner, Jac-Lynn Stark, George Ferencik, Ruth Blomquist, and Ray Bachand.

A kind word or vote of confidence powered me through many a long day holed up in my writing studio. Attempting to mention all these supportive friends would certainly result in my overlooking someone, but know I love and appreciate every one of you.

I'm ever grateful for the support of my dear family: Jessica and Alaska Ferencik, Michael and Rebecca Ferencik, Nancy Cummins, Bob Cummins, the Cruder family, and my husband and greatest love, George Ferencik.

GIRL

IN

ICE

ERICA FERENCIK

This reading group guide for Girl in Ice *includes an introduction, discussion questions, and ideas for enhancing your book club. The suggested questions are intended to help your reading group find new and interesting angles and topics for your discussion. We hope that these ideas will enrich your conversation and increase your enjoyment of the book.*

introduction

VALERIE CHESTERFIELD IS a linguist trained in the most esoteric of disciplines: dead Nordic languages. Despite Val's successful career, she leads a sheltered life and languishes in the shadow of her twin brother, Andy, an accomplished climate scientist stationed on a remote island off Greenland's barren coast. But Andy is gone: he willfully ventured unprotected into fifty degrees below zero weather. Val is inconsolable; suicide is the easy conclusion—but she suspects foul play.

When Wyatt, Andy's fellow researcher in the Arctic, discovers a scientific impossibility—a young girl frozen in the ice who thaws out alive, speaking a language no one understands—Val is his first call. Will she travel to the frozen North, meet this girl, and try to comprehend what she is so passionately trying to communicate? Under the guise of helping Wyatt interpret the girl's speech, Val musters every ounce of her courage and journeys to the Arctic to solve the mystery of her brother's death.

The moment she steps off the plane, fear threatens to overwhelm her. The landscape is fierce, and Wyatt, brilliant but difficult, is an enigma. The girl, however, is special, and Val's connection with her is profound. But something is terribly wrong; the child is sick, maybe dying, and the key to saving her lies in discovering the truth about Wyatt's research. Can his data be trusted? Does it have anything to do with how and why Val's brother died? With time running out, Val embarks on an incredible frozen odyssey—led by the unlikeliest of guides—to rescue the new family she has found in the most unexpected of places.

topics & questions
for discussion

1. At the start of the novel, Val is confined to her personal bubble by her anxiety disorder, whereas her father is confined by old age and the inability to take care of himself, let alone travel. We also see Val and her father butt heads over what they each think happened to Andy. How does this family relationship influence Val's mindset at the beginning of her journey? Is she traveling to get out of her bubble, to find out the truth about Andy's death, or to prove something to her father? Could it be all three?

2. In a flashback scene, Andy is adamant about refusing to have children due to a sense of climate change fatalism. He does not want to bring children into what he sees as a doomed world with a failing environment. How does this desire to protect potential children from the dangers of climate change connect to Val's decision to fly to Greenland to help Sigrid? Do these attitudes from the two siblings toward helpless children seem to match or diverge? Do you share Andy's concerns about how the world is changing for future generations?

3. Sigrid responds emphatically to chocolate and communicates via drawing pictures when she doesn't respond to toys, new clothes, Val's languages, etc. What are ways we can communicate with one another that don't involve speech? What would your version of the chocolate bar be if you were in an unfamiliar and scary situation like Sigrid's?

4. "The word in Inuktun for climate change translates to 'a friend acting strangely'—what a personal and beautiful way of describing a relationship to the natural world" (page 24). The setting of the Arctic almost acts as its own character throughout *Girl in Ice*, informing many of the characters' decisions, impulses, and actions. Discuss each character's relationship to the Arctic.

5. During the ice storm, all of the characters are stuck in the main house with one another. There is an irony in being trapped in a room with several people while stationed in total isolation. The stress of this proximity leads to rising tensions between Wyatt and Val and results in Wyatt and Jeanne forcibly drawing blood from Sigrid. How did your perceptions of Wyatt and Jeanne change at this turning point in the story? Discuss how Val is increasingly wary and distrustful of Wyatt from this point forward. Does Sigrid's fear toward Wyatt and Jeanne actually advance her relationship with Val? With Nora and Raj?

6. *Girl in Ice* is told entirely through Val's perspective. If you could read the book through another character's eyes, whose would it be? How might each of the characters describe one another and the setting of the Arctic, and how would these ideas differ from Val's perceptions of her surroundings? For example, Val finds the Arctic desolate and unforgiving. How would Sigrid's perception of her environment differ from Val's?

7. Each of the characters seems to be in Greenland to cope with death. Val has recently lost her brother, Jeanne has lost her husband and daughter, and Nora and Raj have lost their infant son. Even Wyatt is dealing with cancer and facing his own impending death. How can a new environment help us gain perspective on our problems? How can seeking out a new environment backfire on us?

8. Jeanne is loyal to Wyatt even when he mistreats her and insults her behind her back to the other characters. She even intentionally sabotages his research to try to keep him from leaving the Arctic and her with it. Why might Jeanne go along with his violence, abuse, and scheming throughout the novel, and what do you think causes her to finally turn her back on him? Does she turn against him for her own sake, or for Val and Sigrid's?

9. At what point did you start to suspect Wyatt of being responsible for Andy's death? Do you think that Val became suspicious of Wyatt soon enough, or was she in denial? What do we know about Val that can help us understand why she kept herself from seeing a painful truth?

10. While reading, did you theorize about Andy's death or the mystery of Sigrid thawing out alive? Discuss what you thought might have happened to Andy or how Sigrid could have thawed out from the ice alive. Were you surprised by the ending?

enhance your book club

1. Who would you like to see cast in a movie or TV adaptation of *Girl in Ice*?

2. The characters in the book, especially Wyatt and Jeanne, have had to eat mostly canned, dried, frozen, or reconstituted fare flown over from the mainland at great expense. In one scene, they name a few fresh foods that they crave after having spent more than a year on the research base. What fresh foods would you miss the most if you found yourself in a similar situation?

3. Sigrid and Val overcome a sharp learning curve due to their inability to understand each other's speech patterns and language. Spend five minutes with your group trying to communicate without speaking, then discuss the experience. Can you better relate to Val and Sigrid as characters struggling with communication?

4. After learning what the challenges of living in the Arctic can be like, look into supporting Indigenous groups in Greenland. Some online resources include the International Work Group

for Indigenous Affairs page on Indigenous peoples in Greenland, or Oceans North, which aims to spread awareness about conserving the marine environment and coastal lands in the Arctic in collaboration with Indigenous peoples.

5. What parallels in Sigrid's ancient society do you see in the world today, in terms of competing for resources deemed more and more precious due to climate change?